"Fast, dangerous, a...
swoop out of the da...
book!''
                    author of ...

THE DARKNESS

From out of the black night comes a force no one suspects or has reason to fear.

THE HUNGER

Driven by an unquenchable appetite, the creatures stalk human prey—striking at random, leaving death in their wake.

THE FRENZY

If their fury is unleashed, the killing will explode, utter madness will spread, and horrifying carnage will follow. And the rampage won't end until the flesh and blood of man have disappeared.

THE DEVOURING
What you can't see can kill you.

DOUGLAS D. HAWK

THE DEVOURING

LEISURE BOOKS   **NEW YORK CITY**

For
John and Aaron—
Good sons, Good men,
Well met

A LEISURE BOOK®

August 1994

Published by

Dorchester Publishing Co., Inc.
276 Fifth Avenue
New York, NY 10001

Printed in the United States of America.

Prologue

Roberta Ferris stood at the edge of the clearing, studying the woman's body illuminated under the bank of powerful lights mounted atop the four-wheel-drive truck. Their intensity washed away the shadows, starkly exposing the mutilated flesh and revealing the dark red splotches staining the snow.

The dead woman looked so frail and small. Whatever self-respect and dignity she had possessed in life, whatever hopes and dreams she had harbored, were now lost beneath that uncompromising glare.

Roberta acknowledged these things silently. She couldn't afford to dwell on such things; her stomach was already knotted, and contemplating the horror and brutality the dead woman had suffered would only make it worse. All her mourning and pity would be wasted. The woman was *dead*. Nothing could change that simple, ugly fact.

It was not that Roberta Ferris was a pitiless person. Far

7

from it. In fact, if what she suspected was true—and the manner in which this woman had died appeared to confirm it—perhaps death was better than the fate that had befallen her. Perhaps death was the only escape from a destiny too awful to contemplate.

Two men knelt in the snow near the body. They both wore dark blue coveralls with FBI written across their backs in large yellow letters. The 35mm camera one of them held softly whirred as the automatic shutter recorded every grim detail. The second man, being careful not to touch the body, peered at the assorted wounds.

"It looks like you were right," Richard Case said as he came up behind Roberta.

She turned and looked into his face. The FBI agent's normally morose features were rigid, the lines around his mouth and creasing his cheeks stony and hard. He was assigned to her, bound to follow her orders, but protocol aside, whenever she was near him, Roberta was decidedly unsettled. There was something dark and forbidding in his manner and bearing. She couldn't explain it, but the man exuded a dark and ominous quality that stirred a deep-seated need for caution.

"Damn," she snapped, shifting her gaze. "I was afraid of that."

"It's getting bolder," Case muttered.

"It or *they*," she muttered.

"You really think there's more than one?" Roberta didn't miss the note of excitement and anticipation in Case's voice.

She stuffed her hands deep into the pockets of her leather coat. She was chilled, and not just from the light breeze stirring the towering pines and whipping the hem of her dress around her knees. Her worst fears were all but confirmed.

"If there's just one, then it's an anomaly, but if there's more, then . . ." Roberta left the thought unfinished.

"We still don't know shit," Case growled.

8

The Devouring

Roberta sighed. "Bring me the minicam."

He frowned and spun away. A moment later, he returned with a large, professional-quality video camera. Roberta took it, checked the battery pack and videotape, and then lifted it to her shoulder.

"Tell your men to move away," she told Case.

He called to his colleagues and motioned for them to move away from the body.

Carefully, Roberta began recording the scene. After taping the clearing, she picked her way through the ankle-deep snow, thankful for the insulated boots, and stood above the body. She focused on the face, gritting her teeth as the viewfinder revealed the bloody, empty eye sockets and the mouth opened in a soundless scream.

When she shifted to the dead woman's midsection, Roberta swallowed hard, fighting the bile burning the back of her throat.

Gutted like a fish.

Chapter One

The scratched and dented body of the big, yellow snow tractor churned through the deep snow, its twin treads creating a sparkling cloud of frozen powder. The rumble of its engine, reverberating across the broad, flat snowfield and off the surrounding peaks, caused small showers of snow to tumble from the nearby pines and triggered tiny avalanches on the sheer slopes.

The air was still, the temperature hovering at ten below zero. Inside the Bombardier, the heater emanated a steady rush of warm air, while the defroster struggled with some difficulty against the soft frost coating the inside of the window.

The snow tractor approached a high chain-link fence forming a protective square around a cinder-block building at the far end of the flat area. An array of antennas protruded from its sloping metal roof.

For the hundredth time, Gruff Ryan wondered why these bureaucrats were so damned anxious to come up into this frozen wasteland. Jesus, couldn't it wait until spring?

"Okay," Carl Fenwick called. "We've arrived."

Ryan brought the machine to a jarring halt a few yards from the fence. Snow was drifted against the building's nearest wall, all but obscuring that one side.

"Better put on the snowshoes. It'll be deep," Ryan told the trio.

Fenwick, a big burly man with a massive gray and brown beard, sharp, dark eyes and a gravelly voice, turned in his seat to look at his two companions.

"Let's hope it's just a bad connection," he said.

"We probably won't be so lucky," Mike Crocker whined. Even in his snowsuit, he looked fragile and wimpy. Not that Ryan would hold that against him. What he disliked was the man constantly bitching about anything and everything.

Connie Pruett sighed. "Let's just do this, okay? We don't have time for carping."

Crocker shot her a dark look as he continued donning his cumbersome snowshoes.

Fenwick turned to Ryan. "Better let Mitchell know we've arrived."

Gruff Ryan tried to radio several times, but received only a flurry of static in reply.

"Oh, great," Crocker groaned. "We can't even call down the mountain."

"Mike," Fenwick hissed. "Relax. It's no big deal, just a little interference."

"I wish I wasn't here," Crocker mumbled.

"I wish you weren't here either," Connie hissed.

"Enough," Fenwick growled.

Ryan shook his head. Why did he always get stuck with the geeks? Blaylock got the fun stuff; he ended up with the creeps. Although, he had to admit, the Pruett woman was a looker. He wouldn't mind losing himself for a good long while in those deep, amazingly violet eyes.

11

Wearing snowshoes, their mouths wrapped in heavy mufflers and the hoods of their parkas tightened snugly around their heads, Ryan and his passengers stepped out of the snow tractor, making their way toward the snow-bound building like alien visitors to some desolate, frozen world.

Ryan thought the concrete building looked more like an old World War II bunker than a scientific station. The chain-link fence surrounding it was topped by double strands of barbed wire. Near a locked gate, a sign attached to the fence pronounced this NORAMS Station 23, and cautioned the curious that it was federal property, trespassing was a federal crime and trespassers would be prosecuted by federal authorities.

Ryan's passengers were a technical team working for the North American Atmospheric Monitoring System, NORAMS, a joint U.S.-Canadian project. On the way up the mountain, he had learned that NORAMS had stations scattered through the U.S. and Canada, collecting data on various atmospheric conditions. The information from each unmanned station was fed into a central computer system in Denver, where scientists interpreted and evaluated the readings.

The whole thing sounded tedious and dull. Ryan would much rather be out here, tooling around the Colorado Rockies, than doing what they did for a living.

Fenwick had told him more than he really wanted to know. The project was expensive but revolutionary, and was funded by the Environmental Protection Agency, the National Weather Service, the Canadian government and several large American and Canadian corporations. Apparently, it was helping scientists figure out solutions to a lot of weird stuff like acid rain, ozone depletion, carbon monoxide pollution and other man-made problems.

The signal from this particular station had been lost the previous night and Fenwick and his team had been dispatched to check it out. They had contacted Ryan, who made his living with the big yellow Bombardier, and here he was, running around in this frozen hell wishing he was back in Crystal Wells with a frosty brew and a hot blonde.

Ryan watched as Connie Pruett stood on the wide rubber track and handed Crocker their bags and tools from the rear of the vehicle. Fenwick was already unlocking the gate.

Pulling on his snowshoes, Ryan made his way to the leader.

"This is a bitch," Fenwick muttered through the thick wool muffler.

"Not a good place to get stuck," Ryan grunted as they stepped through the gate and walked toward the snowbound building. Fenwick held another key in his gloved hand.

They both came to a jarring halt when they rounded the corner.

"What the hell . . . ?" Fenwick shouted.

"You got a problem," Ryan snorted, staring at the steel-clad door. It hung by one twisted hinge, its gray paint marred with deep, straight gashes. The bolt of the massive lock still jutted from the door's edge, but it was bent and the doorframe was torn completely away from the concrete wall.

"What is it, Carl?" Connie asked, coming up behind him lugging a heavy canvas bag.

"Take a look," Fenwick cried. "Ripped out of its frame!"

The woman visibly shivered. "What could have done that?" She raised her voice to be heard through her heavy muffler.

Shaking his head, Fenwick moved forward to inspect the damage. He touched the gashes in the metal and fingered the twisted frame.

"I've never seen anything like it."

Mike Crocker moved up beside Ryan and Connie. He said something, but Ryan couldn't make out his words.

13

Fenwick took a tentative step into the station's dark interior. Fumbling for the wall switch to turn on the lights, he cursed.

Ryan peered over his shoulder, just able to see the shredded wires hanging out of the electrical box.

"I'll get the generator," he told Fenwick.

"Don't touch anything until we get some light in there," Fenwick told the others as Ryan moved awkwardly back toward the snow tractor. He pulled the small, gas-powered generator from the back and carried it back to the others.

"Pretty strange," Ryan said when he returned.

Fenwick glanced at him. "You know this country, Ryan. Anything up here that could tear a steel door off its hinges?"

Ryan's eyes slitted. "This time of year? I don't think so. And even in the summer, it'd have to be human. We got elk and deer, cougars and bears, but none of them could do *that*." He gestured at the ruined door.

"Well, it just didn't tear itself off the wall," Mike Crocker blurted out, peering suspiciously into the darkness.

Connie shook her head. "Vandals."

"Vandals?" Crocker growled nastily. "Up here, in the middle of nowhere? Not too likely! During the day it might reach a balmy zero!"

Connie whirled, glaring at him, her violet eyes flashing. "Hey, I don't know who did it, okay? People do crazy things. If you've got a better idea, let me know, okay?"

Ignoring the pair, Ryan peered into the dim interior, only able to see what was illuminated by the splash of light from the doorway. Snow had settled on the floor and was piled against the base of a console holding a bank of equipment. While he couldn't make out much, he could see strands of loose wire hanging from the ceiling and pieces of broken glass littering the parts of the floor that weren't drifted over with snow.

Fenwick knelt to the portable generator. "Let's see if we can rig some lights." He started the generator's small engine. It chugged twice and then erupted into a dull roar. Plugging a powerful spotlight into one of its sockets, he suspended it from a dangling wire. Under the brilliant glare, the full measure of the destruction was revealed.

All four of them crowded through the open door for a better look. Metal racks that had once held delicate instruments were now overturned and twisted into impossible shapes; fragile gauges and expensive computerized hardware were little more than unrecognizable junk. Wiring was ripped out of the ceiling and the light fixtures were broken and twisted. Everywhere was broken glass and crumpled metal.

"What in hell went on here?" Fenwick groaned.

"It looks like a bomb went off," Connie said in disgust. "No wonder we lost the signal."

"I sure as hell can't put *this* back together," Mike Crocker cried, drawing a disdainful look from Fenwick.

Ryan figured Crocker might be some hotshot technical troubleshooter, but as far as he was concerned, the little shit was just another childish asshole, more of the West Coast technotrash that had fled to Colorado over the last few years. He had all the charm of a computer.

"Shit," Fenwick said, shaking his head. "None of us are going to be of any use here. We've got a million bucks of high-tech toys turned into rubble." Again he turned to Ryan. "Any ideas?"

The burly man shook his head. "There ain't any tracks outside and to do this much damage there'd have to be several people. . . ."

"It just snowed," Connie declared. "Maybe the tracks were covered up."

Ryan shrugged. "Yeah, that's possible, but it ain't likely. You said the signal went out last night. Believe me, there was nobody screwing around up here during last night's storm. It was a big one. And even if someone was

15

up here, we'd have seen their trail. The way we came up is the only way to get here, and they sure didn't walk up here. They either had a snowmobile or tractor."

"Still, this wasn't the work of one or two people," Fenwick observed. "Did you see those marks on the door? Looks like they used an ax. And this." He waved his hand to take in the entire room. "This wasn't just some kid's prank. Destroying all of this took a lot of time and energy. Christ, look at that shelving. Nobody bent that steel with their bare hands, that's for damned sure."

"Well," Connie said thoughtfully, "whoever did it had plenty of time and opportunity up here. There's no one around for miles. You could set off a bomb and nobody would hear it."

Ryan scanned the room, his eyes finally resting on an unidentifiable black mass on the floor. Approaching it, loosening his muffler, he knelt beside it. He grunted in disgust as he caught an acrid ammonia stench and recoiled.

"What a stink!"

The others watched as Ryan pulled his muffler back over his mouth and nose and then picked up a piece of splintered wood from a countertop and probed the soft, spongy pile.

"Shit," he muttered.

"What is it?" Connie asked.

Ryan held up the stick, showing her the stained point. "Shit. Excrement."

Fenwick stepped near and inspected the glob of blackish-brown defecation. "Whew!" he whistled, pulling away from it. "Rank. And fresh."

Ryan carried the stick to the door and tossed it out into the snow.

"Some animal must have gotten in here last night or this morning," Fenwick said.

"Not any animal I've ever run into," Ryan said, turning away from the door. "The fence is intact. And besides,

16

like I already said, all the big animals moved down the mountain weeks ago. Hell, that pile is from something big, but it ain't elk or deer or bear."

Fenwick sucked in a deep breath and knelt next to the dung pile. "I've never seen anything like this before either."

"So," Connie said, in a tone of dismissal, "maybe the vandals had a big dog with them."

Ryan shook his head. "Take my word for it, that ain't dog shit."

Crocker frowned and shook his head in frustration. "Who cares what left it there? Whatever did it, it's gone now and that's exactly what we should be."

"Not yet, Mike," Fenwick told him patiently. "We've got to assess the damage and secure the building as best we can."

"But . . ." Mike said, starting to protest, only to be silenced by a wave of the older man's hand.

"Regulations. Let's get started," Fenwick said. "Connie, you inventory the broken equipment. Mike, how about helping me figure out a way to repair that door."

Mike Crocker pressed his lips in a hard, disapproving line, but said nothing.

As the men pulled off their snowshoes, Ryan moved past them and stepped outside. "I'll see if I can raise Mitchell on the radio."

"While you're out there, Ryan, grab my camera," Fenwick said. "Guess I'd better take some pictures of this. We'll have to notify the FBI."

"That'll delay the hell out of getting this station back on line," Mike Crocker observed.

"Can't be helped," Fenwick answered.

"If I can raise him, what should I tell Mitchell about our ETA?" Ryan wondered.

Fenwick tugged up his parka's sleeve and glanced at his watch. "Well, it's already a quarter to four. Sun'll be down in forty-five minutes or so. It'll take us at least that long to figure out this mess. Better tell him to expect us about ten."

"Ten?" Crocker groaned. "It's going to take us five hours to get back? It'll only took two hours to get up here."

Fenwick didn't look at him, but gave Ryan a wink. "Yeah, better tell Mitchell it'll be about ten or so. And tell him to contact the local law and have them get in touch with the FBI."

Ryan nodded and quickly turned to hide his grin. He sat in the Bombardier cab for five minutes, trying to radio the NORAMS man waiting in the truck down the mountain.

When he returned to the building, the two men were trying to decide how best to force the door back into place. He gave Fenwick his camera.

"You get through to Mitchell?" Fenwick asked.

He shrugged. "Maybe. There was a lot of static. I think I heard him calling back, but he was breaking up pretty bad."

The crew chief nodded. "At least he knows we made it."

"I think I'll get a photograph of the door before you move it," Connie said, taking the 35mm camera from Ryan. She clicked off several shots from various angles, the powerful flash popping like a strobe light.

"We'd better not disturb anything until the FBI boys get up here and check it out," Fenwick told them.

Mike brightened. "Does that mean we can get out of here right away?"

Fenwick thought about it. "'Fraid not. We've still got to inventory the damage."

Crocker frowned. "There's nothing worth salvaging!"

"Mike," Fenwick said icily. "It's regulations. We do this by the numbers, understood?"

Crocker scowled and turned away.

Connie Pruett continued moving carefully around the room, using the camera to reveal each area of the chaos all-too-bright relief.

The Devouring

Giving up on the notion of forcing the ruined door back into place, Fenwick found a heavy piece of plywood torn away from the wall and, with Ryan's help, used it to block the opening to keep the bitter cold at bay. In one corner, Crocker found a small portable gas heater. After cursing it for five minutes, he got it lit. It put out enough heat to ward off some of the bone-numbing chill.

While the NORAMS people moved around the room, noting the extent of the damage, Ryan went back out to the Bombardier, returning a few minutes later with a small camp stove, cook pots and several bags of freeze-dried food.

Even in their heavy parkas and insulated clothing, the intense cold made everyone sluggish and irritable. Their breath hung in the still air like amorphous ghosts, their uncovered cheeks and noses grew red and their eyes watered incessantly.

"Nothing seems to have been taken," Connie commented, breaking the silence. "Looks like whoever did this was in it for the kicks."

"Expensive fun," Fenwick snorted.

By the time they were finished, the sun had long since slipped behind the mountains. The temperature plunged and the cold intensified. The small space heater became less and less effective.

"What time is it?" Crocker growled.

"Six-thirty," Fenwick answered. "Took longer than I thought."

Mike shook his head. "Hell, if I was back in Denver, I'd be sitting down to a nice piece of veal and a glass of wine."

"You'll have to settle for beef stew and coffee," Ryan said. He knelt next to the stove stirring a large pot of stew. A metal coffeepot steamed next to it.

"Why don't we just get out of here?" Crocker whined.

"Because the rest of us are hungry," Fenwick snapped, his patience clearly at an end. "You don't have to eat, but

19

Douglas D. Hawk

it's a long trip down and I'm sure as hell not going to drive it on an empty stomach."

The younger man turned away, mumbling under his breath.

Ryan filled their plates and cups and they all sat on the cold floor, eating in silence.

When they finished, he gathered the dirty utensils and pots, stuffing them in an old, greasy backpack. "I'll take these out to the tractor."

Using a flashlight, he walked carefully along their trail to the snow machine. As he was lifting the insulated containers out of the storage area, the hair on the back of his neck prickled and an uneasy sensation crawled down his spine.

He had the oddest feeling he was being watched.

Turning slowly, Gruff Ryan scanned the darkness beyond the chain link. Nothing moved out there. The air was deathly still and the nearby pines stood out like a black wall against the snowy mountain slopes beyond.

"You're getting punchy," he admonished himself as he started back to the station. Nothing was roaming around here. The deer, elk, and smaller animals had long since drifted down to warmer climes, and the bear were nestled in their winter burrows wisely spending these bitter months in hibernation.

But as he trudged back to the building, Ryan couldn't shake the feeling of unseen eyes following his every step. Another cold chill ran down his spine and for a brief, fleeting moment, he wanted to break into a run, dashing for the relative safety of the NORAMS station. Not that he could run particularly well in snowshoes. But he fought the urge and moved carefully back to the building.

Inside, he said nothing to the others. This was a skittish bunch and there was no reason to give them something else to worry about.

But Ryan couldn't shake the feeling that someone or some*thing* had been out there, watching him.

The Devouring

They were sipping the last of the coffee, getting ready to start the long haul down the mountain, when they heard metal groan and the unmistakable sound of smashing glass. Beneath them, the floor trembled ever so slightly.

Ryan leaped to his feet, heading to the makeshift door. "What the hell was that?"

Eyes wide in terror, Mike Crocker slopped coffee down the front of his parka.

Ryan and Fenwick were already pulling back the plywood barrier. Ryan grabbed one of the flashlights and moved quickly outside. The NORAMS team commander was only a step behind. The intense beam probed the darkness, reflecting off the white-silver snow.

"Damn," Ryan snarled.

"What?" Connie asked breathlessly. She moved up behind the two men.

The bright beam of light played off the snow machine. Its yellow roof was caught in the glare and turned the surrounding snow an eerie saffron.

"The damned thing's been tipped over!" Ryan hissed through clenched teeth. The light wavered as his hand began to tremble.

"That's impossible!" Fenwick snapped, looking around quickly. "How the hell could that happen? Those treads are two-and-a-half-feet wide! What the hell's going on?"

"I wish I knew," Gruff Ryan breathed. The damned thing was built so as *not* to tip over.

Crocker's voice suddenly sounded panicky. "How are we going to get out of here now?"

"Shut up, Mike!" Connie said in irritation. She touched Fenwick's arm. "Did the snow just give way under it, Carl?"

"Not a chance," Ryan answered, grabbing his snowshoes, which were leaning against the side of the building. A moment later, he was moving warily toward his toppled machine. He paused by the Bombardier's roof.

"But those things don't just fall over, Ryan," Fenwick called.

"No," Ryan answered slowly, as he stepped turned the light on the ground, looking for telltale footprints. "And the only marks out here are ours."

"Is the radio still intact?" Fenwick asked, as he pulled on his own snowshoes.

Ryan was already crouching on the frozen ground, reaching through the broken windshield for the radio microphone. Holding it in one gloved hand, he set his flashlight aside and fumbled for the radio's knobs. His breath came out in a cloud as he groaned.

"Battery must have been knocked loose," he said in disgust.

The others joined him a moment later.

"This is impossible!" Mike Crocker growled.

Ryan straightened. "Yeah, sure, but it happened."

Fenwick's flashlight roamed through the surrounding darkness. Nothing moved in the vast, frozen plain.

Connie Pruett lifted the camera and, in one flash after another, recorded the latest bit of craziness.

Again, Ryan had the unsettling sensation that they were being watched. Something was out there, beyond the periphery of their lights, their vision. Watching. Waiting.

For what? he wondered, a crawling sensation again creeping up his spine.

There was no way the snow machine could have fallen over without being pushed—and pushed very hard—by something very powerful.

"Now what?" Mike Crocker whined.

Fenwick shook his head. "We'll have to stay here for the night."

"Oh, God . . . !" Even as Connie screamed, they all ducked as a large, black shape swooped out of the darkness above their heads. Craning their necks, they could see two black forms, outlined against the bright field of stars, moving rapidly through the sky.

"What the hell . . . ?" Fenwick hissed, as he tracked the two objects.

"Let's get out of here!" Mike Crocker yelled, turning and moving awkward on the cumbersome snowshoes toward the station.

"Inside, people," Fenwick hissed.

"I'm scared," Connie whispered as they started after Crocker.

"Me too," Fenwick answered.

Mystified, as curious as he was worried, Ryan fell into step behind the others. He continued to study the dark night sky. What the hell was up there? There was nothing—*nothing!*—that big flying around these mountains.

They were halfway back when Ryan sensed, rather than saw, something coming out of the darkness toward them. "Get down!" he yelled, throwing himself into the snow.

Connie started to turn and then, screaming . . .

. . . she was lifted from the ground, one snowshoe flying high and wide as her legs thrashed empty air.

Ryan spun around in time to see her disappear into the darkness.

He yelled even as her voice rose in a high-pitched, hysterical wail.

"IT'S GOT ME. OH, GOD, IT'S GOT ME . . . !"

"Jesus Christ . . . !" Fenwick cried, struggling to his feet.

He and Ryan watched in horror as the woman was carried higher and higher into the cold blackness, a fading splotch dangling beneath dark, flapping wings.

"Connie! My God, CONNIE!" Fenwick cried.

"What's happening," Mike called in panic. He stood framed in the light from the station.

"Connie!" Fenwick repeated. "It got Connie!"

"For God's sake, Carl. What got her? Where is she? What are you talking about?"

Ryan ignored the others and continued to scan the sky. He was sure he could hear the woman's frantic cries echoing hollowly from the distant peaks.

"Ryan," Fenwick cried, his normal composure shattered. "What was that? What . . . ?"

"I don't know."

Crocker moved cautiously out of the station, making his way to the others.

"It got her, Mike," Fenwick panted. "It just snatched her off the ground and carried her away." The older man's voice was tinged with awe and disbelief and his eyes were glassy and unfocused.

"Come on," Ryan urged, grabbing Fenwick's arm. "Let's get inside."

"What . . . are we going to do?" Crocker demanded.

"It just picked her up and carried her away," Fenwick cried as Ryan steered him toward the station. "Just picked her up . . ."

Once inside, a pale, confused Carl Fenwick leaned against a cinder-block wall and slid slowly to the floor. His lips were now moving soundlessly.

Mike Crocker looked at Ryan. "What are we going to do?"

"I'm going out to the tractor, see if I can get the radio working."

"What about . . . ? Did . . . you see what it was?" Crocker asked hesitantly, his voice barely above a whisper.

Ryan shook his head. "Happened too fast. Too damned fast."

"Poor Connie." He looked up at Ryan with terror-filled eyes. "We've got to find her. We've got to get her back!"

"We can't do anything for her now," Ryan answered, keeping his voice steady and firm. "Not right now. What about us? What if whatever *they* are are coming back? We've got to be ready for . . ." He left the thought unfinished. He wasn't sure what they had to be ready for.

Crocker swallowed. "Can you fix the radio?"

"Let's go find out."

Crocker glanced at the open doorway and the darkness beyond. "What about Carl?"

"He's as safe in here as any of us," Ryan answered, already moving toward the door. "If the radio was working, we might be able to reach your man down the mountain and get help."

Ryan tried to keep his voice from betraying his own fear. The idea of going back outside, into the darkness with whatever was out there, with whatever had taken the woman, terrified him. But these people had hired him to get them up here and back.

"Maybe I could get the battery out and rig it to the radio," Ryan speculated aloud, trying to sound reasonable, trying to ease his own fears.

Crocker sucked in a deep breath. "Then do it."

"I want you to come with me," Ryan said, fixing the small man with a harsh gaze. "I need someone to watch my back."

Crocker's eyes slid away.

"I need your help," Ryan prodded.

"All right."

Crocker went across the room to retrieve his toolbox from near the door and then shot Ryan a sorrowful glance. "Let's do it."

The darkness enveloped them like a shroud. They both turned, scanning the sky before starting toward the Bombardier. As they moved away from the station and its light, their flashlights became meager defense against the night and whatever horrors it concealed.

Hurrying as quickly as possible in the cumbersome snowshoes, they moved through the open gate.

"Keep watch," Ryan ordered as he crawled atop the Bombardier. After removing his snowshoes, he lowered himself into the cabin. Fumbling, he finally managed to unlatch the engine compartment's cover. In the intense flashlight beam, he studied the battery. When the vehicle went over, it had been knocked out of its carrier. Although the cables were still attached, other wires were torn loose.

Ryan pulled off one of his gloves, gritting his teeth as the cold's biting sting immediately began numbing his fingers. He fumbled with the wiring, discovered the one he thought went to the radio and reattached it. He was rewarded by a crackle of static from inside the cab as the soft glow of the radio's lights illuminated the interior.

"I got it," he called.

"Hurry," Crocker called.

Tugging his glove back over his tingling hand, Ryan retrieved the microphone, checked the frequency and began calling Mitchell.

"NORAMS station to base," he called twice.

For several minutes there was nothing but nerve-grating static. Then he heard a faint voice.

"This is base. Go ahead."

"This is Ryan," he said.

"Ryan?" Mitchell's voice was tinny and distant.

"Yes."

"What's going on?"

"We need help, Mitchell."

"What's wrong?"

"The machine's wrecked. And . . ."

Outside, Mike Crocker continued to study the sky, but he never saw the dark shaping coming in low above the trees until it was too late. With the force of twin hammer blows, something slammed into his back and sharp, tearing pain shot through his•shoulders. Unable to comprehend what was happening, struggling and screaming in panic and terror, he felt himself lifted from the ground.

Ryan dropped the microphone when he heard Crocker's scream and stood, poking his head out the open door. A dark shape was perched near him.

"Holy . . ."

The Devouring

In one brief instant a flood of images filled his mind: Mike Crocker's flailing body lifting from the ground. A pair of yellow eyes glaring down at him. Huge wings spreading above him, blotting out the stars . . .

And then a bright burst of pain exploded behind his eyes and he was falling backward, crumpling in a heap amid the scattered debris inside the Bombardier.

"Ryan?" the tinny voice cried. "Goddamn it, answer me!"

High in the night sky, Mike Crocker was aware of sticky warmth spreading from his shoulders, rolling down his chest and back.

Futilely he struggled.

Yelling and screaming hysterically, he struck blindly at the dark shape above him. His awkward, ineffectual blows glanced harmlessly off hard, fur-covered muscle. Cold air rushed past his face as he was carried higher and the broad snowfield stretched out below.

Over his head, powerful wings beat the bitter night air with a steady, leathery swoosh.

Suddenly the sharp, stabbing pressure gripping his shoulders was gone . . .

. . . and he was falling.

His screams, hollow cries in the dark night, filled his own ears as he plummeted down, clutching at the nothingness around him.

Chapter Two

Morgan Blaylock crawled out of bed with a groan. Thunder rolled behind his eyes and his mouth tasted the way the bottom of an outhouse looked.

Snatching his robe from the back of a chair and mumbling a curse, he padded into the living room on unsteady legs. He yanked the phone from its cradle just as it rang for the umpteenth time. The shrill twitter ignited another explosion in the nether regions of his head. He was definitely too old for this shit.

"It better be good," he growled into the mouthpiece, shivering in the bitter chill permeating the room.

"Blaylock?"

"It ain't the Easter bunny."

"It's McKissik."

"Yeah. So?"

"We need you and your machine."

"For what?" McKissik was Crystal Wells's answer to Barney Fife. A devious little bastard, he and Morgan had a mutual understanding that disliking one another was not simply acceptable, but cosmically ordained. The fact that the deputy sheriff was now married to Morgan's ex-wife served only to exacerbate their mutual antipathy. "What the hell time is it anyway?"

"It's a little after three."

"In the morning? Why don't you call me back during business hours. Mine start sometime around noon."

"We got a problem up in the mountains," the deputy blurted out.

"Who's we?" Morgan growled.

"Some federal guys," the deputy answered, his voice dripping with contempt.

"What feds? Are you calling for them?"

"Jesus, Blaylock. There are people missing. You just going to let 'em die?"

Morgan grunted. "Who's paying the freight?"

"Feds, probably."

"Probably?" Morgan growled. "Come on, Jasper, I can't run all over the mountains on a 'probably.' I've got expenses. It ain't a hobby, you know?"

He smiled to himself as he heard McKissik cover the phone and speak to someone. After a few moments the deputy was back on the line.

"Regular rate?"

"Regular rate starts at eight. Double rate this time of night."

"Yeah, okay. You love having us over a barrel," McKissik said nastily.

"Hey, Jasper, you can always call Gruff," Morgan hissed.

"Who do you think's among the missing?" McKissik demanded nastily.

"Gruff?" Morgan's stomach did a slow turn.

"Just get over to the truck stop ASAP." Before Morgan could respond, there was a loud click on the other end followed by an irritating dial tone. McKissik had enjoyed

29

dropping that particular bomb shell. Gruff Ryan wasn't just a competitor in a decidedly dicey business.

Morgan trudged into the bathroom, downed four aspirins and then studied his face in the mirror. His green eyes were glassy and puffy, his dark hair was greasy and the skin on his face appeared to be stretched too tightly over his bones. A two-day growth of beard stood out in stark relief against his sleep-pale face. Gone forever was the fresh-faced kid. Somebody had stolen his young body and replaced it with this older, more battered one.

It's a crime. A damned crime.

He was just stepping out of the shower when the bathroom door opened and last night's blonde peeked into the steamy room through blurry blue eyes.

"Whatta you doin' up?" she slurred.

Morgan studied her. Good God, he'd forgotten about her. Not that he could remember much about last night.

"How old are you?" Morgan asked, drying himself on a big bath towel.

"Nineteen."

He sighed. At least she was legal. But he must have been pretty damned drunk to drag home one this young. Cradle-robbing wasn't his style. Hell, he could be her father. And her real father was probably some slab of beef who'd break him in half if he even suspected some yahoo had touched her.

Touched, my ass, Morgan thought as faint memories slowly filtered through his fogged brain. This little number knew more tricks than a Las Vegas hooker.

"I've got to go to work," he told her. "Go back to bed."

She smiled coyly and reached out her hand. "You come on back with me, honey. You can warm me up."

There was a faint stirring in Morgan's loins. It was a very tempting proposition.

He shook his head, disgusted with himself. "No, I got a job. An emergency."

The Devouring

The blonde—Morgan couldn't remember her name—stuck out her lip and pouted. "Well, can I wait here until you get back?"

"Better not. My wife gets off the night shift at eight and she's a real bruiser," Morgan lied.

"You're married?" The girl spat out the word like something with a nasty taste.

"Just go back to bed and be gone before eight. You'll be fine."

"Fuck you," she hissed, whirling and stomping back toward the bedroom.

"Too late," Morgan mumbled softly.

He dressed in the dark, aware of the girl curled in the bed, glaring at him. Morgan hoped the lie about his bruiser wife would hasten her departure. But as a precaution against youthful wrath, he locked the door to the second bedroom, which served as his study. The computer and a laser printer were worth more than he cared to think about. Not to mention the half-finished novel he had to have in New York in two months. Another in the *Half Breed* series. He was one of a half a dozen writers around the country cranking out tales of the oversexed, excessively violent Jackson Black Cloud.

What the hell, Morgan often rationalized, ol' Jackson kept a steady flow of cash coming into the bank. Someday maybe he'd find time to write something that wasn't based on a formula you could write on the back of a cocktail napkin. Until then, he'd keep Black Cloud knee-deep in hard-hearted villains and pecker-deep in wanton women.

Outside, the sky was crystal clear, the air bitterly cold. Smoke drifted from the chimneys of the surrounding houses and the pungent scent of wood smoke was thick and heavy.

Morgan's headache was starting to dissipate and he was starting to feel his humanity reemerging. And with it came a little guilt about leaving the nameless blonde. She was just a kid. But he couldn't afford to encourage her. Better for both of them if she was gone when he got back.

Morgan made his way to the side of his small house, where his big Thiokol 601 snow tractor sat on its trailer behind his battered four-wheel-drive Ford pickup. The snow machine was gassed, its 300-cubic-inch industrial engine tuned and ready to roll. After a cursory check of the chains holding it on the trailer, the hitch and the connection for the trailer lights, he climbed into the truck.

Crystal Wells's streets were empty and the houses dark. Sensible people didn't get up before the sun, and really sensible people didn't even stick their noses out on a night like this. It had to be ten below. God was probably in Acapulco. Welcome to winter in the Rockies.

If the feds were involved—probably the Forest Service—then the emergency was probably real and not some half-baked fantasy cooked up in Deputy Jasper McKissik's mind. And besides, Sheriff Red Crumley wouldn't let McKissik drag Morgan out of bed for anything stupid.

On the other hand, if the feds were footing the bill, why was the Crystal County Sheriff's Department involved?

When Morgan pulled into the snowpacked parking lot of the Aces and Eights Truck Stop on the edge of town, he noted the sheriff's department car, a white Highway Patrol cruiser and a nondescript sedan with a government plate.

Parking out of the way of the 18-wheelers constantly moving in and out of the lot, Morgan left the truck running and wandered into the cafe. A few truckers sat in a booth sipping coffee and swapping lies. Morgan spotted Red Crumley and Jasper McKissik near the back wall, seated around a big table. He recognized the highway patrolman sitting with them, but didn't know the other man and woman from Adam and Eve.

"About time," McKissik muttered as Morgan walked over. He was a slight, small man, not weighing more than 120. His mousy-brown hair was thinning and there was a permanent sneer on his thin lips.

It was always too easy to take a rim shot at McKissik,

so rather than slam the little jerk, Morgan turned to Sheriff Crumley, who nodded toward an empty chair.

"Glad you could make it," Crumley said as Morgan sat down next to McKissik.

True to his nickname, Crumley sported a mop of bright red hair laced with a few threads of gray. He was big and solid, his 48-year-old body still unblemished by middle-aged fat. His ancient and weary eyes studied Morgan.

"I guess Jasper told you about Gruff."

"Just said he was missing." Morgan nodded to Bernie Alvarez, the state cop. He was sitting next to a hard-looking guy, who in turn sat next to a striking brunette with expressive dark eyes. Morgan studied her for a long moment.

Red introduced them. "Agent Richard Case, FBI." Case offered a curt nod. "And Roberta Ferris."

"You with the government?" Morgan asked.

The woman nodded. "Yes."

"FBI?"

"No."

"Is it a state secret?" Morgan's question drew a scowl from Case and a warning frown from Crumley. The woman almost smiled, but didn't.

"What I do . . . Mr. Blaylock, is it? . . . has no bearing on this situation," she answered.

Morgan started to say something, but Red touched his arm.

"Don't press," he cautioned.

Morgan spread his hands in mock surrender. "Hey, just curious. So, what's happened to Gruff?"

"He had three people with him," Red explained. "Technicians checking on a monitoring station."

Morgan looked around the table. "So why is the FBI involved?"

Case shook his head. When he spoke, he sounded as though he was addressing a ten-year-old. "The people up there work for NORAMS. It's a joint project between the

33

U.S., Canada and private business—"

"I read the newspapers," Morgan said, interrupting. For reasons he couldn't understand, he was taking an immediate and visceral dislike to the FBI agent. He'd never trust this man.

Case stared into his coffee cup, obviously annoyed. "Ryan took the NORAMS people up yesterday to check on a monitoring station. They radioed to their man waiting at the base of the mountain. Said there was trouble. He called the sheriff and the sheriff called us."

"What kind of trouble?" Morgan interrupted.

Case sucked in a deep breath and continued patiently. "We don't know." The man locked eyes with Morgan. "It's a federal project on federal land, which means the Bureau has jurisdiction. Not that it's any of your business."

Morgan frowned. All of that might be true, but he had some idea how the FBI worked, and agents didn't show up in a hick town like Crystal Wells a few hours after a report of trouble unless they were either nearby or waiting for trouble.

"Ryan's tough," Morgan said to no one in particular. "He can handle just about anything these mountains can dish out. If there was trouble, I can't think of anyone better equipped to handle it."

Richard Case glowered. "We're not really interested in what you think, Blaylock. You're being hired to get us up there."

Morgan shrugged and glanced at the sheriff. "This'll be fun."

A smile tugged at the corner of Crumley's mouth. "Don't start."

"Fine," he said, standing. "Let's roll."

"How soon can you get us up there?" Roberta Ferris asked, getting out of her own chair. Morgan couldn't help but notice the swell of breasts under the heavy sweater, and how snugly her jeans hugged her hips and thighs.

"Couple of hours, maybe longer," he answered. "Depends on the trail. If we're lucky, we'll be able to follow Gruff's trail."

The woman caught his eye for just a second, and Morgan saw a flicker of concern.

"Fine," she said, looking away.

"Who's going?" he asked, glancing around the table.

"Everyone," Red answered.

"Why so many?"

"Not your concern," Case snapped.

Morgan turned to Ernie Alvarez. "How come you're coming?"

The state trooper shrugged. "Just going as far as you go in the truck. I'm setting up a command post there to relay information."

"Whatever," Morgan said. "The tractor can handle quite a few folks."

"Tractor?" Roberta asked.

"His snow machine," McKissik answered quickly. He shot Morgan a hateful glance. "He's our answer to Dan'l Boone. Don't that just beat it all to hell, ma'am?"

Morgan grinned. "And *he's* our answer to Barney Fife."

The deputy balled a fist and glared at Morgan, but Red stepped between them. "Only warning," Red said. "I don't want any of the crap between the two of you interfering with the search. Understood?"

Morgan clapped the sheriff on the shoulder. "You know me, Red. Mellow as they come."

Red glowered. " 'Bout as mellow as a pit bull in a schoolyard."

McKissik frowned and walked away. Morgan and Red exchanged knowing looks. The others were already walking outside.

"What the hell has Gruff gotten himself into?" Morgan asked.

Crumley shook his head. "Beats me. I got a radio call from some guy named Mitchell. He told me to contact the

FBI staying over at the Crystal Wells Lodge."

"So the feds were already here?"

The sheriff nodded.

"I don't like the smell of this, Red."

Crumley turned and blocked Morgan's path. "Do the job, take the money and keep your mouth shut."

"Is that an order?" Morgan asked.

"A suggestion."

"Noted."

Getting mixed up with the feds, on any level, didn't set well with Morgan. He had a deep-seated distrust of bureaucrats and politicians. Working for the FBI was like a chicken sleeping with a fox.

As a rule, his work entailed searching for lost hunters or ferrying electric company linemen to remote power-line towers. A couple of times he'd helped Red look for fleeing felons stupid enough to risk the wintertime Rockies, and once he'd helped bring down the bodies of a Texas family whose plane had slammed into the side of a peak. Overall, it was mundane, boring work.

As he and Crumley stepped outside, Red whispered to Morgan, "What about that Ferris woman? Nice, huh?"

Morgan gave him a look of mock surprise. "Does your wife know you lust around after other women."

Red smiled. "Hell, I can look, can't I?"

"No. It's bad for your heart."

The sheriff harrumphed. "Speaking of bad for your heart, I hear you left the bar last night with some little girl barely old enough to walk."

Morgan shook his head in mock disgust. "Small towns. No privacy."

"Hope she was legal."

"She was."

"Thank God," the sheriff hissed.

It was agreed Crumley and McKissik would ride with Morgan and the FBI agent and the Ferris woman would go with the patrolman. They left the FBI and sheriff's cars at the truck stop.

Morgan reached the NORAMS truck in less than an hour. A fresh-faced kid, not more than 22 or 23, leaped out of the vehicle as Morgan braked to a stop.

"Nothing more from the station," Paul Mitchell said breathlessly. His acne-scarred face was pale in the faint light and his eyes were hollow and worried.

"I'm going up there with you," he added, acting as if he expected an argument.

Red Crumley shrugged. "Fine." He turned to McKissik. "You get the rifles out of the back of the Blazer. The rest of us will help Blaylock unload the machine."

Morgan was already pulling the steel ramps out of the back of the trailer. He locked them in place as Red and Case began loosening the tie-down chains. In another few minutes the Thiokol's big engine roared to life. Once it was off the trailer, Roberta Ferris hefted a large, padded case into the back along with several pairs of snowshoes. Crumley carefully placed three rifles, a shotgun and a canvas bag of ammunition next to them.

"Expecting a war?" Morgan asked, eyeing the weaponry.

"Just a precaution, Morgan," Red answered.

"Against what?" Morgan had a bad feeling about this whole situation.

Capable of holding ten people, the snow tractor afforded everyone plenty of room. There were two bucket seats in the front and three wide, deep bench seats in the back. Morgan had made a few modifications to the rebuilt machine, including insulation and a more powerful heater.

Roberta Ferris sat in the other front seat, telling Morgan she wanted to have a clear view on the way up.

The tracks of the other snow machine stood out in sharp relief in the tractor's powerful headlights. Morgan slipped it into gear and, with a rolling lurch, the Thiokol started up the winding trail.

Once they were up the first slope, he watched Ferris pull a large, single-lens binocular from her bag.

"Infrared?" he asked.

She glanced at him and frowned. "Yes."

"What're you looking for?"

She shook her head. "Nothing in particular. I just . . ." She left the thought unfinished as she began studying the surrounding area with the binocular.

"You expect to see something?" he prodded.

She turned and studied him, her face an inscrutable mask in the pale green glow of the instrument panel lights. "Just a precaution."

He shook his head, shifting in his seat. "We're taking an awful lot of precautions for a rescue mission."

Roberta Ferris laughed without humor. "You're very suspicious, aren't you?"

"Very."

"Leave it alone, Blaylock," warned Richard Case from the back seat. "Just get us up the mountain."

Morgan decided to keep his mouth shut for the time being, and lapsed into silence. Occasionally, he glance at Ferris, watching the woman as she leaned back in her seat, scanning the darkness through the binocular.

He thought it more than a little odd that she was aiming high, toward the mountaintops and not the surrounding forest.

The twin tracks of Gruff's machine wound through the trees, climbing steadily higher into the wilderness area. For the most part, the going was easy, even in the darkness. Not having to break a fresh trail was a big help.

A few times, he used the radio in a vain attempt to contact Ryan or the NORAMS people. Each time everyone in the snow machine grew silent, unconsciously leaning forward to listen to the crackle and static. And each time he slipped the mike back into its holder, the others sighed and leaned back in their seats.

Crumley and Case shared the rear seat directly behind Morgan. Both Paul Mitchell and Jasper McKissik sat alone. No one spoke.

It was almost six in the morning when they emerged from the trees and onto the broad, flat expanse of a high mountain meadow. The trail left by Ryan's machine angled in a straight line across the otherwise unblemished field of snow.

"Must be close," Red Crumley said, leaning forward to look out the front window.

"At the other end of this clearing," Mitchell said.

Roberta Ferris was again peering intently through the infrared binoculars. And again, Morgan noticed she was scanning the high peaks surrounding them.

As they drew nearer to the station, they could see the glimmer of light coming from the building. When they were within 50 yards, the headlights illuminated the underside of the overturned Bombardier.

"Damn," Morgan breathed. "There's problems here, all right. What the hell did that?" He glanced at Roberta Ferris. "What's going on?"

She returned his look, her eyes flashing in the weak light from the instrument panel. "How should I know?"

"Right," Morgan snorted. "Like you don't know a hell of a lot more than you're saying."

"Back off, Blaylock," Case warned.

Everyone strained to see the wrecked machine. "Take a lot to tip over one of those mothers," Crumley observed.

Morgan stopped his Thiokol and everyone began pulling on snowsuits and strapping on snowshoes. When they climbed out, McKissik handed Red one of the rifles, gave one to Case and kept the third for himself. Morgan brushed the deputy aside and picked up the shotgun. He didn't know what they were expecting to run into, but whatever it was, he didn't want to get caught unarmed.

Roberta Ferris pulled the heavy bag from the back and opened it, lifting out a big, professional-quality minicam.

"Home movies?" Morgan asked.

Her glance was withering. "Are you always such a smartass?"

"As a rule," he said seriously.

She shook her head, picked up the camera and started after Red Crumley, who was yelling at Paul Mitchell's back.

"Hey, don't disturb anything in there," he shouted as the young man moved quickly past the overturned snow machine and through the open gate toward the station.

Light was streaming out the door of the small concrete building and for a second, Mitchell was framed in its bright glow. The others heard him shout something and rush inside.

"It's Fenwick," he cried.

"Who's Fenwick?" Morgan asked Roberta as they moved awkwardly along the now-worn path.

"NORAMS area chief, I think."

Carl Fenwick was lying on the concrete floor. His eyes were open and staring. Ice had formed in his beard around his mouth and the exposed flesh around his eyes was deathly pale.

Paul Mitchell knelt beside him, looking up as the others crowded into the room. "He's alive, but his pulse is weak. We've got to get him to a hospital."

Case and Crumley squatted next to Fenwick and conducted their own hasty examination.

"Doesn't seem to have any broken bones," the FBI man said after a few moments. "Exposure. Probably hypothermia." He looked around the room. "Damn, will you look at this place?"

"Where the hell's everybody else?" Morgan hissed to Red Crumley. "Where's Gruff?"

"Beats me, Morgan. I'll have a look around."

Morgan touched the small space heater. It was cold, its

fuel supply depleted. "Let's get this thing fired up."

"Where is everyone?" McKissik wondered aloud, peering into the dark corners of the room.

Case stood and looked at Morgan. "Forget the heater, I want you to get this man down the mountain right away."

Morgan frowned, automatically bridling at the order. Before he could say anything, Case tapped his own chest. "My department's picking up your inflated tab. No arguments."

Morgan frowned, but nodded. He'd like to have a few minutes to let the kinks in his spine straighten themselves. The tractor was a kidney-buster. But like Case said, he was being well paid for his time and services.

"I'll fix a bed for him in the back," he told the agent. As he turned to leave he almost crashed into the lens of the minicam Roberta held on her shoulder. She was just ready to turn on its powerful light.

Without a word, he moved past her. What in the hell was she doing? None of this made any sense.

It took only a few minutes to rig a stretcher and carry the unconscious Fenwick to the snow machine. Using blankets and a sleeping bag, Morgan made a bed between the two rear seats.

They had just situated Fenwick in the back of the Thiokol when Crumley hushed everyone.

"Listen," he said.

There was a low, barely audible moan from nearby.

The sheriff crouched beside the overturned Bombardier, shoving his flashlight through the broken front window.

"It's Ryan," he spat.

Morgan moved quickly to the sheriff and peered into the Bombardier's dark cab. Gruff Ryan lay in a heap on the passenger-side seat. His face was a dark mask of congealed blood and his beard was coated with ice.

"Jesus," Morgan breathed. "Let's get him out of there."

It took several minutes to maneuver Ryan's bulky body out of the machine. Once they had him in the back of the Thiokol, Morgan and Roberta Ferris flanked him, inspecting the nasty gash just above his right eye.

"Somebody really clocked him," Morgan said, opening his first-aid kit. The cut on his friend's head was straight and clean. "Looks like they used a knife or something else with a sharp edge." When the woman made no response, he glanced at her, and in the faint light saw an odd expression on her face.

"He's awfully cold," she said, not returning Morgan's gaze. "You'd better get him down."

"Maybe you should come with me," Morgan suggested. "To keep an eye on both of them while I drive."

Roberta shook her head. "I can't."

Morgan lowered his voice. "What the hell is going on?"

She pressed her lips together and then looked up at him. "Need-to-know basis. Just get Fenwick and your friend out of here."

"Need-to-know? Lady, I need to know a hell of a lot more than you're telling me."

"Just do what you're being paid for," she snapped. "For hired help, you're awfully damned pushy." An instant later, she was out of the machine.

For a fleeting moment, Morgan wanted to go after her, take her by the scruff of the neck and shake the truth out of her.

Once he had the injured men situated as comfortably as possible, Morgan moved to the front of the machine and started the engine. Just as he was about to depart, Red Crumley opened the door.

"You think those two are going to make it?" he asked.

"I don't know. Neither one's in great shape. It'll take about three, maybe three and a half hours for me to get down and back. I'll radio Alvarez so he can have an ambulance standing by."

"You'd better have him get some food to bring back up and plenty of hot coffee," the sheriff told him.

It was still an hour away from sunrise. The air was still and brutally cold and the heat from the snow machine's interior had already dissipated. Morgan set the heater on high as he slipped the Thiokol in gear and headed it back along the trail.

When he was halfway to the truck, with the sun rising above the jagged peaks in the east, he radioed Alvarez. The connection was staticky, but Morgan managed to give the patrolman instructions.

A few minutes later, Fenwick let out a gasping cry. Morgan, concentrating on the oncoming trail, his mind lulled by the throbbing engine, jumped in his seat.

"Connie?" Fenwick called out. "Connie?"

"She's not here," Morgan said.

The other man's voice was despairing and terrified. "It picked her up. It just picked her up . . . and . . . and carried her away. It just . . . just . . ."

Morgan brought the machine to a grinding halt and climbed into the back, half afraid Fenwick had died. He was relieved to find the man was still breathing, although he looked bad and had again lapsed into unconsciousness.

"Hang in there," Morgan told him. Ryan was breathing deeply and his skin seemed to be much warmer now. Hurrying back to his seat, Morgan sent the snow machine rumbling down the trail.

Something was seriously wrong up there. Two people had simply disappeared and the other two were found half frozen. There was no sign of another vehicle having been in the area nor of any animal—what kind of an animal could overturn the big yellow snow tractor?—and yet the place had been wrecked.

And what was all that crap Fenwick was hollering about *something* carrying a woman away? And what had the Ferris woman been looking for? UFOs? Maybe she's some agent for a top-secret Pentagon project investigating visitors from another world.

Morgan hummed the first few bars of *The Twilight Zone* theme. Aliens inhabiting the mountains outside Crystal

Wells? Not the best place to gather human specimens. But then, maybe they came from a bleak and icy wasteland.

He reached the highway patrolman in another half hour. A big, boxy orange-and-white ambulance sat waiting, clouds of exhaust pouring from its tailpipe. The paramedics, alerted by the roar of his engine, stood ready to transfer the two unconscious men.

A moment later, the efficient young medics had Fenwick and Ryan in the back of the ambulance and, with lights flashing, roared away into the early morning.

"Any idea what happened up there?" Alvarez asked.

"Not a clue," Morgan answered, sipping a steaming cup of coffee. "Something sure as hell tore the place apart and overturned their tractor. I'll be damned if I can figure out what did it."

They loaded two boxes of freeze-dried food, a larger insulated coffee server and a Coleman stove into the back of the tractor. Morgan refilled the Thiokol's tank from the five-gallon cans Alvarez had waiting.

"By the way," the trooper said as Morgan was finishing his coffee. "Charlie Shaw from the paper tracked me down when I was in town. I don't know how he got wind of this in the middle of the night, but he wanted to know what the hell was going on up here. That fed was very explicit about keeping a lid on this. You should warn him that the press is snooping around."

Morgan smiled. "Ah, yes, the ever-present Fourth Estate. I'll tell Case. It's his problem. But I don't know how he's going to keep Shaw away from the hospital."

Alvarez smiled ruefully. "Those medics told us two feds are already *at* the hospital waiting for the ambulance." He shrugged. "At least they *claimed* to be feds. Neither of the medics was convinced."

Morgan mulled over that bit of information. "How'd the feds know I was bringing them down?"

"Beats me," Alvarez answered. "Maybe they were monitoring our calls."

44

Morgan shook his head. "Pretty weird all the way around."

The cop nodded.

The sun was rising rapidly as Morgan piloted the machine back up the winding, twisting trail. He fished a cassette tape out of a compartment between the front seats and jammed it in the stereo player mounted under the dash. Jimi Hendrix's screaming guitar erupted in the snow machine's cab. The music invigorated him, and he joined with the dead musician singing about a purple haze.

As he crossed the snowfield, a flash of light from atop a huge craggy boulder caught Morgan's attention. He braked the Thiokol and studied the outcropping, jutting from the deep snow like a rotten tooth.

The sun was reflecting off something small and bright. Slipping on his dark glasses, Morgan saw a shape sprawled over the top of the rocks.

Curious, an odd quiver in the pit of his stomach, Morgan turned the snow machine toward it. As he drew nearer, he muttered a curse. As he neared the barren rock, the shape became human.

Stopping near the outcropping, he pulled on his snowshoes and climbed outside.

The body was too high for him to reach, but from where he stood he knew the man was far beyond help. White, blood-streaked bones protruded through the heavy winter gear and frozen red rivulets streamed down the rock. Bitter bile rose in the back of Morgan's throat when he saw the man's face. The mouth hung open in an eternal scream and the eye sockets stared down black and empty.

Chapter Three

"Must be Crocker," Richard Case said, standing outside the NORAMS station. "Any idea what killed him?"

Morgan exhaled a cloud of breath. "None. If I didn't know better, I'd say he was dropped on those rocks from pretty high up. But hell, that's ridiculous." Uncomfortably, his thoughts returned to his early, facetious speculation about UFOs.

That was just a little private joke, right?

Case motioned to Roberta Ferris. "Better grab your camera and come with us."

"I'll go too," said Paul Mitchell, appearing very tired and strained, his acne-scarred face now hinting at how it would look when he was an old man.

Case shook his head. "I can't allow that."

"I *knew* Mike!" Mitchell shot back bitterly.

Roberta Ferris touched the young man's arm. "We know he was a friend, but from what Blaylock tells me, you don't want to see what happened to him. You just stay here with the sheriff and his deputy. We'll be back soon."

Mitchell muttered a curse under his breath and turned away.

"That's the last thing we need right now," Case said as he climbed into the Thiokol opposite Morgan.

"The kid's pretty torn up," Morgan commented. "He just wants to be involved."

"I know that, Blaylock," Case said. "But this mess has got to be kept . . . quiet. The less people know, the better."

"Oh, really?" Morgan shot back. "Something going on here that might upset the delicate sensibilities of Joe Citizen?"

Case fixed him with a hard, even gaze. "I'm going to say this one time, Blaylock. You're working for the FBI at the moment. That means you're working for me. I don't need your sarcasm or your attitude. You keep fucking with me and I can promise you your life will become *very* uncomfortable."

Morgan gritted his teeth and studied the FBI man. "Instead of calling you Richard, can I just call you Dick?"

Case grimaced. "You just don't know when to quit, do you?"

"Oh, I get your drift, *Dick,*" Morgan said bitterly. "So, let me share something with you. If you're trying to pull off a cover-up, if you're sweeping something under the rug that's putting people at risk, I swear to God, I'll personally see to it the lid's blown off."

Case started to say something, but Roberta Ferris interrupted. "Richard, please, drop it." She looked at Morgan. "Trust me on this. He's following orders."

"Whose?"

"Mine."

Morgan turned in his seat and appraised the woman. "What I said stands. Call me an idealist or a son of a bitch, or whatever you want, but I won't be part of some bullshit government cover-up."

Roberta pursed her lips. "Fine. You've made your point. Now can we go?"

Morgan smiled humorlessly. "At least you know where *I* stand."

A dark, faraway look washed over the woman's eyes. "Maybe you wouldn't want to know." Case shot her a cautioning glance.

"Try me."

She shook her head and sighed. "Just take us to the body."

They drove in silence to the rock outcropping where Crocker was sprawled on its jagged stone crown, his open mouth screaming and his orbless eyes staring into eternity.

Morgan sat in the tractor while Case and Roberta inspected the area. He watched as the FBI agent started circling the rock, and the woman shouldered the minicam and began shooting video from every angle.

"Hey, Blaylock," Case called, his breath hanging in the frigid air. "I need some help getting up." He gestured toward the massive rock.

"I'm not that kind of guy," Morgan quipped, earning a dark look from Roberta Ferris and an ugly frown from Case.

"Save the wit, Blaylock," the FBI man snapped.

Morgan pulled on his snowshoes and followed Case around the outcropping. The FBI agent pointed to a fissure a few feet above their heads. "Just give me a boost so I can reach that crevice."

Case pulled off one snowshoe and slipped his booted foot in the Morgan's cupped hands. Once the agent had a firm hold, Morgan removed the man's other snowshoe.

"Roberta," the agent called, after a cursory inspection of the body. "Have Blaylock hand me the minicam. I think you'll want this mess on tape. Guy's broken up like a china doll." His voice was husky and strained.

Case had to cling precariously to the surface of the rock to reach the camera from Morgan's outstretched hand.

While the FBI agent stood focusing and taping the grisly remains, Morgan leaned against the boulder and looked at the woman. "I was right, huh?"

She raised an eyebrow. "About what?" She didn't try to hide the note of suspicion in her voice.

He gestured toward the top of the rock. "Crocker was dropped."

She looked away from him and studied the distant peaks. "Maybe."

"Oh, come off it," he said, keeping his voice low so Case wouldn't hear. "You know it and I know it. He was splattered on this rock like an egg. There are no marks or tracks in the snow except ours. And he sure as hell didn't climb up there and bash himself to death."

Roberta Ferris turned, looking at him for a long moment. "You were right, you know?"

"About what?"

"Always being a smartass." Before Morgan could say anything further, she stepped away and, shading her eyes, looked up at Case. "You about done?"

"Yeah," the agent answered. "Guess we'd better get this guy down."

"You ain't puttin' him in my unit," Morgan said to them. "Not without a body bag."

Case glared down. "Look in the back of your machine. You'll find a canvas carrier. Body bags inside."

Morgan swore softly to himself and then looked at the woman. "You two beat everything. You came ready, didn't you? You knew there'd be dead up here."

Roberta looked momentarily stricken and a little ashamed. "We didn't know," she said defensively. "We just . . . wanted to be prepared."

Morgan made a face. "Good answer, lady. Just too ghoulish for me."

She pursed her lips. "Christ, you're really a self-righteous son of a bitch."

"I am that."

Mike Crocker's remains came off the rock easily, if with little dignity. Once Morgan had the body bag unfolded and opened, Case simply shoved the body down. It fell stiffly into the snow, frozen limbs twisted and bent in odd, unnatural angles.

Morgan groaned, his stomach doing a slow, ponderous turn. Roberta looked away, a gloved hand over her mouth. Only Case appeared untouched by the horror sprawled in the snow.

Once the FBI agent was off the rock, he and Morgan struggled to put Crocker's body in the black plastic bag. It took a little doing, but finally they had the zipper secured, the plastic bulging in strange places.

"Now," Case said to Morgan, "I want you to ferry us back to the station and then take the body down."

"Can't it wait until we're all going down?" Morgan asked.

Case shook his head. "I want it autopsied immediately. You tell the patrolman to call the hospital."

Morgan sighed. Another three-hour drive. "You're paying the bill."

The agent smirked. "Glad you remembered that."

When they were back at the NORAMS station, Case gave Morgan a list of items he wanted brought back up.

"Okay," Morgan said skeptically after reading the list. "But I may have a problem with the snowmobiles. I'll have to trailer them up here unless you want someone to come with me to drive them."

Case thought about it for a minute and then turned to the sheriff. "Feel like driving a snowmobile up this mountain, Crumley?"

The sheriff shrugged. "Beats standing around here. Besides, I took samples of that pile of shit in the building. I can send it to the lab with the body."

Case frowned at the sheriff. "Make sure the results are kept strictly confidential."

Crumley frowned and nodded. "Yeah, sure. I may not be FBI, but I know how to conduct an investigation." He shot Morgan a disgusted glance.

"What about you?" Case asked McKissik.

The deputy sullenly eyed Morgan. "Yeah. I'll drive one."

Morgan and Red sat in the front, letting McKissik share the back of the big Thiokol with the body bag. He was obviously uncomfortable with the arrangement, but said nothing. Morgan suspected he'd be even less comfortable sitting up front with *him*.

Listening to a mellow jazz tape Morgan shoved in the player, the three made the trip in silence. Halfway down, Morgan radioed Alvarez, read off the list of items Case wanted and told them to have the coroner's meat wagon standing by.

"You going to keep running up and down that mountain all day?" Alvarez asked as they stood watching the coroner's station wagon pull away.

"One more time," Morgan answered, starting to load the items Case had requested into the back of the snow tractor. "Bring 'em down and then I'm hitting the sack."

It was only noon, but Morgan felt like he'd been at it for days rather than hours. The short night, the healthy blonde and a high-stress morning were all compounding his exhaustion.

Red Crumley yawned. "No kidding, I'm bushed. Jasper and I still have to drive those things back up." He pointed at the two big snowmobiles parked near Morgan's rig.

"So, what do you think?" Crumley asked, keeping his voice low.

Morgan shook his head. "I'm not sure what to think. But one thing's for sure. Whatever caused the mess up there wasn't an animal, at least none I'm familiar with."

51

Red continued to keep his voice low. "It's weird. What do you suppose happened to the woman? Think she's dead?"

"Probably," Morgan sighed.

"You know Charlie Shaw was back up here an hour or so ago," Alvarez said as he dropped the last boxes of supplies into the Thiokol next to the two-by-four lumber. "He was raisin' holy hell about getting no cooperation from the authorities. He accused me of participating in a cover-up. Said he was going to feed a story to the Associated Press, put pressure on the feds."

Red wiped a hand across his ruddy face. "What put a bug up his ass?"

"You know Charlie," Morgan said. "Can't find a story, he'll create one. Trouble is, this time, he's on to a good one."

"We better get going, Red," McKissik called as he straddled one of the snowmobiles.

For the third time that day, Morgan started the trip up the mountain. Crumley and his deputy on the small machines stayed with him for a while, dodging in and out of the trees like porpoises swimming with a whale. Finally, Red motioned that they were going on ahead.

Morgan reached the station 15 minutes after the others. Everyone was milling around, waiting impatiently for the food Mitchell was cooking.

Morgan took his plate of stew and a cup of coffee and retreated to his machine. He was tired, his eyes grainy and his kidneys sore. The aspirins had worn off and the headache was back, a small, nagging pain at the base of his skull. It was nothing 12 uninterrupted hours of sleep wouldn't cure.

"May I join you?" Roberta Ferris asked, opening the tractor's passenger door.

A little surprised, he nodded. "Sure."

She climbed in. Morgan held her plate while she slipped her small booted feet out of the snowshoes. Placing her

52

coffee on the floor, she took her plate and held it in her lap.

"You don't like me much, do you?" she said, matter-of-factly. The directness of her question caught Morgan off guard.

"Gee," he said innocently. "I'd say it was the other way around. I mean, weren't you the one that told me I was a smartass and a self-righteous SOB? Now, don't get me wrong, but I usually take that as a negative in forming any kind of a relationship."

Roberta nodded, a smile again tugging at the corner of her mouth. "Listen, I'm sorry about that. I was . . . well, a little upset. Crocker's body and all. And . . ." She paused and eyed him. "You do have a way of rubbing people the wrong way."

He flashed a crooked smile. "Yeah, I've been told that before. My mama used to say I engage my mouth before my brain."

She laughed. "Are you always so self-deprecating?"

"Does it bother you?"

"A question for a question. You're rather oblique, aren't you?"

"Oblique? Like indirect and evasive?"

"Exactly."

He laughed. "That's me."

"What's between you and what's-his-name, the deputy?"

"McKissik?" Morgan flashed a halfhearted smile. "Ol' Jasper and I have some history."

"Sorry," Roberta said quickly. "It's none of my business."

"Oh, hell, in the Wells, it's everyone's business. Small towns were designed for gossip. Nothing for people to do but invade other people's lives." Morgan offered her a crooked smile. "Doesn't bother me to talk about it."

She remained quiet.

"Jasper's married to my ex-wife," he said evenly.

"Ouch." She winced. "Makes having to work with him kind of tough, huh?"

He shook his head. "Not really. He's got Claudia and, believe me, he's welcome to her."

"I take it the divorce was less than amiable."

Morgan laughed. "Oh, hell, it was more than amiable. It was downright cheerful. She wanted out and I wanted her out."

Roberta shook her head. "It's always too bad when a marriage breaks up."

"Yeah," Morgan agreed, taking a sip of coffee. "But in our case, it was for the best. We were about as compatible as Charlie Manson and Mother Teresa."

"Which were you?" Roberta asked, a twinkle in her eye.

He laughed. "A little of both, I suppose."

Roberta appraised him for several long moments while they ate. Morgan sensed she was trying to find the right pigeonhole in which to slot him.

"What do you do in the summers?" she finally asked.

"I write."

"Really?" She was genuinely surprised.

"Did I fool you with the country-bumpkin routine?"

She blushed. "I didn't mean it that way. It's just that driving this monster around *and* writing strikes me as a very unlikely combination."

"Gotta eat."

"What do you write?" Roberta seemed truly interested.

"Oh, a little of this, a little of that," he said modestly. "Article for Charlie Shaw at the Wells paper, an occasional piece for regional rags, and the last couple of years I've been writing novels."

Unlike many writers, Morgan didn't like talking about his work. It always made him feel self-conscious.

"Might I have read any of your books?" she asked.

He looked at her and grinned. "Only if you like sexy Westerns."

"Sexy Westerns?"

He nodded. "Yeah, the traditional Western genre was pretty well mined by Max Brand and Louis L'Amour and Luke Short and a few hundred others. Sex sells books, Western or otherwise, and publishers aren't in the business for their health."

"So, did you come here to write?" she asked.

Morgan grinned. "How do you know I'm not a native?"

Roberta's brow furrowed in thought. "I'm not sure," she admitted. "You just don't strike me as a native."

"Very perceptive," he acknowledged. "In fact, I did come here to write. The Great American Novel or some such bullshit. I was just out of college, full of myself and sure I could conquer the publishing world given a little time and opportunity."

"And?" she prodded.

"I met Claudia. She was a very available woman and I was a very lonely guy. She kind of liked the idea of hanging out with a writer, I suppose, and I kind of liked . . ."

"The companionship?" Roberta finished diplomatically.

"Yeah, right. So one morning I wake up after a three- or four-day bender and she tells me we're married. We have a license and rings and everything. I haven't enjoyed drinking much since then."

Roberta laughed. Morgan liked the sound of it. It was soft and fragile and not at all like Claudia's braying guffaws. Maybe this woman wasn't such a dragon lady after all.

"I decided if I'd gone off and married her, I should take the responsibility seriously. A guy told me about the kind of money I could make with one of these snow monsters and I bought a used one. Decided to settle down. That's probably when Claudia stopped liking me. I wasn't a writer anymore; I was just another working stiff."

Morgan turned and set his empty plate on the floor behind his seat.

"We lasted a couple of years," he continued, vaguely realizing he'd never really talked to anyone about his divorce. "Actually, the last eighteen months we hardly saw each other. In the winter I was hustling customers so I could pay for this thing, and in the summer I was either planted in front of my computer or working some part-time job. Twelve, fifteen-hour days most of the time.

"Then I came home early one night and who do you suppose was in the sack with my wife?" He offered her a twisted smile.

"McKissik?" Roberta asked, amazed and mildly horrified.

"None other."

"That's terrible, Morgan. What did you do?" There was a note of real concern in her voice. Then she blushed and looked embarrassed. "I'm prying again."

Morgan's green eyes turned inward. "I left them to finish their little party and found the closest bar. Got stinking drunk for about a week. Absolutely can't remember any of it. When I sobered up—in Red Crumley's jail, by the way—I went to my house intent on telling Claudia it was over, but she was already gone."

"It must have been painful for you," Roberta said.

He shrugged. "Not really, although being cuckolded by Jasper McKissik was a blow to my manly ego. It was a pride thing. My delicate feelings were wounded." His attempt to make light of it failed miserably.

"I'm sorry."

"Jasper had been solo all his life and for all of her faults, Claudia is still something of a bombshell. The booze and mileage are starting to take their toll, though."

"That's too bad," Roberta said seriously. "I hate to see anyone destroy herself like that."

"Jasper takes good care of her. Buys her all the stuff she wants. Within his means, of course." Including all the booze she can guzzle, he thought, but didn't say.

They both watched McKissik and Crumley talking near the chain-link fence.

"I guess that explains the bad blood between you and McKissik," Roberta said.

"I never liked Jasper," Morgan said pointedly. "And not because of Claudia. He's a small man with a big mouth and a gun. Bad combination. Red should get rid of him."

They were silent for several minutes, both lost in their own thoughts. Finally, Roberta looked at him. "I hope you understand that Richard and I are just doing our jobs."

He stared out the windshield, squinting against the brightness. "You know more about what's going on up here than you're willing to admit. I've got to tell you, that bothers me."

She sighed. "More than I *can* admit."

He thought about that for a moment and then turned to her, catching her eyes with his own. "Okay. Tell me one thing."

"If I can."

"Tell me that whatever killed Crocker and snatched the woman—she was snatched, wasn't she?"

Roberta said nothing.

Morgan continued. "Just tell me that all of this has a perfectly understandable explanation."

Looking away, studying the mountains for a minute, she shook her head. "It's very complicated."

"Rocket science is complicated. Brain surgery is complicated. I don't think *this* is all that involved."

"You might be surprised," she muttered.

"Try me."

Roberta glanced at him, her eyes now slitted against the brightness. "I can't. It's top secret. Classified."

Morgan rolled his eyes. "Great. I ask a straight question and you give me a bureaucrat's answer."

Her eyes flared and she started to reply, but clamped her mouth shut when Case rapped on the window.

"Come on," he told them. "We've got some things to do before we leave." The FBI agent appeared strained, and he gave Roberta a questioning look which Morgan thought betrayed a basic distrust.

As she climbed out of the snow tractor, he hissed something to her and she reacted as if slapped.

"Don't forget who's calling the shots, Richard," she said testily.

He glanced irritably at Morgan as Roberta walked away.

"What'd she tell you?" Case demanded as Morgan pulled on his snowshoes and came around to the front of his vehicle.

"Stuff you wouldn't like to hear," Morgan deadpanned.

"Like what?" Case's mouth was set in a hard line and his eyes were flinty. He took an awkward step toward Morgan.

"She said it was okay if I called you *Dick*." Morgan smiled and started to walk away. He staggered when Case grabbed his parka and jerked him around. Unable to catch his balance on the snowshoes, Morgan pinwheeled his arms a couple of times and then went sprawling backward.

Case towered over him, aiming a finger at his face. "I've told you, Blaylock, don't fuck with me."

Morgan glared up at the agent, his jaws clenched. Then he smiled. "Sure. Whatever you say, *Dick*. No problem."

The other man stood glaring at him, his eyes smoldering. He abruptly turned and stalked away, leaving Morgan to struggle to his feet.

Morgan's mama always said he'd gotten a double helping of lip and a short ration of sense.

Along with the two-by-four studs, Case had ordered a roll of heavy plastic, a box of folded cardboard cartons, strapping tape, a heavy-duty stapler, various hand tools and other odds and ends. He mobilized everyone to help carry the items into the station.

Case told them he wanted all the smashed equipment gathered and placed in boxes and sealed with the strapping tape. Additionally, he wanted a wood frame built inside the doorway to which he could attach the plastic to help keep the snow out until a repair crew could be brought up to set things right.

While everyone began working, Case asked Mitchell to accompany him on one of the snowmobiles to search the area. Clearly, the young NORAMS man was glad to have something to do.

"What a charmer," Morgan snorted as Case and Mitchell set off across the snow on the whining machines.

"Why's he want all this stuff boxed up anyway?" McKissik asked Roberta. "It's all junk."

"Evidence," she responded. "He wants to have all of it analyzed."

Red Crumley screwed up his face. "Now, I know he's a big-shot FBI agent and all, but when I gather physical evidence I usually make sure the people handling don't get fingerprints all over it."

The three men watched Roberta, waiting for her answer. "I'm not a cop," she answered. "He is. I'm sure he knows what he's doing."

"Glad somebody's sure," Morgan muttered. It earned him yet another dark look from the woman.

While they were gathering the destroyed equipment and placing it into boxes, Morgan saw Roberta Ferris retrieve a small electronic device attached to a cracked computer case. She examined it quickly, a puzzled expression crossing her face, and then, almost furtively, she slipped it into her coat pocket.

Morgan thought it odd, but dismissed it with a shrug. What wasn't odd about this mess?

When the junked equipment was safely packed, Red and Morgan began measuring and cutting the lumber for the makeshift door.

The sun was sliding down toward the mountains when Case and Mitchell returned on the snowmobiles. The whine of their engines had grown and faded throughout the afternoon as they scoured the area.

Morgan noted the expectant, questioning look Roberta shot Case walked into the station.

"Nothing," he said sourly. "We covered the entire area and there's no sign of her."

Mitchell entered, looking dejected and weary. "I can't figure out what happened to her," he said sadly. "She's just gone!"

"We'll find her," Case said confidently.

"Yeah," Morgan said, holding a board while Red prepared to drive in a nail. "The FBI always gets its woman."

"Probably won't find her until the spring thaw," the sheriff whispered.

"These boxes okay stacked here?" McKissik asked Case. The deputy was carrying a box which tinkled with broken glass every time he took a step.

"No. Put them in Blaylock's machine."

Morgan paused and stared at the agent.

"'Scuse me, Dick," he said. "But if you put all that in the tractor, there's going to be no room for anything else, like people."

Case fixed him with a steely-eyed gaze. "Then I guess you'll have to make another trip, won't you."

"Guess again," Morgan said, dropping the hammer he'd been holding. Its head hit the concrete with a bang. "I've been up and down this mountain two and half times. Three's going to make it a full day. Now if you want me to haul these boxes down, that's fine. But you and the others better settle in for a long, cold night, because I ain't coming back up until tomorrow morning."

Roberta Ferris suddenly looked worried. Red Crumley turned away to hide his grin.

"You can't leave us up here, Blaylock," McKissik blurted out.

"Sure I can," Morgan answered affably.

"No," Case said. "That's not how it's going to work. You're going to carry these boxes down, turn around and come back up for us. You don't, and I'll throw the book at you, Blaylock. Your insolence and insubordination are wearing damn thin."

Morgan sensed a test of wills. If he kowtowed to Case, he'd lose face with Red and McKissik. Red he didn't worry about, but McKissik would never let him live it down. On the other hand, if he backed Case into a corner, God and the government only knew what the guy would do.

Morgan might have given in had McKissik not been watching him with wolfish, dancing eyes.

"That's the deal, Dick. I mean, all you have to do is stack the boxes in here overnight and I can come back up tomorrow morning and get them. But I'm sure as hell not going to make another round trip tonight."

"Listen, Blaylock . . ." Case paused in mid-sentence as the unmistakable whine of yet another snowmobile came roaring up to the station.

"Damn it," the FBI agent snapped. "Who's here? That cop is suppose to keep anyone from coming up here."

The intruding machine's engine was suddenly silent, and a few seconds later a small man in a padded snowmobile suit appeared at the door. He tugged off big bubble goggles to reveal wire-rimmed glasses beneath.

"You're on government property. Clear out," Case snapped.

Nonplussed, the little man looked at Crumley. "Hi, Red. Figured I find you up here."

Case glared at the sheriff. "Who is this man?"

"Charlie Shaw," Red said, pointing his thumb at the new arrival. "Meet Richard Case, FBI."

"Who are you?" Case demanded.

"Editor of the *Crystal Wells Journal*. I'd like to ask you some questions." The man was oblivious to the dark frown on the agent's scarlet face.

"I told you about him," Morgan said.

"Get out!" the FBI agent snapped. "You've no authorization to be here."

"Really?" Shaw asked innocently. "Gosh, when I looked this morning, the Constitution was still in effect. In fact, unless I'm very much mistaken, you're sworn to uphold it. First Amendment's part of the package, isn't it?"

"You want a story, see our press officer," Case snarled. "This is a crime scene. You're interfering with a federal investigation."

Shaw looked at Morgan, who had to suppress a laugh when he saw the wicked glint in the editor's eyes. "Is that right, Blaylock? You a federal investigator now?"

"Me? Naw, I'm just the hired help."

"And what about you, Red? You and Jasper turn in your county badges to be Junior G-Men?"

"Giving the FBI our full assistance, Charlie," Red said straight-faced.

"Well, now, Mr. FBI Agent," Shaw said, screwing up his face and fixing Case with a hard stare. "If this is a federal investigation, where are all your federal people?"

Case leveled a finger at the reporter's face. "I'm all the federal people that's needed. This is a classified area. You're trespassing. You want to push me and I'll have you up on a dozen federal charges."

Shaw bristled. "Fine. It'll be one hell of an interesting story." He moved his hand across the empty space in front of him as if read an imaginary headline. " 'Reporter Jailed for Exposing Federal Cover-Up.' It'll make all the wire services, Mr. Case. I'll be a goddamn martyr and you'll look like a horse's ass."

Case drew in a breath and turned away, apparently ignoring the smirks on the others' faces. When he finally spoke, his voice was low and controlled. "This is a very important and sensitive situation, Shaw. In order to conduct a successful investigation, it's important that it remain confidential. However, if you'll agree not to write anything about it until it is concluded, I think I can guarantee you the exclusive of a lifetime."

Morgan watched as Roberta paled when the FBI agent made the offer. Whatever was going on here was definitely something that was never going to be publicized by the feds.

"Bad offer, Charlie," Morgan said, deciding to stir the pot just to see what floated to the top.

Case glared at him. "This is none of your business, Blaylock. You can be replaced."

Morgan smiled sardonically. "Ah, geez, Dick, that'd break my heart. I've been up and down this mountain so many times I feel like a yo-yo."

"You *are* a fucking yo-yo," Case snarled, moving toward the other man. "I'm going to have your ass, mister."

"Morgan, don't . . ." Red warned, taking hold of his friend's arm. "Let it lie."

"Stop it! All of you!" The men all turned toward Roberta Ferris. Her eyes blazed and her mouth was a hard line. "We don't have time for the two of you to play this macho bullshit game. You want to see who's got a bigger dick, fine, do it on your own time. It's getting late. We need to get down."

Shaw cocked his head, noting, as had everyone else, the tinge of fear in her voice. "What's the rush?"

She met his gaze and held it for several heartbeats. "Because we aren't prepared to stay here all night."

The newspaper editor looked around the now-empty station. His eyes lingered on the bits and pieces of broken glass scattered over the floor. "Oh, I don't know, I think we could make do."

"Speaking of going down," Morgan said. "My bus is pulling out in half an hour." He glanced significantly at Case. "Last run of the day."

The FBI agent shook his head in defeat and sighed heavily. "All right. We'll leave the boxes. But let's finish this door so we can secure the place." He turned to Shaw. "You can wait outside."

The editor frowned. "Okay. I've already got enough for a story."

Case grimaced. "Don't write it."

"Is that a warning?" the newspaperman demanded.

"Take it however you want."

Morgan winked at Red Crumley, but kept a straight face. Let Shaw spar with Case for a while. He was tired. All he wanted now was to get home and into his bed. Hopefully, this morning's young blonde would be gone.

Morgan picked up his hammer. "Red, what say we finish up?"

The sheriff nodded. "The sooner done, the sooner gone."

Case slipped on his snowshoes and followed Shaw outside. He returned a few minutes later no longer looking worried.

The sun was down and the sunset was fading into a purple night when they were finally finished. They parked the two snowmobiles inside the NORAMS building and then Case closed the hasp installed on the makeshift door.

"Let's go," he said.

Morgan turned to Shaw. "You going to ride down with us?"

The small man shook his head. "Naw. I'll follow along on my snowmobile." He looked at the FBI agent. "I wouldn't want it to get stolen up here."

"Have it your way," Morgan said.

Everyone piled into the snow machine while Morgan walked to where Charlie Shaw stood straddling his small snowmobile.

"Hey, Morgan," he called, thumbing at the yellow snow tractor lying on its side like some slain beast. "What the hell did that?"

Morgan shook his head. "Beats me, Charlie. Snow trolls, maybe."

"Yeah, right," the editor replied with a laugh. "Or Bigfoot." He pursed his lips and studied Morgan. "How much do you know?"

Morgan shook his head. "Not a lot, but I'll tell you one thing: You weren't wrong about a cover-up. The feds are sitting on something big and, if I'm not mistaken, dangerous."

"How dangerous?" the editor asked.

Again Morgan gestured at Ryan's overturned snow machine. "You decide. One confirmed dead, one missing and two in the hospital."

Shaw leaned forward. "Can we talk later?"

"Sure. I'll give you everything I've got. But like I said, it's not a lot."

"Hey, Blaylock," Case shouted from inside the big Thiokol. "I thought you wanted to get out of here."

"Duty calls," Morgan told his old friend. "I'll talk to you when we get down."

It was dark once they were among the trees. The snow tractor's headlights cut brilliant holes through the ebony night, illuminating the now-well-worn trail. Charlie Shaw's snowmobile stayed behind the Thiokol.

They were just moving over a stretch of small dips when McKissik called excitedly from the back.

"Hey, I don't see Charlie's light anymore."

Morgan braked the tractor to a halt. He craned his neck to look out the rear window. Behind them was a wall of darkness.

"Maybe he took a shortcut," Roberta suggested, a nervous tremor in her voice.

"Not likely," Morgan answered. "This is the only way through this particular stretch. Guess I'd better go back and take a look. He might have had an accident."

"Leave him," Case snapped. He sat in the front seat opposite Morgan. "You're being paid by my agency. We're not responsible for that nosy bastard."

Morgan started to say something and then bit off his words. Instead, he put the machine in gear and executed a tight turn.

"Did you hear me, Blaylock?" Case demanded.

"Richard," Roberta cried in disgust. "We can't just leave without knowing if that man is hurt or not, for God's sake." She sat in the seat directly behind Morgan and Case.

The FBI agent's face grew dark in the dashboard lights.

"She's right," Crumley said. "No way I'm leaving a man to die up here."

Morgan sent his machine back up the trail. As it topped the first hill, he cursed. The powerful headlights fell across the snowmobile. It was on its side. There was a collective gasp when they saw the dark figure crouched nearby, just out of the circle of illumination. As the snow tractor came to a halt, the figure turned, looking up. Round, cold yellow eyes glistened for a second and then the figure was gone.

"What the hell?" Morgan yelled struggling out of the machine and pulling on his snowshoes. He could hear nothing over the rumble of the engine. He scanned the area quickly and saw a huddled shape where the dark figure had squatted. He hurried across the hard-packed snow.

"Don't touch anything!" Case called frantically, scrambling out his door.

Morgan ignored the agent. When he reached the spot, he stopped abruptly and stared.

Charlie Shaw was dimly illuminated, but there was just enough light for Morgan to see the look of utter terror frozen on the man's dead face. The snow around the body was splattered red and tiny streamers flowed from the gaping wound ripped across the editor's throat.

Morgan cursed, kneeling beside his friend. He gagged when he saw the dark, empty eye sockets staring up at him.

Chapter Four

Morgan was enraged. Standing quickly, he turned away from Charlie Shaw's body to confront Case. "What the hell's going on?"

The FBI agent's eyes darkened and he met Morgan's gaze. "Nothing you need to concern yourself about."

"Bullshit!" Morgan roared. "This man was my friend."

An odd look passed over Case's face. "Well, he's dead now."

Morgan stepped forward, his fists balled. "You son of a bitch . . . !"

Before he could throw a punch, Red Crumley was between them, his gloved hands locked on both Morgan's arms. "Enough!"

For several long moments they stood there, and then finally, he let Morgan loose.

"Let's just . . . get this over with," Morgan breathed. He glared at Richard Case. "Got any more body bags?"

Leaning against the snow machine, Morgan watched

67

while Roberta put the grim scene on videotape. Under the minicam's harsh light, Shaw's brutalized body looked small and fragile, like a broken toy smashed by some nasty child.

Case, on the other hand, was ignoring Charlie Shaw and instead knelt next to the dead man's snowmobile. Jesus, he was a coldhearted bastard.

A few moments later, Morgan helped the FBI agent and Crumley slip the dead man's body into one of the heavy black bags.

He was heartsick and disgusted. Charlie Shaw had been a good friend, a mentor. He'd been the first man in Crystal Wells to give him a chance. He had encouraged and badgered and cajoled Morgan. Now he was lying inside a plastic bag with his throat gaping like a second mouth.

Morgan shook his head. He couldn't indulge his emotions now. Charlie was dead, and whatever killed him was still out there, somewhere.

And what did kill him? What was that thing with the evil yellow eyes that had disappeared in a heartbeat?

The Mitchell kid took one look at the body and started to blubbering. It was too much for him. One of his friends was in the hospital, one was dead and one missing.

Leaving Shaw's snowmobile, they loaded his body into the Thiokol. The silence inside the cab was thick and heavy as Morgan started down the mountain. Everyone was lost in his or her own thoughts.

At the truck, they loaded the body into the back of Alvarez's cruiser. Case left for the hospital morgue with the patrolman while Crumley, McKissik and Mitchell helped Morgan load the snow tractor. Roberta Ferris watched with evident disinterest.

The main street of Crystal Wells was empty when Morgan drove into town. He left Crumley, his deputy and Mitchell at the truck stop. Red had decided to take the Mitchell kid home for the night, not wanting to leave him alone in some strange motel room. Besides, Red confided, his wife would enjoy mothering the young man.

"I'm sorry about your friend," Roberta said as Morgan wheeled the truck down the street toward her motel.

"Right," he growled.

"Damn it," she snapped. "You think I don't under-stand?"

Morgan glanced at her. "Frankly, I don't give a rat's ass, Ms. Ferris. All I know is that you've got two peo-ple dead and you and that asshole Case act like it's no big deal!"

Roberta blinked, her eyes suddenly moist. "If that's what you think, then you're . . ." She paused, sucking in a deep breath, struggling against the hot, angry tears burning her eyes.

Morgan sighed. "Look, why don't you and Case go your merry little way without me? I've already lost my stomach for whatever shit you're into."

"Fine," she whispered. "Is there someone else we can hire?"

Morgan shook his head. "Ryan and I have the corner on the market."

It was Roberta's turn to heavy a weary sigh. "We could use your help," she finally said as Morgan pulled to a stop outside the rambling Crystal Wells Lodge.

"Have a nice life," he said sarcastically.

She glared at him for a long moment, and then climbed out of the truck, dragging her minicam case with her.

A few minutes later, Morgan stepped wearily through the front door of his house and wandered into the kitchen for a beer. Physically tired and emotionally drained, he tried to push away the grim image of Charlie Shaw's body. Finding Crocker smashed on the rocks had been bad enough, but he was a stranger and Morgan was detached from his death.

The cold beer did nothing to quell the sick knot in the pit of his stomach. He gulped it down and reached for another.

Leaning against the kitchen counter, Morgan studied some spot in the middle distance. There was something up there in that frozen hell killing people and the feds wanted to keep it all very hush-hush.

His thoughts turned to Roberta Ferris. She was an enigma. When they found Charlie, she had remained stoic and firmly resolved, taking out her video camera and calmly recorded the scene. Yet in the truck, she had been on the verge of tears.

Morgan couldn't figure her. At lunch she was pleasant and engaging, but a few hours later she had turned sullen and icy. She was harboring a deep secret and guarding it with a vengeance. And Morgan couldn't shake his suspicions that the secret would make a lot of people very nervous and uncomfortable if it came out.

And then there was Case. Morgan didn't have much experience with the FBI, but if this guy was a typical agent, then the Bureau was a snake pit of neo-fascists.

Morgan wandered into the living room and flopped wearily on his couch.

What *had* they seen crouching over Charlie's body? It had been a dark blotch against the trees; yellow, inhuman eyes peering at them with cold indifference. And it had vanished in an instant. How was that possible?

Morgan cursed and took another pull on the beer.

Give it a rest, he told himself bitterly. He tugged off his boots, dropping them on the hardwood floor. Finishing the second can of beer, he wandered into the bathroom and flipped on the light.

He was startled by the scrawled letters, and for a second a rush of paranoia flooded over him.

YOU'RE A BASTARD PRICK. The words were written in lipstick across the mirror. Morgan frowned. A parting gift from last night's little-miss-no-name.

"A fan letter." His words sounded hollow and empty in the small room. As he stared at the scrawled words, a deep, despairing sadness settled over him. His life was a circus. He was either hustling customers to keep the payments up on the snow tractor, pounding out formula books on his computer to satisfy his creative needs or, just as often, stumbling home with a gut full of booze and a bimbo on his arm.

And Charlie Shaw was dead. That was the real pain.

Gripping the edges of the sink, Morgan bowed his head and gritted his teeth. He stood there for several long moments, fighting off the images of Charlie Shaw's small body lying in the blood-soaked snow, struggling against his welling sense of despair. Finally, drawing in a deep breath, he washed his face with cold water.

Roberta Ferris had called him self-righteous. And he *was* feeling self-righteous. She and Case were hiding something and whatever it was, it scared the hell out of them. After Shaw's death, he could almost smell their fear.

Something was up there and it was a killer. Maybe it was a rampaging psychopath or some berserk wild animal . . .

. . . with gleaming yellow eyes and the ability to disappear?

Right.

A chill went down Morgan's spine. Maybe it's both, he thought. Some genetic experiment gone wrong. A cross between man and beast . . .

"Bullshit!" he said aloud. UFOs and mutants. It was all a lot of crap.

Using a wet towel and glass cleaner, Morgan wiped the greasy red letters off the mirror. He dropped the towel in the wastebasket, not interested in trying to get it clean later.

He stared at himself in the glass. If possible, he looked worse than he had that morning. His green eyes were red-rimmed and darkly circled and his face was deathly pale beneath the sunbaked tan. The few wrinkles were more pronounced and his cheeks hollow.

Wandering into the bedroom, he noted the faint,

lingering odor of cheap perfume as he straightened the rumpled bedding. He crawled between the covers and drifted into a fitful sleep.

Morgan awoke later with a start, still seeing the twin yellow eyes glaring at him from the winter forest darkness. It took him almost an hour to fall back to sleep.

The insistent pounding brought Morgan awake. He blinked against the bright sunlight streaming in his bedroom window and dragged himself out of bed. It was chilly in the house, and he pulled the heavy wool robe off the back of a chair and shrugged it on.

There was more pounding on his front door.

"All right. All right. I'm coming," he bellowed in irritation, padding barefoot across the living room.

Opening the door, he was mildly surprised to see Richard Case and Roberta Ferris standing on his porch.

"We've been here for five minutes," Case snapped.

Morgan shrugged. "Morning to you too, *Dick*. Didn't know I'd penciled you in for an appointment."

The FBI agent started to say something but was stopped by Roberta. "May we come in, Morgan?" she asked.

He nodded and stepped aside to let the pair enter. *"Mi casa, su casa."*

"How soon will you be ready to go back up there?" Case asked abruptly.

Morgan rubbed his face with both hands and then fixed the agent with a squinty-eyed stare. "Seems to me I quit last night."

Case sucked in a breath and frowned. "You're a real piece of work, Blaylock. I've asked around. You and Ryan are the only game in town. With him in the hospital, you're our only option."

"And I've optioned myself out," Morgan said flatly.

Case took a quick step forward. "Hey, Blaylock, if you want, I can confiscate your machine and you'll be shit out of luck."

Morgan crossed his arms and fixed the FBI agent with

a hard stare. "I'd sugar the gas tank before I'd let you steal it. And if you try, God help you!"

"Don't threaten me . . ."

"Take a hike, Dick. You're undermining my faith in our government."

Case jabbed a finger at Morgan. "I need your vehicle. Either I get it or I'll take it."

Morgan's grin evaporated and his jaw clamped shut hard. His eyes grew dark and when he spoke there was a dangerous edge in his voice. "You touch it, Case, and they'll be looking for a new FBI geek. You got that? You touch and I'll take you apart!"

"The two of you sound like spoiled children," Roberta spat angrily. "Sandbox childishness. I've had enough of it. Richard." She touched the agent's arm firmly. "Go wait in the car. I'll talk to Morgan alone."

Case turned and glowered at her. "Roberta, let me handle this. We're supposed to be working together."

"Just go out to the car, will you?" She was exasperated and weary, her face etched by sleeplessness and fatigue.

Case shot Morgan a harsh parting glance and then stalked out of the house, banging the door shut behind him.

"What a nice guy," Morgan snorted. "Where do they find people like that?"

Roberta shook her head and pulled off her heavy parka. Tossing it on the couch, she glanced around the small living room. Her eyes stopped when she saw the three bookcases packed with hardbacks. She moved to it and studied the titles. After a moment she looked up at Blaylock and smiled. "I'm impressed. Hemingway, Fitzgerald, St. Augustine, Plato, Dickens. Quite a library. I haven't seen *On the Early Education of the Citizen-Orator* since I was in college."

Morgan shifted. "Quintilian. Fascinating stuff, really.

Not that anyone cares in these post-literate days."

Roberta studied him for a moment. "You're awfully cynical."

"I have reason to be," he said pointedly.

She straightened, holding her arms and studying him. "About last night . . . I'm really sorry about your friend. I know you don't trust Richard or me, but we need your help."

Morgan frowned. "Look, I don't know what's going on, but it has a bad feel about it."

"Whatever we're paying you, we'll double it," Roberta said.

Morgan nodded. "That's a hunk of change. But it's not about money."

He studied her. Damn, but she was beautiful. If it wasn't for all this intrigue and deception, Morgan thought he'd enjoy getting to know her better.

"Want some coffee?" Without waiting for an answer he started toward the kitchen.

"If it's ready," she answered, following him. "I shouldn't keep Richard waiting too long."

"It'll only take a few minutes. Let him cool his heels for a while. Do him good."

Roberta watched Morgan while he slipped a fresh filter into the coffee maker and spooned in a liberal amount of dark coffee.

"French roast. Hope you like it," Morgan told her. "I always need something strong to jump-start my heart."

"It'll be fine." Roberta scrutinized the kitchen. It was neat and clean, everything in its place. The frilly curtains on the window over the small table showed a woman's touch.

"Want something to eat?" Morgan asked as the coffee maker began to gurgle and pop.

She shook her head. "I've already eaten."

He moved to the refrigerator and pulled a bag of English muffins from one of the shelves. He removed one and dropped the two halves into the toaster.

Roberta crossed her arms beneath her breasts and leaned against the door jamb. She looked rather sexy in her blue jeans and bulky sweater.

"I really need your help, Morgan."

He turned to her and frowned. "I'm not sure I want to get involved any further."

"Because of Case?"

Morgan shot her a critical glance. "That's part of it. He doesn't bother me as much as whatever's going on up there." He jerked a thumb toward the mountains visible through the kitchen window.

She sighed. "I wish I could tell you more."

"But you can't, right?"

She nodded.

"Look, I'm no rocket scientist, but it doesn't take a genius to know whatever's up there is as dangerous as hell. Now, if you want me to risk my neck, then you're going to have to tell me what you and Case are up against. What *I'll* be up against." Morgan kept his voice level and reasonable, a contradiction to his mixed feelings of annoyance and paranoia.

Roberta looked down, studying the pattern on the tiled floor. "All I want you to do is take us up there. You're perfectly safe during the daylight. I guarantee it."

He looked at her. "Safe in daylight, huh? What's that supposed to mean?"

"Just exactly what I said," she answered, and then rushed on. "And don't ask me any more questions. I can't tell you anything else."

"Don't tell me you can't get a snow tractor from the Forest Service or some other agency."

"Yes, I could," she admitted. "But I can't afford to get more people involved."

"That bad, huh? What're you covering up?" An icy note had crept into his voice.

Roberta looked up at him, her eyes flashing. "You don't

want to know what's up there, Morgan. Believe me, you don't want to know."

"But you know, don't you?" It was an accusation.

She sighed. "Not for sure. Only a vague idea. A theory."

"And that is?"

"I can't tell you, damn it!" she snapped. "Can't you get that through your thick head?"

Morgan frowned. "Look. If you expect me to help, I damn well want to know the score. I'm not some army grunt blindly following orders from some guts-and-glory general."

Roberta straightened. "Fine. I'll show myself out." She vanished from the doorway. Her boots clattered across the living room floor.

"Wait a minute," he called, going after her. She was standing in the middle of the room, her coat in her hands. "Okay, I'll take you and Dick up there. But I want a few answers."

"I told you," she said wearily. "I can't tell you anything. Frankly, you already know too much."

He smiled crookedly and gestured toward the kitchen. "Coffee's done and my muffin's getting cold. Let's talk. You tell me what you can."

She shook her head. "You just don't listen, do you?"

"I'll just ask a few questions," Morgan persisted. "Answer whatever you can."

"It won't be much," she said, sounding a little defeated.

They sat at the kitchen table, steaming mugs of coffee in front of them. Morgan smeared butter over a muffin half and then looked up at the woman.

"Let's play twenty questions, okay? I'll ask and you answer."

Roberta looked skeptical and rolled her eyes. "If you must."

"Okay. Do you know who or *what* killed Crocker and Shaw?"

"No."

"Can you tell me what you *think* it is?"

"No."

Morgan took a bite of muffin and chewed it thoughtfully. He tried a different tact. "What agency do you work for?"

"I'm a member of a jointly funded task force," she answered flatly.

"Funded by whom?"

She shook her head. "Sorry."

"Are you in the military?"

"No."

"CIA?"

She almost laughed. "I'm not that devious."

"Oh, don't underestimate yourself," he said. "You're remarkably devious. Does this task force investigate unusual phenomena?"

Her eyes shifted. "Yes."

"Ah-ha," Morgan cried in mock triumph. "I'm finally getting somewhere. Are you part of the Pentagon's UFO investigation team?"

"No." She sipped her coffee, watching him over the rim.

Again, Morgan munched on the muffin and thought. This was tedious, but he'd give it the old college try. "Have other people died like Charlie Shaw and Crocker?"

She didn't answer immediately. Then she bobbed her head.

"Recently?"

"Yes."

"Around here?"

"Yes."

"How many?" He asked the question earnestly.

"One."

"So three people have died, not counting the missing woman, right?"

"Yes."

"And the Pruett woman is probably dead. So that makes four."

"We don't know that she's dead," Roberta said too quickly, her eyes growing large and concerned.

"You think she's still alive? Why?"

"I can't tell you that."

Morgan sighed. "Okay. Are you and Case the only people investigating this?"

"No. There are others. We're the only ones on-site right now." She took another drink. "Can we go now? We really need to get up to the station and get those boxes down."

Morgan got up from the table. "Sure, we can go. But one more question. Was the other person killed a man or woman?"

Roberta looked away from him, a darkness filling her eyes. "A woman."

He nodded. "Two men and one woman killed and a woman missing. Where they killed the same way?"

Roberta looked back at him. "I thought you only had one more question."

Morgan screwed up his face. "Hey. I don't like playing this silly game any more than you do. Did the other woman die like Charlie?"

Roberta made no response.

"Yes?" he prompted.

"She died . . . more slowly."

He thought for a moment. "I guess I'd be wasting my time to try to get more out of you, huh?"

"Morgan," she said, getting up from the table, "I don't like this either. It's not my style, but I don't have much of a choice." She looked into his eyes. Her voice was barely a whisper. "The woman was eviscerated. We think she was pregnant."

"God," Morgan groaned. "That's sick."

"What's really sick," Roberta said flatly, "is that she wasn't pregnant when she disappeared last summer."

Morgan let that settle in. "So she was . . . what? Raped,

impregnated and then the baby taken after a few months? It wouldn't even be much more than a bit of shapeless tissue."

Roberta remained silent. The look on her face told Morgan she had already told him too much.

"Okay. Give me ten minutes and we'll leave." As if on cue, a car horn blared outside.

"Richard," Roberta said. "He's getting impatient. I'll go out and wait in the car."

Morgan took a quick shower, pulled on fresh, insulated clothes and went out to the car. The engine was idling. Richard Case sat in the driver's seat, impatiently drumming his fingers on the steering wheel. When he saw Morgan, he rolled down the window.

"You follow us in your truck," Case ordered. "Maybe we can salvage some of this day."

Morgan gave him a snappy salute. "Lead on, Dick." He saw Roberta turn away, hiding a faint smile.

They reached the base of the trail in good time and Morgan had the snow tractor unloaded in minutes. As they were getting ready to leave, Red Crumley arrived.

"Weren't planning to go without me, were you?" he asked Morgan.

"Didn't know you were coming."

"He's not," Case growled.

"Wrong," Crumley answered. "Two people are dead."

"On federal land."

"In my county. I'm coming."

"There's no problem, Sheriff," Roberta said as she climbed into the back of the tractor with her padded minicam bag. "You're more than welcome."

Case scowled, but kept quiet.

Red sat in the front with Morgan. Case and Roberta retreated to the far back seat where they talked in low voices. Occasionally, the FBI agent's voice would rise, but neither man in the front could make out any of the conversation.

"I talked to Doc Reed this morning," Red said quietly.

Morgan looked at him expectantly. "And?"

"Had to pry the information out of the old goat," the sheriff whispered.

"So, I have to pry it out of you?"

Red smiled. "Doc was pretty worried about telling me anything." The sheriff glanced back toward Case and Roberta Ferris and, satisfied they weren't listening, continued. "He said the feds came down pretty hard on him."

"Yeah, okay, I get the message. So what'd he say?"

"He did the autopsy on Crocker. The guy had almost no blood left in him." Red gave Morgan a meaningful look.

"He bled a lot . . ."

"Yeah, but Doc said the blood was drained from him. *Sucked* out. Arteries and veins were collapsed." The sheriff made a face.

"What about Charlie?" Morgan asked, feeling his stomach do a slow turn.

Red shook his head. "No autopsy yet. Scheduled for this morning. But his preliminary exam seemed to indicate a lot of blood loss. More than what he lost from the throat and head wounds. And Doc said the throat wound was made by teeth."

Morgan thought about that for a second, replaying the grisly scene from the previous night in his mind's eye.

"Teeth? Damn!" He swore too loudly. In the back, Case stopped talking.

"What's wrong?" the agent demanded.

"Nothing, Dick," Morgan answered in a forced falsetto. "Everything's okeydokey up here."

The agent glowered and then resumed his conversation with Roberta.

"How's Gruff?" Morgan asked.

Crumley made a face. "He's not in the hospital."

"What?"

"The feds spirited him and Fenwick away not long after they arrived."

Morgan chewed on that bit of unsettling information for a moment. "Any idea where they took them?"

"None."

"All of this is starting to play like a James Bond movie, Red."

"And I'm getting sick of it," the sheriff hissed.

Morgan stopped when they came across Shaw's snowmobile. It was still lying on its side. The front cowling was cracked. A nearby pine bore evidence of the impact.

"What's the holdup?" Case demanded.

"Just want to take a look at Charlie's snowmobile," Morgan called out. "Only take a minute."

Case started to protest, but Roberta touched his arm and shook her head.

Morgan and Red slipped on their snowshoes and trudged to the snow machine.

"Ran right into the tree," the sheriff observed.

Morgan's eyes scanned the broad, flat path left by the machine's tread. A few feet away from the tree, the track twisted sharply twice before angling into the tree.

"Something got him right there," he said. They moved to the spot. Several frozen red splotches were visible in the snow.

Red glanced down toward the snow tractor. "Must be twenty feet from where we found him."

"Yeah, something pulled him off the snowmobile, dropped him over there and killed him." Morgan stared at the bloody marks in the snow, and then peered at the area around the snowmobile's clear track. "Not a footprint anywhere. What got him?"

"I don't know," Red said thoughtfully. "Something big and strong and very dangerous."

Morgan looked at his friend for several moments. Finally he voiced what he'd been thinking about all morning. "Something that can fly?"

Red Crumley returned his gaze. "It'd have to be awfully big, Morgan. Something that could lift a man off the ground . . ." The sheriff shook his head. "I can't buy it."

"There's no tracks, except the ones we made last night," Morgan said, emphasizing his point by making a broad, sweeping gesture around the area. "None. But something lifted Charlie off the snowmobile and carried him twenty feet without leaving a mark."

"Yeah, Morgan, but . . ."

"And we all saw those eyes last night and then whatever the hell was there was gone. Like it flew away."

The sheriff adjusted his dark glasses and shook his head. "Pretty fantastic."

Morgan nodded. "And what about Crocker? His body was smashed on those boulders. When I found it, there wasn't a mark in the snow."

"Hey, let's get going!" Case yelled, his head thrust out the Thiokol's door. "We're wasting daylight."

As he and Red walked back, Morgan wondered why the FBI agent and Roberta weren't more interested in the snowmobile.

They reached the station without further incident. Everything was just as they had left it. The chain-link gate was locked, the makeshift wood-and-plastic door was still secured and there were no fresh marks around the area.

"Blaylock," Case said. "Will you help Roberta load those boxes? I'd like the sheriff to come with me on the snowmobiles."

Morgan nodded. "Sure."

"Good." The FBI agent turned to Red. "Sheriff, what say we take another look around. Maybe we'll find something the kid and I missed yesterday."

After the pair dragged the snowmobiles out of the concrete building and filled their gas tanks from the cans in the Thiokol, they took off amid whining engines and clouds of powdery snow.

Morgan and Roberta set about loading the boxes into the tractor. They took up much less room than Morgan would have believed. When they finished, he refilled the space heater, started it and then lit the Coleman stove. Before long, a pan of water was boiling over the open flame. Morgan sat on the floor near the heater and invited Roberta to join him.

In the distance, the snowmobile engines reverberated and whined, oscillating as they drew nearer and then further away from the small station. "Case seemed almost human when we got up here."

"I spoke to him," Roberta said quietly.

"Telling him what?"

"That I'd have him shipped out if he didn't lighten up." She gave Morgan a devilish grin.

"Can you do that?"

She spread her gloved hands in front of her. "I honestly don't know. But I don't think he wants to find out. That's all that matters."

Morgan laughed. "I like your style."

She blushed and looked away. "I like yours too. Sometimes." She added the last word with a mock frown. For a few moments an uncomfortable silence grew between them.

"The ever-popular pregnant pause," Morgan chirped.

It was Roberta's turn to laugh. She looked at him for several seconds and her smile faded. "I'm sorry I can't tell you more, Morgan. I really am. But security is very important and . . ."

He motioned with a wave of his hand. "Forget it. Let me try a theory on you." He got up and filled two cups with boiling water before adding instant coffee from a jar he carried in his machine. Roberta took the offered cup and blew on the steaming brew. She kept watching him closely.

"What's your theory?" she asked.

Morgan held his cup between his two hands, the insulated leather gloves keeping the hot metal from burning his fingers. He stared toward the patch of blue sky visible outside the partially opened doorway.

"Let's say there's something that lives up here that's very big and has a penchant for human blood," he began, pausing when he heard Roberta's sharp intake of breath. Glancing at her, he saw her staring into her coffee cup.

"And let's say this certain something doesn't prance around on two or four legs like other critters, but has wings. It swoops down, snatches an unsuspecting snowmobiler right off the back of his machine, carries him a few yards and drops him like a sack of meat." Morgan was watching Roberta now and he saw the blood drain from her face. He was very close to the truth.

He pressed on. "Then our mysterious widget beast rips out the snowmobiler's throat and starts sucking out his life's blood." Morgan took a drink of coffee. "Sound like a reasonable theory to you?"

Roberta breathed deeply several times and then looked at him. He was startled to see the moistness in her eyes. Maybe he'd laid it on a bit too strong.

"You're very perceptive, Morgan," she said in a strained voice. When she said nothing further, he reached over and touched her arm.

"Sorry, I didn't mean to sound so flippant."

She met his gaze and held it. "I can't say anything, Morgan. How many times do I have to tell you that?" He didn't miss the note of frustration in her voice.

He got up and walked to the door, resting his forearm on the jamb and studying the white wilderness surrounding them.

"I don't get it, Roberta," he said, his back still to her. "You know something's going on. You know I'm pretty damned close to the truth. You and Case are up here running around gathering data. Probably putting together a report to whatever hush-hush agency you work for. I just can't figure out if you're more interested in stopping this thing, or covering it up."

As he spoke, his voice rose. When he turned around, lashing out with his foot and kicking an empty metal cabinet, Roberta came off the floor and looked at him with wide, frightened eyes.

"People are dying!" he hissed. "People are getting killed and I don't see that you and Case are doing one damned thing to stop it. It's the kind of fucked-up mess I'd expect from the government, but . . ." He threw his hands in the air and turned away with a muttered curse.

Roberta stood slowly, watching him warily. She was breathing fast and her mouth was twisted into an unattractive frown.

"Don't judge us too quickly, *Mister* Blaylock," she hissed. "Don't you dare insinuate I'm not doing all I can do. You're just some backwater hack writer who happens to have a snow tractor we need. You aren't part of this. After today, I'll see you never have to be part of it again."

Her voice was low and controlled, but Morgan knew he'd pushed too hard and the slender thread of trust starting to build between them had been severed. He wanted to tell her he was sorry, but there was still a hard, ugly knot in the middle of his gut. Whenever he closed his eyes he could see Charlie Shaw's gaping throat and those empty, black eye sockets.

"Fine," he spat, dismissing the whole thing with a wave of his arm. "This stinks! I want no more of it."

"Don't worry," she snapped back. "You won't be involved after today!"

They stood glaring at each other across the cold, dim room. Outside the snowmobile engines came screaming up to the building, and in another few seconds Red Crumley came rushing into the room. He saw Morgan and Roberta glaring at each other and stopped.

"Sorry to interrupt," he said, catching his breath. He looked at Roberta. "Case wants you to get the minicam. We found something."

"What?" she demanded, already pulling on her snowshoes.

"You'd better have a look." The sheriff shot Morgan a questioning glance and then turned to leave.

"Roberta," Morgan said. "I . . ."

Without another word or look, she moved past him and followed Crumley outside.

Chapter Five

They crossed the stark, barren snowfield and then angled east and north from the NORAMS station. Morgan rode behind Red Crumley on one of the big snowmobiles. They followed Case and Roberta, who led the way on the other machine.

Morgan could still feel the sting of the woman's words. He'd pushed and she'd pushed back. He let his temper run ahead of his reason and, almost instinctively, she'd known exactly what to say to cut him to the quick. Maybe he deserved it, but being called a hack was like being assaulted with a racial slur.

Roberta had zeroed in on the one thing that could make his psyche bleed.

Whatever she was hiding, it scared her, made her defensive. Morgan could see it in her eyes. She was running on fear. And whatever was up here in these mountains utterly terrified her. She wanted it found, wanted it stopped, but at the same time she wanted everyone kept in the dark.

It both frustrated and infuriated Morgan. People were at risk, so why in the hell did Case and Ferris want to keep everything hush-hush? What the hell was the point of letting other unsuspecting souls wander into a death trap? If nothing else, they could have cordoned off the area.

Why weren't they calling in the damned marines?

Once across the snowfield, the FBI man angled toward the tree line, finally stopping near a heavy stand of pines. Crumley pulled the other machine next to them.

"We have to walk from here, Morgan," Red told him when he'd cut the engine. "Not too far."

Moving awkwardly on their snowshoes, they made their way into the trees. The snow bore the imprints left by Crumley and Case on their earlier visit.

"Watch where you step," Case cautioned as they neared a spot relatively clear of snow in the center of the pines.

Morgan studied the area.

"That's what drew our attention," Red told him, pointing at a blue parka tangled in the lower branches. Morgan hadn't noticed it as they approached.

The sheriff gestured toward a series of impressions in the virginal snow. "When we walked over here, we saw those marks."

Roberta pulled the minicam from its bag and began putting the scene on tape. Morgan saw her zoom in on the heavy jacket hanging in the tree and then on the impressions in the snow. She moved carefully about the area, recording every telltale mark and sign. At one point, she laid a red plastic ruler segmented in centimeters next to one of the prints and then videotaped it.

Morgan stepped closer to inspect odd marks. They were footprints. No doubt about it. Snow had drifted into to them, softening their edges, but he could still see the deep holes left by sharp claws and narrow toes. Distinctly non-human.

Roberta slipped the camera back into its case. "We

can get the coat out of the tree now. Maybe it has some ID in it."

Case tried to retrieve the jacket, but it was out of his reach. Without being asked, Morgan returned to the snowmobiles, started one and drove it under the branch. Standing carefully on the seat, he pulled down the coat. Roberta took it without comment.

She searched the coat's pockets, fishing out a woman's billfold. Morgan watched as she opened it, noting the darkness pass over her eyes as she studied the driver's license tucked inside a plastic sleeve. After a moment, she handed it to Case.

"Constance Pruett," she sighed. "The missing NOR-AMS woman."

Case shoved the billfold back into the parka's pocket and then surveyed the area.

"No sign of her," he said to no one in particular. "No bloodstains. No other clothing. Not even a human foot-print . . ."

"Richard," Roberta snapped in warning, shooting him a hard glance.

"Don't worry, Ms. Ferris," Morgan said flatly. "Red and I can tell those aren't human." He pointed at the prints in the snow. "We may be a couple of country bumpkins, but we're not stupid."

He saw her wince.

"Blaylock," Case said wearily. "All you're supposed to do is drive the damned snow tractor up and down the mountain. If we want any input from you, we'll ask."

"Mr. Blaylock will not be working for us after today," Roberta told the FBI agent, who responded with a crook-ed smile.

"Good."

Red Crumley studied Roberta and Morgan curiously, but said nothing.

"Yeah, I think so," Morgan said to Case. "Give me a chance to sell this story to one of the newspapers."

"What?" the FBI agent cried. "You better be talking out of your ass, pal."

Morgan smiled. "I'm serious. You two spooks can try to keep a lid on all this crap if you want, but I know a good story when I see one, and more importantly, I know when a story needs to be told."

"You're bluffing, Blaylock," Case said halfheartedly. "This is a matter of national security."

Morgan shook his head. "Don't hand me that bullshit, Dick. Every time some bureaucrat wants to hide a fuckup, he cries 'national security.' Well it won't wash. You can't stop me and you know it."

"Don't bet on it."

Morgan didn't respond. He plopped down on the snow-mobile's seat and turned to Crumley. "What say we head back to the station, Red?"

The sheriff shrugged and climbed on behind Morgan. They left Case and Roberta staring after them as they shot out across the snow.

"Were you serious, Morgan?" Red asked when they were back in the small concrete building sipping fresh cups of instant coffee.

Morgan brushed a hand through his hair and nodded. "Damned straight. This whole thing stinks. Let those two play secret agent if they want. I'm more concerned to make sure no one else gets killed up here."

The sheriff shook his head. "That Case fellow is dangerous, Morgan. I've seen his type before. He's totally dedicated. The mission is everything. If you get in the way, he'll bring so much shit down on you, you'll need an umbrella."

"Maybe. But they can't take me to court. They couldn't afford the publicity. What are they going to charge me with? I can't violate any confidences; I never signed anything swearing me to secrecy." Morgan sipped his coffee and then smiled at his friend. "Besides, I've just stirred the pot a little. I'm always interested to see what floats to the top."

Red frowned and stared at his cup for several minutes. "Let's hope it's not your body, pal. You're being naive. You're assuming you have some kind of rights."

"Like Charlie asked yesterday, ever hear of the Constitution?"

The sheriff spat on the floor. "Yeah, Morgan. Great document, beautiful ideology. But if you think it's going to protect you, my friend, you're sadly mistaken. Those two are bureaucrats. Your rights, my rights, nobody's rights amount to a pile of monkey nuts if they decide to go after you. You think they give one flying leap at the moon about your rights? Check out the IRS or the military or the Justice Department. A self-perpetuating bureaucracy is also self-*protecting*. You get in their way and they'll make you curse your mother for ever having fucked your old man to bring you into this world."

Morgan looked at his friend in surprise. "Holy cow, Red, you're a closet anarchist."

"I'm a damned realist," the sheriff shot back.

Morgan laughed. "My God, you sound like some paranoid right-winger."

Red's face suddenly matched his name. "Damn it, Morgan! I'm trying to tell you these people are interested in one thing and one thing only: protecting their interests and their jobs. They don't give one good spit in hell about you."

Morgan started to reply, but the whine of the other snowmobile's engine cut him off. A moment later Case and Roberta trudged into the building. The FBI agent walked to Morgan, towering over him.

"We need to talk, Blaylock."

"About what?" Morgan asked innocently.

"Don't play games with me. Roberta tells me you're a writer. I didn't know that. So maybe you weren't bluffing about writing an article on this." He gestured around the room. "I'm telling you flat out. Don't do it."

Red Crumley gave Morgan an I-told-you-so look.

Morgan got out up from the floor slowly and met the FBI agent's gaze. "Or what? You'll have me *neutralized?*" He glanced at Roberta, mildly surprised to see her face was now ashen. "Isn't that what you do to people who get too troublesome? Just take them out in a field somewhere and blow their heads off, make them disappear?"

"This isn't one of your paperback novels, Blaylock. You aren't the hero and, believe me, you can't win." Case spoke firmly and evenly. Morgan felt an icy chill run down his spine followed instantly by a hot flash of anger. A tiny, rational part of his mind sent out a cautionary alarm, but too late.

"Hey, Dick," Morgan snarled, grabbing a fistful of Case's coat. He jerked the man around and slammed him into the wall. The impact drove the wind out of the fed's lungs with a whoosh and his eyes grew dazed.

Still holding Case against the wall, Morgan turned toward Roberta, who was watching in disbelief. "I'm going to say this just once, *Ms*. Ferris. Keep this asshole on a leash or I'll . . ."

Too late, Morgan felt Case tense. Then the air exploded out of his lungs and a fierce burst of agony exploded in his body as the FBI's agent's knee drove into his crotch. Gasping, he staggered backward, reeling to the floor on his hands and knees in pain. As his anger evaporated into gut-wrenching paralysis, a second blow hammered into his side and he was sent tumbling across the room. His head banged on the unyielding concrete sending bursts of red and yellow fireworks exploding behind his eyes.

Before Case could kick him again, Red Crumley grabbed the FBI agent from behind, pinning his arms to his sides.

Swirling in a black fog, Morgan was vaguely aware of a confusion of yelling, cursing voices. He tried to speak, tried to make sounds, but all that came out was a series of gasps. And then the black fog enveloped him, smothering him in its merciful embrace.

Chapter Six

"What in hell were you thinking?" Roberta Ferris demanded hotly. She and Richard Case stood just outside the front door of Crystal Wells Municipal Hospital.

"He had it coming," the FBI agent snapped, glowering at her.

Roberta seethed. She didn't need this kind of incident in the middle of such a sensitive investigation.

Red Crumley, furious with both of them, had threatening to arrest Case for aggravated assault and if that didn't stick, he'd take Morgan Blaylock's story to the press himself. Roberta had spent the better part of an hour calming the sheriff down, and only succeeded by using a thinly veiled threat to bring charges against *him*. He'd properly pointed out that they'd never stick, but they both knew the blow to his career could prove fatal.

"If he's permanently injured, your ass is in a sling," Roberta now hissed, keeping her voice low as two nurses walked into the hospital.

Case turned to her, his eyes blazing. "Don't threaten me. Don't ever threaten me! I've dealt with prissy little bureaucrats like you all my life." Roberta found herself retreating a step as he thrust his face close to hers. His voice was low and deadly. "You want it both ways: a nice clean investigation with no complications and you want a lid kept on it. Well, it doesn't always work that way."

He moved away from her, his eyes darting around the area. "You make trouble for me, *Ms*. Ferris, and it'll be *you* with your pretty little ass in a sling." He turned back to her, his dark eyes boring into her like twin lasers. "And don't think I can't do it."

Before she could answer, Case spun on his heel and stalked down the broad sidewalk toward his car.

Roberta stared after him, her anger suddenly blunted by his not-so-subtle threat. She shivered in the late afternoon chill, for the first time accepting the fact that Richard Case only worked for her on paper.

"Can we talk?" Red Crumley asked, stepping through the glass doors.

Brought out of her reverie, Roberta turned and studied the sheriff.

"Ms. Ferris?" Crumley said, eyeing her suspiciously.

She blinked. "Yeah, sure. Let's go someplace less public and a little warmer."

They found a small, unoccupied alcove off the waiting room and sat opposite each other in wobbly plastic chairs.

"He's still unconscious," Crumley said without accusation.

Roberta heaved a weary sigh. "What does the doctor say?"

"Concussion and some badly bruised ribs. Doc Reed thinks he'll survive."

Relieved, Roberta brushed absently at a loose strand of raven hair and leaned back in her chair. "I'm really sorry it happened."

Crumley chewed on his lower lip for a few moments and then caught her eye. "Case is a dangerous man. Why don't you get him replaced?"

Why don't I indeed, she mused. "I'm not sure I can," she finally answered. "I didn't pick him."

"You know," Crumley continued, "if I hadn't stopped him, I think he'd have kicked Morgan to death. I don't know how he got into the FBI, but he's not particularly stable."

Roberta had no response. Of course the sheriff was absolutely right, but she wasn't certain there was anything she could do about it.

Feeling boxed in, trapped by the sheriff's questions and Case's threats, she got to her feet. "Look, I'm truly sorry about what happened. God knows, it's not the way I wanted it. Morgan pushed too hard. Believe me, Sheriff, he's in over his head."

Crumley looked up at her. "And you aren't?"

Roberta turned away. "Keep me posted," she said, hurrying toward the front doors.

His chest was encased in a steel band. Each breath he drew into his lungs was hard and painfully. His midsection was numb and sore and there was a knot in the pit of his stomach. A bass drum was pounding a steady beat at the back of his skull.

Morgan opened his eyes. The room was starkly white, illuminated by hidden lights in the ceiling. The window across the room was dark and the bed next to his empty.

"How you doing, pal?" Morgan turned his head to his right until he could see Red Crumley sitting in a chair. An open copy of *Time* was draped across his lap. The sheriff looked strained and tired and his face sagged.

"So'd you give the guy a ticket?" Morgan croaked, his throat and mouth dry.

Crumley looked momentarily confused.

"The guy in the truck," Morgan went on.

The sheriff's smile was rueful. "The one that hit you?"

Morgan nodded, sending a fresh waves of pain bouncing around the inside of his head. "How long have I been here?"

Red peered at his watch. "About ten hours." He filled a glass of water from a pitcher and handed it to Morgan.

After taking a long drink, Morgan closed his eyes. "Guess I should stick to writing and toolin' around the mountains and quit trying to be a testosterone cowboy, huh?"

"Sounds reasonable."

Morgan looked up at Red. "Speaking of testosterone and all that macho stuff, I take it you kept the rabid fed from turning me into ground meat."

The sheriff nodded. "He wanted to kill you right there and leave you for the buzzards."

"Thanks," Morgan told him. "What's my prognosis?"

"Doctor ruled out brain damage," Crumley answered, a glint in his eyes. "Said you have to have one to get it damaged."

"I ain't got no drain bamage?" Morgan quipped, dredging up on old Eddie Murphy line.

The sheriff grinned. "Always the joker." His smile faded as quickly as it had come. "Actually, Reed says you'll live, thanks to a head filled with more rock than brain. You've got a a nasty knot on your skull, Case used your ribs for punting practice and your balls may be sore for a while. You're more bruised than anything."

"Gee," Morgan quipped in a weak falsetto. "Not so bad."

"Look, I gotta get home. You know Ruth. We'll talk tomorrow."

Morgan caught the note of concern in his friend's voice. "Talk about what? Why I shouldn't sign for a title match?"

Red's smile was crooked. "We'll talk about it tomorrow."

"Give me a break, Red. You want me to lie here all night wondering what kind of crap's coming down?"

Red sighed, pulled his chair closer to the bed and sat down. "It took some doing to get Case calmed down. The jerk would have left you there if Roberta Ferris hadn't lit into him like a wounded she-cat. She tore him a new asshole.

"So all the way down the mountain—I drove, by the way—he kept going on about filing charges against you for attacking a federal officer. Let me tell you, Morgan, you've got an enemy there. With a capital E. He wants you hung out to dry."

"I never won any personality contests."

Red screwed up his face. "I'm serious, Morgan. The guy's going to nail you one way or another."

"With Roberta's blessing?" Morgan asked. He shifted in the bed and groaned as his battered body protested.

Red thought for a minute. "That's one complex lady. She was pissed at Case, but you weren't on her hit parade either. I'm not sure how it works. She's supposed to be calling the shots, but Case seems to have a pretty free hand."

"They won't file charges," Morgan said flatly.

Crumley snorted. "You're counting on Case not wanting to take you to court. But he could put you into the federal system, hop you around the country for quite a while. It's done all the time. Before you could find a lawyer, they'd have you so discredited, you'd spend the rest of your life trying to figure out what went wrong. Government does it to people every day."

Morgan smiled. "You're sounding paranoid again."

The sheriff leaned forward. "Just because you're paranoid . . ."

". . . doesn't mean they're not out to get you," Morgan finished for him. "Yeah, I know."

"And something else," the sheriff said.

"Yeah?"

"The Mitchell kid."

"What about him?"

Red shook his head. "He's gone. My wife said some-body showed up after I left this morning and took him away."

"Where?" Morgan asked.

"Beats the hell out of me," Red answered. "First Fenwick and Ryan, now the kid." He shot Morgan a meaningful look.

"You think I'm next?" Now he was starting to feel acutely paranoid.

Just then the door opened and a middle-aged woman walked in wearing a crisp white uniform and a stern scowl. She gave Morgan a smile and glowered at Red.

"Red Crumley," she scolded. "I told you to let me know when Mr. Blaylock woke up. Now you get home to your wife, you hear me?"

The sheriff nodded. "All right, all right, I'm going. See you tomorrow, Morgan."

"Dr. Reed told me to call him as soon as you came around," the nurse said as Crumley left the room. "He'll probably come over in a little while."

Morgan nodded mutely.

The woman checked his temperature, blood pressure and other vital signs, and apparently satisfied, left him alone.

Bustling into the room like a man with a mission, Dr. Milo Reed arrived 15 minutes later. A short, rotund man with a fringe of wild, white hair surrounding a bald pate, mischievous eyes gleaming from behind gold-rimmed glasses and a toothy grin, he was Crystal Wells's resident curmudgeon.

"Blaylock, you've got more gall than wit," the doc-tor barked by way of a greeting. He glanced quickly at the chart hanging from the end of the bed, and then unceremoniously began inspecting the red, tender lump on Morgan's forehead.

98

"What in the hell possessed you to take on a federal agent? My God, boy, they don't hire those guys because they're weaklings. Damned good thing Red was there. I'd be fitting you for a body bag the way I hear it. Hell's bells, you're a strong, healthy man, but your momma must have dropped you on your head when you were a baby. Lucky you—"

"Nice to see you too, Doc," Morgan cut in. "Ouch! Hey, that hurts."

Doc Reed stopped probing at the lump. "It should. Lucky you didn't crack open your fool head."

"You'd have fixed it."

The doctor harrumphed. "It's hard enough to keep people healthy without having them go out looking for trouble."

"I hear a lot of your patients are disappearing," Morgan said.

A frown crossed Reed's face and his eyes narrowed. He stopped his poking and prodding and glanced at Morgan. "I'm not happy about it." The doctor shook his head. "They've all been spirited away."

"Feds?"

"No, by Santa Claus," Reed snapped sarcastically. "Of course by the feds. They brought their own ambulance, loaded Ryan and that Fenwick fellow in and cleared out."

"Where to?"

"If I knew, it wouldn't be a secret." Reed resumed his examination and then stopped, suddenly dropping his gruff demeanor and leaned closer to Morgan. "I heard they had a helicopter outside of town. Don't know why they didn't just use our helipad. That's what it's there for. Hell, we got it with a government grant."

"Didn't want to attract too much attention," Morgan reasoned.

Reed grunted, threw back his shoulders and rubbed the small of his back. He pulled the chair closer to the bed, sat and eyed Morgan curiously. When he spoke, his banter and mockery were gone and his voice was low and earnest.

"What the hell's going on up there?"

Morgan shifted with a groan to better see the doctor. "I'm not sure, Doc. Something's killing people and the feds don't want to talk about it."

Reed leaned back, pulled off his glasses and pinched the bridge of his nose between thumb and forefinger. "Tell me about it. That Case fellow—very unpleasant man, by the way—gave me all manner of grief about not saying anything to anyone about Fenwick and Ryan or that Crocker fellow and poor old Charlie."

"He threaten you?" Morgan wondered.

"He tried. I told him to take a long walk off a short cliff. Hell's bells, I'm a doctor. I don't talk about my patients." He looked around guiltily. "Not too often anyway."

Morgan cleared his throat. "I hear Crocker was bled dry."

Reed slipped his glasses back on, fussed with the temples until they fit right and then stared at the ceiling. "Yeah. Amazingly devoid of blood. All busted up too. His legs, arms, chest, skull, all fractured. Lost a lot of blood when he hit those rocks, but there still should have been *some* left in his body. What there was wouldn't have filled an eyedropper."

"So what took the blood?"

"I don't know," Reed said quietly. "Both Charlie and Crocker had teeth marks in their throats."

"Animal, I assume."

The doctor studied Morgan for a moment before answering. "Yeah, animal. Fangs, really. Very sharp and very long."

"No idea from what?"

"Not from the autopsy," Reed answered dolefully. "I guess I should have had a veterinarian assist me."

Morgan studied the doctor. "But you know something, right?"

Reed's tongue explored the surface of his teeth while he considered his answer. "Too weird for an old secular humanist like me."

"I'll listen."

Reed eyed his patient for several long moments. "You know Red sent that specimen to the lab with Crocker's body?"

"The feces?"

"Yeah."

"What about it? You see a lab report?"

Reed shook his head. "No chance. The feds had their own man here doing the tests."

"They didn't send it to Denver or Washington?"

"Nope," the doctor answered, sounding puzzled. "Did it right here. A guy showed up, took over a lab, brought in some of his own equipment and went to work."

"And?" Morgan prompted.

"And one of our nurses was assigned to help this guy out. Not with the tests, just to make sure he had everything he needed, including *full* cooperation." Reed's disgust was obvious.

"Anyway," he continued. "He got a phone call and the nurse transferred it into a small office off the lab. While she was waiting for him to return, she saw something on his computer screen."

"His report?" Morgan was growing impatient, but knew the good doctor was being unintentionally circumspect while building up to something important.

"Yeah. She didn't even know what it was, but she read enough to send her to me all flustered and worried."

"What'd it say?"

"Well," Reed said, breathing the word out in a long stream. "According to what she told me, the technician couldn't say conclusively, but the feces was very much like . . . wait a minute, that's not what she said. The words were 'scatologically similar to Chiroptera guano.'"

"Chirop-what?" Morgan asked, frustrated.

Reed smiled humorlessly. "In layman's terms, Morgan, bat shit."

"That's crazy," Morgan spat. "I saw the droppings. Big as a damned cow pie. You sure she read it correctly?"

"That's why she came running to me," the doctor explained. "She couldn't understand what was going on, but she knew what Chiroptera meant. She's one of those people with a bat house in her backyard. You know, the bats-are-our-friends type. It flustered the hell out of her. She was worried these people were going on some kind of bat hunt."

Morgan tried to sit up, found his bruises and abrasions too painful and leaned back with a grunt. "You're saying that there's a big fucking bat flying around up there killing people and drinking their blood?"

Reed lifted his round body out of the chair quickly and turned away. When he spoke, he was brisk, sounding defensive and embarrassed. "I'm not saying anything. I'm telling you what I was told. Hearsay evidence. Maybe the nurse was mistaken. I don't know."

He turned back around and peered at Morgan over the tops of his glasses. "You can probably go home in a couple of days. I want to keep you around just to make sure the bump on your head doesn't result in anything worse."

Morgan nodded. "Listen, Doc, I'm sorry. I didn't mean to question your . . . information."

Reed frowned. "Yeah, well . . . I know how you feel. The more I thought about, the more I wondered. But . . ." He stopped and gave Morgan a long, intense gaze. "What in the hell does it mean?"

"I don't know, Doc, but I'd like to find out." He gestured at his body. "I already got stomped for my trouble."

"You got your nuts crushed and the shit stomped out of you because you were stupid," Reed told him flatly.

Morgan forced a laugh. "Yeah, that too."

Reed started to say something more, but the nurse came barging into the room. "Doctor, they want you in ER."

Reed started for the door. "What's up?"

"That FBI man . . . he just brought in some guy who's pretty bad," the nurse said breathlessly. As she turned to leave, she looked over her shoulder. "Looks like he was attacked by some kind of animal."

Chapter Seven

Morgan Blaylock's dreams were a kaleidoscope of jumbled images: gleaming, yellow eyes, blood-drenched fangs and dark, winged shapes moving through the darkness of his mind.

It was mid-morning the next day before Milo Reed showed up again. The bulbous doctor came strolling into his room looking very tired and not a little grumpy. His eyes were puffy and dark-circled and his normally wild fringe of hair was greasy and limp.

He stopped at the end of the bed and scanned Morgan's chart. "You're pretty healthy. No fever. Blood pressure's normal."

"So what went on last night?" Morgan asked impatiently.

"I think you can go home tomorrow," Reed said, ignoring the question and refusing to look at him.

"Doc?"

"What?" There was an edge in Reed's voice.

The Devouring

"I asked you what went on last night."

The doctor rubbed a hand over his face. "That nasty man Case was very upset, but also very emphatic. I'm not to say a word to you or anyone else."

"Say a word about what?"

A twinkle appeared in Reed's eyes and a wry smile briefly touched his lips. "About the man he brought in last night with gashes all over his body and suffering from severe shock and trauma caused by loss of blood. He was adamant that no one knows this other FBI agent was attacked by an *'animal'* up in the mountains. Sorry, Morgan, but I just can't tell you about the claw marks on this man's back and chest or the bite marks on his throat."

Morgan smiled. "Okay, fine. Don't tell me. See if I care."

Reed held his hands in front of him, wrists together. "My hands are tied."

"Patient's condition?"

"Bad. Coma."

"What about—"

"Sorry," Reed said. "I've got to go home. You know when a fellow my age has to sew over two hundred and fifty stitches into someone, it takes a lot out of him."

Morgan whistled softly. "I'll bet."

"Gotta go," Reed said, yanking open the door.

"Take care, Doc."

Alone again, Morgan considered all he'd learned. Case and another agent must have gone back up to the station or certainly into the area. Whatever was stalking the wilderness had attacked and damned near killed one of the men. Who now had 250 stitches and massive trauma and was now in a coma. There was one mean, vicious son of a bitch prowling—or *flying*—around up there.

Red Crumley came to see him that afternoon. Self-consciously, he carried a bouquet of flowers in a clear glass vase.

105

"Oh, Sheriff," Morgan said. "I didn't know you cared."

"I don't. They're from Ruth," he growled, placing them on the table next to the bed. "When do you get out?"

"Tomorrow."

Red grunted.

"Know anything about the guy they brought in here last night?"

Red looked surprised. "No."

Morgan told him about the mauled FBI agent, and then recounted everything Doc Reed had told him about the laboratory tests on the feces they'd brought down a few days before.

"Bat shit?" Red shook his head. "That's crazy."

"Hey," Morgan said, spreading his hands. "Who's arguing?"

"Well," Red said thoughtfully, "I didn't get any report on this attack. Guess I'll talk to Case. Maybe if I raise a little hell, he'll tell me more."

"Don't count on it."

"Case is a fed and all that, but he's not Superman. I can pull a few rabbits out of my hat too. I'm getting sick and tired of all this James Bond action."

Morgan cocked his head. "Is this the same Red Crumley who told me to back off, stay away from the feds or they'd have my balls in a jar?"

"Was I wrong?"

Morgan flushed. "No. I just don't want you to end up as my roomie." He pointed at the empty bed next to his.

"I won't. I'm going to go talk to Case right away. If I can find him, that is."

They talked another few minutes and Red left, telling Morgan he'd come by in the morning to drive him home.

"It's for you," Ruth Crumley called from the kitchen, her hand covering the mouthpiece on the wall phone. When her husband appeared from the living room, she shot him a frustrated glance. "You need a night off, Red. Tell whoever it is it'll have to wait until morning."

She was an apple-cheeked woman with soft brown eyes, shoulder-length hair dyed dark brown and a ripe figure.

Crumley looked at her and smiled wearily.

She handed him the phone with a shake of her head and returned to the stove where a pot of stew bubbled.

"Sheriff Crumley?" an unfamiliar voice asked.

"Yeah, who is this?"

"You don't know me," the man answered. "But, I think there's a problem out on the road to Coronado Lake."

"What kind of trouble?"

"I . . . seen somethin' out there, Sheriff. Somethin' mighty peculiar."

"Did you call the station?" Crumley snapped. He was too tired for flights of fancy.

"No, sir. I . . . thought maybe you'd want to hear this your ownself. 'Sides, I don't want this gettin' all over town and makin' me look like a fool."

Crumley decided to play along. A lot of the folks who lived in the mountains around the Wells were borderline hermits and social outcasts. If they thought it was going to earn them unwanted notoriety, they'd let the Devil himself pass their way without a word to anyone.

"Okay, what did you see?"

There was a pause at the other end of the line. "Well, Sheriff, I don't rightly know *what* it was. But right after sunset, I was out back of my place and I swear I seen somethin' flyin' round Stovepipe Rock."

Red Crumley's hand tightened around the phone and his stomach clenched. He turned his back to Ruth and lowered his voice. "What was it?"

"Well, Sheriff, I . . . ain't sure. But it was big. Huge. Bigger than any eagle or turkey buzzard I've ever seen. And it . . ." The man on the other end of the line paused.

"And it what?" Crumley pressed.

"Honest to God, Sheriff, I ain't makin' this up, but . . . well, it had wings like a bat. Only they was real big."

Crumley muttered a curse. "Where's your place?"

"Three miles down the Coronado Road. Ol' Stockton place. You know it?"

"Yeah, I know it."

"Now, listen, Sheriff," the man said earnestly. "I don't want this gettin' out. I came here to get a fresh start. I don't want people thinkin' I'll some loony-tick."

"I understand, Mr. . . . ? I'm sorry, I didn't get your name."

There was another pause. "Clem. Just Clem."

"Okay, Clem, what say I meet you there in . . ." Crumley glanced at Ruth, saw her frown and then looked at the wall clock above the kitchen table. "Say an hour?"

"I'll be waitin'." The line went dead.

"Honestly, Red," Ruth Crumley admonished. "Why don't you let Jasper or one of the others handle some of these things."

He smiled sheepishly. "Oh, it's probably nothing. The guy sounded kind of worried, so maybe if I drive out there and talk to him, he'll calm down and, in the long run, think better of the Crystal Wells Sheriff's Department."

Ruth shook her head. "Honestly, you're too good for these people. What did he see, anyway?"

"Funny lights in the woods," Red lied. "Thought it might be a UFO or something."

"Or something is right," she said, filling a bowl with steaming-hot stew.

After eating, Crumley climbed into his car and drove to the Coronado Lake Road. This time of year, there wasn't much traffic on the narrow two-lane blacktop. Coronado Lake was a summer resort and in the winter, most of the locals hightailed it for warm climates.

As Crumley recalled, the old Stockton place was a ramshackle collection of crumbling outbuildings surrounding a dilapidated house. If someone was setting up housekeeping there, more power to him.

Crumley's memory was accurate. The house sat 50 yards off the road with its back to a high, rocky bluff. He stopped the car at the gate, which was open and, from the looks of it, would never again close.

There wasn't a flicker of light from the house and in the spillover from his headlights, Crumley noted that the snow between the gate and the house was utterly unblemished.

No one had been there recently.

Suddenly, Red Crumley had a very bad feeling.

On instinct, he jammed the car in gear and cranked the wheel in a hard turn. The road was too narrow and he had to maneuver it around before he was aiming back toward the highway.

As he was about to hit the accelerator, a shadowy shape fluttered just beyond the periphery of his lights. Crumley's foot stayed on the brake as he peered out the side window and into the blackness.

"What the hell . . . ?"

Sensing something behind him, Red Crumley turned just as the passenger window exploded, showering him with tiny jagged shards of safety glass. Instinctively, he reached for his gun, but a shrill screech immobilized him.

He looked up and into the face of a demon. Huge yellow eyes peered at him with unmistakable hatred and blood lust.

His fingers touched the butt of his revolver. . . .

Something slammed into the car. There was a frenzy of tearing metal and smashing glass. The car rocked and bucked.

In desperation, Crumley jammed his foot down hard on the gas pedal, but instead of carrying him to safety, the tires spun and the car lurched toward a ditch paralleling the road. The front end nosed into the shallow depression, the impact slamming the sheriff against the steering wheel.

Dazed, he shook his head and again reached for his gun. The window at his side shattered and before he could react, he was literally ripped out of the car.

Fetid, rancid breath washed over his face. Powerful claws pierced the padded nylon of his jacket and burrowed into his skin.

Red Crumley thrashed and struggled against the thing holding him, but its strength was awesome.

The last thing he saw was a huge, yawning mouth filled with impossibly long, sharp fangs.

Then pain exploded in both his eyes and a tearing, vise-like pressure constricted his throat. . . .

Red Crumley heard a terrible, wet retching and, as his mind dimmed, he knew it came from himself: the sound of a man choking on his own blood.

Sometime after midnight Morgan awoke with a start. The room was dark except for the muted street light reflecting off the snow to cast weak shadows on the far wall. The hospital was graveyard quiet.

He listened. Something had awakened him. Maybe an orderly had dropped a bedpan. Or maybe it was the wind. He glanced out the dark window. The night was still.

As he studied the far wall, a large shadow flitted across the light, momentarily blotting it out.

Curious, Morgan climbed stiffly out of bed and limped slowly to the window. Leaning against the sill, he peered out into the wintry darkness. There was nothing moving. The street bordering the hospital was empty, as was the sidewalk and the broad, snow-covered lawn.

He glanced toward the street light just as a dark, fleeting shape swooped through the air a scant ten feet from the ground. For the briefest instant, Morgan thought he saw two yellow eyes glimmer. Then the dark, flying shape made an impossibly sharp ascent and vanished. In its wake, Morgan thought he could hear a keening whine, an echoing animal cry lingering long after the presence had disappeared.

"What in the hell?" he muttered, an icy chill shaking him.

From somewhere in the hospital, a high, piercing scream broke the quiet. It echoed in the hall for several seconds and was followed by an ominous silence. Then there was a growing murmur of alarmed voices coming from everywhere. Morgan heard people rushing down the hall outside his closed door.

He pulled his robe from the edge of the bed and tugged it on. His ribs throbbed and Morgan groaned against the pain.

A nurse went rushing by as he stepped into the hall. The lights had been muted for the night and in the dimness, he could see her join several other people outside a door at the far end of the long corridor. Other patients were emerging timidly from their rooms and milling together in small groups.

All conversation ceased and every head turned as another scream reverberated through the hospital.

Morgan started moving toward where the people were gathering. As he neared the spot, a young orderly stepped from the room. Deathly pale, his eyes wide and glassy, he leaned against the wall and wiped the back of his hand across his mouth.

Morgan tried to see into the room, but his line of sight was blocked by a burly man in a white lab coat standing in the partially opened door.

"Okay," said the man. "Nothing to see. Everybody back to bed or your duties." He clapped his hands to emphasize his point. "Come on, let's go."

Muttering and mumbling, people began to drift away. Patients returned to their rooms and nurses and orderlies wandered off, whispering apprehensively.

"You too, sir," the man in white said to Morgan. "You can go back to your room now."

Morgan eyed the guy. He'd never seen him before. "FBI, right?"

The other man blinked and his face took on a confused expression. Then a knowing looked filled his eyes and he nodded, pointing down the hall. "Go to back to bed, Mr. Blaylock."

"You have me at a disadvantage," Morgan said affably. "You know my name and I don't know yours."

The man flushed and scarlet streaks climbed from beneath his collar. He started to say something, but at that moment, a burly man came hurrying toward them. The man at the door brightened.

"Escort Mr. Blaylock back to his room, Nias," he told the newcomer.

Morgan eyed Nias. He stood well over six-six and weighted in at about 275. He had massive arms, tree-stump legs and a dark scowl.

"You're quite the side of beef, ain't ya, Nias?" Morgan said blissfully. "And I'll bet your IQ matches your belt size."

The man's face grew darker. "Get outta here," he said menacingly.

"Nias," the other man said warningly. "Don't make a scene, just help Blaylock to his room."

"Yeah, Nias," Morgan taunted. "If you make a scene, Mr. Case won't let you out of your cage for a month."

The huge man suddenly roared and lunged at Morgan. "I'll tear your . . ." He didn't finish his threat. As he came at him, Morgan stepped aside, thrust out his leg and tripped him. Nias grunted as he smacked hard on the floor. Pushing himself up, he glared at Morgan. The other man rushed between them, but Nias brushed him aside.

"He's mine," Nias snarled.

By now, several of the staff had returned, watching the scene in amazement.

"No!" the goon in the lab coat yelled. "Don't do anything."

Nias kept moving toward Morgan, who, in turn, was backing away, a wry smile on his face. He tried to ignore the sharp pain radiating from his battered ribs.

"Hey, Nias. Your mother have any babies that lived?"

Morgan's taunt was too much for the man. He bellowed like a gored bull and charged, launching a punch at his antagonist's face. Fortunately, he was off balance and Morgan easily ducked aside.

"Better call him off," Morgan called. "Case's going to have your ass as it is."

"Maybe not, Blaylock," Richard Case said, coming up behind him. He shot Nias a fierce look and the big man backed away, mumbling to himself.

"Get out of here," Case told the two men. "We'll discuss this incident later."

"Yeah," Morgan called, unable to control himself. "He's going to give you both a good tongue-lashing." He looked at Case and smiled. "I'll bet you'd like that, huh?"

Case saw the smirking faces of the hospital staff and the few patients still milling around and reddened. He turned to Morgan.

"You don't know when to give up, do you?"

Morgan spread his hands in mock innocence. "Hey, I was just hanging around and your gorilla started coming after me."

"Yeah, right," the FBI agent spat in disgust. "I suppose you wanted to rubberneck like the rest of these people."

Before Morgan could answer, Case pulled out his credentials and flashed them at the other people. "FBI. I'm in charge here. There's nothing more to see. I suggest you all go back to what you were doing."

His words had the desired effect and the rest of the crowd dispersed. When they had gone, he turned back to Morgan; only Morgan wasn't where he was supposed to be. Instead, he was pushing open the door to the room the screams had come from.

"Get away from there, Blaylock," he snapped.

"Mother of God," Morgan breathed, staring into the interior. A chilly breeze rushed into the hall, carrying with it the unmistakable coppery stench. Blood was splashed over the walls and floor. The bed was a tangled mess of red-stained sheets. The window was broken and pieces of glass gleamed in the light.

Lying near the foot of the bed, like the discarded limb from a department-store mannequin, was a bloody leg. A severed arm, the flesh ragged and ripped around the shoulder joint, was leaning against the far wall. Another arm and hand, a ring on one nerveless finger sparkling in the light, hung over the edge of the hospital table.

Morgan fought back bile as he surveyed the scene.

"That what you wanted to see?" Case asked bitterly. "One of my men. Slaughtered."

"What did this?" Morgan asked, his mouth dry, his throat tight. This must have been the man brought in the previous night.

Case didn't answer. Morgan whirled around. "It was that damned thing that killed Charlie, wasn't it?"

"You've seen it," Case said softly. "Now why don't you go back to bed so we can clean this mess up before . . ."

"A panic starts?" Morgan snarled. "Before somebody else discovers what you're covering up?"

Case drew in a deep breath. "Don't push me, Blaylock. I've already kicked your ass once, I can do it again. You keep horning in and I'll have you busted so fast you won't have time to piss."

Morgan studied the FBI man, measuring him. "You won't do squat and you know it. If you bust me, I'm in court sooner or later. You can't have that happen." Morgan shrugged. "Of course, I suppose you could kill me. That's probably more your style."

Case was silent for several moments. When he spoke again, his voice was very low and he pronounced each word carefully. "That's right, Blaylock. I could arrange for you to die. It's relatively simple. One phone call and bye-bye pain-in-the-ass. They won't find your bones until spring. Don't think I won't do it."

Their eyes locked. Morgan's skin crawled and tiny streamers of cold sweat coursed down his sides. After long, tense seconds, he flashed a smile.

"Dick, you're a predictable man. Cunning, but not too bright, and very predictable." Morgan brushed past the FBI agent and returned to the hall. He turned and leveled a finger at the agent. His smile was now gone. "I figured you for a government hitman first time I saw you. All bluster and bullshit, but no brains.

"If Red hadn't stopped you, you've have killed me up on the mountain. You think I don't know that? You think I've been in here playing with myself the last couple of days? Hell's bells, I wrote down everything I knew about what's going on and had a nurse mail it to a lawyer friend in Denver. If I get an infected hangnail and die of blood poisoning, everything goes to the press. Everything."

He took a perverse pleasure watching Case's face pale. Then he turned and walked away.

Talk about bluster and bullshit. He'd just cornered the market.

"It'll never see the light of day, Blaylock," Case hissed to his retreating back.

"Clean up your mess, Case," Morgan called over his shoulder. "All you need for that one is a mop and a box. For the big one, you're going to need a damned good lawyer."

Back in his room, Morgan slumped on the bed and reached for the phone. It took several moments to get the hospital operator, and then he was told his call could not be completed. Before he could ask why, the line went dead. He tried again. This time a more hostile voice came on, telling him that no calls were going out for the time being.

Morgan banged the phone down, cursing Case. He pulled a handful of change out of his pants hanging in the closet and, still in his robe, moved to his door. Opening it a crack, he glanced into the corridor. Several people were bustling around the room where the FBI man had been murdered. Morgan waited until they were all inside before he slipped out his door. He hurried up the hall fighting the pain in his side that came with each step.

There was a bank of pay phones just off the lobby. Morgan went to one and dialed Red Crumley's number. The phone rang half a dozen times before sleepy woman's voice answered.

"He's not here, Morgan," Ruth Crumley said. "He was called out several hours ago."

"Sorry to wake you, Ruth," Morgan apologized before hanging up.

He dialed the sheriff's office. The dispatcher—he remembered her as a plump little Hispanic woman with bright, dancing eyes—answered.

"No, Sheriff Crumley's not here," she said in answer to his question.

"Do you know where he went?"

"Home. Hours ago."

Alarm bells went off in Morgan's head. "I just talked to his wife. She said he was called out on an emergency."

The woman sounded concerned now. "Not by me. This has been a very quiet night. No calls."

"Listen," Morgan said intently. "Have you received any kind of call from the hospital?"

The woman sucked in her breath. "No. Is it something to do with the sheriff?" There was genuine concern in her voice.

"No. But there's been an . . . accident at the hospital. You should dispatch the cops right away. And if Red comes in, tell him to see me pronto."

As Morgan hung up, he heard someone coming up behind him. Instinctively, he ducked and spun. A huge meaty fist missed his head by scant inches and slammed into the plastic and metal phone box.

Nias shook his hand in pain and then his left fist shot out at Morgan's face.

Morgan saw his opening and drove his bare foot into the bigger man's groin. With a resounding cry, Nias grabbed his crotch and slumped to his knees. Morgan aimed a short jab into the man's jaw. The blow sent waves of jarring pain down his side, but he smiled as Nias tumbled over, his eyes rolling up in his head.

"Who'd have guessed? A glass jaw," Morgan mumbled, turning and starting back to his room. Just as he reached his door, he heard a siren whine in the distance and smiled wolfishly. Now Case could explain all this to the cops.

Morgan knew that Case and God knows how many of his men would be looking for him very soon. If discretion was indeed the better part of valor, Morgan decided he'd better get the hell out of there.

Slipping back to his room, he pulled his clothes from the closet, dressed quickly and left. Down the hall, two local police officers were trying to get past Richard Case. The FBI agent was gesturing with his hands and speaking in a low, earnest voice. He saw Morgan, pointed in his direction and shouted something.

Morgan didn't wait to find out what. He simply started running, made a sharp turn and ducked into the first door he came to. A second later he could hear the thud of footsteps running just beyond the door.

It wouldn't take them long to figure out he hadn't left the building. He flipped on the light. It was the janitor's storeroom, filled with boxes of toilet paper, cleaning supplies, pails, mops and other paraphernalia necessary to keep the hospital clean and functioning.

Tugging off his parka, Morgan took a pair of white coveralls off a hook and pulled them on over his clothes. Stuffing his coat into an empty mop bucket mounted on casters, he grabbed a mop and pulled open the door. The hall was empty.

Using the mop to both push the bucket and conceal his coat, Morgan started toward the lobby. When he heard people coming his way, he leaned the mop against the wall and quickly knelt, as if scraping something off the floor.

"Where'd he go?" someone demanded.

"He was here a minute ago and he hasn't gone outside," another answered. Morgan dared not look up.

"Hey, buddy," one of the pair asked him. "You see a guy running this way?"

Morgan kept his head down. He could see the cop's shiny black shoes. He pointed with his thumb down the way he had come. "He vent dat vay," Morgan said in his best German accent.

"He's doubled back on us," the second cop said, trotting off.

As soon as the pair was around the far corner, Morgan rose, grabbed the mop and again started toward the front of the building. When he neared the lobby, he saw Nias hulking in a chair, his face chalky white and his hands massaging his inner thighs.

Morgan scanned the area. Outside the main door, a man in a dark trench coat moved back and forth, watching the front of the building. No doubt the emergency entrance was covered too.

Abandoning the mop and retrieving his coat from the bucket, he ducked into the restroom near the now-closed cashier's window. The stalls were all empty. The one on the far end was directly below a narrow window mounted high in the wall. Morgan stood on the toilet and studied the opening. Unlatching it, he found that it tilted back about a third of the way, held in place by a chain. A flimsy screen was mounted on the outside.

Morgan had the chain loose and the window opened wide in a matter of seconds. Shivering in the blast of cold air, he held onto the window's frame for balance and used his free hand to push on the screen until it popped free.

118

"So far so good," he breathed, wincing as his injured ribs spasmed.

Hauling himself out the opening proved almost more than he could bear. Levering himself up with his arms, placing tremendous strain on his bruised side, he managed to maneuver himself until his head and shoulders were out the window while his feet dangled down the inner wall.

A thick pine tree blocked his view, but also concealed him from anyone watching the area. As he started to drag himself out the window, there was a commotion in the bathroom.

"There he is!" someone yelled. Morgan cursed as a pair of hands clamped around one of his booted ankles. Without thinking, he lashed out with his other foot, rewarded to feel his heel connect. A man cried out and his ankle was free.

Fighting the pain, Morgan let himself tumble out the window. His short fall was broken by a spreading juniper bush. He closed his eyes as his face ground into the brittle needles.

The night was bitter and icy. Although there was no wind, the cold stung Morgan's eyes and numbed his face almost instantly. With each breath, frigid air shocked his mouth and throat.

There was more shouting inside the restroom. Clutching his tortured ribs, Morgan limped to the dark shadows along the brick wall. Twice he stumbled over low bushes, but he reached the alley behind the hospital unobserved.

Leaning against the building, catching his breath, Morgan looked back the way he'd just come. Several flashlights bobbed and wavered as men shouted to one another in their search.

He had scant minutes to get clear of the area. Gasping, he pushed away from the wall and started racing down the snowpacked alley. As he ran, his feet repeatedly slipped and slid, threatening to fly out from under him. What with the tenderness in his crotch and the steady ache in his side, each movement was a small agony.

At the end of the alley, he paused to study the street. Nothing was moving. Morgan darted out of the shadows and started across the avenue. When he was halfway across, a car came roaring around the corner to his right. Its headlights swept back and forth across him as the driver fought to keep the vehicle from spinning out.

He had no way of knowing whether or not the car carried any of his pursuers and he wasn't waiting to find out. Still holding his side, Morgan crossed the street and ducked into the alley.

The car's engine whined as the tires spun on ice and then squealed as they hit dry pavement. Headlights glanced down the alley just as Morgan dashed into an unfenced backyard and plowed through the snow toward the front of the dark house.

He heard the car stop as a powerful spotlight danced across the snow near him. He dodged close to the house's wall and kept moving. He could hear someone shouting and the sound of a car door slamming.

They were attempting to flank him, cut off his escape. He sensed someone dogging his trail, and he was sure a car would come down the street in front of him.

For one panicky second, Morgan was ready to quit, but the thought of Case's cold, calm threat galvanized him. Better to make them work to get him than to simply fall into their waiting arms.

You forced him to do this, Morgan reminded himself as he ran across the front yard of the house and into the street. Couldn't keep your big mouth shut.

At the far corner, the car's headlights flashed at his back. Behind him he could hear the man on foot closing the distance between them.

The pain in his side was growing worse. His breath was now coming in labored gulps and the brittle cold air made his throat raw and his eyes sting. His knees were shaky and weak.

The Devouring

The car was roaring down the street; the man chasing him was only a few yards behind. Morgan suddenly stopped in the street and turned. His follower, a big bulky man wrapped in a long overcoat, faltered for an instant when his quarry stopped. His feet hit a slick spot and he swung one arm wildly for balance. Morgan saw the gun held in his fist.

With the car closing fast, Morgan lunged at his pursuer. He kicked hard at the man's kneecap, feeling it crunch under his boot. The gun went flying as the man squealed and sat down hard on the icy pavement.

The car horn suddenly blared. Morgan looked up and jumped at the same time. The driver had jammed on the brakes and, without control, the car was careening sideways. The howling man in the street saw the car coming and tried to drag himself out of its path. Too late. The driver's door caught him solidly and sent him spinning across the snow and ice. The rear end of the car swayed and then moved ahead of the front end, angling toward the curb.

Morgan staggered to the opposite side of the street as the car plowed backward into an old, solid elm tree. The resounding crash of twisting metal and breaking glass was sure to wake the entire neighborhood.

The man who'd been hit was still moving. The icy street, Morgan decided, had probably saved his life. He was dragging himself to the curb. Inside the car, the driver was rubbing his head and neck.

Up and down the street, porch lights winked on and curious, frightened people peered warily out of their warm houses to discover the source of the racket that had drawn them from their warm beds.

Breathing hard, Morgan started limping away from the wreck. He'd bought himself some time and he had to use it to get away, find a place to hole up.

It was only a few blocks to his house, but he knew that going there would likely put him right back into

Case's hands. He could go to Gruff's, but that was another likely place to start searching. On the other hand, Red Crumley was already involved. If Morgan could stay with the county sheriff, he would at least have some measure of protection from Case until he could figure out a way to blow the lid off this whole bizarre affair.

And blow the lid off was exactly what Morgan intended to do. Rationally, he knew this was way out of his league. The people mixed up in this were cold-blooded and vicious. They would probably stop at nothing to keep the public from learning about whatever was *flying* around the mountains.

Still, he couldn't just walk away and forget about it. He'd found Crocker's battered body. He could still see those black, empty eye sockets and the streamers of frozen blood running down the rock. And he'd never be able to erase the memory of Charlie Shaw lying in the bloody snow, his throat ripped out, his eyes torn from his skull, nor of what he had seen at the hospital tonight. These were nightmares he'd have to contend with the rest of his life. Which, admittedly, might be very short.

Maybe if the public found out, they'd be panicked and frightened. But better a terrified public armed with the truth than unsuspecting victims falling prey to some unknown killer stalking the wilderness.

Morgan could again see the dark shape gliding past his hospital room window. He shivered at the memory and hunched his shoulders as much against the cold in his soul as the frigid air.

As these thoughts cascaded through his mind, a white-hot ball of fury grew in his gut. He'd talk to Red, convince the sheriff that their only recourse now was to call in the media, lay everything out for them.

Sure, Morgan reasoned, the government would try like hell to make them out to be total and complete nutcases, but there were others to corroborate their story. Sooner or later, the truth would come out and when it did, Case and

Ferris and their cohorts could kiss their well-covered asses good-bye.

Lumping Roberta Ferris in with Case brought on a pang of guilt. Call it gut instinct, but Morgan just couldn't picture her as a cold-blooded mercenary. On the other hand, she had the answers to this whole mess and Case was working for her. And too, the FBI agent had beaten him and threatened him. It was hard to believe he was acting without her approval.

Of course, she might simply be a figurehead. For an FBI agent, Case was particularly freewheeling. It was hard to tell whether Roberta was giving him orders or vice versa.

When Morgan neared Red Crumley's house, an icy hand clutched at the pit of his gut. Two sheriff's cars, a highway patrol cruiser and Doc Reed's station wagon were parked out front. A couple of parka-clad deputies were standing on the front porch. They watched as Morgan approached.

"Jesus, Morgan," Jasper McKissik said, coming down the steps. "It's terrible." Morgan could see the man's bloodless face and red-rimmed eyes and knew he had been crying.

"What?" he demanded, a knot of dread creeping over his heart.

"It's Red. He's dead, Morgan. Dead . . ." McKissik turned away, his voice thick with despair. He wiped at his eyes with a handkerchief.

"How?" Morgan asked, feeling an odd wave of sympathy for the little man. Red Crumley had probably been the only person in Jasper's life to give him an even break.

McKissik turned back around. "We found his car out on the Coronado Lake Road." The deputy's eyes turned inward, recalling what he had discovered. His voice became a flat monotone. "It was on the side of road, in the ditch. The windows were all smashed. Red was . . . next to it. He'd been . . . Jesus, Morgan, he'd been torn to pieces.

123

I . . . I've never seen anything like it in my life. . . ."

Morgan had.

The deputy looked up, his eyes searching Morgan's face. "Who . . . would do that? What kind of . . . a maniac would do that?"

Morgan shook his head, the knot of fury in his stomach now a sickening ball. "I don't know, Jasper. I really don't. But you saw what it did the night when Shaw was killed."

McKissik looked at him with pleading eyes. "Is that what killed Red? Was that . . . *thing* what did it?"

"Maybe, Jasper. Maybe. I sure as hell intend to find out. Will you give me a ride to the motel? I gotta talk to someone. I'm going to find out just what in the hell is going on around here."

Chapter Eight

Roberta Ferris sat up in bed, her heart pounding. Someone had banged on the motel room door. Either that, or she was having another nightmare. She'd been having a lot of them lately.

Again, a fist thudded several times against the metal door.

Roberta tossed back the covers and groped for her robe draped over the nearby chair. Standing, she pulled it on and stepped cautiously to the door.

Her common sense told her to simply call the desk, tell the night clerk someone was trying to break in. Of course, she recalled the night clerk, a disinterested little man who spent most of his time in the office sitting behind the desk watching old movies on a small TV. Besides, if her late-night caller was Richard Case, Roberta couldn't risk creating a scene.

She paused at the door.

"Yes? Who is it?"

"Blaylock."

Roberta frowned. What the hell was he doing here?

Hesitantly, she snapped open the dead bolt, but left the night chain secured. Peering through the narrow crack, she was shocked at his appearance. His bruised face was haggard, his clothing was filthy and his eyes were bright with anger.

"Morgan," she hissed. "What are you doing here?"

"We have to talk," he gasped, a hand pressed against his side.

"At this hour? It's . . ."

"I know what time it is," he barked. "And frankly, I don't give a damn if you miss your beauty sleep. We're going to talk. Now are you going to open the door, or do I kick my way in?"

Seeing the look in his eyes, hearing the dangerous edge in his voice made Roberta's heart clutch. She had no doubt he could and would batter down the door. Suddenly the safety chain seemed fragile, absurdly inadequate.

Behind Morgan, the carpeted hall was hushed. The other guests had long since retired to their rooms.

"Well?" he demanded, his dark eyes flinty and unwavering.

"You're crazy," Roberta said, starting to slam the door. Before the latch caught, before she could snap the dead bolt, Morgan drove his shoulder into the heavy door.

Roberta cried out as the screws in the night latch tore away from the jamb. Terrified, she spun and ran toward the telephone.

He hit the door again. Wood splintered as the screws holding the chain in place were ripped loose. Behind her, Roberta heard the door fly open and bang against the wall.

She lunged for the phone.

Breathing in shallow gasps, Morgan rushed her. Just as she started to punch the button for the desk, he caught her by the collar of her robe and jerked her backward. Her legs collided with the side of the bed and she sprawled atop the tangled covers.

Rape! The thought sliced through her mind like a razor-sharp knife. This enigmatic man who fostered such ambivalence, whom she grudgingly admired and reluctantly distrusted, was going to violate her. . . .

Before Roberta could scream, Morgan clamped a hand over her mouth while his other hand corralled her flaying fists.

"Stop it!" he snapped, his voice a raspy hiss. "I'm not going to hurt you. I just want answers."

For long seconds, they stared at each other, his eyes fierce and hard, hers filled with frustration and fear.

"I'm going to take my hand away," he panted. "Don't scream. Just give me five minutes. For God's sake, just hear me out."

Roberta's mind raced. Wasn't that the kind of thing a rapist or murderer would say? Isn't that exactly what some pervert would tell their victim, just before they brutalized them?

"All right?" he asked.

Roberta continued to glare up at him. The hand covering her mouth was hard and callused, but she could feel it trembling. Nervous fear or dark anticipation? She wanted to trust him, wanted to believe him. Since they'd first met, she'd developed a curious admiration for him. Yes, he was arrogant, self-righteous and condescending, but he had a strong set of values, a strong sense of right and wrong.

But this was over the line. Was he some violent psychopath, masking his base desires behind the cynical facade of a crusader?

Roberta nodded her head.

Morgan appeared visibly relieved as he pulled his hand away from her mouth and released her hands.

The instant she was free, Roberta rolled across the bed, swung her legs to the floor, intent on getting out of the room.

Mumbling a curse, Morgan leaped across the bed and circled wide, blocking her path.

"You're not a very honest woman, are you?" he snapped, clutching her arm. "But then, I suppose that goes with the territory, doesn't it? I mean, two more people are dead and here you are, sleeping like a baby."

Roberta felt as if she'd been slapped. She stared into Morgan's face, his angry words washing over her like a hot, stinging wind.

"Two more?" she asked in a whisper. "What are you talking about? Who's dead? Is this some sick joke?" Her fear was now turning to an icy fist squeezing at her heart.

"No joke, Roberta," he barked, still clutching her shoulders, his eyes still burning with fury.

She studied his face for several seconds. "Go shut the door," she whispered.

Morgan limped to the door, glanced out in the hall and then pushed it shut, snapping the dead bolt.

Shakily, Roberta moved around the bed and reached for one of the chairs at a small round table near the curtained window. Her mind was reeling. She slumped into the chair and watched as Morgan moved back into the room and sat wearily on the edge of the bed.

"Who was killed?" she asked.

"One of Case's agents," he said. "At the hospital."

Roberta continued to stare at him for several moments and then, as she realized what he had just told her, her mouth opened. "The hospital?" She looked around as if trying to find some misplaced item. "Dear God, it's . . . getting bolder."

"And Red Crumley," he blurted out. "Outside of town. In his car."

Roberta stared at Morgan in disbelief. Hot tears welled in her eyes and she covered her face with her hands. "Crumley?" she said, the dead sheriff's name coming out of her mouth in a long gush of air. "Oh, Morgan, I'm sorry. I'm so sorry. I . . ."

Morgan reached for her hands, gently pulling them away from her face. After a moment, her eyes met his.

"What's going on?" he demanded. "What in the hell is happening?"

"I can't tell you. . . ."

"Don't give me that," he said quietly. "All that crap about *national security* doesn't wash." His voice grew more intense. "People are dying. Red Crumley was one of my best friends. He was a good man, a good cop."

Roberta peered into his eyes and saw his pain.

"Are you afraid of Case?" The question took her by surprise.

"What are you saying?" she asked defensively. Memories of her confrontation with Richard outside the hospital flooded back and she shivered.

"He's a dangerous man," Morgan answered flatly. "You and I both know it." He released her hands, but continued to hold her eyes with his own.

"What's Richard got to do with . . . look, I'm sorry he attacked you," she said, meaning it. Case was not the man she would have selected to help with her investigation. But then no one asked her opinion. And if the gossip back in D.C. was true, he had pulled a lot of strings to get the assignment. "He's . . . *sometimes* he just can't control his temper. You pushed him and he . . ."

"Roberta," Morgan growled, cutting her off. "Don't apologize for the bastard. I really don't give a damn about all that." He probed his tender ribs and flashed her a humorless smile. "Well, maybe a little."

Roberta fished a tissue out of the pocket of her robe and wiped her eyes and blew her nose. "What's happened tonight?"

She listen in shock as Morgan told her about the savage murder of Case's man, his own confrontation with Nias, his subsequent narrow escape and Red Crumley's death.

As Morgan spoke, the cold emptiness in the pit of Roberta's stomach expanded, consuming her in icy ball of fear.

Since almost the beginning of this operation, she had realized Case was a man to be watched. After he attacked Morgan, she knew his propensity for violence extended beyond verbal assaults, but now, hearing Morgan detail everything he'd been through, she understood how truly unscrupulous and dangerous he was.

When Morgan finished, Roberta reached out, touching his arm gently. "I swear to you, I didn't know about any of this. After he put you in the hospital, I complained to . . . my superiors. They told me they would see to it that he stayed in line."

"But?" he said, studying her face.

Roberta sighed. "But I don't think they'll do anything."

Morgan got up, shaking his head. "Either Case has gone totally rogue or your superiors can't be trusted."

Roberta adjusted her robe, carefully covering her knees and the lacy hem of her nightgown. How much could she tell this man? According to the briefing she'd had before coming to Colorado, anything she told him was too much, but Case's actions were compromising security beyond anything she could do by opening up to Morgan Blaylock.

Still, Roberta was honor-bound to adhere to the operation's security. If anyone found out she'd spilled her guts, she could kiss her job and maybe her career good-bye.

"Richard is obsessed," she ventured.

"With what?" Morgan asked, leaning back on the bed, supporting himself on his elbows. Each time he shifted, he grimaced.

She averted her eyes. She wanted to tell him the truth, but was the risk justified? Finally, after a long, tense silence, she looked up, catching Morgan's eyes. "With . . . that damned thing in the mountains."

"What is it?"

"I don't know," she sighed. And it was the truth. "At least, I'm not certain what it is."

"But you have a good idea," he said quietly. "My guess was pretty close, wasn't it?"

"Yes," Roberta conceded. Hoping to avoid further discussion of that particular subject, she changed the subject. "You shouldn't be out of the hospital. You're not well."

Morgan was ashen, his eyes feverish and his face coated in a thin sheen of sweat.

"No kidding," he groaned. "You're ducking the issue."

"Morgan, you're sick."

He shifted on the bed, squeezing his eyes shut. "Got any aspirin?"

Roberta got up and went into the bathroom. She returned with three white tablets and a glass of water. He swallowed them and then stretched out on the unmade bed.

"Too much exertion," he breathed. "Too much . . ."

Roberta stood, watching him, as almost immediately, he dropped into a deep sleep.

Morgan awoke with a start. He didn't know where he was, and for a moment couldn't remember why he wasn't in the hospital. Then, memories flooded back, settling over him like a dark, stifling shroud.

He sat up in the bed.

Heavy curtains were drawn tight across the room's window. Suddenly realizing he was alone, he felt a rush of panic overwhelm him. Then he saw the closed bathroom door.

"Roberta?" he called. His voice was dry, a hoarse crackle.

The bathroom room door opened and he squeezed his eyes shut against the glaring light.

"Roberta?"

"No, it's not Roberta," a familiar voice replied. "She's gone."

"Reed? What are you doing here?" Morgan peered at

the rotund doctor through slitted eyes.

"She called me," Milo Reed answered dryly, wiping his hands on a towel. "Said you konked out on her bed. I was intrigued." The last words came out accompanied by a lascivious smile.

"Thought you were at . . . Red's."

Doc Reed sat down heavily in one of the chairs and frowned. "Just long enough to give Ruth a sedative. She took the news rather badly, I'm afraid."

"Where'd Roberta go?" Morgan asked. He still wasn't convinced he could trust her. One word from her and he'd be in shit up to his neck.

"She didn't say and I didn't ask," the doctor answered. "She left about an hour ago. Said she'd be back soon. She wanted me to tell you not to leave the room. Something about that nasty Case fellow."

Morgan started to get out of bed, realizing he was naked beneath the covers. His ribs had been retaped.

"I wanted to put you back in the hospital," Reed explained. "But she told me what happened there last night. We both decided you'd be safer here. However, I want you to stay in bed for today at least. Between your concussion and those cracked ribs, you're in no shape to be gallivanting around."

"Have you been to the hospital?" Morgan asked.

"No. Jasper McKissik called me from Red's, and I'd barely gotten home from there when Ms. Ferris phoned. Don't worry, I'll check into it when I go in this morning." He took off his eyeglasses and wiped the lenses on the damp towel he still held.

"Morgan, do you understand any of this?" There was an all-too-familiar weariness in the man's voice.

"Some. All I've really got are suspicions. I think Case is trying to pull off a cover-up, but I'm not sure why."

Reed reached for something on the table and handed it to Morgan. Turning on the bedside lamp, Morgan unfolded the newspaper. It was one of the Denver papers, opened to a middle page.

"Read that article at the top," Reed instructed.

Morgan looked at the headline.

Two Killed in Freak Accident

Crystal Wells—The editor of the *Crystal Wells Journal* and a second man were killed in a freak accident near here, federal authorities reported yesterday.

Charles Shaw, 53, a 25-year resident of Crystal Wells and an award-winning newspaperman, and Michael Crocker, 23, a technician for the North American Atmospheric Monitoring System, were killed earlier this week in what authorities describe as a "freak" snowmobile accident.

According to a NORAMS spokesman, the pair were riding a snowmobile across a snowfield when they apparently lost control and sent the machine off a 200-foot cliff.

Morgan stopped reading and threw the paper on the floor. "That's bullshit!" he snarled.

"Of course it is," Reed said placidly. "Utter nonsense. But the feds got the word out first. Now when someone tries to refute them, they'll have already planted the seed in the public's mind. Whoever tries to debunk the official story will look like a liar.

"If you had read the rest of the story," the doctor continued, "you'd discover that both men were killed instantly when they landed on the rocks at the base of the cliff. And you'd find that the time delay in reporting the tragedy was due to the time it took rescuers to find the bodies."

"It's all so much crap," Morgan said in disgust. "They can't cover up what happened at the hospital last night.

Too many people saw the condition of that room and the . . . body parts scattered around." Morgan looked at the clock radio next to the lamp.

"Almost ten o'clock. Let's see what's on the local news." He turned on the radio, tuning in one of the two local stations.

After a series of commercials for a supermarket, a truck sale and the local feed and grain store, a bass-voiced announcer came on with the news.

"Topping our news at this hour: A massive search is underway for a suspect in the murders of County Sheriff Roscoe 'Red' Crumley and a second man killed at Crystal Wells hospital overnight.

"A massive manhunt has been launched for Crystal Wells resident Morgan Blaylock following the overnight slayings."

The voice droned on, but the words were lost on Morgan. His stomach lurched, and Doc Reed looked first at Morgan and then at the radio, his eyes wide in apprehension.

"Although information is still sketchy, FBI Agent Richard Case, in town on an unrelated investigation, said Blaylock was a patient at the hospital recovering from injuries received when he attacked a federal agent earlier this week. Case would only identify the victim at the hospital as an FBI agent, also hospitalized after being attacked in a related incident.

"According to Case, sometime during the night Blaylock allegedly crept out of his room and killed the FBI agent. The suspect and Sheriff Crumley are known to have been friends, and it is believed Blaylock lured Crumley to the hospital, forced him to drive him away and then killed him.

"Authorities said Blaylock is armed and should be considered extremely dangerous."

Morgan turned the radio off. The room tilted, and there was a sudden, intense throbbing that the back of his head. His stomach turned and for a moment, he thought he was going to vomit.

"That bastard really nailed me down," he hissed.

Doc Reed nodded. "No shit."

Morgan sat on the edge of the bed, running his hands through his greasy hair. "I've got to get out of here. Jasper McKissik drove me here last night. He knows where I am. I can't believe no one's been here yet."

He tossed off the covers and reached for his clothes piled on the floor.

"Where can you go?" Reed asked, concerned. "You're in no condition to be acting out *The Fugitive*."

"Maybe not, but my life won't be worth a damn if I stay here. Hell, if Roberta hears that news, she's as likely to turn me in as not. She won't know whether or not I'm guilty."

He was tying his boot lace when the door opened. Turning quickly, he saw Roberta Ferris hurry into the room. She was now wearing a smartly tailored business suit, gray skirt, matching jacket, a crisp white blouse and high-heeled black patent-leather pumps. Her hair was stylishly swept back.

Morgan appraised her transformation in one long look.

"You've got to get out of here," she hissed.

"I take it you heard," Morgan said. "Where have you been, anyway? Meeting with the Rotary?"

Roberta frowned. "There are people here from Washington. I had to see them." She shot him a concerned glance. "I know none of it's true, but I can't do anything about it right now. Case has outflanked me. Now come on, let's go." She handed him his coat.

"Where *can* he go?" Reed asked, pushing himself out of the chair.

"I've got another room in the hotel. They'll search mine but they won't think to search the other one." She handed Morgan a key.

"But if it's under your name . . ." Morgan said.

"It's not. Now come on." She turned to Doc. "Please, don't say anything about coming here."

The small, fat man shook his head. "Not a word. I'm afraid I know too much of what's been going on to want to help cover up any more."

Roberta bit her lip and looked at the doctor. "It was never supposed to go this far. Please, believe me."

"I do," the physician answered.

She hurried to the door, looked up and down the hall, and satisfied it was clear, motioned for Morgan to follow her. She led him to the stairs.

"One flight up, Morgan. I got it under a fake name. The desk clerk downstairs is new—at least I've never seen him before. He had no idea who I was. I paid cash." All of it came out in a whispered rush. She pressed a key into his palm.

"Put out the 'Do Not Disturb' sign and wait until I come. I'll bring you food." With that she wheeled, and hurried back down the hall to her own room.

Morgan went up the stairs, found the room number and let himself in. After slipping the sign on the door, he closed it and sat wearily on the edge of the bed.

Did Case really believe he could pull off this elaborate hoax? Or was he simply buying time? He couldn't silence everyone; there were too many people with pieces to the puzzle. It wouldn't take much for a few of them to gather their individual bits of knowledge and assemble a mosaic of his treachery and deceit.

In the meantime, as Doc Reed had pointed out, Morgan would be playing fugitive. He'd never had more on his record than a few traffic tickets. Oh, he'd been in a few barroom brawls and he'd had his share of heated "discussions" with cops, but for all his verbal defiance of authority, Morgan Blaylock was actually a regular John Q. Citizen.

Now, he was a suspected killer. There were probably a hundred cops crawling over Crystal Wells and the surrounding area looking for his ass.

That was a hard reality to accept.

Morgan glanced down at his hands and saw that they were shaking. With something like amazement, he realized he was utterly terrified.

God in heaven, Red was dead. Dead. Not just gone away. Not just sick, but dead. The big one. And there was no getting around it; no hiding from it. Dead is dead.

His friend was dead . . .

. . . and the omnipotent *they* were accusing him of the murder.

This was insanity. The whole thing was right out of some Hitchcockian fever dream. Morgan was trapped in a nightmare he neither had created nor understood. Although, ruefully, he admitted to himself that he'd stuck his head in the lion's mouth by baiting Case at every turn. Was it any wonder the lion had taken a bite?

Confused, his thoughts jumbled, Morgan stretched out on the bed and tried to make sense of everything that was happening. Roberta Ferris was helping him hide from Case. Yet Case supposedly reported to her. The lady was truly an enigma. One minute she could be remarkably compassionate and the next, amazingly hostile. The only consistent trait she exhibited was fear. She was frightened of something. Maybe it was the thing in the mountains. Maybe it was Case. More likely, it was both.

When he thought of her, something inside stirred. In spite of everything, he found himself thinking about the depth of her eyes, the appealing curves of her figure, those long, sensuous legs. . . .

"Damn," he muttered. This was no time to lust after a woman he hardly knew, especially since she held his very life in her hands.

Maybe she'd bring Case back here. Maybe her offer of sanctuary was a ruse, a cheap trick to lull him into trusting her so she could get good ol' Dick and together they could . . . what? Kill him? Use him as a scapegoat to explain the murders of Crumley and the FBI agent and maybe even the disappearance of the Pruett woman?

Douglas D. Hawk •

And if she did betray him, if Case or his men came into
the motel room, guns blazing, who would question their
actions? Morgan had already been fingered as a murderer.
His death could easily be explained away as the necessary
use of deadly force against a dangerous felon.

For a moment Morgan thought about bolting from the
room, the hotel, the town. He knew the area well. He could
take back streets and roads until he was well away. Once
he was out of the area, he could find a place to hole up
until he could plan his next move.

"You're paranoid, Blaylock," he told himself. Roberta
called Doc Reed. Hadn't she gone to the trouble and
risk of renting this room? Those weren't the actions of
a deceiver. If she was in it with Case, all she'd have had
to do was call him after Morgan passed out.

No, better to sit tight and play out this hand. Roberta
Ferris was the only one who could help him now and she
held all of the cards.

His only real concern for the time being was McKissik.
The deputy had brought him to the hotel. Why hadn't
he turned Morgan over to Case? Certainly not out of
any sense of loyalty, and not in his wildest fantasy did
Morgan believe the little deputy would protect him, even
if he knew he was innocent.

Morgan's headache was numbing and the tight, throbbing ache in his ribs made each breath labored. Lying
back on the bed, he sighed heavily and forced himself
to relax. There was nothing he could do until Roberta
returned.

He was watching an insipid afternoon game show with
its panel of washed-up performers and has-been celebrities
when Roberta stepped quickly into the room. A plastic bag
of groceries dangled from one hand and a large padded
case was held in the other. Morgan recognized latter as
a VCR carrier.

"We going to watch movies?" he asked, getting off
the bed.

138

She gave him a sour look. "Something like that." Putting down the VCR and the bag, she pulled out a loaf of bread, a package of sliced salami and a six-pack of beer.

"Feast fit for a king," Morgan said, starting to make a sandwich.

Roberta didn't answer. She was pensive and distant, quietly taking the VCR out of the case and hooking it up to the room's large TV.

"So," Morgan said with forced levity. "What're we watching? A videotape of *The Fugitive?*"

"Not funny," she snapped, frowning at him.

He pulled two bottles out of the six-pack and twisted off their tops. "Here," he said, handing her one. "You look like you could use it."

She took the bottle. "You're always so damned glib. God, you're up to your neck in shit and you don't even care."

"Oh, I care. Believe me." A sardonic grin crossed his lips. "Of course, if Case was here, he'd say there wasn't enough shit."

Roberta's mouth almost curled up at the corners, and Morgan could see she was making a conscious effort to keep from smiling. "Old joke," she said.

"Yeah, but it applies." Morgan took a long pull on his beer and then studied the woman. "What's the situation? Have you talked to Mr. FBI?"

Roberta sighed and nodded. "I talked to him." Her mouth pressed into a hard line. "He's completely out of control. He wants you and he wants you in a bad way."

"Seems like he's done a pretty good job of getting me." He frowned at her. "Explain something to me. I thought he reported to you. How come you can't call him off?"

She looked away, moving to one of the chairs. "In theory, he does report to me. But in fact, Richard does whatever the hell he wants to do. Like I said, I reported his behavior to people in Washington, and they all gave me the same line of patronizing crap: 'Work with him. Try to see things from his prospective . . . blah, blah, blah.' It's all a big joke!"

Morgan saw the tears in her eyes and had an overwhelming urge to go to her, comfort her. But he didn't. That would be adding insult to injury. Whatever else Roberta Ferris was, she wasn't some simpering schoolgirl. She was bright and capable. If those jerks in D.C. couldn't see that, it was their loss.

"What I don't understand," Morgan said after a long silence, "is why Case decided to set me up. I mean, sure, I'm a bonafide pain-in-his-ass, but to frame me for two murders? It's nuts. He can't get away with it." Morgan's voice rose as he spoke, and when he stopped he suddenly realized he had been close to yelling.

Roberta stared at him and then shook her head. "The trouble is, he *can* get away with it. Half the town already has you tried and convicted. By tonight every radio station, TV station and newspaper in the state will have a story on Morgan Blaylock, the homicidal maniac. The Denver media will have a field day. Nothing they like better than trying and convicting people in the court of public opinion."

Morgan looked at her as he considered her words. "That still doesn't tell me what Case is so afraid of. Nor you, for that matter."

If the remark had touched a nerve, Roberta face didn't reveal it. She picked up her large purse and pulled out a videotape.

"The why is between you and Case. *Macho* bullshit, I suppose. As for the what, I think I can shed a little light on that." She held up the cassette.

"You've already put a lot of it together," she added, getting up and repositioning her chair. She kicked off her shoes and sat down, propping her legs up on the edge of bed. Her skirt rode up to mid-thigh. Appreciatively, Morgan cast an admiring eye at the silky length of those legs. She didn't appear to notice.

"Remember the other day at your house when you were asking me all those questions?" she asked rhetorically. "I told you about a pregnant woman who was killed."

Morgan nodded.

"Well," she said. "It was very bad, very messy." Her voice was flat, lifeless. "It was worse than Crocker and your friend Charlie Shaw."

"Because she'd been pregnant?" Morgan pressed.

Roberta turned up her beer bottle and took two long swallows. She was silent for a moment, and then glanced at him. "She disappeared from a weekend cross-country ski trip last March. She was from Las Vegas, a cashier in one of the casinos. Came to Colorado alone to get away from a rocky relationship or some such.

"Anyway, she was staying here in town, spending her days skiing and the evenings hanging around the local watering holes. Seemed to be a pretty decent woman. Twenty-five, pretty, very responsible. So, one day she went out to do a little cross-country on the approved trails and that was the last anyone saw of her until about three weeks ago."

Roberta paused to take another sip of beer.

"And when she was found, she wasn't eight months dead?"

Roberta nodded. "Exactly. She'd been alive until maybe twelve hours before a couple of hunters stumbled over her body."

"So where had she been all that time?"

Roberta's eyes grew dark. "I don't know."

Morgan was surprised to again see tears brimming her eyes. And again, he wanted to hold her, comfort her.

"Someone . . . some*thing* had . . . torn the baby from her womb. It was . . . savage. The most savage thing I've ever seen . . ." She wiped a hand over her eyes.

Morgan breathed a curse, trying not to visualize a pregnant woman eviscerated.

Roberta got up and, without a word, went into the bathroom. Morgan heard water running and a few minutes later, she returned looking pale beneath her light makeup.

"You okay?" he asked.

She shrugged. "No. Not really." Returning to the chair, she sat down wearily, propped her legs on the bed and leaned back, closing her eyes.

"Do you know what *Desmodontinae* is?" she asked.

Morgan made a face and shook is head. "Sorry, my Latin is terrible."

"It's Greek," she corrected. "It's the scientific name for certain species of bats."

"Bats? Little furry rodents with wings?"

She flashed a crooked half smile. "Yes. *Hematophagous* bats to be exact." Roberta watched him carefully for reaction.

"Hema . . . what? Like they eat blood. Vampires?" Morgan shivered, recalling the lab report Doc Reed's nurse friend had seen. The substance they had found in the NORAMS station had been very similar to bat guano.

"This is starting to sound a lot like a fifties B-movie," he muttered.

Roberta's laugh was hollow and empty. "As they say, you ain't seen nothin' yet."

"Meaning?"

She got up and slipped the videotape into the VCR. She stood with her finger poised over the start button.

"This was shot about a month ago by . . . one of my assistants." A sadness filled her eyes. For an instant, they clouded as she peered into the middle distance; then she blinked and continued. "He was using special infrared equipment and a very powerful lens." Without another word, Roberta started the tape and returned to her chair.

The TV screen was black for several seconds, and then abruptly a hazy, reddish picture appeared. It took Morgan several seconds to recognize the image: a craggy mountain peak, fuzzy, but distinct enough to make out the sharp, barren rock escarpments.

After several moments a dark shape glided into view from behind the peak. It flew on massive wings, descending and ascending with incredible maneuverability, soaring around the rocky ledges. The picture was too hazy to make out much detail, but Morgan could see that the thing was unnaturally large and its wings fluttered effortlessly.

The camera followed the smooth, easy flight of the creature for several minutes. It appeared content to sail on the air currents and glide in the downdrafts, although occasionally it would flap those huge wings and achieve incredible speed. More than once it sped out of the picture, the cameraman unable to keep up with it.

"Amazing," Morgan said. Roberta touched his arm and pointed at the screen.

"Just watch."

Abruptly, the soaring creature wheeled and with amazing speed came streaking down the face of the sheer mountain. Its powerful wings were a blur as it dropped to the base of peak and came toward the camera's position on a low, straight trajectory.

The picture wobbled for an instant as Roberta's assistant had adjusted the camera. The telescopic lens was so powerful, depth perception was impossible. Too late, the man behind it realized the creature was coming directly at him. The camera tilted back. A dark, leathery wing filled the screen, and then the picture jumped as the camera fell backward. For a second there was eerie red darkness, and then dark liquid splattered across TV screen and the tape ended.

"My God," Morgan breathed. He realized he was holding the beer bottle in a white-knuckled grip. He turned to Roberta. She was staring sightlessly at the TV screen, tears running slowly down her cheeks.

"I'll never get used to watching it," she said in an empty, faraway voice. "Never."

Douglas D. Hawk

Morgan cautiously touched her shoulder. "There was nothing you or anyone could do. How could anyone know . . . ?"

She blinked and looked up at him. "He was just a kid, Morgan. I didn't know what was up there. I had people scattered around the area with cameras. We didn't know what we'd get, but . . ." She stopped, unwilling to continue.

"You can't blame yourself," Morgan soothed.

"I know," she said, pulling a tissue out of her purse and blowing her nose. "But it doesn't make it any easier. Hell, I've seen that tape fifty times. And it never gets any easier."

"So what did I just see?" Morgan asked.

"I call it *Homo Desmodus*. Human bat."

"Human bat? That sounds . . ."

"Melodramatic?" Her tone was thick with sarcasm. "Maybe it is, but I think that's exactly what we have."

Morgan mulled over her assertion. This wasn't something he could just accept without question. But what was it he had seen out the hospital room window? What had been crouching over Charlie Shaw's body? What had ripped Case's man limb from limb and what had killed Red Crumley?

"Where did it come from?" he finally asked, sinking into the other chair.

Roberta spread her hands, palms up. "Who knows. What you just saw is all we know about it, other than the carnage it's left behind."

"Is there only one?" Now that Morgan had seen the tape, he had a thousand questions.

Her answer came in a flat monotone. "I don't know. Could be a hundred."

"Where does it . . . they live?"

Roberta shot him a despairing look and he fell silent. "I don't know, Morgan," she cried, desperation edging her voice. "I just don't know. I don't have any answers."

144

Morgan was quiet for a few minutes. "It was here last night, Roberta."

She didn't look at him, but nodded. "I know. It killed the FBI agent in the hospital and Sheriff Crumley."

"Has it ever come down this far before?"

"Probably." She drew in a deep breath. "I've done some research in the last few months."

"Into giant bats?"

"More or less," she nodded.

"And?"

"And," Roberta said with a sigh, "I've come up with some interesting, if enigmatic bits of information."

"Such as?"

"Well, there's the story of one Oliver Larch. He was eleven years old in 1889. Lived on an Indiana farm with his parents. On Christmas Eve, while the family was entertaining a houseful of distinguished guests, the boy went outside to the well for water. There was fresh snow on the ground. The family heard the boy scream. They ran outside. The only prints they found were his, but they could hear him screaming from above them, from the air. It was reported he cried, 'They have me!' "

Morgan listened to Roberta's story, feeling cold and sad. When he realized his mouth was suddenly very dry, he sucked on the beer bottle.

"Th . . . they ever find the kid?" he asked.

"Nope. Not a trace. Other guests—including a minister and a judge—confirmed the story."

"What else?" Morgan prompted, not sure he wanted to hear more.

"Well, in December 1990, some archaeologists around Mexico City uncovered a black ceramic statue of a 'human bat.' " Roberta voice remained flat and emotionless. She was simply reciting facts, hard data used to back whatever theory she had formulated.

"The find was significant," she continued. "Not so much because it was a human bat, but because it was one of only a handful of such ceramic figures ever discovered. The statue's face was particularly ferocious. The researchers weren't sure of its origins. Maybe it's Aztec. I haven't bothered to follow up."

"So what does it have to do with what's up there?" Morgan asked, gesturing vaguely in the direction of the mountains.

Roberta shrugged, crossing her legs, still propped on the edge of the bed.

"I'm not sure," she said thoughtfully. "But I did a little more digging. The Mayan and other civilizations had bat gods. The Aztecs believed in nine levels of the underworld. Some researchers suspect this human bat was a representative guardian of one of those levels."

"And you think it was more than just mythology, right?"

"Yeah, I do," she answered, looking at him for the first time since the video ended. "I think maybe it was a representation of a *real* creature. Something with which they were familiar."

Morgan looked at her curiously. "So you think . . ."

She cut him off. "I'm not sure *what* I think."

Getting up carefully, Morgan began pacing the room. "I just don't get it."

She exhaled. "I've been over every aspect of it a thousand times. I don't understand it either."

"It came down last night and killed two people," Morgan said thoughtfully. "But *how* did it know where to find that agent and Red? They sure as hell weren't random acts."

Frowning, Roberta stood, smoothed her skirt and walked to the VCR. After hitting the rewind button, she folded her arms and turned to Morgan.

"Case brought that FBI agent to the hospital after that thing attacked him," she said.

"Yeah," Morgan nodded. "I figured that out."

"And you know what I think?" she asked quietly. "I think that it . . . whatever it is . . . has considerable intelligence and I think it has some sense, some capacity to locate its prey."

"It actually came down looking for him?" Morgan found that hard to believe.

"Revenge."

"For what? Hadn't it already savaged the guy?"

Roberta agreed. "Oh, yeah. It savaged him good. But when he was attacked, he had a gun with him and, according to Case, he used it. He wounded the thing."

Morgan turned this new information over in his mind. "But what about Red? He never even saw the thing, except for that brief glimpse when we found Charlie's body, let alone confronting it."

She shrugged. "I don't know, Morgan. Honest to God, I just don't know."

"But you have your suspicions," he said, reading the truth in her face.

She reached for her purse, pulled out a plastic bag and held it up to the light.

Inside was a small plastic device, broken with loose wires trailing from it like entrails.

"I saw you pocket that up at the station," Morgan said, taking the bag and inspecting the device.

Roberta snorted a small laugh. "And I thought I was being so discreet."

"What is it?"

She shook her head. "I'm not positive, but I think it's a homing device of some kind."

The full impact of what she was suggesting was overwhelming. "You think someone used that to *attract* those flying bastards?" he asked.

Roberta shrugged. "I'm not sure what to think."

Chapter Nine

Morgan and Roberta ate in silence, a pall hanging over them like an invisible shroud. Sitting across from each other, they self-consciously avoided eye contact and thereby conversation.

The image of the winged anomaly soaring around the craggy mountain escarpments flickered through Morgan's mind again and again like a bit of film caught on an endless loop. Caught in a desperate need to explain it rationally, he considered a score of explanations, discarding each as being too elaborate or as implausible as the winged creature on the videotape.

The lamp suspended above their table was turned low, casting dim, vague shadows. Other than the whisper of air moving through the heating grates along the baseboards, the room was still and hushed.

Roberta twisted the top off her third bottle of beer. She was flushed, and had already shrugged out of her jacket and tossed it on the bed. She'd never been much of a drinker, and it took very little alcohol to fog her mind and unbalance her equilibrium. The alcohol was breaking through her self-imposed mental barriers, letting deep-seated torments rush to the surface.

Not that she cared. Too much tension, too much pain. At some point, she had to let the pent-up emotions out or risk toppling over a psychological precipice into a sea of boundless despair.

"Cheers," she mumbled, hoisting the bottle and sucking down a long gulp.

Morgan cocked his head and regarded her. "I think you've had enough. Your eyes don't look like they're focusing too well."

"What's wrong with my eyes?" she demanded.

He stared into them, peering into their dark, liquid depths. "Actually, nothing." He smiled as she blushed.

"Was that a pass?"

"Huh?"

She leaned back in her chair and flashed him a mischievous smile. "A pass. You know, a come-on?"

"I know what a pass is. And it wasn't." He continued to watch her.

She showed him an indignant frown. "What? I don't warrant a pass from the town's legendary lothario?"

Morgan eased his chair back, clasping his hands behind his head and stretching gingerly. "The key word is here legendary. My reputation exceeds my exploits."

"Not what I heard," Roberta teased.

"Oh? And what have you heard?"

She smiled coyly. "That you're a . . ." She stopped and looked away. "I'm sorry. That was spiteful. I guess it's the beer. Your personal life's none of my business." She closed her eyes and reached back with both hands to massage her shoulders. "God, I'm as tense as a coiled spring."

Morgan got up and moved around to stand behind her. He put his hands on her shoulders and began gently kneading muscles in her neck. He could feel their tight resistance to his gentle probing. "Never apologize, it's a sign of weakness."

"What?" Roberta breathed, making small sounds of pleasure and pain as his thumbs rolled over the knots. "Who came up with that asinine bit of nonsense?"

"John Wayne. Be careful, you're besmirching an American icon," he told her.

"I don't think I've ever seen any of his movies," she admitted thoughtfully.

"Where were you raised? Siberia? How can someone grow up in America and not see at least one John Wayne movie?" He was genuinely intrigued.

"Someone raised in a backwater Kansas town by a father who happened to be a minister and believed movies and television were tools of the Devil."

"Seriously?" Morgan asked incredulously.

"Yes," she answered. "Daddy was a very stern man. Not mean and never abusive, but very stubborn and steadfast on certain things. Usually things having to do with fun."

"Must have been depressing."

She shook her head. "Not really. You don't miss what you don't know. Besides, he insisted we read. He gave us mountains of books. When I reached high school, I'd already read all the books our literature teachers assigned. The others kids thought I was from Mars."

Morgan continued to work her muscles, pleased to feel them loosen beneath his fingers. "You sound like the typical preacher's daughter, forced to set an example."

Roberta was quiet for a few minutes. "Yeah, I suppose I was." There was something wistful about the way she said it. Morgan could sense a sadness in her voice and it stirred something in him.

"That's so much better," she said, arching her back and hunching her shoulders, testing the muscles. She got up. "I've got to go to the bathroom." As she started past Morgan, she touched his face lightly with her fingers.

"You're an interesting man," she whispered.

When Roberta returned, she reached for her jacket and looked for her shoes. Finding them, she slipped them on and stood unsteadily for a moment until she had her balance.

"I'd better go to bed," she mumbled.

"It's early," Morgan said, not looking forward to passing the long hours alone in the room.

She shook her head. "If I stay here any longer, I might do something I'll regret."

"Really?" he asked innocently. "Like what?"

Roberta gave him an unfocused glance and a grin. "Use your imagination."

"I already have," he said unabashedly.

Again, she blushed and started to reach her hand out to him and then withdrew it. "Nope. I've got to go back to my room. What if Case checks up on me?"

"Is he in charge of your personal life?" The mention of the FBI agent irritated Morgan.

The darkness returned to her eyes.

He moved in front of her, put his hands on her shoulders and stared into her eyes. She stood stiffly in his grasp, her eyes squeezed shut. Then, like the mournful wail of a lost, frightened child, a deep, gut-wrenching sob tore from her throat. Suddenly she was shaking violently, fists clenched, her nails biting deep grooves into her palms.

"Let it out," he whispered, pulling her close, holding her tightly. And she clung to him like a frightened, lost child.

They stood there in the dimly lit room for long minutes, holding each other. Roberta's face was buried in Morgan's shoulder, the tears flowing freely. When they subsided, he brushed his hand across her cheek. She looked up at him.

His kiss was gentle, tentative, and then, as she responded, it grew more urgent. She pressed against him and he slipped his hands down her back and stroked her hips. He held her, lifted her. Clinging to him, Roberta suddenly ground her body against his.

They breathed in fast, shallow gasps as their lips crushed together and their tongues probed one another's mouth. Morgan's hands slowly, erotically lifted Roberta's skirt. She moaned softly as his lips kissed her neck, caressing it with his tongue.

"Are you sure . . . you can do this?" she breathed. "I mean, after what . . . ."

Morgan silenced her with a hard kiss. "I'm not hurt that *bad*."

He pulled her to the bed and lowered himself across it. She knelt, her fingers deftly unfastening his jeans. Carefully, quickly she pulled them off his legs and then freed him from his shorts.

Her tongue flicked over his hardness and then, she took him in her mouth. Morgan writhed, his fingers clawing at bedding.

Finally, unable to contain himself, he reached for her, pulling her to him. Lying next to her, he kissed her throat, his fingers fumbling with the buttons of her blouse. As he exposed her white flesh, his lips traced a hot pattern between her breasts and down the taut muscles of her stomach. Her hips responded, thrusting eagerly.

Breathing hard, Morgan pulled down the silken panty hose and tossed them away. Roberta rolled on her side, reached back to unfasten her bra and then quickly unzipped her skirt. Morgan tugged the items off her body and she lay naked on the bed.

Her fingers undid his shirt and as he shrugged it off, she lightly touched the heavy tape circling, protecting his ribs.

Morgan shifted on the bed until he could caress her calf with his mouth. His tongue flicked up her leg, inside her thigh. Roberta's fingers buried themselves in his hair as his mouth moved to the moistness between her quivering thighs.

The Devouring

Morgan felt her body tense and writhe as his own ardor became almost unbearable.

"Now," she hissed. "Oh, God, now!"

He hovered above her, as her legs parted and wrapped around his waist. When he entered her, she made a soft noise deep in her throat. She matched his every thrust as their passions became demanding, reckless and violent.

Their bodies ground together in a quickening, ancient rhythm, and Morgan let out a groan as he exploded inside her and she responded in a frenzied climax.

Gasping, they lay in each other's arms for a long time. Roberta made a hiccuppy sob as a fresh flood of tears burst forth.

"It's been so long," she whispered. "So long." Morgan stroked her hair, pulled her close.

As their sweaty bodies began to chill, he tugged the bedspread free and covered them. They cuddled close for warmth, their bodies pressed close together.

"I feel as if I took advantage," Morgan said. She put a finger against his lips, silencing him.

"You didn't."

They were relaxed now, temporarily secure in the shelter of one another's arms, drifting on the borders of sleep. The sudden pounding on the door brought them both fully awake in an instant.

"Who could it be?" Roberta asked, panicked.

He motioned for her to be silent.

The pounding came again, more insistent this time.

Roberta pulled away from him, swung her legs off the bed and quickly gathered her clothes. Carrying them, she hurried into the bathroom and shut the door.

"Open up, Blaylock," Case called from the hallway. "I know you're in there. Open the damned door or I'll kick it down."

Morgan retrieved his pants, pulled them on and then grabbed his shirt. He glanced around the room. There was no way out. The room was four stories above the street, and there wasn't even a balcony from which to attempt an escape.

Case slammed his fist against the door a third time. His voice was loud and menacing. "Open up, Blaylock!"

Morgan sighed in resignation. If he didn't open the door, the FBI agent would probably kick it down and shoot him to boot. As he moved to the door, Roberta, now dressed, emerged from the bathroom. She watched as he slipped off the night chain and pulled the door open.

Richard Case stepped into the room, a wolfish grin on his face. When he saw Roberta, the grin turned into a hard frown. "Well, isn't this cozy? It wasn't enough for you to hide this bum, you had to fuck him too?"

"Watch your mouth, Dick," Morgan snarled. He made a move toward the agent, and was brought up short when the cold steel of a revolver was pressed hard against his cheek.

"Go ahead, Blaylock," Jasper McKissik hissed. The deputy's eyes were wide and wild and there was a sheen of nervous perspiration on his face. Morgan stood very still, watching Case.

The FBI agent returned his stare. "You're quite the cocksman, I hear." He looked at Roberta. "Is that true? Did he set your soul afire?" His mocking tone was cruel and malicious.

Roberta Ferris stared at the gun touching Morgan's face and then hurried over to Case. "Richard," she said sharply. "Tell him to put the gun away."

Case regarded her coldly. "You really screwed up, Roberta. Do you know that? You really screwed the pooch." He glanced meaningfully at Morgan. "By the time he gets out of prison, you'll be an old hag."

Roberta continued to glare at him, refusing to back down. "Tell him to put the gun down, Richard." She pronounced each word carefully, precisely.

Without taking his eyes off her, Case motioned toward McKissik. Frowning, the deputy holstered his weapon.

"I can't believe what you did to me, Blaylock," McKissik said bitterly. "Had me drive you over here, pretending you were all upset about Red. When it was you who killed him. You son of a bitch!" In his mounting anger, McKissik sucker-punched Morgan in the side. With a grunt, he crumpled to the carpeting, gagging, holding his ribs.

"McKissik!" Case growled in warning. "That's enough."

"Not by half," the deputy cried. He cocked his leg to kick Morgan, but as it swept forward, his intended victim grabbed the booted foot and twisted. With a cry of pain and surprise, McKissik spun around and thudded hard on the floor. Grunting from effort, Morgan pulled the gun from the deputy's holster and leveled it at the surprised FBI agent.

"You can't get away, Blaylock," Case said. "There's no place to run, no place to hide. We'll find you. *I'll* find you and when I do, by God, I'll kill you!"

"Maybe," Morgan agreed, breathing hard against the agonizing pain in his ribs. "And maybe not."

Case turned to Roberta, who was now standing well out of his reach. She was pale, clearly stunned by everything that had just transpired. "Tell him," Case said. "He's being crazy. You know we'll catch him. You know it! Look how easily we found him today. We knew McKissik brought him here to see you. Nobody remembered seeing him leave, but they remembered seeing that hick doctor come and go." The wolfish grin had returned to the FBI man's face.

"While you were out meeting with . . ." He paused, reconsidered what he was saying and then continued. "While you were at your meeting, we searched your room. When we didn't find Blaylock there, we started checking the register. Took us quite a while to track down the clerk that was working this morning. But when we did, he identified you as the woman who rented this room."

Case continued to stare at Roberta, his eyes piercing, penetrating. "Tell him, Roberta. He can't get away with it."

Her eyes flickered from Case to Morgan and back. "Maybe he can't," she said emphatically. "But you've backed him . . . us into a corner. If he goes with you he'll never come to trial. You'll kill him." She was badgering him now and enjoying it. "You'll kill him because if you don't he'll blow the lid off this whole thing and that'll blow the lid off your career, your life!"

He took a step toward her. "You don't know half of it!"

"Don't, Case," Morgan warned. "Don't give me a reason to put a hole through you." The FBI agent stopped and stared at the gun. It was held rock steady, and when he looked at Morgan's eyes, he knew it wasn't an idle threat.

"If you go with him, Roberta, you'll be an accomplice to murder," Case said.

"I'll take that risk," she answered.

Morgan glanced at McKissik. The deputy was sitting on the floor, his back to the door. A trickle of blood was leaking out of the corner of his mouth and he was watching Morgan with hate-filled eyes.

"Okay, boys," Morgan said. "Take off your clothes."

"What?" Case exploded.

"Take them off. Now!" He cocked the revolver.

Fuming, Case began to strip. McKissik got slowly to his feet, wiping the blood from his swollen lip with the back of his hand. He followed the FBI agent's lead.

"Roberta, take their belts and tie their hands behind their backs." Keeping the gun trained on the pair, Morgan pushed himself to his feet.

Doing as instructed, in a matter of minutes she had the two men seated in separate chairs, their hands bound behind their backs, their feet tied to the chairs' legs with lengths of torn bedding. Giving the gun to Roberta, Morgan took two wet washcloths from bathroom, forced them into the men's mouths and then securely gagged them with more of the bedding.

"Now go back to your room," Morgan told Roberta, taking the gun from her. "Pack your stuff." He shot her a hard, questioning look. "That is, if you're really going with me."

"I am," she assured him.

About 15 minutes later, Roberta returned carrying two suitcases with the video camera case slung over her shoulder by its strap. She retrieved her cassette from the VCR.

"Case," Morgan said, before leaving. "What she said is true. You boxed me in. You and I both know *what* killed your man and Crumley. I'll be damned if I'm going to let you railroad me."

McKissik turned to stare at Case.

"That's right, Jasper," Morgan told him. "You can hate my guts, but you know I'd never kill anyone, especially Red. You know it, even if you don't want to believe it."

They made certain the "Do Not Disturb" sign was still on the door, and then left the two naked, bound men. In the hall, Morgan stopped Roberta.

"Are you sure you want it this way?" he asked her.

She nodded her head. "Yes."

"You don't have to do this. You could give me a couple of hours and then call the cops. Case won't do anything to you. He can't afford to."

She smiled humorlessly. "I think he'd kill me." She snapped her fingers. "Just like that. Like turning out a light switch. It wouldn't faze him one iota."

Morgan nodded. "Okay. If you want it this way. I sure as hell can use your help."

He took one of the suitcases from her and headed toward the back stairs. Roberta carried the other suitcase and the VCR down to the lobby, checked out and met him in the parking lot behind the hotel.

Once they were in the car, Roberta behind the wheel, she looked at him worriedly. "Where to now?"

Morgan shook his head. "Case is right. If we run, they'll catch us. But if I can get proof that *thing* killed Red and that agent, maybe I can come out of this all right."

She shot him a wide-eyed stare. "You're not serious? You can't believe you can . . . capture one of those creatures? Jesus, Morgan, they're primitive, bloodthirsty, and very smart. You saw what it can do."

"It's my only chance. If you don't want to go with me, I understand. But I have to go." They looked at each other for a long time. Finally, Roberta took a deep breath.

"Okay."

Morgan hadn't been to his house for several days. It smelled musty and stale, but there were signs that someone had been there recently. Probably Case and his men searching for him.

Parking Roberta's car in his garage, Morgan gathered his insulated clothing, and packed a canvas bag with enough freeze-dried food to last them for several days.

Roberta changed into jeans, a heavy sweater and stout, insulated boots, opting to wait until they were in the high country before changing into her heavy arctic jumpsuit.

Standing in the kitchen, Morgan saw her shiver and went to her, slipping his arms around her and pulling her close.

"Cold or scared?" he asked.

"A little of both."

Red Crumley had carefully parked Morgan's truck and the trailer holding the Thiokol in its usual spot. There was plenty of gas in the truck, but he knew he'd have to fill the snow tractor's tank. He put eight ten-gallon cans in the back of truck. When they went up into the mountains, he wanted to make sure they were prepared.

In the garage, he climbed up a stepladder and reached into a recess formed at the juncture of the rafters and a side wall, and lifted out his .30-06 rifle in a dusty, padded case. He fished around in the recess a second time, and pulled out a box of ammunition and an extra four-shot clip.

Not a hunter, Morgan always felt vaguely uncomfortable around guns. This one had been a gift from Red Crumley years before, when the sheriff was trying to convince him that stalking deer every fall was a sacred rite of manhood.

Morgan never had gone hunting with his friend. Now, oddly, he wished he had, just to have made the guy happy.

Thinking about Red brought a pang of hurt and guilt. He hadn't even begun to mourn. There was too much going on around him to allow himself to grieve. When there was time—if there ever would be—he'd give Red his due.

Morgan had fired the rifle several times and although he was no marksman, he knew the weapon's particular feel. Now, going into the mountains looking for God only knows what, he wanted it with him.

Roberta came out of the house with the video camera and a small paper bag holding a change of jeans, another sweater and toiletry items.

After Morgan locked up the house, they climbed into his truck.

"This is going to be tricky," he told her. "The cops are looking for me, so it stands to reason they'll have a description of my truck. But I've got to get gas for the tractor, so we'll have to chance it."

"Can't we take back streets until we're at the edge of town?" Roberta wondered.

"Yeah. There's a convenience store outside of town, not far from the turnoff."

They were both tense as Morgan drove his truck with its long trailer through the quiet, deserted side streets. They breathed a collective sigh of relief when they reached a rutted back road at the edge of town.

Morgan pulled next to the gas pumps in the empty convenience-store lot. Roberta went inside with enough cash to pay for the gas. The bored clerk, a kid barely old enough to shave, paid little attention to either Morgan or his rig. He did, however, openly leer at Roberta, who distracted him with an alluring smile.

Five minutes later, they were back in the truck. Rather than take the truck all the way to the end of the road where Morgan had previously unloaded the snow tractor, he pulled off and followed a snow-covered lane that wound among barren pine and aspen trees.

"There's an old barn back here. We'll leave the truck there and take the tractor the rest of the way," he told Roberta.

After unloading his machine and placing the gas cans in the back, Morgan pulled the truck and trailer into a weathered, dilapidated barn. It had no door and the roof was missing almost as many boards as were still attached, but it would hide the truck well enough for the time being.

A sliver of moon hung above the cold, dark mountains, shedding faint light across the snow-shrouded terrain. Morgan powered the tractor up the now-familiar trail, its powerful lights flaring into the darkness.

Roberta sat quietly next to him, wrapped in her own thoughts. Morgan popped a cassette into the tape deck and the soft, sensual sound of John Klemmer's saxophone filled the Thiokol's interior, drowning out the steady rush of air from the powerful heater.

The slice of moon was now appearing and disappearing as wind-driven clouds scudded across a lowering sky. The wind buffeted the tractor and sent snow swirling and spinning around them. Above the quiet music, the wind moaned and wailed. Occasionally a burst of snow would obscure their visibility completely and Morgan would have to slow the machine until it subsided. On either side of them, the darkly silhouetted trees swayed and danced in the wind.

The Devouring

It took longer than usual to reach the NORAMS station. Morgan didn't want to stay there, but he needed to check for recent signs of the creatures. There was plenty of room in the tractor to sleep, and long ago he had fashioned insulated foam window covers which would contain the heat and block the cold. He would feel much more comfortable in the tractor than in the concrete bunker.

He stopped near Gruff Ryan's overturned tractor. "You stay here," he told Roberta. "I'm going to have a look around."

Morgan pulled on his snowshoes and slipped the .30-06 out of its case. Roberta eyed it as he loaded one of the four-shot magazines.

"Do you think you'll need that?"

He shook his head. "In this weather, I doubt it. But it'll make me feel more macho," he answered, trying to sound jovial. "You know, a phallic symbol."

She didn't smile. "This is all pretty crazy, Morgan." She shook her head and looked away.

He reached over and touched her shoulder. "It's only a precaution."

"I know," she sighed, still staring out into the cold, windswept night.

Morgan left the engine running and the heater on. "I'll be back in five minutes."

Even in his down-filled snowsuit, the bitter, wind-driven cold chilled him as he stepped out of the tractor. Even though he carried the rifle in one hand and a heavy military spotlight, powered by a six-volt battery, in the other, Morgan felt vulnerable.

He made his way slowly to the building, stopping abruptly when he saw the wooden and plastic door splintered and shredded. He moved the light around the area. Blowing snow had drifted around the building, but the smashed boards were uncovered. There were fresh marks in front of the entrance and he moved closer to inspect them.

Morgan stopped a few feet from the doorway, his light

playing over the clawed footprints. Kneeling, he noted the clear impression of a broad flat foot, about the size of his palm, with the five long, clawed toes jutting from it.

His blood froze as a fierce shriek echoed from inside the building.

As if physically struck, Morgan recoiled, lost his balance on the snowshoes and sat down heavily. His light fell from his gloved fist, landing several feet behind him on its lens. Suddenly he was surrounded by total darkness and howling wind.

A second ear-splitting screech shattered the night.

Panicked, he lifted the rifle, aimed in the general direction of the door and fired. In the microsecond of the muzzle flash, Morgan saw a dark, inhuman shape in the doorway. His shot was instantly followed by a scream of pain and rage.

Something came hurtling toward him, a dark, yellow-eyed shadow flying in the night. Morgan rolled to one side as he felt sharp talons rake the back of his snowsuit, ripping the nylon fabric.

Wildly, he fired a second shot, and rolled and started to belly-crawl toward his spotlight. Even as his fingers wrapped around the metal handle, he heard a shriek of tortured metal, followed instantly by Roberta's scream.

He aimed the light toward the snow tractor. The circle of illumination caught Roberta flaying against a dark shape. Her door hung on one hinge and the creature was reaching for her with its long, clawed feet. It hovered scant inches above the ground, its wings, at least 15 feet from tip to tip, beating the air in a fast, steady rhythm.

Morgan saw it all in a split second. As the light shone on the thing's face, it again screamed, ducked its head, trying to shield its eyes. Then, with impossible speed, it shot straight up into the night sky on its leathery wings.

In its wake, it left a final, piercing cry that momentarily reverberated and then was lost on the wind.

The Devouring

Morgan tried to follow the fleeing creature with the spotlight, but it was far too fast. Turning the light back on the snow tractor, he let out a strangled cry. Roberta hung half in and half out of the ruined door. On the ground below her were dark, red splotches in the virginal snow.

Chapter Ten

Richard Case gritted his teeth as he flexed his muscles against the belt holding his hands behind his back. He was unmindful of the leather biting into his wrists and continued to work the stiff cowhide. He had been at this for hours. His body was coated in sweat, great salty drops rolling down his face, into his eyes.

What Blaylock and the bitch hadn't taken into account was his determination. He'd come too far, put too much on the line to be stopped now.

Next to him, Jasper McKissik also worked at his bounds, but his efforts were halfhearted. Clearly, the deputy was content to wait for someone to find them.

Case was not.

But the deputy was a problem. He knew too much and had already served his usefulness. He'd have to be eliminated.

The FBI agent felt the belt slip. Just a little, just a fraction, but enough to encourage him. With renewed determination, he twisted his wrists, feeling the leather rubbing his skin raw.

A few minutes later, his right hand came free.

Deputy McKissik looked at him in awe and satisfaction.

After catching his breath, Case cast off the belt and untied his legs from the chair.

McKissik was grunting, rocking in his chair, urging Case to free him.

"Sorry, Deputy," the FBI agent said, getting to his feet and rubbing his chaffed wrists.

McKissik's eyes widened, his eyebrows arching questioningly.

Ignoring him, Case pulled on his clothes and without so much as another word or a backward glance, left the room.

He returned a few minutes later, stopping to shake his head at the hapless deputy, who was now struggling frantically, his wrists smeared with blood.

"You can stop," Case said casually, one hand held behind his back.

McKissik stopped, looking in anger at the FBI agent. He grunted again, motioning with his head for Case to untie him.

"Sorry, Jasper, but I won't suffer a fool." In one smooth motion, Case's right hand appeared from behind his back, producing a long-bladed, double-edged knife. One side was razor-smooth, the other serrated with wicked, barbed teeth.

For one long second, Deputy Jasper McKissik's eyes locked on the knife, and then his body was jerking in spastic convulsions as Case drove the blade into his throat.

Jetting from McKissik's severed jugular vein, a fountain of blood splattered across the walls and draperies.

Lurching in the snowshoes, Morgan rushed to the snow tractor, his spotlight bobbing and bouncing across Roberta's motionless form. Setting the light on the cowl of his machine and leaning the rifle against it, he gently lifted her until she was again upright in her seat. He inspected her face, her hands, her throat. . . .

No wounds.

His breath came out in a long, cloudy stream.

Roberta's eyes fluttered as she groaned. Then suddenly, her eyes flew open and she started to scream, her arms flaying wildly at Morgan's face.

"Roberta, it's me!" he cried, pulling her to him. She resisted, still striking blindly. Then her eyes focused and, with a strangled sob, she clung to him, her head buried against his shoulder.

"It was horrible," she cried, hugging him close. "It was . . ." She couldn't finish; there were no words to describe her revulsion.

"You're okay," he soothed. It was as much the bone-numbing cold as his ministration that calmed her. Realizing her exposed hands and faces were stinging and growing numb, she withdrew from Morgan and moved closer to the heater.

"Get in the back," Morgan ordered. "There's a couple of sleeping bags back there. Roll one out and get in it. I've got to fix this door."

Roberta obeyed without question.

The door had been torn loose. The part of the hinge attached to the tractor's body was intact, but the corresponding part on the door was badly damaged and the linchpin gone. The door itself was twisted and warped.

Grabbing the light and his rifle, Morgan moved to Gruff Ryan's machine. Crawling on top of it, he inspected its door. Both custom cabins had been built by the same manufacturer and he decided he could make it work.

It took a good half an hour to remove his smashed door and replace it with the one from the yellow snow machine. Throughout the process, Morgan constantly stopped to scan the wintry sky and listen for the rustle of leathery wings.

The Devouring

By the time he finished, the wind had died down and large, heavy snowflakes were falling. Grateful to be out of the wind, Morgan crawled inside and moved to the back where Roberta lay huddled in one of the sleeping bags. She had spread it on the floor between the second and third seats.

"You okay?" he asked.

"Yes," she said, her voice low and shaky.

"I'm sorry I left you. The damned thing was inside the station. I . . ."

"It's okay," she said. "I'm okay."

"I saw the blood and . . ." The blood. There had been blood in the snow. If it wasn't Roberta's, then it was the creature's. Morgan felt a perverse elation. He'd hit the bastard. Maybe not fatally, but he'd hurt it. And to know it could be hurt gave him a renewed sense of hope and bolstered his courage.

"That thing was bleeding from its side, I think," Roberta said quietly. "I'm not sure. It all happened so quickly. God, Morgan, its face. It was awful. It wasn't anything remotely human."

"Don't think about it," Morgan told her, knowing she would be hard pressed not to think about anything else for a long time.

"What was it doing inside the station?" Roberta asked. "It must have a permanent home, a cave or something, in the mountains."

Morgan considered her question. This was the second time the creature had broken into the station, yet Roberta was right. It had to have some other, much more secure place where it lived.

"If you're right about there being more than one, doesn't it stand to reason that one of them might be an outcast or a loner, seeking a place to stay, away from the others?"

Roberta shrugged. "Or maybe it's a guard, a kind of sentinel, to keep humans out of here, out of their territory." She yawned. "I'm so tired." Her voice was groggy

167

and distant. For a fleeting instant, he wondered if she had taken a blow to the head during the attack.

"No," she said in answer to his question. "I just fainted. What a wimp, huh?"

"I wouldn't say so. You put up a hell of a good fight." He touched a tender spot on his cheek where she'd hit him.

Morgan sat there for another few minutes, until he heard her rhythmic breathing. He then returned to the driver's seat and put the machine in gear. He wanted to get away from the station tonight, while it was snowing. If, or more precisely when, Case and McKissik were freed, the FBI agent would look for them and sooner or later, he'd look here. Better to not leave too noticeable a trail to follow.

He headed the Thiokol across the broad expanse of the snowfield. When he was near the rock outcropping where they had recovered Mike Crocker's body, he guided the tractor behind it and cut the engine and lights.

Morgan too was exhausted, but he didn't dare risk falling asleep, not until sunup. He moved carefully to the back of the machine and found the canvas bag containing the heavy, dense foam pads for the windows. Custom-made, they were rigged to cover the windows with a series of snaps riveted into their fabric covers. It took only minutes to cover all the openings.

Sprawled on one of the seats, the spotlight on his lap and the .30-06 next to him, he began the long vigil.

In the darkness, Morgan considered the creature he had seen so briefly. *Homo Desmodus* Roberta called it. Human bat. How human was it? How human could it possibly be? It was savage and cunning, and unlike its smaller cousins, it could live in these sub-zero conditions.

And most importantly, it could be hurt.

Where in the hell had they come from and how did it come to be here, of all places? Was it, as he had earlier speculated, some bio-engineered monstrosity, or as Roberta believed, some ancient, primordial beast suddenly thrown into the world by some cruel trick of nature?

There were just too many unanswered questions.

Roberta probably knew more than she was telling him, and while her reluctance to talk about it was frustrating, Morgan decided not to press her.

She still hadn't discussed her meetings with the mysterious people from Washington.

Time crawled through the night, and Morgan struggled to stay awake. He let his aching head and throbbing ribs keep himself awake.

At five, he groped in his toolbox, still sitting on the front passenger seat, and found his crescent wrench. Working blindly and very quietly, he knelt on the floor and began removing the bolts securing the middle seat to the floor. When he had it free, he carefully moved it forward, opening a wide space next to Roberta.

Stepping over her, he found the second sleeping bag in the back and spread it beside her. Peeling off his snowsuit, shivering as the warmth was immediately drawn from his body, he crawled into the bag. Holding the snowsuit in the darkness, his fingers explored it, finding the three ragged gashes in the slick fabric. An icy sensation touched his heart when he realized how close he'd come to death.

Morgan lustfully wished the bags were zipped together so he could hold Roberta, touch her, share her body heat and passion.

He was strongly attracted to her and it was more than just sex. She was tough and straightforward with brass and guts and stony determination.

It'd been a long time since he'd known a woman with such alluring qualities. As a rule and perhaps as a measure of self-defense, Morgan was generally attracted to only one thing in a women. He made no bones about his womanizing, nor did he apologize for it, although it was nothing he took pride in and he never bragged about it to his bar buddies. In point of fact, he chose women who were safe and asked nothing more than a one-night stand. Wham, bam, thank you, ma'am.

Roberta was a definite departure from that.

As he lay in the darkness, the fatigue washed over Morgan like a smothering wave. It was more than merely physical exhaustion. In the span of a few days, he'd lost two friends, witnessed brutality beyond his experience, been beaten and hospitalized, watched his life and reputation disintegrate in a dark cloud of false accusations. Now he was a hunted man.

He was drifting into the twilight between wakefulness and sleep when the snow tractor rocked violently under a hard, crashing blow. The machine groaned on its treads as the right side was lifted and dropped.

In the darkness, Roberta gasped, calling out for Morgan. He was already scrambling out of his sleeping bag, groping for the rifle.

Again, the machine was hammered, the sheet-metal roof screeching as it buckled under a tremendous blow. More blows rained on the roof, filling the interior with deafening thunder.

"They're back!" Roberta cried.

"Stay there," he ordered, as he yanked down the insulated pad from the window of the side door. He gasped when he saw the two yellow eyes glaring at him from the swirling maelstrom of snow. Before he could react, the window exploded in a shower of tiny glass fragments and a sharp, powerful talons ripped the front of his shirt.

Morgan staggered back, his chest ablaze with pain. He landed hard on the edge of the seat he had unbolted, and cried out as his already cracked ribs slammed against unyielding steel. Tiny sparks leaped behind his eyes and his head swam with a red agony.

Again, the vehicle rocked hard, and there was another cry of tortured metal as the side door was torn away and flung into the swirling darkness. A bitter cold blast of air and frigid snow raced into the snow tractor, sucking out what little warmth it held.

Gasping, Morgan struggled for the toggle switch on the spotlight. Finally, his fingers found it, flipped it to the side. Nothing happened.

Again, the creature's powerful talons slashed at him, and Morgan avoided having his face laid open by rolling toward Roberta.

Still gripping the light, he banged it on the metal floor. Bright light exploded inside the Thiokol's cabin. The thing at the door emitted a terrible howl as the light flashed across its eyes, and instantly it was gone.

Morgan struggled up and painfully staggered to the opening. He aimed the beam of light into the darkness. The crystalline flakes still cascading around them caught the light, refracting it into a dazzling, jeweled radiance.

The spotlight, designed for navy divers, pierced the swirling darkness, boring a hole through the snow. Crouching in the doorway, the cold numbing him, Morgan scanned the sky for any sign of the winged monstrosity.

Much to his amazement, he saw the beam touch the low, gray clouds, hanging well below the level of surrounding peaks.

Sweeping the beam from side to side, Morgan let out a shout of triumph as it caught a distant, fleeting shape.

As if physically impaled by the light, the winged creature darted away with a muffled, echoing cry.

Morgan swung the spotlight and again found the creature in the darkness. And again it maneuvered with astounding speed.

"My God," Roberta whispered breathlessly as she crouched beside him, her eyes following the beam. "It's diving."

Morgan tracked the dark, distant shape through the swirling snow. It rocketed down toward the base of the mountain directly in front of them, veered impossibly near a rocky ledge, dove behind a craggy escarpment and was gone.

"Fantastic," Roberta whispered. "Come on, get back in here. You'll freeze."

Morgan nodded, suddenly aware of the incredible cold.

"Are you okay?" he asked her.

"Yes." In the bright glow from the spotlight, she saw his torn shirt and the bloody stains around the shredded material. "You're hurt."

"Nothing a good plastic surgeon can't fix."

"Let me look at it," she insisted.

"Later," he groaned, finding his snowsuit. "Right now I've got to do something about that door. We'll freeze to death if I don't get it plugged with something."

Donning the insulated suit, Morgan stepped out into the storm. Roberta, again in her own snowsuit, crouched at the open door holding the .30-06.

Carrying the spotlight, his snowshoes tracking across the virginal snow, Morgan searched for the missing door. He found it 20 yards from the tractor. It was bent, but not beyond repair.

Carrying it back to the tractor, Morgan used a hammer from his toolbox and the tractor's floor as an anvil to straighten the crimped metal. Each blow clanged and reverberated into the night. Finally satisfied, he fitted the door into the opening. The hinges were worthless, and in order to affix the door he used heavy duct tape he routinely carried for a variety of emergencies. The cold metal made it difficult for the tape to adhere, but finally he had the door reattached.

Back inside the tractor, he placed the insulated pad over the window opening and then started the tractor's engine and turned the heater on high. Within minutes, the interior was decidedly warmer. He turned on the inside lights and sat down wearily.

With the door back in place, Roberta knelt in front of him and made him open his snowsuit. She examined

172

the two bloody slashes ripped through the tight bandages wrapping his chest. The wounds were not deep and the bleeding had stopped.

"Have you got any first-aid cream I can put on these?" she asked him. He pointed at the first-aid kit under the driver's seat. She pulled it out, found a tube of disinfectant and began ministering to his wounds.

"Now what?" she asked as she worked.

He winced as she carefully smoothed the ointment into the cuts. "I've got to get some sleep. I'm running on empty and feel like hell." He glanced at his watch. "It's almost six-thirty. The sun'll be up soon. I'll try to sleep a few hours and then I'm going after that son of a bitch."

Roberta paused and stared up at him in disbelief. "You can't, Morgan. You haven't the equipment; you don't know what you'll be up against."

"It's my only chance," he said desperately. "I either go up there and find that thing or I go back down the mountain and take my chance with Case. I'll have better odds against that flying freak."

"There has to be another way," she hissed.

She was pleading with him, and he found it strangely pleasing, a sign she cared.

"Besides," she continued, "how can you possibly get up there in this weather?"

"It may not be as difficult as it sounds," he said, wondering if that was really true. "I can drive the tractor as far as it'll go and then climb the rest of the way."

"But, Morgan, that thing is . . ." She paused, then: "You'll be hurt . . . or worse." Her voice caught in her throat.

"True," he agreed. "But it hates bright light. That's a distinct advantage." He remembered the shadow of the thing as it passed by his hospital room window. Certainly the streetlights hadn't bothered it nor kept it at bay.

"Then I'm going with you," she said flatly.

"Not a chance," he said emphatically.

"Morgan . . ."

"No. It's out of the question." He got up and stepped around her.

Her eyes flashed. "No it's not, damn it! If you're going after that thing, then I'm going with you. I won't let you leave me behind like some simpering wuss."

"I can't let you," he said, his back to her.

"Why?" she demanded. "Is this some macho bullshit pride thing?"

He whirled, grabbing her, pulling her close. "No," he snapped, glaring into her face. "It matters to me to know you're safe. Okay?"

Roberta searched his face, studied his eyes. Her anger evaporated and she hugged him close. "Oh, Morgan," she said sadly. "Why does it have to be like this?"

He sighed. "It just is."

After several moments, he gently pulled away from her and moved to the front of the tractor to turn off the engine. It was relatively warm inside the cabin now and he wanted to save fuel.

"I'm going to sleep," he said. "If you get cold, start the engine."

A few minutes later, they were both curled up in their insulated bags, sleeping.

Morgan awoke with a start. Outside he could hear the deep, throaty *whamp-whamp* of helicopter blades beating the air.

"Wake up," he hissed, shaking Roberta's shoulder.

Startled, she looked at him in confusion.

"I think we're about to have company." As if on cue, the helicopter roared low over the snow tractor.

Crawling out of his bag, Morgan made his way to the front seat, slipping on a pair of dark goggles before pulling down one of the insulated pads covering the window. The snow clouds had disappeared and the sky was a deep azure, the sunlight blinding as it bounced off the fresh snow.

"What'll we do?" Roberta asked, joining him.

Morgan shook his head. "I don't know. We'll have to wait to see who it is." But he knew. Case had come to gather the fleeing felons.

About 50 yards away, a huge, jet-powered helicopter, distinctly military in design but free of markings, settled down amid a huge cloud of sparkling snow.

As they watched, three men looking like avenging ghosts in their white winter jumpsuits emerged from the mini-storm created by the helicopter's still-spinning blades. Each held a rifle.

Roberta made a small noise deep in her throat when she saw the men and their weapons.

"This doesn't look promising," Morgan quipped.

"Case," she spat. "I don't know where he's getting the men and equipment, but I underestimated the bastard."

"Is he getting private money?"

Roberta nodded, glaring out at the advancing men. "Could be."

Morgan stared at her. "Maybe they're feds."

"I doubt it," she answered. "I think Richard's gone into business for himself." Again she shook her head. "He'll never let us live."

Morgan looked at her. "He won't just kill us. He couldn't get away with it."

"Oh, but he can."

"It's too late to run. I was too cocky last night. I should have parked us in the trees, camouflaged the tractor."

"Come out with your hands in the air," a metallic voice boomed from an external loudspeaker mounted on the helicopter.

Morgan and Roberta exchanged glances.

"We'll have to give up," she said, reaching for Morgan's gloved hand. "Say nothing about what we saw last night. Absolutely nothing. It may be our only bargaining chip. If things get bad, we'll use it as leverage."

Morgan swallowed. He acknowledged his own fear, but when he searched Roberta's eyes, it wasn't fear he saw, but a deep, almost primal fury.

"You have thirty seconds," the metallic voice boomed.

"Ready?" he asked. Roberta nodded.

"Twenty seconds!"

Glancing outside, Morgan saw that the three men had taken up positions 20 yards away, their weapons held at the ready.

He forced open the damaged door. The three men brought up their rifles, aiming in unison. He thrust his empty hands out to show he had no weapon, and then slipped on his snowshoes.

"We'll get through this," he told Roberta just before stepping into the glaring morning sun.

"Come forward slowly," the voice ordered.

Morgan complied, keeping his arms in the air. When he reached the men, one of them advanced and ordered him to turn around. Heavy handcuffs were snapped on his wrists.

Roberta still hadn't emerged from the rig.

What was she waiting for?

"Take him," the man told one of the other two.

His guard grabbed him roughly, and started pulling him toward the helicopter. Even as he marched toward the open bay door, Morgan craned his neck, trying to catch sight of Roberta, terrified when he saw the two men still advancing on his machine.

A fourth man inside the big helicopter helped Morgan climb through large door.

From inside, Morgan watched anxiously as the pair stopped 20 feet from the snow tractor. One of them made a hand gesture and the metallic voice boomed again.

"Come out now, Ferris. We know you're in there. You have thirty seconds and then we open fire!"

"Come out, Roberta," Morgan hissed through clenched teeth. "Get out of there!"

"Shut up!" snapped one of the two men flanking him.

"Fuck you," Morgan snarled.

"Don't give me a reason to kick your ass," the larger of the pair cried. "I'd like that!"

Vaguely, Morgan recognized the man from the hospital. Nias.

Why wasn't Roberta coming out? What was she waiting for? Didn't she realize these thugs were serious?

He watched tensely as the two men standing near the tractor raised their rifles and aimed.

"Ten seconds," the metallic voice warned.

Still, there was no sign of Roberta.

"Five seconds."

Morgan turned to Nias. "For God's sake, don't let them kill her."

"Shut up!" the man roared back.

"Fire!" the voice on the loudspeaker ordered.

Like seeing a nightmare in slow motion, Morgan watched the two riflemen jam their weapons against their shoulders and with the practiced, casual indifference of trained killers, spray the Thiokol with automatic gunfire. Glass exploded, dimpled pockmarks appeared in lines along the metal body. Metal-jacketed slugs tore ragged holes in the cowl, ricocheted off steel in bursts of yellow sparks. Bits of metal and glass showered in the air.

"GOD, NO!" Morgan screamed, tearing free of his captors and lurching out the opening and into the snow. Without his snowshoes, he sank to his knees into the powder. Behind him, Nias was yelling.

And then the world exploded. In a geyser of flaming fuel and flying metal, the snow tractor burst into a million pieces. It lifted from the snow, fire pouring out of the shattered windows, and then came back down, sinking several feet into the snow.

The concussion knocked Morgan backward. Shrapnel tore into the helicopter. One of the two riflemen screamed, as his weapon flew into the air and he clutched at his bloody, punctured throat.

A second explosion ripped through the machine. Fuel splattered over the rock outcropping behind it and hissed into the snow. Thick black smoke poured into the air.

"You sons of bitches!" Morgan screamed, struggling in the snow. "You motherfuckers!"

Powerful gloved hands grabbed him from behind and spun around, and he was staring into Nias's astonished face.

"Let go, you goddamn butcher!" He tried to jerk away, aware of his other guard running at him as a third man dashed toward the two riflemen sprawled in the snow.

Morgan was yelling incoherently now, his outrage and shock consuming him, blinding him.

"You killed her," he screamed Nias. "You fucking butcher! You goddamned . . ."

Then suddenly, unexpectedly, the back of his head exploded and he was engulfed in a black, painful void.

Chapter Eleven

Somewhere in the back of Morgan's head, a particularly sadistic drummer pounded out a sharp and steady beat. He didn't want to open his eyes; he wanted to go back into the black void, away from the pain. He tried to rub his temples, but his hands were stuck behind his back, a fact he couldn't at first comprehend.

As he sucked in great gulps of air, wincing against the sharp jabs stabbing his ribs and chest, the memories came screaming back like a flood of vile sewage. The helicopter. The men with guns. The explosion . . .

. . . Roberta!

"Roberta!" Her name escaped his lips in a hoarse, panicky cry. His mouth and throat were painfully dry.

"He's awake," grated a familiar voice.

Morgan opened his eyes. For a few moments, his vision was blurry, but gradually he made out a figure seated nearby, and a moment later he was looking into Richard Case's smirking face. He was wearing a dark suit, his legs indolently crossed and a tumbler of amber liquid held in his left hand.

"Welcome back, you dumb son of a bitch," Case said nastily.

Morgan was lying on a bed. As his eyes adjusted to the light, he glanced around the room. It looked like the same hotel room he and Roberta had shared, certainly the same hotel. Nias sat at the table to his right, eyeing him with obvious contempt.

Although the light above the table was off, he could see dark splotches on the far wall and curtains.

Morgan looked at Case. "See you found some clothes."

Case's contemptuous smile never wavered. "You've returned to the scene of the crime. How fortunate. For me."

Morgan didn't know what the hell the FBI agent was talking about.

"You should have killed me, too," Case added, glancing at Nias.

Morgan shook his head. "I don't stoop to your level." His words came out in a raspy croak.

The FBI agent flashed a wolfish smile. "Oh, really? After what you did to my man and to Crumley? You've stooped well below me."

Although fuzzy on the particulars, Morgan could feel the noose tightening.

"You know what killed them," he hissed. "We've both seen it. Me a little more recently than you."

Something passed over Case's eyes and he leaned forward, glaring at Morgan. "When?"

Morgan ignored the question. "Why'd you have to kill Roberta?"

"She wouldn't surrender," Case answered easily. "We're still waiting for the fire to die down so we can find what's left of her."

In his mind's eye, Morgan again saw his snow machine exploding in a ball of fire. Suddenly, he was tasting bile at the back of his throat and his stomach was knotting. "You didn't have to send in the commandos, Dick."

Case shrugged, but Nias stood and leveled a finger at Morgan. "Yeah, right, asshole. One of our men was killed up there and another one's in the hospital."

"What should I do, squeeze out a few crocodile tears?"

The man started toward him, but Case waved him off. "He's not worth the trouble, Nias. Blaylock's just trying to bait you."

Nias thought about that. "Death. They should give him the chair. I've never seen anyone who could be so . . ." He groped for the right words. "So evil."

Nias's massive frame and powerful shoulders strained the fabric of his white shirt. And even though his midsection was running to fat, the way it will in a man who forsakes physical exercise after pursuing it for years, he was still formidable. But what struck Morgan most was the lackluster glint in Nias's eyes, as if thinking was just too hard. He had seen it before at the hospital. He had no idea who the guy was, but it was a sure bet he wasn't FBI.

"You've been listening to Case, Nias. I can tell. Whenever anyone hangs around this joker for long, they wind up thinking I'm Jack the Ripper."

Nias screwed up his face. "Jack the Ripper? You make him look like a lightweight. A bush-leaguer." He walked to the dimmer switch, turned it on and pointed to the corner near the table.

"Take a good look, Blaylock, you pathetic piece of shit!"

Straining against his bonds, trying to ignore the pain, Morgan followed the man's pointed finger. In the harsh light he saw the dark, brownish stains splattered over the wall and curtains.

"Killing a man," Nias continued, his voice high and strained, "I can understand. But butchering him like . . . like an animal . . . That's somethin' I can't stomach."

Morgan shot Case a questioning look. "What the hell's he talking about, Dick?"

Case rubbed his forehead. "Oh, don't play dumb, Blaylock. I'm just grateful I got away."

"What the hell are you two talking about?" Morgan asked.

Case glanced at Nias and then shook his head. "I told you, he's psychotic. Probably doesn't even remember."

And then Morgan knew. Deputy Sheriff Jasper McKissik was dead. It was his life fluids staining the walls. Oddly, he thought about his ex-wife. Now she was a widow.

He shot Case a hard, knowing look and something in the FBI man's eyes shifted.

"Nias," Case said, turning to the other agent. "I'd like to talk to him alone for a few minutes."

Nias's dim eyes slitted and he made a face and glanced at the mess on the walls. "I don't know, Case. . . ."

"Just go."

Reluctantly, the other man nodded, pulled his jacket from the back of his chair and stalked to the door. Before he went out, he shot Morgan another damning glance.

"He really thinks I did it," Morgan said, eyeing Case. "What's your game? How is framing me for three murders going to stop that thing up in the mountains?"

"It won't," Case answered, still sitting calmly in the chair. "But it'll stop you. Not that you'll ever go to trial."

Morgan nodded. "Attempted escape. A bullet in the back of the head and *poof!* No more problems with Blaylock. That about it?"

"You're a liability, Blaylock. In my world, liabilities have to be recognized and eliminated." Coldly, almost casually, Case pronounced his death sentence and Morgan felt a chill run down his spine.

"And Roberta?" he hissed. "Was she a liability too?"

Case didn't bat an eye. "Roberta turned into one. She chose the wrong side."

"Side? What side? Aren't we all interested in stopping those flying freaks?"

Case smirked. "Some people are."

Morgan nodded. "You don't want them stopped. You're trying to protect them."

Case stood and straightened his jacket. "What I want is of no concern to you. In your situation, I'd be thinking about"—he looked into Morgan's eyes—"who was going to deliver the eulogy at my funeral."

"If there is one."

The FBI agent smiled as he tugged on the cuffs of his shirt, bringing them down below the edge of his sleeve. He picked a piece of invisible lint from his jacket. "Oh, there will be."

"You know where the creature lives?" Morgan asked.

Case stared at him. "What do you care?"

"Do you?" he prodded.

"No, but it's only a matter of time." Case didn't sound as certain as his words implied.

"*I* know."

Case stopped fussing with his clothing, his eyes growing a little more excited. He studied Morgan for another moment and then turned away, walking toward the door.

"Nice try, Blaylock. No cigar."

"Roberta and I saw it last night. Hell's bells, I shot it, wounded it! I know where it lives."

Case paused, his hand on the doorknob. He turned and studied Morgan suspiciously, weighing the information. A shadow of doubt flickered across the man's face.

"How do I know this isn't just a line of bullshit?" he finally asked.

It was Morgan's turn to flash a wolfish smile. "You don't." Lying on the bed, forcing himself to relax, he met Case's gaze. This was the court of final appeal. He'd already been tried and judged. All he could do now was shoot for a stay of execution.

Before Case spoke, the shift in his eyes told Morgan he'd won. "Okay, Blaylock. I'm going to gamble that you're telling the truth." He pointed a warning finger at Morgan. "But I swear to God, if you're jerking me around, I'll cut off your balls and make you eat them! You got that?"

"Yeah, I think I get your drift." He didn't try to hide his insolence nor his contempt. "Think of it as a business deal, Dick."

Case again smiled. "I'll do that. And you can think of it as a reprieve. Just a reprieve." With that, he jerked open the door and disappeared into the hall.

Morgan let out a long breath. "Screw you too, buddy."

When he was alone in the room, an overwhelming sense of loss washed over him. Roberta was dead. Hell, he'd only known her a few days, but in that time, in those last few hours together . . .

She was gone. All gone. In one mindless, terrible second everything that had been Roberta Ferris was consumed by a hellish ball of fire.

Morgan shook his head at the irony. For a long time, he'd wanted to find a woman with whom he could connect on more than just a physical level. And when he'd found her, she'd been suddenly taken from him in one mindless act of mad violence.

He was snapped out of his dark reverie when the door burst open and Nias came back into the room. He gave Morgan another withering look, took off his jacket and flopped down in one of the chair.

"I don't know what kind of deal you cut with Case," Nias said nastily. "But it sucks."

"Yeah, life's a bitch and then you die."

Nias glowered. "You won't die soon enough for me. I just want to live long enough to piss on your grave." He came around the bed, unlocked the cuff on Morgan's left arm and reattached it to the bedpost between two crossbars.

"Help the lilies grow, huh? Very considerate," Morgan deadpanned. Nias continued to glower, but made no reply.

"How long you been in the FBI?" Morgan prodded, catching Nias completely off guard.

"I'm not FBI."

"Oh?"

"Case hired me . . ." The man caught himself. "Hey, it's none of your business."

Morgan nodded knowingly. "Right. Just curious. You don't look the type to hang around with feds."

Nias frowned. "Yeah, well, money's money."

"That it is," Morgan agreed. "That it is."

"Why don't you just shut your pie hole?" Nias growled, his eyes filled with dark anger.

"Ah, gee, did I hurt your feelings?" Morgan's sarcasm was thick and bitter.

Nias looked at him curiously. "You're a real psycho, you know that?"

"So everybody tells me."

"You'd have to be to do something like that," Nias said, pointing at the bloodstained walls.

Morgan decided to try a different tact. "You really think I did that?"

"Of course," Nias answered emphatically.

"With what? My bare hands?" Morgan snorted a disgusted laugh. "A chain saw, maybe?"

Nias looked confused. "A butcher knife. I saw it."

Morgan shook his head. "Where would I get a knife? And if I killed McKissik, how come I didn't kill Case? I mean, even you can tell there's no love lost between us."

"Case told me what happened."

"And that was?" Morgan asked curiously.

"Don't play stupid. He told me he got loose before you'd finished with the deputy. Before you could catch him, he was out of the room and you and the broad bolted."

"Geez," Morgan said in wonder. "Is that what happened? Gosh, I must have been so filled with bloodlust I just blanked out."

Nias glowered. "You're a fuckin' loonie!"

"Yeah, and maybe you're a child molester. What's it matter? Case's has his hooks into both of us." Morgan realized too late he'd gone too far. Nias was across the room in three long strides, towering over Morgan.

"Smart mouth. Really funny man, aren't you?" His face was twisted in anger and his eyes flashed with outrage and hate.

"I'd match wits with you, but you're unarmed," Morgan spat.

The blow came fast and hard. It snapped Morgan's head to the side and sent sparks showering in front of his eyes. The second blow caught him just behind his left eye and cracked his head to the opposite side.

"Wiseass bastard!" Nias snarled.

Morgan shook his head, trying to clear it. He could taste blood in his mouth. His right jaw and left cheek ached and dizzying sparks still flared before his eyes. He looked up at his enraged attacker.

"Your dick hard now, tough guy?" He'd be damned before he'd let this Neanderthal cow him. The old self-destructive trait, never knowing when to keep his mouth shut, kicked in again.

The third blow stunned him. Nias's balled fist slammed into his right cheek like a line drive off a fast pitch. Morgan's mind clouded and momentarily he slipped into a spinning vortex of pain and bright fireworks.

When he came around, his head thundering and warm sticky blood trickling down his cheek, Nias had moved away, looking more alarmed than sated.

"Hey, big man," Morgan said groggily. "Make you feel pretty tough? I'm not exactly in the position to defend myself."

"Don't play with me, Blaylock," Nias barked.

"I don't need to. You play with yourself enough for both of us." Morgan spat the words with as much venom as he could muster. "Now go tell Case the deal's off. If he's going to kill me, fine. But I'll be damned if I'm going to be a punching bag for a no-brainer like you."

Nias appraised him, a worried look slowly spreading over his face. Clearly he had no desire to tangle with Case and just as clearly, he didn't want the deal, whatever it was, affected because he'd gone off on Morgan in a fit of rage.

"Look, Blaylock," Nias said, suddenly sounding conciliatory. "I blew up. You pushed me. So why don't we just call it even?" He absently rubbed the palm of his right hand on his pants leg. He glanced at Morgan, unable to disguise his worry. "So what's your story? Why would Case set you up?"

Morgan shifted uncomfortably. Forced to hold his arm awkwardly, it was now numb and stiff, but considering the rest of his battered body, it was only a minor inconvenience.

"What difference does it make?" he asked, spitting a wad of blood on the pillowcase. "You've got me tried and convicted, right? Let's just forget about it and you go tell Case the deal's off."

Nias made a face. "Case won't like it."

"Tough. Tell him to sue me." He watched the other man closely. He didn't want to push him to further violence, just keep him a little off balance.

"You're really serious, aren't you? You really don't give a damn if Case hauls you off to jail." Nias sounded genuinely amazed.

"Jail?" Morgan laughed. "Nias, you're so far behind in this game you need instant replay to catch up. Case isn't taking me to any jail. I'm going to be back-shot trying to escape. Or maybe he'll be more creative and arrange a convenient accident."

"That's crazy, Blaylock. He's not going to let anything happen to you." Regardless of his words, Morgan detected a worried note in the man's voice.

"Fine, whatever. Just go find Case and tell him what I said."

"I'm not telling him squat."

Morgan shook his head in disdain and Nias continued to look worried.

They both glanced at the door as a key turned in the lock and Richard Case came into the room. He stopped and stared at Morgan for an instant and then looked accusingly at Nias. In turn, Nias lowered his pale, bloodless face.

"What the hell happened?" Case demanded.

"I . . . ah . . ."

"My fault, Dick," Morgan said. "I tried to get loose and . . . Nias here stopped me." He tried to sound sheepish, and watched with secret amusement as Nias's face took on an expression somewhere between shock and relief.

"Is that true?" Case asked Nias.

"Ah . . . yeah. I guess I got a little carried away when I . . . ah . . . grabbed him," Nias explained haltingly. "He was pretty hard to stop."

Case's frown turned into a broad, malevolent grin. "You're going to have to learn when to quit, Blaylock. Nias could take you apart, you know that?"

"So I found out," Morgan said, meaning it. Nias was still watching him curiously. The guy was completely off balance now. Morgan had set him up and then bailed him out. It might have been foolish, but it also might have planted a seed or two of doubt in that less-than-high-speed brain. Whether or not he could use it to his advantage later would remain to be seen.

Case sat in one of the chairs and studied Morgan. "All right, Blaylock. You've had your fun." He turned to Nias. "Go on to bed. We've got an early morning."

188

Relieved, Nias nodded, shot Morgan one last questioning look and then left.

"Now, we'll find out if you're bullshitting me or if you really know where to find *Homo Desmodus*," Case said after Nias was gone. "I suppose you tried to convince Nias that there was a flying monster in the mountains."

Morgan shook his head. "He's too dumb." He touched his bruised face. "Besides, I pissed him off once. Why run the risk of doing it a second time?"

"Why indeed?" Case agreed. "Now here's how it works tomorrow. We go up there and you show us where the creature lives. For your sake, I hope you're not screwing around with me."

"I'm not."

Case leaned forward in the chair, his face suddenly intent, etched with concern. "You said you shot it. Are you sure you didn't kill it?"

"I don't think I did more than puncture its wing or maybe graze its side. It bled a little."

"Good." Case got to his feet. "I've got a man outside the door and the phone's dead. Don't try anything. Just get some sleep. We're leaving before sunrise."

"How about letting me go to the toilet and clean up my face?" Morgan asked seriously, his bladder ready to burst.

Case made a face. "No tricks?"

Morgan nodded.

Case let him use the bathroom, with the door opened. He washed his face, staring at the pinkish smears on the white cloth, then drank a glass of tepid tap water and let Case reshackle him to the bed.

"I'll be back in the morning," Case said, heading for the door.

"I'm all atwitter," Morgan quipped.

Ignoring him, Case walked out of the room.

When he awoke, Morgan found his shackled arm stiff and sore, and when he moved his arm, there was a distinct grating in the socket. Sitting up, he massaged the joint and surrounding muscles, grimacing when the numbness turned to a fierce tingling as the blood began to again flow. He probed his face with his fingers, feeling the puffiness around his left eye. His jaw ached and his tongue found a couple of loose teeth. At least his injured ribs seemed to be better, and while the wounds on his chest were tight and itchy, they were no longer painful.

Cold comfort, of course. Morgan Blaylock felt like a bag of shit that had been dropped from a very high place.

His shirt collar and hair were damp with sweat and his mouth was again dry and his tongue swollen.

It was still dark outside and from the sound of the wind, another storm had swept in during the night. Unable to reach the curtain, Morgan imagined the wind-driven snow swirling around the town, blanketing it in a fresh coat of white, piling drifts in doorways and turning the streets into skating rinks.

At best, his sleep had been fitful. His mind had returned to his capture and he'd been haunted with nightmarish images of poor, dead Roberta and the winged monstrosity. There had been sharp images of his snow machine exploding in a fireball overlaid by glaring, inhuman yellow eyes.

Cursing and rubbing the sleep from his eyes, he tried to drive away the dark images. It wouldn't do to let himself be distracted today. He couldn't give into the depression lurking near the edges of his mind. The cards were all stacked against him. At this point, no matter which way the deal went, he'd lose unless he could play his one ace.

Case came into the room five minutes later. He was wearing a heavy flannel shirt, blue jeans and a pair of heavy boots. There was a worried, distracted glint in his eyes.

"You're up. Good. I want to leave in half an hour," he said.

"Sounds like a bad storm outside, Dick. Could be impossible up in the mountains . . ."

"Hey," Case snapped, cutting him off. "I'll decided what's impossible and what's not. We're leaving in half an hour. Nias is coming in to watch you. Don't try anything."

"Wouldn't dream of it," Morgan answered.

"Your gear's in the closet," the FBI man told him. "Nias will let you shower. But be ready in half an hour." With that Case left, and a few minutes later beefy Nias arrived.

"What's eating Case?" Morgan asked him.

The big man shrugged. "What's it to you?" He moved over and unlocked Morgan's handcuffs. "Don't try to pull anything."

"I won't."

At that moment, Morgan was only interested in getting into the bathroom. After relieving his aching bladder, he peeled off the grubby clothes and showered. Dressing under Nias's watchful eye, he found his snowsuit and boots heaped on the floor of the room's closet.

"Why'd you cover for me last night?" his guard asked quietly.

Morgan glanced at him. "What good would it have done to piss off Case? He might have taken it out on me. I didn't need the grief."

"I can't figure you out," the other man admitted. There was a bewildered look in his small, beady eyes, and Morgan realized his attempt to plant seeds of doubt, or at least throw the big man off, had worked.

"Oh?"

"Yeah, I mean, a guy that kills three people and then . . ." He searched for words.

"Covers up for someone holding him hostage?" Morgan filled in.

Nias grimaced. "Something like that, I guess. It doesn't figure."

"Maybe I'm not the killer."

Nias didn't answer.

"You going with us today?" Morgan asked, lacing up his boots.

"Yeah."

"It'll be a real education."

"What's that suppose to mean?"

Morgan looked at him and smiled. "You wouldn't believe me if I told you. Just take my word for it. But you'd better take a change of underwear. When you finally figure this out, you'll need 'em."

Again Nias looked worried. "Come on, Case's waiting for us." Morgan pulled on his coat and gathered his snowsuit.

Nias led him down the back stairs to the parking lot. A big pickup truck with a six-man cab was parked near the side door. A gray cloud of steam plumed from its exhaust and there were heavy chains on its rear tires. Case sat behind the wheel and three other men filled the back seat. Morgan recognized one of them from the helicopter.

Wind-driven snow was swirling in a torrent and there were already five or six inches on the ground. It was piling up on the parked cars and drifting against the concrete wall around the lot.

Not a good sign. If it was this bad in town, you could bet it was many times worse up the mountain. Case must be desperate to risk a winter storm on what might very well be a wild-goose chase.

Morgan had said he knew where the creature lived, which was more than a mild exaggeration. Now, faced with the prospect of actually leading Case and his men to the site, he was beginning to reconsider the wisdom of his words.

Then again, if he hadn't convinced Case that he could help, he'd be as dead as Red and Jasper and Roberta. . . .

He shrugged off a pang of remorse. This was no time to think about the dead.

Morgan was made to sit in the front seat between Case and Nias. As he slid across the wide seat, he could feel the eyes of the three men in back studying him. He kept his mouth shut.

"This is cozy," Morgan told Case sardonically. "Now you boys keep your hands to yourselves."

"Shut up," Case snapped. There was still a worried look in his eyes.

"You really think we can get up there in this mess?" Morgan asked seriously.

Case shoved the pickup into gear. "We'll make it." He didn't sound as confident as he wanted everyone to believe.

As they drove out of town, the tire chains clanged and rattled on the snowpacked, icy streets. The snow was coming down so hard, it was difficult for the wiper blades to keep up with the onslaught. The highway out of town was bad, but Case seemed not to care, pushing the truck well beyond the limits of safety.

When they reached the familiar turnoff, he geared down and stomped on the gas pedal, plowing the truck through the heavy drifts. There was another set of tracks to follow, but he had to move more slowly now.

At the spot where Morgan had unloaded his own machine, he was surprised to see a familiar rig and a snow tractor with Park Service markings parked at the base of the trail. It was running and he could see the figure seated behind the wheel.

"Gruff?"

"He decided to help us out," Case said with a note of triumph.

"Better than being held prisoner, huh?" Morgan mumbled.

"Get out."

Nias took Morgan to the snow tractor while Case and the others unloaded boxes from the back of the pickup. Morgan took note of the machine pistols each of the others carried. Case might want that thing in the mountains alive, but he wasn't taking any chances.

"Good to see you, Morgan," Gruff Ryan said solemnly. He smiled behind his bushy, untrimmed beard, but it didn't touch his deep-set eyes. The corner of a white bandage was just visible below the hood of his snowsuit.

"Hey, yourself, Gruff. Looks like you've fallen in with a bad crowd."

Ryan made a face. "Don't it, though."

Morgan could tell his friend was not at all happy about the arrangement.

"Every cop in the county's been lookin' for you," Ryan hissed. "They say you . . . ah . . . you killed Red and that dim-witted deputy of his and some other fellow."

"You believe it?"

Ryan shook his head. "Of course not. You? A killer? You ain't the type."

Nias fixed Ryan with a curious look. "So who *is* the type?"

Ryan's smile exposed his crooked, yellowed teeth. "Me." He laughed when he saw Nias's expression shift.

"Asshole," Nias muttered under his breath, only loud enough for Morgan to hear.

Ryan shot Morgan a serious look. "I don't like this one bit, Morgan. But . . . hell, they've had me locked up in a damned room for the last few days, and besides, they're paying me five times my rate."

Morgan flashed his friend a smile. "Lighten up, Gruff. I'd do the same thing. You gotta look out for yourself, make the bucks while you can. I just hope you got it up front."

Ryan smiled. "Half. Safely stashed away."

"Good." Morgan nodded. "Can't trust these government boys."

They left in another few minutes. Case sat in the front with Ryan. Morgan was sandwiched between Nias and one of the others, and the two remaining men occupied the back seat.

The snow was falling hard, and Ryan had to keep the tractor's speed down as he negotiated the winding course through the trees. The heater failed in its struggle to keep up with the bitter cold and after a time, one by one, Morgan, Nias and the others struggled into their snowsuits.

The leaden sky had lightened by the time they reached the broad snowfield. The towering peaks were obscured by the heavy clouds and raging snow.

"Okay, Blaylock," Case called from the front seat. "Where to?"

Morgan thought for a minute. "Snow makes it hard to get my bearings. Gruff, can you take us over to that rock formation in the middle of the plain?"

"Sure."

"Why do we want to go there, Blaylock?" Case demanded, again a worried look on his face.

Morgan sighed. "Because from there I can figure out which way we need to go."

"I hope you're not bullshitting us."

"No chance, Dick. You've cornered the market." Morgan turned to Ryan. "Go on."

The jutting rocks, partially obscured by the blowing snow, rose out of the ground like spiky teeth. Seeing them, remembering what had happened there only yesterday—yesterday? It seemed like a lifetime. A knot started twisting in Morgan's gut.

"Go around to the far side," Morgan told Ryan, ignoring Case's nasty glance.

"Jesus!" Ryan snorted as they rounded the rock. "What was that?"

Blackened, twisted metal poked out of the snow like the bones of some prehistoric beast. He stopped near the wreckage.

"My rig," Morgan answered flatly. "This is where your employer killed the Ferris woman."

Ryan shot a glance over his shoulder at Morgan and then turned to Case. "She's *dead?*"

"Yeah," Morgan sighed.

"Cut the crap, Blaylock," Case growled. "Which way do we go from here?"

Morgan moved toward the window and peered out into the storm. He tried to remember where he had shone the powerful spotlight the night he and Roberta had seen the creature vanish into the mountains.

"Gruff," he said. "Head that way." He pointed over Ryan's shoulder, aiming across the snowfield toward a peak now obliterated by low clouds and swirling snow.

"Okay."

Case flashed Morgan a hard look. "You sure, Blaylock?"

"As sure as I can be, Dick. It's a little hard to see anything in all this shit."

"Okay," Case told Ryan. "Go ahead."

The tractor plowed across the snowfield. When they came to the thick tree line, Gruff Ryan stopped the machine and looked at Case for instructions.

"Can you get this thing up the slope?" the FBI agent asked.

Ryan looked dubious. "I can try. You pay for any damages?"

Case glowered. "That's the least of your worries. Go on!"

Ryan looked back at Morgan and raised an eyebrow, but said nothing. He slipped the tractor in gear and started up the slope.

Morgan knew what Ryan was feeling: The machine was powerful and surefooted, but it wasn't a tank. Or a mountain goat. And it sure as hell couldn't go beyond the first line of cliffs Morgan remembered seeing at the base of the peak.

The steel treads fought the ice-covered ground as they struggled for purchase. Once Ryan had to make a hard turn to avoid a boulder which loomed out of the storm, and in doing so the tractor canted precariously on one track before he managed to right it and get back on course.

"Can't go much farther," Ryan said. "You'll have to climb from here. If you're dumb enough."

"He's right, Dick," Morgan said. "In this snow and wind, we'll never get up the slope."

"We're going to try," Case said flatly. "And you're going with us."

Gruff Ryan turned around to look at Morgan. "This ain't too smart, Morgan. How far up you goin'?"

Morgan thought for a second, aware Case and Nias were also waiting for his response. He calculated the distance as best he could.

"At least five hundred feet. Maybe more, but not much less."

"That's a long way in this crap," Ryan observed, rubbing his beard with a meaty hand. "So much snow you couldn't see your pecker when you piss."

"Let's get started," Case said, ignoring the sarcasm. He looked at Ryan. "You stay right here until we get back."

The big man nodded. "Long as I'm getting paid, it's fine with me."

Case and his men pulled on goggles, and climbed out into the bitter wind and began unloading their equipment. Morgan and Nias joined them, leaving Ryan alone in his tractor.

They're crazy, Morgan thought as he watched the others take out heavy hemp rope and tie themselves together. Insulated in their white snowsuits, they all carried climbing picks and heavily laden packs. Their machine pistols were slung over their shoulders. Case motioned for Morgan.

"You lead the way," he said, handing him the end of the rope. Reluctantly, Morgan looped it around his waist. He was no better off than a rat in a trap. But there was nothing to do but play it by ear and go up the mountain. In the storm, he'd be hard pressed to find the particular rock formation behind which the flying creature had vanished. But if he didn't find it, it would be a long time before anyone found his bones.

Chapter Twelve

The first one died halfway up the mountain.

After leaving Ryan's big Parks Department Sno Cat, Morgan led Case and his men into the teeth of the storm. Every step was a battle against the raw wind and relentlessly snow. It tore at their clothing, hammering them with rock-hard ice pellets and blinding clouds of powder. It howled and raged as they picked their way along the patches of barren rock, threatening to pluck them from the face of the mountain and send them tumbling down the steep slope.

Struggling at the head of the line, Morgan knew this trek was sheer insanity. One misstep, one miscalculation, and they could all die before any of them realized what had happened. Even in the best of weather, at the height of summer, this climb was dangerous. In the dead of winter, in the middle of a snowstorm it was madness.

He continually searched for passable trails, leading them along precarious ledges and treacherous rock escarpments.

Inside his insulated gloves, his hands felt raw and sore as they clutched at ragged rocks and clawed their way around ice-encrusted boulders.

God only knows what the temperature was, but with the wind, the chill factor had to be 40 or 50 below. If any of them should lose a glove or their goggles . . .

Morgan let the thought evaporate. Freezing to death wasn't how he wanted to die. But then, neither was catching a bullet in the back of his skull.

Much to his amazement, they made steady, if slow progress. When the going became difficult, he found, more out of luck than either skill or knowledge, a series of cuts and trails through which they were able to ascend.

As they were moving cautiously along a particularly treacherous precipice, Morgan felt the rope go tight around his middle. He clutched desperately at a finger of rock thrusting out of the cliff face next to him. Holding it tight in his gloved fist, he let out a cry as the rope bit into his middle, squeezing out his breath and reigniting the fiery pain in his ribs. Glancing over his shoulder, he saw Nias scrambling for purchase. Below him, the others too were struggling to find handholds. The rope vanished over a ledge as the last man swung free, threatening to drag all of them over the edge.

Morgan's hands started to slip. He dug in with his boots and adjusted his hold on the rock. The pressure around his gut grew tighter. Then, quite suddenly, it ceased. Again, looking over his shoulder, he saw the others leaning against rocks, clinging to them in relief. Case, now the last man in line, held a huge knife in one hand, the severed end of the rope in the other. The FBI agent motioned impatiently for him to continue the ascent.

Morgan shuddered as he started up the slope. He forced himself not to think about the man Case had just murdered, and instead focused on the climb. He had to find a way up the cliff face. If memory served—and he wasn't certain it did—once they were atop the next cliff, it was only another 20 or 30 yards to the spot where the flying creature had vanished.

But how could he be sure? What he and Roberta saw had been masked by darkness and the storm. He could easily be wrong.

On the other hand, Case had been fully prepared to snuff him out without a thought. Coming here had been his only option. The raw, unforgiving weather aside, Morgan knew he stood a better chance of survival out here than he had tied to a bed in a Crystal Wells hotel room.

Picking his way along a narrow ledge, refusing to look down, he finally rounded a protruding rock formation which offered some shelter from the wind. Just beyond it was a deep, narrow fissure in the cliff face, just wide enough to allow a man to move up if he braced himself between the opposing walls.

He waited for the others to catch up, and then motioned for them to gather around him.

The germ of an idea was sprouting in his mind. It was a dangerous gambit, but one he was willing to take.

Case pulled up the mask shielding his face, exposing his mouth. He leaned close to Morgan to be heard above the wind. "What is it?"

"A way up," Morgan replied, yelling. "It's about fifty feet and too dangerous for me to go up there with all of you tied to me. Let me go up with the rope and then I can tie it off and you can come up one at a time. It's the safest way."

Case was quiet for a minute, perhaps considering his options, or remembering the man he had just sent to his death in order to save the others.

"All right," he finally said. "Toss the rope back down when you get to the top."

Morgan freed himself from the rope and waited for the others to untie themselves. Case handed him the coiled hemp and he slipped it over his shoulder.

"Don't be a hero, Blaylock," Case yelled above the

wind. "There's no place for you to hide from me. Not up here. Not anywhere!"

Morgan nodded. "I'm crazy, Dick, not stupid."

Making his way back to the cut in the cliff, he spent several moments studying it before wedging himself between its narrow walls. With his back against one wall and his feet against the other he started moving upward.

It was a slow, arduous process. The bulky snowsuit hampered him and his bruised ribs protested each step, but by using handholds and keeping his back pressed against the rock, he carefully edged his way up the jagged rocks.

Below, Case held a machine pistol aimed at him.

If it had not been an insane risk, Morgan would have tried to find a nice, hefty rock to pitch down at the FBI agent. As it was, it took all his concentration to make the climb. At least he was sheltered from the snow and wind, although there were several patches of dangerous ice on the exposed rock.

Nearing the top, Morgan was again buffeted by the raging wind and pelted by clouds of gusting snow. It would be extremely dangerous up there, exposed to the raw elements sweeping down from the towering peaks.

For one long moment, he thought he might abandon his desperate plan.

But what did he have to lose? Pragmatically, he knew he was dead regardless of what options he chose. This way he was giving himself the choice of dying on his feet and not like an ignorant sheep lead to slaughter.

He struggled out of the fissure and rolled wearily atop the windswept rock. He glanced around, saw several large rocks scattered near the opening and then quickly motioned to Case. He held up the rope, indicating he was going to find a place to tie it off.

But once he was out of the FBI agent's line of sight, he went to one of the large rocks nearby. Getting behind it, he pushed, gritting his teeth against the stabbing pain in his side. At first it refused to budge, but once he found a foothold, he managed to move it a few inches. Bracing his feet, he shoved again. This time the rock rolled forward. He scrambled after it, guiding it toward the fissure.

Stopping the boulder, he looked down the cut and waved at Case. The FBI man made an impatient gesture and Morgan extended his middle finger of his gloved hand.

He returned to the rock and pushed it into the opening. In one brief instant, he saw Case stare up at the descending boulder and then leap out of sight.

The rock tumbled down the narrow gouge in the cliff, breaking loose smaller pieces of rock and starting a tiny avalanche. It lodged two-thirds of the way down, completely blocking the opening.

Quickly, Morgan looked around for more rocks. In moments, he had three smaller ones wedged into the opening, effectively sealing the fissure from below.

As he was pushing the final one into the opening, rock exploded near him and he threw himself backward as a hail of slugs stitched along the cliff's edge and buzzed above his head.

Rolling over on his stomach, Morgan crawled up behind the small boulder poised above the opening. With one hard shove, he sent it down, satisfied when he heard it bang against its mates.

The wind howled in Morgan's ears and the snow swirled around him as he lay panting on the hard, frozen ground. Wearily, he moved against the rock behind him and sat down.

He had escaped, but had trapped himself in the process. He had the rope, but finding a way down would be difficult with Case and his goons waiting below.

Still, this was better than leaving himself to the mercy of the FBI agent. At least that's what Morgan kept telling himself.

His only regret was Gruff Ryan. Case might take out his vengeance him. Not a pleasant thought.

After a few minutes, he started moving along the wide ledge until he was 20 or 30 feet away from the fissure. He crawled on his belly and peered over the cliff.

Through the flying snow, he saw Case, Nias and the other two below him, frantically searching for another way up. They moved cautiously, continually scanning the rock face, their machine pistols held ready.

Morgan found a basketball-sized rock and eased it to the edge of the cliff. Positioning it, he waited for them to move directly beneath him.

If it hit someone, it would probably kill them. A sobering thought. Morgan had never taken a human life. Like most people, he had contemplated it in the abstract, but never seriously considered it. The thought of actually *killing* someone was repulsive. When he was a boy, his mother had repeatedly told him that killing another person was a mortal sin. While he had largely abandoned his religious beliefs as an adult, sitting there, the very real prospect of having to take a life staring him in the face, Morgan realized that murdering one of the men below would make him no better than Richard Case.

Then again, he was fighting for his life.

When they were directly beneath him, he realized he couldn't do it. Maybe the men below were cold-blooded killers. Morgan was not. Shifting his position, starting to roll the large rock away from the edge, he inadvertently dislodged a small stone which went flying toward the knot of men. When it hit the rock in front of Nias, he whirled around and pointed toward Morgan. The others too swung their machine pistols up, unleashing a barrage of gunfire.

Forced to jumped back, Morgan saw the boulder he had been holding rolling over the edge. An instant later, the machine pistols fell silent.

He waited for several minutes before moving back and peering cautiously down. He stared at the scene below in a mix of fascination and horror. One of the men lay on the ledge, the hood of his snowsuit stained crimson as steam rose from a spreading pool of blood around his head.

The others were nowhere to be seen.

Morgan rolled back, retching. He gagged violently for several moments, afraid he was going to puke into his mask, maybe choke himself to death. Finally, when the spasms stopped, he crawled to the back of the ledge, again peering down, not allowing his gaze to linger on the dead man.

After a few moments, Morgan realized that the wind was dying and the snow slackening. In the distance, he could see a patch of blue on the horizon. The storm was breaking up and with any luck, the sun would be out before noon.

There was no way to know where Case and the other survivors had gone. If they were smart, they were heading back to the snow machine.

Morgan couldn't worry about any of that now. He needed shelter. Moving along the wide shelf, searching for a way up, he found it came to an abrupt end at a wall of rock. Picking his way carefully, he retraced his steps past the now blocked fissure. Again, he found the rock shelf terminated at a sheer drop. The slope descending from the peak was at his back. He was effectively trapped.

But at least for the moment, he was safe from Case. If he couldn't get down, they sure as hell couldn't get up.

Morgan stopped and listened as the unmistakable reverberation of an engine far below. For a moment, Morgan thought it was Gruff's Sno Cat, but it was too shrill a whine for a tractor engine. More likely a snowmobile, he decided.

The engine abruptly ceased. He waited for several long minutes and then heard a staccato crack of gunfire. In another second, he heard the deep, throaty roar of the snow tractor's engine.

The clouds were lifting now and the sun was peering tentatively through the hazy mist. Morgan could see the broad expanse of the snowfield. In amazement, he watched a snowmobile, two riders hunched low on its back, cut across the white expanse. A moment later, the Park Service snow tractor lumbered into view, following, more likely pursuing, the smaller machine.

Morgan watched as the snowmobile angled toward the NORAMS station, a snow-covered lump in the distance, and then abruptly turned and vanished into the distant line of trees. The slower snow tractor dogged the other machine's trail and soon followed it into the tree line.

Suddenly, Morgan felt very alone. Unable to get up the cliff and vulnerable to attack from above, Case and his men had abandoned him. They were probably forcing Ryan to follow the snowmobile.

Who the hell had it been carrying?

Case would be back. Maybe not today, but certainly tomorrow.

Not that it would matter. By tomorrow, Morgan knew he'd be dead or close to it.

In truth, his odds of surviving the night perched on the broad, open, rocky plain were bleak and none.

Finally, needing to take some action, he gathered the rope and returned to the fissure. It would be impossible to get down the mountain before dark, and even if he tried, the best he could do would be to build a snow cave for the night. The possibility of making it to the NORAMS station without snowshoes was remote.

The sun broke out of the clouds, bathing the ledge in bright, welcomed light. Morgan was shocked to note that it was already afternoon. The morning had passed far too quickly, and sundown would come in a matter of hours.

He patted the pockets of his snowsuit. He had a small aluminum tube of matches, his pocketknife and nothing else. At least with a knife and matches he might be able to survive the night if he could find someplace to hole up.

He studied the mountain behind him. The sloping rise led to the peak. Here and there, massive, jagged points of stone jutted from the mountain like protective armored spikes. Scanning the area, Morgan paused, staring at a black, yawning cavity near the base of one of the spiky projections. He hesitated, studying it, then glanced at the sun.

There was time to investigate the opening and return to attempt a climb down the fissure. But did he want to be stranded on the ledge below with a dead man?

Still, he was too close now not to at least attempt to find the lair of the flying monster.

And then what? If he found it, what would he do? He was no match for those creatures.

"Don't be stupid," he told himself, even as he started looping the rope over his head and under his right arm and began climbing.

The wind was gusty and bitter, but nowhere as severe as it had been earlier. He adjusted his goggles, tugged down his mask and tightened the scarf across his cheeks and mouth. The wind chill was still deadly and Morgan didn't want to have to contend with frostbite on top of his other worries.

Bending at the waist, he clawed with his hands and braced himself with his feet as he climbed toward the dark opening 30 yards above him. The slope was not as difficult to ascend as he would have thought, although the climb, particularly in the thin air, was strenuous. By the time he flopped down on the rock just below the opening, he could feel trickles of sweat moving down his back and sides inside the heavily insulated gear.

After resting for a few moments, he hauled himself up until he could look into the dark mouth. Morgan was immediately disappointed. It was only a hollow depression in the rock. Although the light was bad, he could make out the back wall a scant ten feet away. From the opening, no more than six feet wide and half as high, a rocky incline dropped gently down to the rear of the cavity.

Tired from the long morning, weary of the buffeting wind, Morgan climbed into the opening and slid down the gentle slope. The floor cave was littered with small, brittle sticks and twigs undoubtedly caught by upslope winds and trapped in the narrow recess.

So much for the lair of the flying freak, Morgan thought ruefully, deciding to stay in the cave until he was ready to make his descent.

Sitting there, he was abruptly aware of his gnawing hunger, and tried to remember when he had last eaten. Holding out his gloved hand, he saw it shaking and realized his blood sugar was plunging.

"Great," he hissed to himself. If the cold didn't kill him or one of those winged freaks, he'd die of starvation or go into hallucinations and stumble off a cliff.

Morgan considered the dead man lying on the narrow ledge. The guy was wearing a pack. Could there be food in it?

The sun was now about halfway to the horizon and the wind was gusting, sending icy clouds of snow swirling across the barren mountain. Readjusting his scarf, Morgan climbed out of his burrow and carefully scrambled down the slope.

The body was still lying where it had fallen, the pool of blood now frozen into a reddish-brown mass. The pack was still strapped on the dead man's back.

At the fissure, Morgan tied the rope around a large boulder and then tossed it down. Looping it in his fist, he descended. Negotiating the boulders he'd used to block the passage was physically taxing, but after long minutes, Morgan stood on the narrow ledge.

Sucking in a deep breath, Morgan went to the body. It was lying facedown on the barren rock, and Morgan didn't have to look into the dead man's face. It wasn't that he was squeamish about death—he'd seen his share—he just didn't want the features of the man he'd killed forever haunting him.

The Devouring

Fumbling open the pack's stiff straps, he probed inside. It was a veritable treasure trove. He fished out a flashlight, a thermo blanket, a small bag of trail mix—which Morgan ripped open, pouring a goodly helping into his mouth—a box of ammunition, a package of beef jerky, a canvas-encased mess kit and, at the very bottom, a pair of heavy wool socks and two bags of freeze-dried food. On the dead man's belt was an insulated canteen.

It was more than he could have hoped for.

Munching on the frozen trail mix, Morgan felt his body react to the food. His light-headedness disappeared. He was just pouring more of the mix into his mouth when he heard the unmistakable beat of helicopter blades.

"Son of a bitch," he snorted, scanning the afternoon sky. In the distance he saw a big, jet-powered chopper thumping above the snowfield.

Morgan's heart quickened. Stuffing his booty back into the pack, he struggled frantically to free it from the dead man's stiff limbs.

When one strap was off the man's shoulder, he started working on the other one. The thump-thump of the helicopter was growing steadily nearer. He had to roll the body slightly and as he tilted the corpse on its side, something slammed into the rock a foot from where he crouched. Instinctively, Morgan jerked back, his foot colliding with the dead man.

The helicopter now hovered over the snowfield, and a man leaning against its open door was aiming a long-barreled rife.

A second shot whined off the rock just behind Morgan. He threw himself flat and then felt himself being dragged across the barren rock.

A sick panic clutched him as he saw that the dead man was now hanging above the chasm, a stiff arm caught in the strap of the pack. Morgan held the other strap, unwilling to give up its meager contents even as the body's weight threatened to pull him over the edge.

Struggling, he tugged at the strap, still aware of the helicopter hovering nearby.

Morgan's fingers clawed into a crack in the rock, and he heaved with all his might. The body bobbed above the edge of the precipice . . .

. . . and Morgan was looking into the dead, blood-streaked face. The man's eyes, rolled back, bulged white as a streamer of frozen blood trailed over shattered teeth like red drool.

A third shot slammed into the rock face inches below where Morgan clutched for purchase. Tiny pieces of rock pelleted his goggles and mask.

He jerked frantically on the pack, trying to dislodge the body.

Another shot whined off the ledge and simultaneously the body came free. The horrible face vanished and with the weight gone, Morgan's straining arm slung the pack onto the ledge. Driven by fear, he scooped it up and started back to the rope.

Chancing a glance at the helicopter, he saw the steam from the powerful jet engine as it maneuvered closer, bucking as it fought the updrafts. The gunman was now attaching something across the open door.

Morgan groaned when he saw the barrel of a heavy machine gun in a sling thrust out the opening. Almost instantly, a stream of gunfire hammered the rock just behind him.

Throwing himself down, Morgan crawled around the rocky protrusion to the base of the fissure. Reaching for the rope, he jerked back as another barrage of machine-gun fire pounded the surrounding rocks.

He pressed himself into the cut. If he tried to make it up the rope now, he'd be exposed, but he couldn't stay where he was for long. Sooner or later, by skill or luck, he'd be cut down.

The helicopter circled, the pilot trying to get a better angle. It wasn't the same copter Case had used before.

The Devouring

This was a leaner, meaner machine.

Morgan watched the door gunner swing the machine gun toward his position, and instinctively dropped from the fissure to sprawl prone on the cold, narrow ledge. Bullets and splintered bits of rock ricocheted around him.

When the barrage stopped, he glanced up. Although he could still hear the copter's prop beating against the wind, the machine itself was out of sight, no doubt circling for another pass.

Grabbing the pack, Morgan slung it over his shoulder and started hauling himself up the cut in the rock. Inside his insulated suit, sweat rolled down his sides, prickling his flesh.

The helicopter swooped into view like some giant, predatory bird. Morgan heard it pass above and in front of him and then it was on his right. It was only a matter of seconds before the gunman would have an angle on him.

Panting and gasping, he desperately clawed at the rope and struggled over the sharp, jagged rocks.

Morgan was just starting over the first boulder wedged in the fissure when the helicopter came thundering up behind him. His back muscles tingled and squirmed in anticipation of the fiery burst of slugs which would no doubt hammer out his life.

The rope in one hand, his other grasping at the rough surface of the large boulder, Morgan tottered, his body now balanced on the rock. He heard another burst of machine-gun fire, and thought he could feel fragments of stone and lead plucking hungrily at his legs. Gripping his lifeline in both hands he heaved himself forward, slamming hard into the deep stone cut. Bullets rained around him, cut across the boulder at his feet, fractured the rock inches above his head. A terrified animal scream filled his ears and he realized it was his own voice.

Then the firing stopped and the helicopter was again circling.

Lying between the narrow rock walls, Morgan considered his options. He couldn't go back down, but above, once he was out of the passage, he'd be totally exposed until he could reach the small cave.

The sun was much lower now, hanging just above the mountaintops. If he waited until dark he could make a break for the cave, but he ran the risk of encountering one of the creatures he'd been brought here to find.

Hearing the steady chop of the helicopter blades echoing off the mountains, but not seeing it, Morgan gritted his teeth and continued up the fissure. His arms quivered from strain, the muscles threatening to collapse. His aching body protested every move.

The wind was picking up again, howling like a wounded beast. Morgan paused just below the top of the fissure. Before he could make a break for the small cave, he wanted his attackers to make their next move.

It came swiftly and unexpectedly.

Although he could hear the helicopter, Morgan couldn't see it. With the wind whipping across the mountain he couldn't pinpoint its location.

Then it was there, rising from beneath the ledge below him like an ominous monster. It was dangerously close to the cliff wall. Swaying and bucking, Morgan saw the pilot battling the stick, fighting against the dangerous winds. The jet engine roared. The door gunner, strapped into a harness, was swinging the .50 machine gun around.

Groaning inwardly, Morgan saw his death coming. In another few seconds, the gunner would have him dead on and with one squeeze of the trigger, Richard Case would be rid of him forever.

Without thinking, without planning, Morgan moved. Tumbling out of the fissure, he scooped up a fist-sized rock, stood and pitched it high above the whirling rotor blade. Apparently, the pilot saw his sudden move. The copter lurched. The door gunner lost his grip on the machine gun and it swung free in the sling. The rock sailed harmlessly down the cliff.

Elated, Morgan scooped up two more good-sized stones, poised to hurl them at the helicopter's blades. But it was moving away now, heading out over the snowfield. Keeping his eyes on it, he stooped and untied the rope. Coiling it quickly and slipping it over his shoulder, he hurriedly started up the incline.

At his back, the helicopter now hovered over the snowfield, a predator biding its time before the final, fatal attack.

As if reading his thoughts, the pilot wheeled the copter and came roaring toward him. As its engine echoed hollowly between the mountains, Morgan turned and scrambled frantically up the slope.

The machine gun's roar cracked above the thump of the blades and a line of slugs stitched their way up the incline a dozen feet to Morgan's right. He veered, his boot hit a rock and suddenly he was falling, rolling. He slid on his back, his outstretched arms flailing blindly, seeking something, anything to stop his descent. The edge of the cliff loomed closer.

He tried to kick his heels into the frozen, rocky ground, but they skidded, refusing to dig in.

Above him the helicopter roared and the machine gun chattered.

At the last instant, his foot collided with a large rock. A jolt of pain shot up his leg as his slide came abruptly to an end. The rock tottered on the edge for a second and then fell.

The helicopter, bucking and pitching in an updraft, veered away from the mountain peak.

Morgan felt dizzy and light-headed. His stomach was roiling and he was again nauseated.

The sun was already slipping behind the distant peaks. Soon twilight would spread over the mountains and Morgan wanted to be safely inside the small cavern before darkness—and the creatures it concealed—arrived.

The helicopter was turning slowly over the distant snowfield.

Adjusting the pack and rope, Morgan got to his feet and began clawing his way up the slope. He paused and looked back, a sixth sense screaming a warning. Still hovering, the helicopter was at the edge of the snowfield, just above the tree line. Someone was again at the door, strapped into a harness and holding what Morgan thought might be a bazooka.

Not that it mattered. An instant later, there was a flash from its open door and a long trail of flame shot toward him.

Chapter Thirteen

Morgan screamed something mindless, a cry of utter terror as he saw the rocket streaking toward him. He threw himself to his left and landed hard on his stomach and elbows, his arms instinctively covering his head.

The concussion was devastating. There was a deep, awesome *swoosh* and then a thunderous eruption. Even with his head down, the flash seemed to sear into his closed eyes. The ground beneath him quivered and shook. Shattered rock rained down, pounding his already battered body with a frightening relentlessness.

He open his eyes just as a second rocket whined through the sky and slammed into the mountain. Again, there was a jolting, earthshaking thunderclap and a blazing flash. And again he was bombarded by a downpour of stone shrapnel.

Morgan lay very still for long minutes. Breathlessly, he awaited yet another attack, but it never came. As the ringing in his ears began to subside, he listened for the helicopter, but heard only the whining wind.

Stiffly, he got to his feet, tiny rock fragments cascading off his back. Surveying the area, he swore deeply, bitterly. The rockets had missed him, but one of them had slammed directly into the protective burrow. The opening was now twice its former size, half the roof blown away, leaving a jagged, smoldering wound in the rock.

Morgan shook his head in disgust, overcome by a profound sense of confusion and despair. Relentlessly pursued for reasons he couldn't begin to fathom, he was staggered by the lengths to which Case had gone, and would go, to stop him.

It was incomprehensible.

Consumed by defeat, Morgan sat on the ground for several minutes before wearily climbing up the slope toward the now-smashed cavern. It would have to suffice for the night. He needed to rest, to sleep, to plan.

Kneeling, he peered into the maw that had been his shelter. Large rocks filled much of it now. The large, comfortable area in the back was buried in a mound of small boulders.

. Sighing, Morgan shrugged off the pack and the coil of rope. He fished out the bag of trail mix and munched on it as he studied the mess. His fatigue was beyond anything he had ever experienced and his body ached and throbbed.

After several minutes, he started rolling the stones aside, pushing them up the incline, attempting to build a crude, protective wall for the night.

At the very back of the cavern, under the remaining shelf of roof, Morgan strained to roll a large boulder aside. It had been hammered into the wall and for several minutes refused to budge. Morgan braced his feet and circled his arms around the top of it. Sucking in a deep breath, he pulled, groaning and cursing as his bruised ribs protested. The rock came loose, rolled backward, forcing Morgan to scramble aside lest his leg get pinned beneath it.

The Devouring

A heavy, foul odor flooded into the small area. Even through the mask, Morgan could smell it. He knelt and crawled to the small opening. It was about two feet in diameter, its edges broken and jagged.

He peered into the dark hole and then tugged off a glove and thrust his hand inside. The gaseous odor was flowing out on a rush of oddly warm air.

Excited and not a little curious, Morgan pulled on his glove and dug the flashlight out of the pack. He shoved it into the opening, and its sharp, clear beam of light bored through the darkness. Morgan lay prone and put his face close to the hole in order to see inside.

He swung the light, gasped and rolled away. Staring up at him from the darkness had been a skull. His light had illuminated its dark eye sockets and the grinning yellow teeth.

His eyes wide, Morgan breathed deeply for several seconds and then, his composure regained, pulled himself back to the hole. He let the light play on the skull again. Wedged between two small stones, it grinned from the rock-strewn floor.

Moving the beam away from the death's-head, he swept the light along the floor. Other bones, brown and brittle, were scattered about haphazardly. The floor sloped gently away and appeared to turn sharply some yards down the dark shaft. The warm air was flowing from around that bend. Shining the light in the other direction, he found the terminus of the chamber a scant few feet beyond the skull.

The shaft might have been a volcanic chimney or simply a channel carved by ice and water. Morgan didn't particularly care. It was shelter and that was enough.

The irony of this new situation wasn't lost on him. Case's last attempt to kill him might very well prove to be his salvation.

Gathering the pack and rope, Morgan wriggled his way through the opening. The warm air moving from below carried a faintly bitter, acrid stench, although it was not as strong as that initial burst, which had likely been from a pocket of gas released when he moved the rock.

Hesitantly, Morgan picked up the skull. He knew precious little about anthropology and could tell little about its age or origin. There was a splintered break at the back of the skull. Shining the light on the teeth, he knew it couldn't be too old. Silver fillings winked back at him.

It was a puzzle Morgan had neither the time nor inclination to solve.

"Sorry, pal," he muttered. "There ain't room enough for both of us." Unceremoniously, he tossed the skull through the opening, hearing it clatter on the rocks outside. He quickly gathered the other bones, noting they all appeared to be human, and pitched them out the hole. If there was more time and under different circumstances, he would have bundled them to take back down the mountain for some enterprising anthropology student to ponder.

He quickly unloaded the pack, placing the boxes of ammunition aside as useless. Finding the two packets of freeze-dried food, he scanned the cave for something to use as fuel. There wasn't so much as a twig on the rocky floor. Poking his head through the opening, he retrieved several of the bones and some of the small twigs and branches scattered in the collapsed cavern, and piled them all on the floor near the end of the passage.

It took only a few minutes to build a fire, but eventually he had a moderate blaze going. Opening the mess kit, he poured half of the canteen's water into the pot. Using one of the bones and two piles of rock, he suspended it over the fire and waited for it to boil.

Soon, he was eating a huge helping of chicken stew and washing it down with gulps of the stale, metallic-tasting water.

Morgan could not remember a meal tasting so good.

With his appetite sated, Morgan decided to explore his shelter. He needed sleep, but someone or something had left the bones—or, more likely, a body—in there. At the back of his mind was the image of the dark, flying creature.

The chamber was about three feet wide and not much higher. He crawled on all fours along the passage. As he moved further away from the opening, he came across more bones. The warm air continued to flow unabated, forcing Morgan to pull back his hood and unzip his insulated suit.

After moving 15 or 20 yards down the passage, Morgan reached the abrupt turn. Cautiously, he peered around the bend, his heart pounding when he saw a faint glimmer of light some distance away.

The passage floor was carpeted with discarded bones, and Morgan was forced to move them aside in order to proceed. Although not all of them were human, he found several skulls and what appeared to be humerus, femur and tibia bones, distinctly human.

When he was within a few feet of the light, he turned off his flashlight. The opening was not large, perhaps half the size of the passageway, and the light coming in was faint. Crawling to the opening, he peered out, muttering in amazement as he scanned the large cavern. Streaks of phosphorescent minerals laced the walls, giving off the dim illumination. Huge stalactites hung from the high ceiling, and equally large stalagmites jutted from the floor 20 feet below his position.

The opening through which Morgan peered was between the ceiling and cavern floor. From his vantage point, he could see most of the interior. Opposite his position was a dark entrance to what Morgan assumed was another chamber. Sparkling drops of water rolled down the stalactites, dripping ceaselessly on their glistening counterparts rising from the floor.

It had the appearance of any number of similar caverns Morgan had toured or viewed in photographs. In the center of the chamber, a pool of water bubbled like a cauldron on a low fire, fed, no doubt, by a natural underground hot spring. They were common in the surrounding area and explained the cavern's warmth.

The acrid smell was strong, and Morgan searched the area for its source. Possibly it was from the pool, but he doubted it. The odor was too pungent and not at all like a sulfur spring. It was distinctly an *animal* smell.

As he was gazing into the cavern, he caught a movement out of the corner of his eye. Pulling away from the opening, he squinted in the faint light. In a recess along the far wall, a few feet above the damp, smoothly worn floor, something shifted in the shadows. It appeared to be a bundle of rags. As he continued to watch, he felt his heart skip a beat as a human arm emerged from beneath the rags. They were dragged slowly aside and Morgan saw a figure emerge stiffly. It crawled to the edge of the recess and lowered itself to the floor.

Morgan's heart thundered in his chest and cold, icy sweat suddenly beaded his forehead as he stared at the woman. She was naked except for a ragged bit of cloth tied around her waist. Her blond hair was tangled and matted and dark streaks of filth ran down her face and body. She walked listlessly, and even from where he lay amid the bones and decay, Morgan could see her blank, uncomprehending stare.

Like an automaton, the woman moved to a small pool of water below a massive stalactite. Squatting, she bent forward until her lips touched the water. She drank deeply.

"Who the hell are you?" Morgan whispered. He watched her move to the large, bubbling pool. Again she squatted and took hold of a line running from the edge of the hot spring down into the murky water. She pulled it out. Suspended from the end of it was the carcass of some small creature. The woman stared at it for several moments, then sank her teeth into the steaming flesh, chewing without enthusiasm.

She looked pathetic, so alone and dehumanized. Morgan wanted to call out to her, to let her know he was there, but at what risk? There might be others and Morgan was in no position to fight off a horde of . . .*whatever*.

The hell with it, he thought, his curiosity overwhelming his caution.

"Hello," he called. The woman cocked her head. "Here," he called again, thrusting his arm out the opening, signaling her.

She stared at his arm, not comprehending. Then something changed in her eyes, a light that had not been there sparked. She waved back, feebly, then with an increasingly frantic intensity.

"Who are you?" Morgan asked.

She furrowed her brow, her lips moving. She mumbled something Morgan could not hear.

"What?" he called.

"Connie . . ." she said, her voice raspy and grating.

"Connie Pruett?" he called.

"Yes," she cried, still dazed. "Connie Pruett. Yes."

"How did you get here, Connie?" he asked.

She was silent for a moment, suddenly looking around the cavern. "*They* brought me here," she answered, a tinge of fear and panic in her voice as she scanned the cavern furtively. As if coming out of a dream, she looked around in open horror. "Oh, God, they'll be back. Help me! Please, help me! Help me!" She cried the words in an hysterical chant, her voice growing louder, more hysterical with each word.

"I will," Morgan called down. "I've got a rope. I'll get it. Wait for me."

"Hurry! They'll be back. They'll be back. And they'll . . ." Sobbing, shaking violently, she sank to her knees and covered her face with her hands.

Morgan started crawling as fast as he could along the passage, brushing aside the scattered bones.

221

The small fire was still burning when Morgan reached the campsite. He was reaching for his rope when he heard something outside. His stomach lurched as he raised the flashlight toward the hole above him.

A terrible face peered down at him, and Morgan let out a startled cry. It was not human. Not remotely. Its large, luminescent yellow eyes were filled with malevolence as they glared at him from its leathery, fur-covered face. The gaping mouth was filled with sharp, spiky teeth and its flat, upturned nose twitched as if testing his scent.

Staggering backward, Morgan shone the light into the creature's eyes. It screamed and pulled back from the opening. He clutched one of the burning bones in his fire and when the hideous face appeared again, he thrust at the gaping mouth. Caught in the draft, the flames flared. In one brief instant, Morgan saw the thing's fur dance with fire.

Its scream echoed down the passage and sent a heart-stopping burst of terror through Morgan. It howled and raged as it vanished from the opening. He could hear the screams recede as the creature fled.

They'll be back!

Morgan hesitated a moment, then thrust his flashlight through the opening. When nothing happened, he careful poked his head and arm out and flashed the light into the darkness. He again heard a cry of pain echo through the night, but the creature was gone.

Gathering the rope, Morgan paused, searching for something to burn. Quickly he grabbed the pack and held it over the fire. The dry canvas caught almost instantly and began to burn. It was the best he could do. If the creatures came back, the fire might deter them.

With the rope slung over his shoulder, he started back down the passage.

They'll be back!

The thought propelled Morgan. He was no longer aware of his fatigue nor his aches and pains. The knees of his snowsuit gave him protection, but the fabric was wearing out and tufts of insulation were poking out of a dozen small rips and tears. Similarly, his padded gloves were tattered in a score of places.

Morgan reached the opening breathless and frightened. He peered into the cavern.

"Connie?" he called.

She appeared from behind one of the stalagmites, looking up at him anxiously.

"Oh, God, help me," she cried. "Please!"

"I'm going to lower a rope. Tie it around your waist and I'll pull you up. Do you understand?"

"Yes. Yes. Hurry. Oh, God, hurry." She rushed to a spot just below the opening. Morgan looped one end of the rope around his wrist and dropped the other end. There was more than enough. He watched as the woman circled it around her narrow waist. Her fingers trembled as she fumbled to make a crude knot.

"Please hurry," she panted. "Please, please, please."

"Hold on tight," Morgan instructed as he wrapped the rope around his own waist and started backing away from the opening, hauling the woman up. His already sore, strained muscles flared with renewed pain and the rope prodded his injured ribs into fresh spasms.

Inch by inch, foot by foot, he lifted her from the cavern. The rope slid smoothly along the opening.

He could no longer see the woman, but he could hear her murmured pleas for him to hurry.

They'll be back!

He had backed about 15 feet from the opening when Connie Pruett screamed. Her voice was high and hysterical, filled with abject terror. It was unlike anything Morgan had ever heard. Almost at the same second a dark, fleeting shadow passed near the opening.

Again, the woman screamed. This time it was a mindless, soul-wrenching cry of despair.

They'll be back!

Suddenly, the rope went slack and Morgan sprawled on a heap of clattering bones. Before he could get to his feet, he was jerked forward, the rope still wrapped around his waist dragging him toward the opening. Frantically he clawed at it, trying to free the knot even as he was steadily drawn along the rough passage floor.

The opening loomed five feet away.

He continued to struggle against the rope as it bit into his midsection. The pain was agonizing.

As he was about to be dragged through the hole, his fingers undid the knot and the rope came free, the loose end flying through the opening and out of sight.

All the while, Morgan could hear Connie Pruett's screams, ceaselessly reverberating in the chamber and through his mind.

Panting for breath, he edged toward the opening and looked cautiously into the cavern. What he saw sickened and disgusted him.

Below, partially hidden behind a stalagmite, he saw the grotesque creature, distinctly bat-like, yet vaguely humanoid, holding the hysterical woman from behind by the clawed thumb and forefinger projecting from the top joints of its massive, folded wings. The leading edge of the thin, leathery wings were supported by the elongated forelimb and one "finger." The creature's legs were attached to its massive wings.

Connie Pruett's struggles were useless. The thing turned its head, its large ears twitching, sharp fangs glistening, and stared directly at Morgan. Its evil eyes bored into him and if it was possible, Morgan thought the monster smiled, exposing its two dagger-like upper teeth. As it moved behind the woman, it turned and touched the back of her soft, white neck ever so gently with those sharp fangs. A moment later, a thin streamer of blood flowed down her quivering, naked back. She stiffened and writhed, but made no effort to escape. Slowly, almost caressing the flesh, a long, dark tongue lapped up the blood.

Then the creature cocked its head and locked its powerful jaws on the back of the woman's neck.

For one terrible moment, Morgan thought the monster was going to kill her, snap her neck between its powerful jaws. But its hold was so precise it didn't even break the skin.

Eyes squeezed tightly shut, her body trembling violently, Connie Pruett screamed as the creature drew her to him, bent her forward.

"NO!" she cried, the word ending in a long, piercing wail.

As the creature released his hold on her neck, it straightened, letting Morgan see its engorged penis. It glared up at Morgan, challenging him, taunting him.

"LET HER GO, GODDAMN YOU!"

Morgan watched in horror as the creature forced Connie Pruett's legs apart and then, with one final glance toward him, thrust savagely into her.

Her scream was shrill and mindless, and mingled with Morgan's own cry of disgust and outrage. Bile filled his mouth and he turned away, unwilling to watch the unholy coupling.

Chapter Fourteen

Connie Pruett's mindless screams followed Morgan as he crawled frantically along the passageway. They held a hopeless terror that reverberated off the narrow stone wall until he made the turn; they continued to echo in his mind much longer. Stunned and confused, his body throbbing and his mind numbed, he collapsed by his meager fire.

The remains of the backpack were still smoldering. Morgan stirred the ashes and was rewarded with a small burst of flame. Although the snowsuit staved off the worst of the cold, his hands were shaking as he unfolded the thermo blanket. A weight had settled in the bottom of his stomach like a stone.

Moving to the opposite side of the fire, placing his back against the terminus of the passage, he pulled the blanket across his body.

Trapped in this hellhole, fleeing both the law—or, more properly, Richard Case—and the predators lurking only scant yards away, he accepted that his death was only a short time away.

The nightmare was continuing. The creatures knew where he was hiding, probably knew he was all but helpless against them. Sooner or later, they would come.

Morgan desperately needed sleep. His mind was fuzzy, his thoughts a chaotic jumble, ragged at the edges. His eyes were gritty and sore. The aches and pains in his body all fused into one great malaise, sapping his strength and eroding his will.

Again he saw the thing, the *monster,* violating the woman in an act beyond anything in Morgan's worst imaginings, beyond anything in his worst nightmares. . . .

Great gut-wrenching spasms suddenly gagged him and he doubled over on the floor vomiting in agony.

Sitting up, wiping his mouth on the tattered sleeve of his snowsuit, Morgan leaned back against the wall and closed his eyes. He had failed that poor woman. After promising her he could help, promising he could get her out of there, he'd fucked up royally.

If he had been just a little quicker, a little stronger, he might have succeeded. If he hadn't been forced to confront that thing here at the fire . . .

If only he had a gun . . .

If . . .

It was an endless cycle of lost possibilities; a vortex of tortured thoughts and maddening self-accusations, tumbling and twisting in a dark corner of his mind like a knot of venomous snakes.

The small fire guttered, casting strange and ominous shadows across the rocky wall of the narrow passage. Morgan stared at the dying flames, waiting, almost longing for the encompassing darkness. In spite of his predicament, he would welcome the comfort of cold blackness. If only he could achieve the same effect in his mind, turn off the dreadful image of Connie Pruett with the monster; shut out her screams.

*   *   *

He was in the cavern. It was empty now, the illumination from the mineral deposits streaking the walls flickering and dancing. The smooth stone floor was slick and shiny. The sharp, pointed stalactites and stalagmites glistened crimson in the wavering light like savage, bloody teeth.

He was near the bubbling, steaming pool, staring into its murky depths, his vision weak and blurry. He stepped toward it, and his movements were awkward, off balance. His arms were ponderously encumbered and his legs unnaturally weak.

There was a rope—his hemp rope—trailing over the side of the pond and down into the slowly churning water. He reached for it with one foot. It was neither an odd nor an awkward movement. It was quite natural.

His long, powerful toes curled around the taunt line. The weight it bore was heavy, but rose easily as he skillfully dragged the long line out of the water.

He looked down at the bounty . . .

. . . Connie Pruett's soft, spongy face stared up at him with oozing, melting eyes. As he raised the body, the flesh first sagged and then began to slowly fall from the gleaming white bones. . . .

He saw his reflection in the pool; the cruel saffron eyes, the flat face, the gaping mouth and bloody fangs . . .

Morgan woke with a strangled cry, his body soaked in sweat, his breath coming in ragged, panting gasps. Again, his mouth was dry, his throat sore.

Those terrible eyes stilled stared back at him from the darkness.

There was a movement to his right. Groggily, struggling from one nightmare to the next, he realized the faint light from outside had been cut off. And the two points of yellow fire glaring at him were not remnants of the dream.

The Devouring

Cursing, he groped for his flashlight. His gloved hand struck the metal cylinder and it bounced away.

He heard gasping as a wave of rancid, coppery breath washed over his face. The leering eyes drew nearer, moving violently from side to side.

As terror washed over him, Morgan realized one of the creatures was struggling through the hole.

Another sound, further away, drew his attention toward the far end of the passage. Two more piercing eyes loomed in the darkness, for an instant holding him transfixed. His hand slammed at the rocky floor searching for the light. He touched it, fumbled with the switch and then it sent a brilliant beam of light streaming down the passage.

It was there, moving on powerful, taloned feet, wings folded tightly against its dark, furry body. Its long tongue flicked in and out of its huge mouth, caressing its needle-pointed teeth. The fingers protruding from the apex of the wings flexed and clawed at empty air.

Morgan turned the light toward the creature struggling through the opening. As the beam hit its large, luminescent eyes, it let out a painful cry. In the bright light, Morgan could see the coarse hair around its mouth and below its left eye was blackened and curled from the flaming brand he'd used to drive it away earlier.

It hissed, spitting at him, but its wings were trapped in the tiny opening and there was no way it could reach him. The cruel thumb and forefinger at the elbow of the wing slashed harmlessly.

The other creature, however, was steadily clawing its way forward.

Galvanized by fear, Morgan moved in one fluid motion. Pulling the thermo blanket off his legs, he swung it up and over the creature trapped in the opening. It screamed, its jaws snapping at the thin, tough material. Morgan grabbed the two ends draped over its head and bundled it below the snarling mouth, twisting the fabric tight.

Douglas D. Hawk

Now, the creature tried to pull away. It jerked and thrashed struggling to draw its head back, extract itself from the trap. Morgan held on with all his strength, his battered body and strained muscles screaming.

"Fuck you, rodent!" Morgan cried, bringing the flashlight crashing down on the covered head. It howled and screamed, almost pulling free of the confining shroud.

The light flickered and blinked out. For a panicky instant Morgan was plunged into darkness with the two monsters. Halfway down the narrow passage, two large, luminescent pits of yellow glared at him.

Then the light flickered and flared on.

The creature in the passage paused now, caught in the circle of light. It studied Morgan with evil intelligence, emitting a throaty, warning hiss. Powerful muscles rippled beneath the heavy pelt and its wings fluttered ever so slightly in the narrow confines of the rock chamber.

Morgan had his back braced against the wall now, his feet against the opposite wall as he held onto the blanket with one hand. With his other he attempted to keep the flashlight trained on the second creature.

The thing he held started shaking its head violently from side to side. As his arm was whipped and wrenched, Morgan could hear it thump sickeningly against rocks as its tried to free itself in a mad, thrashing frenzy.

The creature watching began to draw back. Morgan sensed it was not intimidated by the light, but appeared distressed by its companion's manic, self-destructive struggle. It let out an oddly soothing cry, soft and tranquil.

The trapped thing continued to punish itself against the rocks, but its efforts had grown less frantic. It was again attempting to pull itself out of the small opening. Morgan felt it brace itself for one titanic effort. Placing the flashlight down, its beam aimed at the second creature, he gripped the blanket with both hands.

When the creature jerked its head back, the slick fabric pulled free of Morgan's gloved hands. He clawed at the

230

blanket as it was dragged out of the opening. Abandoning it, Morgan clutched his light and scrambled away from the opening. Outside, in the cold darkness, he heard the creature moaning and crying.

Crouching behind the embers of his dead fire, Morgan watched the monster in the passage continue to withdraw. He turned the light to the opening. A corner of the thermo blanket hung from the aperture. Still keeping his eyes on the creature down the passage, Morgan leaned forward and yanked it back through the hole. It fell at his feet and he shone the light on it for a second. Thick streaks of clotted blood and clumps of fur stained one side. Morgan felt a swelling sense of victory and vindication.

"Rot in hell, you bastard!" he snarled, his words tinged with hysteria.

As if in answer, a high, keening cry issued from beyond the bend in the passage. Involuntarily, Morgan shivered.

Its companion had now vanished around the bend.

He wanted to turn off the flashlight, conserve the batteries, but he now feared the darkness. No longer did it provide shelter and comfort. It was a black tomb and there were things in it he did not want to face again.

Morgan had no idea what time it was now. For the first time all day he realized he didn't have his watch. Maybe he'd left it in the hotel, or more likely, lost it during the insanity on the mountain.

It was all madness. Nothing made sense. His world was so far out of kilter, he wondered if he would ever be able to right it again. Men hunted him by day, monsters by night.

Insanity . . .

They'll be back!

In spite of his best efforts to stay awake, Morgan again drifted off into a fitful, shallow sleep. His dreams were filled with winged abominations and terrible image of a woman brutalized. Dark shapes skirted the periphery of his dreamscape, their unseen talons and snapping fangs seeking his throat, his blood, his life. . . .

He was awake again, his body shaking in a cold, fever-ish sweat.

He looked around, amazed to see faint light gleaming around the small opening. The sun was coming up. For long moments Morgan had to assimilate its significance. He had survived the night. The things had not returned. It was a fresh day and . . .

. . . and Case would be back.

A pall fell across him like a curtain of black despair. The thought of another day on the run, another day fight-ing for his life, was unimaginable.

Stiffly, his joints creaking, Morgan got to his knees and opened the canteen, taking several swallows of water to relieve the harsh pain in the back of his throat. His bladder was painfully full and with some difficulty, he opened his snowsuit and relieved himself. His body was clammy and he grimaced as he got a whiff of his own stench.

And he was hungry, but there was nothing to use for fuel. Somehow, he doubted the second packet of freeze-dried food would be much good unprepared. There were bones around the bend, but he had no desire to go for them. God only knows what would be there, waiting.

Morgan pulled himself through the rocky opening. In the remains of the small cavern, he stretched. It was good to be out of the dark tunnel, good to breath the cold, harsh air.

The false dawn was still and gray. The sky was cloud-less and the sub-zero air was bitter and biting. His breath quickly froze around the mask and scarf covering his face, and he drew his hood tighter around his head and slipped on his snow goggles.

Scanning the area, he suddenly drew back into the shattered cave. There, up near the top of the peak, he saw one of the creatures. Its massive wings beat the air as it glided through the shadows on the western side of the mountain. It banked and dove at fantastic angles, swooping dangerously close to craggy ledges. Morgan watched in awe as it dropped straight down the face of the barren rock toward the boulder-strewn slope, and at the last possible second pulled up and shot back into the sky.

For one brief instant, the creature was silhouetted against the lightening sky. The elongated bones supporting the thin, translucent membrane stood out in stark relief, and Morgan saw the thing's dark pelt shine reddish-brown in the light of the coming dawn.

With a sudden cry, the creature wheeled and dove toward the rocky slope. Streaking scant feet above the ground, it soared toward the enclosure where Morgan crouched.

He reached down, picked up a hefty rock and cocked his arm. If it came close enough, by God, he'd peg it between its beady eyes.

The thing shot down the slope. Morgan waited until it was close, then sprang from behind the rocks and hurled the stone with all his strength. It missed its mark when the winged monster veered away, soaring high. It wheeled in the air and let out a high, undulating cry.

Morgan cursed, sensing its mocking laughter. He readied himself for an attack, but the creature simply circled above him, screeching ever louder until its cries reached an echoing crescendo.

Then it was silent. Beating its leathery wings against the air, it soared away and vanished over the cliff face.

Morgan stood alone in the silent, frozen dawn, thinking about the winged demons and the woman they held in the cavern.

How could he get her out of there? What could he do to save her from . . .

. . . a fate worse than death?

He shook his head. His rope was gone and he had no gun. But even if he was armed with one of Case's machine pistols, Morgan wasn't convinced he would be a match for those things. He had been lucky last night. There had been no skill involved, just dumb luck. The next time he confronted them, he couldn't depend on mere chance or dumb good fortune. Lady Luck had been in his corner yesterday and last night, but he couldn't count on such largess the next time.

Morgan was brought out of his reverie by the distant, high-pitched whine of an engine. For an instant, he considered crawling back into his burrow, but the thought of going back inside the cloying darkness was too dispiriting.

Quickly, he moved down the slope to the edge of the cliff and gazed over the snowfield's pale blue expanse. In the middle of the plain, he saw a small, red Kristi snow tractor rocketing toward his mountain.

"Gruff," Morgan laughed, recognizing his friend's Porsche-powered machine. He watched until the Kristi reached the trees and vanished behind the line of towering pines.

Elated, he hurried back to the collapsed cavern to retrieve his flashlight, the canteen and, as an afterthought, the two boxes of ammunition. He left behind the gore-encrusted thermo blanket and the mess kit.

As Morgan reemerged from the cave, the distinctive *thump-thump* of a helicopter broke the silence. Cursing, he hurried back to the cliff and studied the horizon. It took him a second, but he spotted the helicopter coming in low over the snowfield. The early morning sun glinted off the ugly barrel of the machine gun protruding from the open side door.

Morgan crouched low. He should be running for his life, but Gruff was down there and Case wouldn't hesitate to kill him.

Suddenly the machine gun clattered. The gunner swung the weapon back and forth, his arms jerking with the steady recoil. Morgan saw the flicking tongue of fire flaring from the barrel as it sent a barrage of lead into the trees. The gunfire ceased as the copter banked, circled out over the snowfield and prepared for a second pass.

As it drew near, a single rifle shot cracked and echoed in the bitter morning air. The helicopter wobbled and banked again. The door gunner pitched wildly in his harness, loosing his grip on the machine gun.

Second and third shots echoed across the mountains, and a puff of smoke appeared from the chopper's engine. It rocked violently, sinking toward the snow as the pilot fought for control. The smoke turned an oily black as the helicopter continued to buck and pitch.

The pilot steered it toward the NORAMS station at the far end of the broad clearing. Morgan watched in amazement as it descended quickly, then rose and finally slammed down hard in a cloud of snow and smoke.

Morgan let out a wild, triumphant cry.

Without the rope, getting down the blocked fissure was tricky and dangerous. When he reached the three boulders blocking the way, he had to hoist himself over them and then drop down, clawing at the exposed rock to keep from tumbling to his death.

Gasping for breath, knowing his time was short, he stumbled and staggered down the mountain. Once, he lost his footing and with a cry, pitched forward, rolling across the snow and ice and rock. He came to a thudding stop against the bole of a dead pine tree.

Stunned, he struggled to his feet. He was running on reserves and they were nearly exhausted. If he didn't get out of here soon, the backpackers would find his bones in the spring.

Holding his battered ribs, he picked his way along the trail he'd broken yesterday. It was now all but obscured by the fresh snow. His head felt light and hot and he was sweating. His vision blurred momentarily. Twice he had to stop to lean against a tree until his equilibrium returned. A wave of nausea tightened his gut and brought up more bitter bile to burn the back of his throat.

When the ground began to level, Morgan moved among the heavy trees bordering the broad snowfield. He froze when he heard the snap of a tree limb nearby.

"Hold it right there," someone ordered from behind.

"Gruff?" Morgan breathed, recognizing his friend's voice.

"Morgan?" the other man whooped, coming from behind a mound of rock. "By God, you *are* alive." He had a rifle cradled in the crook of his arm.

Morgan turned around as the big man approached. He frowned when he saw the streak of blood staining Gruff's parka.

"You hurt?"

Gruff's face was covered by a dark blue mask. He shook his head. "Naw. That bastard with the fifty-cal blew the hell out of a big rock. Got hit with a piece of it. Just a cut on my cheek."

"Make it hard to sit down, won't it?"

It took the burly man a second to get the joke. "Screw you, Morgan. Ain't *that* cheek."

"So . . . what the hell are you doing up here?" Morgan groaned, again overwhelmed by a wave of dizziness.

Gruff grabbed Morgan's arm. "Jesus, Morgan, you're not in too great a shape." The big man tugged his mask up, flipped on his rifle's safety and leaned it against a tree.

"No kidding. I've had better days," Morgan answered.

"I've been lookin' for you. I was watchin' you guys through my binoculars yesterday and I saw Case cut his man loose." He made a face. "Ain't never seen a man murdered before. Liked to turn my stomach. Felt kinda good to knock that damned chopper outta the air."

He lifted Morgan's mask. "Jesus, boy, you're sick. You don't look so good."

Morgan groaned, his knees suddenly wobbly. He clutched at a tree from support. Gruff grabbed one arm to steady him.

The Devouring

Leaning against a tree, Morgan breathed deeply. "Dizzy." He looked at his friend. "What happened to you yesterday?"

Gruff started to answer, and then stopped as someone stepped into the small clearing. Morgan looked, trying to focus his eyes.

"I happened to him," Roberta Ferris said casually.

Morgan stared at her in disbelief, the fiery explosion that had consumed his snow machine replaying once again in his mind's eye. He tried to pull himself forward, found it too difficult and sagged back against the tree.

Roberta hurried to him. She pulled off a glove and touched his face. "You're burning up."

"I thought . . ."

"That I was dead?" she asked through the heavy mask.

"Yeah. I saw the tractor go up like a Roman candle."

"I slipped out the driver's door and circled around the rocks."

"How . . . ?" he mumbled, finding it hard to concentrate. Her masked face swam before him, growing blurry and faint.

"Later," she said. "Gruff, we've got to get him out of here. He's on fire with fever."

"What about . . . Case?" Morgan groaned.

"Why did you think I brought that little jackrabbit? It's got purely awesome speed." The big man smiled. "Hell, we thought you was dead, but we had to be sure. We had to know."

"I'm glad you did," Morgan answered. He swallowed hard, his throat raw and swollen. He rubbed his temples against the dull ache behind his eyes.

"Let's go," Gruff Ryan said, slipping an arm around Morgan's waist. "It ain't far." Roberta moved to Morgan's other side and pulled his arm over her shoulders.

"Did you see the . . . creatures?" she asked as they walked slowly through the trees.

"Yeah, I saw them."

237

"How many?"

"I'm not sure. Three or four at least." He thought about the other woman. "God, I found Connie Pruett. . . ."

"She's alive?" Roberta asked, her voice low and frightened.

"She'd be better off dead," Morgan answered, his voice hoarse and raspy. He was finding it hard to think, hard to keep his mind focused. "Believe me. I . . . I tried to help her . . . honest to God, I tried."

Once they were inside the small machine, Roberta pulled off his goggles and mask and studied him. He was pale, his skin taut and his eyes bloodshot and sunken.

"Let's get the hell out of here," she said

Gruff fired up the powerful engine. After slipping his rifle into a case mounted along the seat, the big man skillfully wheeled the machine around.

Morgan and Roberta sat behind him.

"Hang on, folks," Gruff roared, sending the machine shooting forward through the trees and out onto the snowfield.

They glanced toward the NORAMS station. Smoke still drifted into the morning air from the helicopter. They could just make out the broken rotor blades and upper body of the craft. It was impossible to tell if anyone was moving around the downed machine.

Gruff throttled the Kristi across the open plain. When he reached the trees on the opposite side, he turned, heading down the mountain. His driving skill was only matched by his recklessness. Fading in and out of lucidity, Morgan was vaguely aware of trees streaking past, of sharp turns and bone-jarring thuds as the machine sailed over rough terrain.

"Let's load her up and get the hell outta here," he heard Gruff shout, and realized they were parked next to his friend's truck.

Then Morgan was inside the truck. He felt cold and clammy, his throat now so dry and swollen, he thought for a minute he was going to strangle. There was a tremor in his hands and he swiped at his eyes, trying to clear his vision. The morning sun on the snow burned them, intensifying his headache.

Roberta was next to him . . . he felt her arm around his shoulder . . . smelled the faint scent of her perfume . . . heard the throaty growl of Gruff's truck . . .

Finally, mercifully, he slumped against her.

Chapter Fifteen

Morgan faded in and out of reality. Roberta was there, feeding him something warm and good, and then he was looking into Connie Pruett's accusing eyes. He was lying in a soft bed, and then was back in the narrow, cramped rock passage. Doc Reed's face swam before his eyes; he saw the hypodermic needle; then it was Richard Case holding a gun. He heard someone scream as Case's face melted into the leering, slathering face of one of the bat creatures. Gruff was talking to him, and then Case was screaming at him.

At once he was burning up and shivering from terrible cold. He smelled his own sweat and urine. He tasted a bitter brackishness in his mouth and moved his tongue over dry lips. He heard himself cry out in pain. . . .

Muted, defused light cast the room in a golden glow. Log walls were covered with painted mountain scenes, pieces of varnished pine root, a bamboo fishing pole, an

240

old cheese-cake calendar. A fire crackled in a moss-rock fireplace on the far wall of the room.

The soft bed was uncomfortable and as he moved, Morgan's back muscles protested. There was a kink in the small of his back and his shoulders were tight and sore. He turned his head and saw the water glass sitting on the small nightstand. Reaching for it, his trembling fingers only brushed it and it dropped from sight, breaking on the hardwood floor with a loud pop.

"Morgan?" said Roberta tentatively, appearing at the wood-planked door. "Are you . . . okay?"

"Yeah." His voice was a hoarse, dry whisper.

Roberta glanced over her shoulder. "Gruff, he's awake." She moved to him, her shoes crunching on broken glass, and placed a cool, dry hand on his forehead. "I think the fever's broken."

"How ya doin', buddy?" Gruff said, standing at the end of the bed.

"How long . . ." Morgan licked his lips. "How long have I been in la-la land?"

"Day and a half," Gruff answered.

"Where are we?"

"Doc Reed's cabin," Roberta said, bending to pick up the shards of glass.

Morgan nodded. He knew the cabin well. It was a few miles out of town, nestled in a grove of trees, out of sight of the highway, but with a relatively easy access road.

"Why here?" Morgan wondered. He shifted on the bed, searching for a more comfortable position.

Gruff drew up a chair and sat down wearily. He shrugged. "Couldn't go to my place. I think Case would like to string me up by my nuts for leaving him. Leastways, that seems reasonable. I ain't seen him since I boogied off the mountain the other day."

Morgan groaned and pulled himself up. Roberta grabbed another pillow and put it behind his back as he settled into a sitting position.

"How did Reed get involved?" Morgan asked.

Roberta smiled. Like Gruff, she looked strained and tired. Her eyes were darkly circled and her skin was pale. "You were really out of it. I was worried, so Gruff gave him a call and he told us to come up here. He's been here twice to check on you."

"What's the prognosis?"

Gruff leaned back and rubbed his big hands over his face. "You were worn out, beat all to shit. Hell, yer body just decided it was time for a holiday and damned well took one."

Roberta excused herself, returning a few minutes later with a steaming cup of soup and a fresh glass of water. He took the cup and sipped.

"Chicken soup? I must really be sick."

"Very funny," she said dryly. "You need to get back your strength."

Morgan winked at Gruff. "How about a big, thick T-bone with a side of home fries?"

"Drink your soup," Roberta said sternly. She sat in a second chair. "Feel like talking?"

Morgan nodded.

"What you told us when we got you," Gruff said. "About the Pruett woman. Did you really find her?"

Morgan's eyes clouded. He looked into the empty cup and nodded. Dark visions flowed back into his mind like fresh blood on virgin snow. Again, he saw the dimly lit cavern, the naked, traumatized woman, the creature with its teeth on her neck, bending her forward . . .

"Those things . . . have her." In a quiet, hushed voice, pausing occasionally to draw in a heavy breath, Morgan told them what he had witnessed.

"Mary, Joseph and the Kid," Gruff hissed through clenched teeth when Morgan finished. "You tellin' me them things are . . . breedin' with women?"

Morgan closed his eyes and nodded. "Yeah."

"It explains a lot," Roberta sighed. "I mean the woman

they found with her child . . . cut out of her . . ." She faltered, her voice momentarily breaking. She gasped, cleared her throat and pulled in a heavy breath. "They're trying to reproduce their own kind."

"Damn," Morgan breathed, putting the cup down and picking up the water glass. "Is that possible?"

Roberta furrowed her brows. "I don't know. They're trying to procreate." Something shifted in her eyes and a note of excitement crept into her voice. "Those things may be all male. Without females to bear their young, they'll die out unless they find suitable hosts for their young . . ."

"You don't have to sound so damned pleased about it," Morgan snapped. Again the scene in the cavern flashed before his eyes. "It was . . . sick!"

Roberta glanced away. "I know," she said in a small voice. "But it . . . tells us a lot about them. It's a major piece of evidence."

"I've got to get the Pruett woman out," Morgan said, his voice rising. "I've got to get her out. We've got to get guns and go up there for her. We've got to kill those fucking monsters!"

"Easy, Morgan," Gruff said. "Take it easy. There's a few things we've got to work out first."

"Work out?" Morgan demanded. "You didn't see what I saw. Jesus Christ, we've got to get guns and get her out!"

"We will, Morgan," Gruff assured him. "Damned straight we will."

There was a long silence in the room. Morgan looked at Roberta, reaching a hand out to her. She took it, held his fingers tightly.

"Sorry," he said quietly. "I didn't mean to bite your head off." His eyes explored her face. "I really thought you were dead. I can't believe you got out of the explosion and away from Case and those other feds."

"First of all," she said, a steely glint in her eyes, "they

aren't feds. They're Case's private army."

"I guessed as much." He turned to study Roberta's face. "How the hell did you get away?"

"Once I was out the driver's door, I circled around the rocks. After those trigger-happy cowboys blew up the tractor, I headed out on my snowshoes. I kept the rocks between me and the fire. I reached the trees before the helicopter took off." She paused to caress his face. "With you on board."

Morgan arched his eyebrows. "It was that easy?"

She made a face when she heard the incredulous note in his voice. "What's wrong? Can't a woman take care of herself?"

He smiled. "Obviously, you can."

"So I waited until it was clear and then made my way to the NORAMS station," Roberta continued. "It took a while, but when I got there I grabbed one of the snow-mobiles and got the hell off the mountain."

Morgan shook his head in amazement. "What I can't figure is how your tracks went unnoticed."

Roberta shrugged. "With the explosion, the fire and all the excitement, I think it was a while before anyone thought to check. Besides, they assumed I was dead."

Morgan nodded. "Where'd you stay after you got the snowmobile?"

"In a motel outside of town. I left the snowmobile hidden in an old farm and walked to the highway. Caught a ride in a couple of minutes." She smiled at Morgan mischievously. "Truck drivers are so accommodating."

"I'll just bet," he said with a leer.

"Anyway," she went on, "I couldn't go into town and I hadn't a clue where they'd taken you. I wanted to call Washington, but . . ." She frowned. "Who can I trust? I'm not sure how many people are involved in all of this."

"All of what?" Morgan asked pointedly. "I'm still a little confused."

"You and me both," said Gruff Ryan.

The Devouring

Roberta looked first at Gruff and then back at Morgan. "Okay, let me fill you on what's going on from *my* end. Just remember, this is classified."

Morgan shrugged and Gruff made a face.

"I'm part of a government team financed by funds from virtually every major government agency. There are only a dozen of us, and in reality, we don't use that much money. We investigate unusual phenomena."

"Like UFO's and haunted houses?" Morgan asked. "And bat people?"

She shook her head. "Not UFO's, not ghosts or psychic stuff. But yes, like these bat creatures in the mountains. We go wherever there are strange reports. For a time, we had a team in the Northwest looking for Bigfoot."

Roberta stopped when Gruff snorted a laugh. "I'm sorry," he said. "I mean, this all sounds pretty damned weird."

Her mouth twisted into a crooked smile. "Yeah, I suppose it does. But given what we *know* is up there in the mountains . . . well, it validates our work."

"What *about* those flying bastards?" Morgan prompted.

Roberta got to her feet and began pacing the room, arms tightly crossed. "The first reports we got were about a year ago. We came out here. . . ." Her eyes clouded for a minutes and Morgan knew she was remembering her dead assistant.

"We set up some monitoring stations in the areas where some backpackers said they'd seen something flying around the peaks just after sundown." She glanced at Morgan. "You saw the videotape. It killed poor Joe. After that, my other assistant asked to be transferred to another project."

"Where did Case come in?" Morgan asked.

"I'm getting to that," she said. "I took that videotape to my boss in Washington. Needless to say, he was staggered. He insisted that if we were going to continue this investigation, we needed protection. He already had an

245

alliance with the FBI, so he met with the Director and Case was assigned to me. He's a kind of troubleshooter for the Bureau. He takes on unusual situations."

"Damned psycho!" Morgan spat bitterly.

"I can't argue with that," Roberta agreed. "It was only later that I learned he'd finagled his way into the assignment. I don't know how he knew what we were after, but he must have known something. There were a couple of other agents with us, but he managed to get them reassigned." She shrugged and then continued. "And at the time, it made sense. It was a waste to have so many people just hanging around."

Gruff grunted. "So why'd he go out of control?"

"And what about this private army of his?" Morgan asked.

"I'm not sure," she answered thoughtfully. "All I know is that shortly after the other two agents left, his goons showed up. When I asked him about it, he just said that, given the situation, he had brought in some 'specialists.' "

"Government-speak for professional hitmen," Morgan said.

"We found the missing woman's body and after that, he really changed. It became difficult for me to control him. He started doing things I wasn't even aware of until it was too late." A pained look filled her eyes. "Like what happened at the NORAMS station."

Morgan shot her a look. "What do you mean?"

"When we first went up there with you, I found a device I couldn't identify. I'm no expert on what equipment environmental scientists use, but this thing was definitely not a monitoring device. It was smashed, but . . ."

"You pocketed it," Morgan said. "Yeah, I saw that. I'd forgotten about it."

She smiled at him. "Guess I'm not a very good sneak thief."

"Guess not," he said.

Roberta shot him a mock frown. "I sent it to Washington. The meeting I had other day was with one of the men from my group. He flew out because . . .well, things are getting weird with my organization too. My boss had a heart attack and is in an 'undisclosed location.'

"The guy I met smelled trouble and decided to come out here to meet with me personally. As it turned out, he had to come here anyway because our *temporary* chief wanted to talk to me, to all of us, about Case."

"Like maybe having him removed and locked up in a rubber room somewhere?" Morgan asked cynically.

"I'm confused," Gruff said.

Roberta nodded. "It's confusing, I'll admit. But that's how it came down. My colleague from D.C. said the device was a transmitter. He was still trying to figure out the exact signal, but it was definitely not part of the NORAMS equipment."

Morgan started to ask something, but she waved him silent. "Secondly, the temporary chief said that, in response to my complaints to Washington, he was here to tell me Case would be staying on and I was not to lodge any further complaints against him. Of course, it was a veiled threat. If I persisted in stirring up trouble, I'd be replaced."

"So, as it stands," Morgan said, "your boss has basically disappeared, you don't have anyone in authority in D.C. you can trust and Case has very powerful allies."

"In a nutshell," Roberta said, tossing her hands in the air. She looked from one man to the other. "I think that transmitter was used to attract the creatures to the NORAMS building."

Gruff Ryan frowned. "Jesus."

"Do you know how bats navigate?" Roberta asked, her eyes suddenly very alive.

Morgan thought about it for a second. "Kind of a radar, isn't it?"

Roberta nodded. "Echolocation. Bats with echolocation send out sound waves that bounce back to them, like natural radar. Of course some species just have normal vision."

Gruff eyed the woman. "What're you gettin' at?"

Still pacing, Roberta continued. "Let's suppose these . . . creatures have the same natural ability. They use a kind of radar to navigate. It's something I've speculated about for weeks."

Morgan and Gruff exchanged glances, but remained silent.

"Now, let's say some sort of high frequency could be transmitted that would . . . attract them," she said. "And suppose Case planted that transmitter at the station to bring those things down."

Morgan shivered under the covers. "God, that would explain a lot." His eyes grew hard. "Like the attack on Charlie Shaw. Case was screwing around with the snow-mobile after the attack."

Roberta nodded. "That's highly possible."

Gruff rubbed his tangled beard, his eyes slitted. "Yeah, okay. But it was those scientists that got clobbered. Case and his boys were nowhere around."

Roberta's was silent for a minute. When she finally spoke, her voice was low. "Maybe Case had some idea that if he attracted them there he could capture one. Besides, I have no idea how long that transmitter was sending out a signal. It could have been hours, days or even weeks."

"So why was the NORAMS station trashed?" Gruff wondered.

Morgan thought about it for a second and glanced at Roberta. "If the transmitter was inside the building and if its frequency aroused or agitated the creatures, then it's logical they'd want to find the source. Maybe they just trashed everything until the transmissions stopped."

Roberta agreed. "That's as logical an explanation as any."

Gruff looked at her. "If what Morgan's sayin' is true,

how much trouble would it be to put one of them transmitters in Red's car? Lure these bat things right to him."

"But . . ." Roberta started, then paused as she sat on the edge of the bed. "Is Case . . . that crazy?"

"It could explain why that one came down to the hospital," Morgan said quietly.

Roberta looked at him with pleading eyes. "That was Case's *own* man! Would he do something that . . . vicious to one of his own?"

Morgan reached across the bed and again took her hand. It was as cold as ice. "Believe me, after what he put me through up on the mountain, I'd say he'd do anything to get what he wants."

"I wonder why," Roberta said thoughtfully.

"Who knows," Morgan said. "Maybe the man was a problem; maybe Case wanted him out of the way and the first time he was attacked he wasn't killed. Or maybe it was just a test."

"Test?" Gruff asked.

"Yeah," Morgan said sourly. "Maybe he just wanted to see if he could lure one of those bastards out of the mountains."

Another long silence settled over them.

After a time, Morgan turned to Roberta. "Tell me something. How did you know they would take me back to the mountain?"

She smiled weakly. "I didn't know. But I knew, sooner or later, Case would be going back up there. The motel where I stayed was close to the turnoff. I was up most of the night and saw Gruff's truck head up there. I decided to investigate."

"Yeah, but why'd you get Gruff out of there?" Morgan asked.

Gruff laughed. "She thought you might be in my snow tractor. When she saw you and the others goin' up the hill, she came to check out the machine."

"Just before I arrived," Roberta continued, "Gruff saw

Richard's men shooting at you. When I arrived, he was ready to get out of there."

"No shit." Gruff glowered. "I figured I was definitely expendable too." A pained expression crossed Ryan's face. "It wasn't that I was leavin' you, I just . . ."

Morgan nodded. "You made the right choice. Why didn't you just take the tractor?"

Gruff gestured wildly. "Hell, I was goin' to, and then Case and his boys came outta the woods lookin' mighty pissed. I was standin' there talkin' to Roberta and we just jumped on the snowmobile and made tracks."

Morgan smiled. "No wonder Case was so pissed off and nervous the other morning at the motel." He glanced at Roberta. "He knew *you* were alive. He was worried. Maybe a little scared. You were a loose cannon."

Roberta looked away. "He's made us all fugitives."

"Hey," Gruff said indignantly. "We ain't down and out yet. We can still beat that son of a bitch!"

She looked at the big, bearded man, a wistful smile twisting her mouth. "Yeah, I think we can." She moved closer to Morgan, squeezed his hand and gazed into his eyes. "Now, if you're not too tired, tell us what happened on the mountain."

Images cascaded back into Morgan's mind as he slowly, painfully recounted everything after his escape from Case and his night in the dark passage. When he finished, he looked from one to the other. "It was beyond a nightmare. It . . ." His voice trailed off.

"Don't torture yourself," Roberta said soothingly.

He nodded and looked at her for understanding. "I just can't get the image of the woman and . . . that monster out of my mind. God help me, I tried to get her out of there."

Roberta continued to hold his hand tightly while her eyes roved his face. "Morgan, it's not your fault. It's not your fault she's there and not your fault you couldn't get her out. You did the best you could do."

"But . . ."

"But, nothing," she said firmly. "You did what you could. Should you have let yourself be killed? Would that have saved her?"

Gruff piped in. "Face reality, pal. You did what you could at that moment. That's all that can be expected of any of us. You do what you can do when you can do it. It's that damned simple."

Morgan leaned back against his pillow and closed his eyes. He was tired again. His strength was sapped.

"Yeah, I know," he sighed.

Roberta released his hand and got up. "I'll get you some more soup and then I want you to sleep."

Morgan nodded, not opening his eyes.

Before Roberta returned, he was sleeping peacefully.

Morgan awoke slowly. The room was dark, except for the faint glow of embers in the fireplace casting pale orange light across the walls. It took him a few moments to remember where he was, but when his mind clicked into sync, he tossed off the covers, swung his stiff legs to the floor and turned on the lamp.

Easing himself out of bed, he felt momentarily light-headed and unsteady. His bladder ached painfully. When he was sure he could navigate, he took an old terry-cloth robe draped over one of the chairs and shrugged it on.

Stepping into the cabin's spacious living room, he saw Gruff Ryan curled up on the couch near the fireplace. The man's chest rose and fell in a steady rhythm. He crept to what he thought was another bedroom and peered inside. Roberta, burrowed under the heavy covers of a massive bed, was also soundly asleep.

For an instant, he thought of going to her, slipping between the sheet and gently rousing her. But he was too damned beat up and she needed the sleep.

A clock ticking quietly on the mantle told him it was just after four. He'd slept another 12 hours.

In the bathroom, Morgan stood in front of a full-length mirror mounted on the back of the door and opened his robe. He studied his body with a critical eye. His ribs were still heavily taped and beneath the tape he could see the large bandages covering the wounds on his chest. His legs and arms were a mass of purple-blue bruises and minor scratches. His face was haggard and thinner than he remembered. Dark circles stood out starkly beneath his hollow, lackluster eyes.

"Who said you looked like death taking a shit?" he mumbled at his reflection. "You look worse. Roll out the casket."

In the small kitchen, Morgan opened the refrigerator and began rummaging for food. After stacking packages and jars on the table, he built two huge salami sandwiches.

"Eat your heart out, Dagwood," he said, washing down a mouthful of sandwich with a swallow of cold milk.

Just as he finished eating, he caught movement outside the small kitchen window. Instantly, his muscles tensed. Sucking in a deep breath, he edged to the glass and peered into the winterscape. The snow was blue-white in the light from the quarter moon and the trees were dark and barren. Nothing moved.

Was it one of those flying monsters? The question traced a hot, frightening welt through his mind and he felt cold sweat trickling down his back. It seemed unlikely. Other than Doc Reed, no one knew where they were hiding. The creatures were powerful and possessed a cunning, animal intelligence, but he doubted they could so easily locate them.

He considered waking Gruff, but to what end? The man was exhausted.

Morgan again stared out into the night. Still, nothing moved save the dark snow clouds boiling above the treetops to the west.

"You're spooked, Blaylock," he whispered to himself, deciding the movement had either been a reflection on the glass or a phantom in his own, jittery mind.

Too bed-weary to seek further sleep, Morgan returned to the bathroom for a hot shower. In the bedroom, he found his clothes freshly washed and hanging in the closet. Dressed, he returned to the living room, turned on a dim lamp and quietly placed wood on the dying fire.

He pulled an old rocker close to the fireplace and sat there brooding.

What to do next? Roberta had been right: Case had made them fugitives. He weighed their options. They could try to contact a law enforcement agency other than the FBI. Maybe the Colorado Bureau of Investigation or even the sheriff in the next county. But none of those ideas seemed viable. Not now. It wouldn't be so bad if Morgan hadn't been accused of killing Red. No one would listened to a cop killer.

What would the fictional Jackson Black Cloud do in this situation? Morgan mused ruefully, absently wondering if they'd let him write the novels in prison. If he was ever brought to trial. If he wasn't dead.

The rising howl of the wind roused him from his morose introspection and he got up to look out the window. As he was clearing a spot on the frosted pane, Gruff groaned and sat up on the couch. He rubbed his eyes with the heels of his hands and then looked at Morgan.

"What're you doin' outta bed?"

"I think I've had enough sleep. Sorry if I woke you."

"You didn't," Gruff breathed. "Damned wind. Sounds like all hell's breakin' loose out there."

"Yeah. It's picking up, going to be a rough one," Morgan said, turning away from the window. "I guess we're as safe here as anywhere."

Gruff Ryan got up and stretched, joints popping and snapping. "Jesus, ya turn forty and your body starts fallin' apart."

"Kill all the men and screw all the women," Morgan muttered.

Gruff shot him curious frown. "What?"

Morgan laughed softly. "That's what ol' Jackson Black Cloud would do in this situation. That's his style. Take no prisoners, leave no virgins."

Gruff continued to eye him suspiciously. "You get into Doc's hooch or did you just knock your brain funny up on that damned mountain?"

For some reason, the comment struck Morgan as hysterically funny and, unable to suppress it, he belly-laughed until tears streamed down his face.

"Maybe I should be a comic," Gruff said as he joined in.

They hooted and whooped until Roberta, blurry-eyed and confused, appeared behind them. "Can anyone join this club or is it just for insomniacs and lunatics?"

Morgan continued to chuckle as he looked at her sheepishly and wiped tears from his cheeks. "Sorry. We woke you, huh?"

She summoned a sour expression and folded her arms. "No, I always get up when I hear the loons crow."

"Loons . . . don't crow," Gruff panted, struggling to catch his breath.

She turned back toward her bedroom. "My point exactly."

Gruff started to say something in reply when the window behind Morgan exploded in a shower of glass and snow and a dark, winged shape crashed into the room.

Chapter Sixteen

In one heart-stopping instant of chaos, the creature was in their midst.

With a sweep of a powerful membranous wing, it sent the offending lamp tumbling to the floor. Now illuminated only by the flickering fire, it hissed and screamed at the frightened trio of humans.

Roberta stifled a cry as Gruff vaulted the couch, lunging for one of the shotguns near the front door. Morgan dived to the floor with an painful grunt, and rolled away from slashing talons that still managed to raked his back.

"Morgan . . . !" Roberta yelled in warning as the thing advanced on him; its inhuman yellow eyes glistened in the dim light. Morgan was scrambling to his feet as the creature's head darted at him with the speed of a striking snake. Fangs snapped shut scant inches from his face.

In Roberta's bedroom, another window exploded and a second creature lurched into the cabin. Acting almost instinctively, Roberta banged the bedroom door shut.

Heavy furniture in the room crashed into the wall and then the door was ripped from its hinges in a cacophony of splintering wood and tortured metal.

"Roberta!" Gruff yelled from behind the couch, a shotgun jammed against his shoulder. "Get down!"

She dove for cover as Gruff squeezed the trigger. At the same instant, the creature ducked back into the bedroom. Buckshot splintered the door frame.

Roberta scrambled around the couch to join Gruff.

The creature pursuing Morgan cornered him in the kitchen. It crouched low, blocking the back door. Its black tongue flicked over its fangs as if already tasting his hot blood.

Morgan stared into the hideous face, as his hands groped frantically for anything to use as a weapon. The monster's lipless mouth spread in a grotesque parody of a grin. Its eyes glowed with bloodlust and triumph.

In the living room, Gruff and Roberta waited for their attacker to reappear at the bedroom door. Hands sweaty and slick, Gruff's finger quivered on the shotgun's trigger.

At their back, there was a tremendous thud and the front door was staved in. A heavy, jagged chunk of broken timber slammed into Gruff's back. The shotgun flew from his hands, spinning over the couch, hitting the floor and erupting with an explosive tongue of fire.

Roberta screamed as yet another of the bat creatures crossed the threshold. In a fraction of a second, she saw the blood welling around a dagger of wood protruding from Gruff Ryan's back and saw the creature lurching toward her.

Roberta threw herself backward and rolled, trying to get the couch between herself and her pursuer.

Ignoring Ryan, the creature glared at Roberta. Its tongue flickered and saliva drooled from its open jaws. She gasped when she saw the erect member jutting from between its fragile legs.

The Devouring

Now the creature in the bedroom stepped into the guttering firelight, its black shadow dancing over Roberta. It too studied her, something dark and evil flaring in its large eyes. It snarled a warning at its companion. The other creature's head snapped to the side, fangs flashing.

In the kitchen, Morgan watched as the bat creature advanced. The talons on the end of its long, finger-like toes clicked on the wooden floor. He saw the thumb and forefinger on its wing/arm open and close in anticipation. Its foul, fetid breath, smelling of blood and rotted meat, washed over him.

His hands groped blindly on the countertop, searching for a weapon. He retreated into a corner, his back touching the rough logs. From the living room, he could hear other creatures snarling and growling.

Morgan couldn't allow himself to think about what was happening in there.

The creature's powerful leg muscles bunched beneath its leathery hide.

Morgan's left hand touched the wooden handle of a knife and his fingers curled around it.

The creature sprang.

Morgan ducked, bringing the long, wide blade slashing up and out. The creature's weight and momentum slammed him back against the wall, but as he was driven down, he felt the leather hide yield with a sickening ripped.

The creature's howl was high and pained. It sprang back, its right wing partially opened. A long, bloody rip, like a tear in a sail, split the leathery membrane. Screaming and howling, it eyed its wound and then snarled at Morgan.

Gasping for breath, fighting a dizzying wave of nausea, Morgan sensed his opening. He pushed off the wall, shifting the knife to his right hand. The creature snapped its jaws at him, tried to move aside and then lashed out with one powerful, taloned foot.

Morgan sidestepped and the beast's foot only brushed his thigh. He feigned to his left and as the creature moved to defend a second attack, Morgan threw his weight to his right and drove the knife through the tough, furry hide and into the massive chest.

This time, the bat creature's scream was piercing, an undulating death wail. It lashed out blindly with its feet, slammed its flexing wings into the countertop, smashing dishes and scattering jars. The wall phone clattered to the floor. Thick, black blood splattered the walls as it poured from the raw, ragged wound. Frantically, fruitlessly, the creature's fingers clawed and clutched at the knife's hilt buried in its chest.

Morgan backed away, watching in sick fascination as the thing slammed its head into the wall and left a dark smudge on the logs. He saw the yellow eyes momentarily flare with utter hatred and rage, and then dim, growing lackluster as the creature's life fluids pooled on the floor.

Meanwhile, in the living room the two creatures cornering Roberta had continued to snap and growl at each other as they advanced on her. Then the larger of the pair, the one from the bedroom, turned and rushed at the other. It met the charge and they clashed amid flashing teeth and talons.

A second later, the high, keening death wail issued from the kitchen, but the pair in the living room were too intent on their brief but savage rivalry to notice.

As they clashed, Roberta pounced on the shotgun lying in front of the couch. Her foot tangled on the corner of a throw rug and she pitched headlong on the wooden floor, the gun a foot from her outstretched fingers.

Then the smaller creature howled, its shoulder suddenly bloodied by sharp fangs. It backed away, its erection dwindling as its long tongue licked at its own blood.

The victor, towering above Roberta, made a guttural sound deep in its throat, a sound like a maniacal chuckle.

The long, clawed toes on one foot grabbed her leg and held it fast. She cried out as sharp talons sank into her flesh.

The creature bent over, its wings rustling as its fingers took hold of the terry-cloth robe and yanked her to her feet. Desperately, she struggled, but was drawn back against the creature's hard body. Its wings began to fold around her. . . .

Panting from pain and exertion, Morgan, dashed into the living room, startling both the bat creatures. He took in the scene in one glance and jumped for one of the shotguns.

The thing licking at its wound, standing near the smashed front door, made a move toward him, while the one embracing Roberta screeched at its companion.

Morgan scooped up the shotgun, pumped a shell into the chamber, whirled and fired at the smaller bat creature. But Morgan was off balance and his aim was poor. The brunt of the blast missed the thing's face by inches, and only a few stray pellets furrowed bloody grooves across its already bleeding shoulder.

The beast howled.

Again pumping the weapon, Morgan crouched. He held it aimed at the now-unmoving monster. Something flickered in its eyes.

"Kiss your fuzzy ass good-bye," he hissed, but he refused to fire for fear the other creature would retaliate against Roberta.

For several heartbeats neither creature moved. A log popped in the fire sending a shower of sparks up the flue. Icy wind and snow billowed into the room through the broken window and door.

Still held firmly by the thing, Roberta was trembling violently. Hot breath washed over her neck, the creature's powerful muscles flexed against her and she felt an intruding hardness pressing against her hip.

Barely conscious, moaning softly, Gruff Ryan groped blindly at the splintered piece of wood buried in his back.

Morgan pressed his advantage, advancing a step toward the smaller creature. It hissed in rage, but stepped back. Its companion screamed and flung Roberta away.

Morgan sensed a measure of victory. They knew he could kill them.

He took another step forward. Again the creature staring down the bore of the shotgun backed away. The other one bared its fangs and hissed, its eyes watching Morgan's every move.

Watching the creature that had released her, fearing it would try to reclaim her, Roberta edged toward Morgan.

Gruff Ryan let out a loud, agonizing cry as his bloodied fingers freed the jagged piece of wood. Both creatures looked toward the injured man. Roberta dashed to the fireplace, pulling off her robe and flinging one end into the crackling fire.

In one blinding, terrifying instant, the larger creature lunged at Morgan, just as he fired the shotgun at the second one. The gun erupted at the same instant a vicious kick caught him in the chest. Again, the blast missed its intended target and tore a ragged, round hole in the plywood ceiling.

Morgan rolled and Roberta threw her flaming robe into the face of the creature that had attacked her. The burning material enveloped the creature's face for an instant. It screamed as the flames sparked in its fur and seared its hide.

Bellowing in pain, it tore the robe free and flung it aside. Wisps of smoke rose from its face as it turned and sprang to the shattered window. The smaller one glared at Morgan for another second, then with a piercing cry wheeled and moved out the door and took wing.

Morgan jumped to his feet and raced to the door. He saw the two creatures soaring into the howling, snowy darkness. A painful scream momentarily echoed and then faded away.

Returning to the living room, he found Roberta kneeling over Gruff. The big man was pale and there were flecks of blood on his lips. He gagged and let loose a wet cough.

"He's badly hurt," she said. "We've got to get him to the hospital."

"I'll call Doc Reed." He looked at Roberta, who was crouching in a nightgown. "You'd better get a blanket or something. You'll freeze."

Hurrying into the bathroom, she grabbed two towels and returned to Gruff. His head wound was oozing blood, but it wasn't deep. The wound in his back, however, was bubbling.

"I think his lung's punctured," she called to Morgan.

Shredding one of the towels, she wrapped it around Gruff's head and pressed the other over the back wound. "Morgan!" she cried. "Tell Doc to hurry!"

In the kitchen, Morgan picked up the phone, praying it still worked. Stepping over the dead creature sprawled in a wide pool of blood, he reattached the phone to the wall. He sighed when he heard the dial tone.

He had to waste precious seconds dialing directory assistance for Dr. Milo Reed's number. After he punched it in, Morgan was mildly surprised when Reed answered on the first ring. Rather than thick with sleep, his voice was hesitant and shaky.

"Gruff's been hurt," Morgan blurted out. "He's in bad shape. We need to get him to the hospital." The words came out in a breathless rush.

There was a long pause.

"I . . . can't help, Morgan." The dejected, defeated note in the doctor's voice sent an icy spasm through Morgan's stomach.

"What? What are you saying . . . ?"

There was a commotion on the other end, and then another, sickeningly familiar voice came on the line.

"I'm impressed, Blaylock," Richard Case said. "Very impressed. I thought you'd be dead by now."

"You bastard!" Morgan hissed through clenched teeth, his fingers gripping the telephone so hard they ached.

"All a matter of perspective, Blaylock. When I hang up, I'll call the sheriff's department. They'll love it. They can get the guy who killed two of their own." Case chuckled.

"Listen," Morgan said, fighting to keep his voice level, his temper in check. "If you let Doc come out here to take care of Ryan, I'll turn myself in to you, to anybody you say."

Again, Case laughed. "That's funny, Morgan. Very funny." His voice suddenly became steel-hard and steady. "What do you take me for? A fool? I've known where you were hiding since last night."

"Then why didn't you just come here and kill us?" Morgan demanded.

There was a grunt. "I wanted our winged friends to take care of the matter for me. It seemed so . . . poetic. Unfortunately, I have to assume they failed."

"Seems so," Morgan spat. His eyes strayed to the dark, ugly body near his feet. "We didn't."

"What does that mean?"

"We killed one, Case," he answered, suddenly inspired. It was a long shot, but better than nothing.

"You're lying, Blaylock." There was a nasty sneer in Case's voice. "You haven't got the stones to kill one of those things."

"Tell you what, Case. You let Reed come out here with an ambulance for Ryan and I won't pour gasoline over this dead body and torch it."

There was a pause. Morgan heard Case breathing heavily, no doubt weighing his options.

"Why don't I just come out there and see for myself?"

Morgan smiled. This just might work. "No dice, Case. Here's how we'll play it. I'll drag the body outside, douse it and wait with a pack of matches. If the ambulance arrives, with just the paramedics and Reed, then the body's yours. If you show up before the ambulance is clear of the cabin . . . poof! One barbecued bat. Got it?"

Another pause.

"Okay, Blaylock. But if this is a trick, I'll cut your—"

Morgan banged the phone down and hurried back into the living room.

Gruff was still lying on his stomach. Roberta had covered him with two heavy comforters and placed his head on a pillow. Her hand was under the covers, holding the compress on his wound. His shallow breathing was raspy and wet.

Wrapped in a blanket, Roberta was gazing out the ruined door. Her face was etched with fatigue and worry.

"How is he?" Morgan asked, kneeling beside her, slipping an arm around her shoulder. He felt her stiffen.

"Not good," she answered haltingly, her voice flat, emotionless.

"Are *you* okay?"

"Just afraid."

"Me too."

"Is Reed coming?" Roberta asked.

Morgan sighed. "Yeah."

She turned and looked into his face. "What it is? What's wrong?"

Morgan looked away.

"Morgan?" There was a trace of the old fire in her voice now.

He told her about the deal with Case.

"Are you crazy?" she demanded, now angry. "He'll never keep his part of the bargain. You know that!"

"I was thinking about Gruff. I don't want him to die because I . . ." He paused, shrugging.

She continued to stare at him.

"Get dressed," he told her. "I want you to leave here. There are snowshoes on the back porch, skis if you prefer. I want you to get out of here before Case arrives."

Streaks of color bloomed in cheeks and her eyes grew hard. "That's bullshit. I'm not leaving."

He took her shoulders in his hands. "I didn't cut the deal so Case could get both of us."

"Oh, Christ, how damned noble!"

Morgan released her and stood, turning his back.

After a long silence, punctured by Gruff's occasional groan, she whispered his name. "Aren't we in this together?" she asked.

He turned, glancing down at her. "I don't want you hurt. I don't want Case to get you."

She reached upward, touching her fingers to his. "And I don't want him to get you either."

Staring into one another's eyes, Morgan again knelt and pulled her close.

How quickly he had become committed to this woman.

Too bad they'd never have a chance to explore their relationship. Other than his decidedly iffy gambit, Morgan saw no way out for either of them.

"I love you," Roberta whispered, her head pillowed on his shoulder.

"And I you," he breathed, squeezing her close. Then, quite gently, he stood. "That's why I want you to leave. Now. Why should both of us be in jeopardy?"

She shook her head. "You don't understand. I *love* you. I don't want to be separated from you. If we have to deal with Case, then I want us to do it together."

"Please," he said.

Roberta shook her head. When she spoke, her voice was firm and steely. "No *macho* nonsense, Morgan. No asinine chivalry. We're in this together, we'll get out of it together."

In the distance, came the staccato whine of a siren.

"Besides," she said in forced joviality, "our company is almost here." She pulled back the comforters and peered at the wound in Gruff's back. "It's not bleeding too badly now. I'm going to get dressed." She stood and retreated into the bedroom. A moment later, as Morgan was heading toward the kitchen and the dead creature, he heard her curse. She appeared at the doorway, a disgusted look on her face.

"What?" he asked anxiously.

"One of those bastards shit in here!"

Morgan shook his head, remembering the guano they had found in the NORAMS station. "Must be a sign of disrespect."

"Terrific," she grumbled.

Gruff Ryan moaned softly and Morgan saw his friend's eyes flutter open. He went to him and knelt.

"Can you hear me?" Morgan asked.

"Yeah," he replied in a barely audible whisper. "Ain't I dead yet?"

"No. And you won't be. You'll be fine," Morgan said, trying to sound more confident than he felt.

"Then why do I feel like somethin' my dog coughed up?" His mouth twitched at his attempted joke.

"Hang on, pal," Morgan said. "The doctor's on his way."

"Good," Gruff sighed. "Tell him I need drugs. Lotta drugs."

Morgan made certain his friend was well covered, then pulled on his parka and hurried into the kitchen. He pulled on a pair of heavy gloves, then grimaced and picked up the body of the dead creature. It reeked with a rancid and sour odor, the smell of the cavern.

Carrying it through the living room, he went outside. He moved to the end of the porch and placed the creature on the ground. Snow quickly started covering the dark form.

The siren was closer now, near the turnoff leading to the cabin.

Moving quickly, Morgan went to Gruff's truck parked behind the cabin and found a can of gas. Then he stood over the corpse, ready to douse it. If push came to shove, would he actually burn this thing? From a scientific point of view, it was of incredible value. Destroying it would be tantamount to destroying some rare archaeological find. Would he burn the Dead Sea Scrolls or smash the Rosetta Stone?

Yes.

If burning this creature could save Roberta's life and his own, or at least buy them more time, he'd do it without hesitation. Case had to know he wasn't bluffing.

He poured the gas over the inert form.

As he returned to the cabin for matches, Morgan wondered if Case would simply have a sharpshooter ready to kill him once he was stationed above the body? The snow would make a clear shot difficult, but not impossible. Who could say what kind of high-tech sighting devices Case had at his disposal? Hell, he had helicopters and rocket launchers. How much trouble could there be in securing some super-sophisticated infrared scope?

Not much.

It was a chance Morgan would have to take.

In the kitchen, he found a book of matches and an old rag. He hurried into his bedroom and pulled a blanket from the bed, promising himself to buy Doc Reed a new one. Assuming, of course, Morgan lived long enough to get to a white sale.

Outside, Morgan could see the refracted lights of the ambulance, its red and blue lights streaking across the swirling white. It was near the top of the hill separating the cabin from the highway.

Morgan waited. He noticed footprints, now half covered with drifting snow, running along the side of the cabin. They weren't his and were too big to be Roberta's. They could be Gruff's, but Morgan was sure he hadn't come outside during the night. These prints had to have been made recently.

Glancing toward the oncoming ambulance lights, he turned and quickly followed the tracks to the rear of the house below the window to the bedroom Roberta had used. They mingled with the fresher, more distinctive prints left by the bat creature.

Morgan found a small plastic box, almost covered in snow, fixed to the sill. Retrieving it, Morgan swore vehemently. It was another transmitter.

"I *did* see someone out here," he muttered.

The ambulance was almost to the cabin. Pocketing the device, Morgan trotted back to the front, took the rag and tied it around a broom handle. He splashed gas on it and struck a match. The makeshift torch flared, surrounding Morgan in a yellow circle of flickering light.

A moment before the big, four-wheel drive ambulance slid to a stop, Morgan tossed the blanket over the corpse. He wasn't interested in explaining the creature to the paramedics.

Morgan tensed as the ambulance doors swung open and people climbed out. In the flashing lights, he couldn't determine if Case was among them.

Doc Reed and two paramedics hurried toward the cabin.

"What's with the torch?" one of the paramedics asked. "A signal beacon?" He glanced at the covered form. "That for us?"

Morgan shook his head. "Forget this one. Take care of my friend inside."

The guy eyed the covered body suspiciously for another instant, then nodded and followed his partner into the cabin. Roberta met them at the door.

"Sorry you're mixed up in this, Doc," Morgan said to Reed.

The old doctor grunted. "Not your fault. Case is, in clinical terms, off the fuckin' deep end."

"How'd he know you had us up here?"

Reed blew out a long breath, a cloud of steam enveloping his face. "I think he used a little deductive reasoning. Figured out who'd be likely to help you and came up with me. Bastard showed up at my house, put a gun to my head, and I spilled my guts." A dejected look passed over the doctor's round, fleshy features.

"Better than getting killed, Doc. A lot better," Morgan told him.

"Doesn't make me feel any less guilty."

"Looks like he's keeping his end of the bargain," Morgan said.

"He is. When you told him about this"—Reed nudged the body with his foot—"he got pretty excited. He believed that you would destroy it."

"He has reason to worry," Morgan said. "I half expected to catch a sharpshooter's bullet standing here."

"Don't think it didn't cross his mind," Reed said emphatically. "But I don't think he wanted to take the chance."

Just then one of the paramedics appeared in the cabin door. "Hey, Doc, you better have a look."

Clutching his medical bag, Reed went across the porch. He glanced at his smashed door and then went inside.

Morgan remained with the body, the torch flaring in the storm.

Ten minutes later, the paramedics brought out Gruff. He was strapped on a gurney. An IV tube snaked out of his arm to a plasma bottle held in the air by one of the medics. They loaded him into the ambulance.

"See you later, Doc," one called to Reed as he stood on the porch. The driver wheeled the ambulance around and, tires spinning on the slick driveway, roared away.

"Why're you staying?" Roberta asked, walking up behind the doctor.

"That's the way Case wanted it," Reed answered bitterly.

"Why?"

The portly doctor flashed her a grim smile. "He has a little project for me."

Morgan started to say something further when he saw a figure appear on the far end of the porch. His gut tightened. Was it one of the creatures, back to finish what they'd started? But then he saw the big automatic leveled at Roberta.

"Toss the torch down, Blaylock," Case called. "Or you can keep yourself warm with her obituary."

Roberta and Reed both whirled around when they heard Case.

Morgan tossed the torch into the snow, where it hissed and flickered out.

"Good boy," Case said with a sneer. "Now get inside." He stood back as first Roberta, then the doctor and finally Morgan trooped into the cabin. At that moment, a truck came roaring down the road.

"Hands on top of your heads," Case ordered. He remained in the doorway, holding the gun on them, until the truck stopped and armed men, led by Nias, appeared.

The FBI man relaxed. "Okay. You can sit down now." His four men, weapons filling their hands, positioned themselves around the room.

"Now, Doctor," Case said, smiling wolfishly at Reed. "Shall we bring our guest of honor in from the cold?"

Reed glowered. "You're calling the shots."

"Damned right I am." He motioned to Nias and one of the other men. "Bring it in." They nodded and hurried outside.

Case glanced around the room. He noted the hole in the ceiling, the broken window, the smashed doors and scattered furniture. "Some party, eh, Blaylock?"

Morgan stood, ignoring the gunman nearest him who raised his .38, and reached into his pocket. "Don't worry, *Dick,* I haven't got a gun. Just something that belongs to

269

you." He pulled out the broken transmitter and tossed it on the floor at Case's feet.

"That's how they found us," he said acidly. "That's why Crocker ended up smashed on a rock and why the Pruett woman is . . ." He choked on the thought and then continued. "Why she's being held by those monsters."

Case leaned against the wall and nodded, smiling with condescension. "Very good, Blaylock." His voice hardened. "What's your point?"

"That's why they killed Red, isn't it? There was probably a transmitter in his car. And your man in the hospital. There was probably one in his room." Morgan watched as the two men keeping them covered frowned.

Case remained against the wall. A crooked smile twisted his lips. "Oh, you are something. You're right about the station and Crumley and the cabin. But"—he glanced at his subordinates—"as for my companion in the hospital. You're wrong. I don't know why it came there and killed him."

Morgan knew Case was lying. He could see it in his eyes. The lie was for the benefit of his men.

"What threat was Red Crumley to you?" Morgan demanded.

Case shook his head almost sadly. "He was a cop, Blaylock. He knew too much. I had to stop him before he told the whole fuckin' world about this little mystery."

"And McKissik?"

Case shrugged. "He was a waste of humanity. Besides, I needed him to really tie up the case against you. And guess what? It worked."

"I suppose you killed Jasper yourself?" Morgan asked.

"Killing him was easy. The rest . . . well, it was unpleasant. Now let's quit playing games, shall we?"

At that moment Nias and the other man came in carrying the still-covered body. Nias had heard his boss confess to having killed McKissik and glanced at Morgan in confusion. Morgan hoped he was remembering their conversation in the hotel room; remembering Morgan's denials.

"Put it on the table," Case ordered, motioning toward the old dining room table against one wall.

Morgan looked at Reed questioningly.

The doctor raised an eyebrow. "Autopsy."

"Here?" Roberta blurted out. She studied Case. "Why don't you just pack it in ice and ship it off to whoever you work for?"

Something dark passed across the man's face. "What I do or don't do is no concern of yours," he snapped.

"Richard," she said, her voice tightly controlled and very steady, "how can expect to get away with all of this? How can you possibly think you won't be caught?"

The twisted smile returned. "Because by the time anyone figures out what's been going on, I'll be long gone. Out of the country, out of sight and very safe." He turned to the doctor. "Let's get started, shall we?"

Reluctantly, Reed pushed his bulk out of the chair and picked up his medical bag. He looked at Case. "Too bad we aren't in a lab. What I learn from doing this autopsy here will be nothing compared to what will be lost by not having the proper equipment and facilities."

Case clicked his tongue and shook his head. "That's too bad, Reed. I always want to advance the cause of science. But circumstances being what they are"—again his voice grew hard and his eyes flinty—"just cut the son of a bitch open, okay?"

Chapter Seventeen

Dr. Milo Reed insisted the table be moved into the cabin's kitchen. He set several lamps and mirrors around the room in an effort—reminiscent of Thomas Edison's efforts a century before, Morgan noted—to intensify the light.

In addition to the rancid odor from the creature, the room stank of gasoline and blood. In spite of the snow and cold already whistling through the cabin, in an effort to ventilate the area Reed opened the window above the sink.

If anything, the harsh glare of the lights intensified the creature's repulsive countenance. Its face was distinctly bat-like, yet remarkably human in some of its qualities. Its large eyes, now closed in death, sat low at the base of the broad forehead, just to either side of its squashed, pug nose. Exposed in the lipless mouth, the twin rows of razor-sharp fangs still glistened in the light.

Everyone in the room stood breathlessly, waiting for Reed to begin. The doctor pulled the kitchen knife out of the monster's chest with a wet sucking sound. Then, scalpel poised in his meaty hand, he lowered his surgical mask and scanned the onlookers.

"This is probably going to create quite a stench. I just want to warn you." With that, he pushed the sharp blade into the creature's left shoulder and, finding the hide tougher than human flesh, sawed a diagonal cut to just below the creature's stomach. He repeated the procedure from the right shoulder. At the intersections of the two incisions, Reed cut straight down to the pubic area forming a large Y on the body.

"I'll worry about the head later," Reed muttered.

"Don't talk, Reed," Case growled. "Just work."

The doctor nodded mutely and continued. He poked his gloved fingers through cuts, and again there was a wet, slurping sound as he folded back the fur-covered flesh to expose the creature's glistening viscera.

True to Reed's warning, the smell of gasoline was overwhelmed by a sickly sweet stench. Roberta gagged and Morgan covered his mouth. The doctor seemed unaffected.

"Interesting," he muttered, studying the organs. "Very similar to humans." When he began cutting out the heart, it was too much for Roberta. She and Morgan retreated to the living room. Nias, his big face pale, seemed relieved to follow them.

"They're such an anomaly," Roberta said. "So alien, yet so much like us. It's . . . almost frightening."

"Frightening?" Case asked sardonically, walking up behind the pair. "Strange perhaps, bizarre even, but not frightening." He fixed Morgan with a steely gaze. "I hope you appreciate what I did for you."

Morgan scowled. "Yeah, you're a regular Mother Teresa."

"I let your friend Ryan leave here," Case said indignantly. "Frankly, after what he did to me in the mountains, I'd as soon let him die." The FBI agent's face grew dark with memory. "He destroyed a helicopter and stranded us up there for most of the day. Believe me, when the time comes, I'll kill him."

"It's a two-way street, Dick," Morgan said evenly. "You just lost a battle, that's all." He let a smile touch his mouth, gratified to see the FBI agent's frown.

Case rubbed his face wearily. He looked tired, his eyes red-rimmed and bloodshot. When he lowered his hand, his eyes were large, the whites showing all around the dark pupils. "Yes, a battle. But not the war, Blaylock. Not the fucking war!"

"What war are we talking about?"

The man shook his head. "The one I'll be winning today." He gestured vaguely toward the mountains. "Up there."

"Richard," Roberta said quietly, wary of the fanaticism in the man's voice and the madness in his eyes, "you can't be thinking of going after those . . . things?"

He glared at her. "Of course. And not just me. All of us. You and Blaylock too."

Morgan tensed. "No way we're going back up there."

Case turned, shoved his face close to Morgan's. "Really? I think you're wrong." His hand shot out and roughly grabbed Roberta's arm and jerked her away from Morgan. "I think if you don't, Ms. Ferris is going to have a very unpleasant time. Do you understand me? Very unpleasant."

For several seconds, their eyes locked. They stared at each other, as if peering beyond the outer shell and into one another's soul. Case's hand tightened on Roberta and she grunted in pain.

Morgan's face grew hard.

"Do we understand each other?" Case demanded again.

"Let her go," Morgan snapped. "You've made your point."

With the speed of a snake, Case released Roberta and flicked his wrist, backhanding her across the mouth. As

Morgan started to reach for Case, Nias pressed cool steel against the back of his head.

"Don't give me a reason," Nias hissed.

Morgan eased back and knelt beside Roberta, who was dabbing at blood from her split lip.

"You okay?" he asked.

"Yes." She shot Case a withering look.

Morgan turned to Nias, but nodded his head toward Case. "He's the one who hacked up McKissik. Not me."

"Shut up, Blaylock!" Case snarled. He looked at Nias. "Have you checked on the helicopter?"

Nias nodded. "It'll be here in half an hour."

"Good."

Morgan stood, helping Roberta to her feet. "You really think you can kill all of these things?" he asked Case.

Case rubbed his face. "Kill them? Hell, we're going to take them alive. Dead"—he motioned toward the kitchen door—"they're only so much meat to be carved on. But alive . . ." He stopped.

"But alive they're what?" Roberta prompted. Case looked at her and smiled.

"They're worth twice their weight in gold."

Morgan shook his head. None of this was about stopping the killing. It was about money. Pure, simple greed. He'd suspected as much.

"Who'd you sell out to, Dick?" he asked.

"Not your worry, Blaylock. You just think about staying alive."

Morgan all but laughed. "If I were you, going up after those things, that's what I'd be worried about too."

"Then we both can worry, asshole!" Case turned and returned to the kitchen. Nias continued to hold his gun on Morgan and Roberta.

"Relax, Nias," Morgan said easily. "You act like your shorts are riding up your ass."

"Keep quiet," Nias barked.

"Sure," Morgan said. "Just remember what I told you in the hotel. Remember who turned McKissik into hamburger."

Nias flushed. He gestured toward the couch with his gun. "You two just sit down and keep your mouths shut!"

Gladly they sat, Morgan slipping his arm around Roberta's shoulders, pulling her close. Nias pulled a chair up and sat opposite them.

After almost half an hour of stony, uncomfortable silence, one of Case's men went outside. Morgan stood, ignoring Nias's scowl, and watched the man light several flares, positioning them around the broad, flat area just beyond the driveway. Within moments, he heard the deep *thump-thump* of a helicopter.

"Their nervous system may not be that much different from ours," Reed said, walking out of the kitchen with Case. The doctor was wiping his hands on a towel. "It's possible you could render them unconscious with a tranquilizer. However . . ."

Morgan and Roberta watched the pair.

Case glanced at Reed. "What?"

The rotund doctor turned to the FBI agent. "You'll be running a serious risk. You don't know their metabolic rate. You might kill all of them."

"Let *me* worry about that, Reed." Case turned away from the doctor and went to a window. "Excellent. Right on time." He turned to the others. "I suggest you get ready. We're heading into the mountains in ten minutes. Nias, keep an eye on Blaylock and dear Ms. Ferris. Doctor, you can help the others get our little dissected friend ready to load."

"You're not really serious about going up there in this storm?" Morgan asked.

Case smiled. "Of course. I haven't time to wait it out. Now either get on your winter gear or wear what you've got on."

276

Morgan looked at Roberta and shrugged. She nodded, and they went to find their snowsuits and other cold-weather clothing. Nias kept them company.

Five minutes later, they were ready.

Outside, the big helicopter—Morgan believed it was the same one used when his vehicle was destroyed—sat, illuminated by flares and its own running lights. Its whirling blades were slicing and swirling the snow.

"What are we going to do?" Roberta asked as they watched two of Case's men carry the now-wrapped corpse of the bat creature out of the cabin.

"I'm not sure," he whispered, conscious of Nias standing several feet away. "But we've got to figure out something pretty damned fast. Between the storm, Case and our mountain friends, our survival rate doesn't look promising."

Roberta nodded. "If we could get a gun . . ."

"Hey," Nias barked, moving his bulky frame closer to them. "Knock it off."

Morgan turned and smiled at him. "Always the lively conversationalist, aren't you?"

"Shut up, asshole."

Morgan winked at Roberta. "He's got such a command of the language. It makes me shiver."

A scowl crossed Nias's face. "Just give me an excuse . . ."

"Let's go," Case shouted from the doorway. "I want to get out of here before sunrise."

As Roberta and Morgan were about to step out the smashed door, a gunshot cracked. They exchanged worried looks.

"Move," Nias prodded.

Outside, Roberta gasped. Richard Case stood holding a gun. Dr. Milo Reed lay sprawled in the snow at his feet, blood leaking from a hole in the man's forehead. His bulging eyes stared sightlessly into the stormy sky.

The FBI agent glanced at them. "His usefulness was over."

"Christ," Morgan yelled, vaulting off the porch. He stopped when Case leveled the gun at him.

"Like to join him?"

"Kill me and you'll never find those things!"

Case glanced at Roberta knowingly. "Don't bet on it, Blaylock. You'd lose!"

"Morgan," Roberta cried. "Don't . . . !

He turned to her and saw the fear in her eyes. Glancing down at Reed's body, Morgan shook his head sadly. "What a waste."

"Get in the chopper," Case ordered, motioning with his gun.

Morgan and Roberta complied, and were made to take seats in the back. The body of the bat creature, wrapped in black plastic, rested next to them. Nias sat nearby, his gun in his lap.

Case made a gesture to the pilot, and the engines whined and then screamed as the large craft lifted off.

The helicopter moved smoothly through the snowy air for several long minutes. But as it ascended toward the mountain peaks, it began bucking and rocking. The jet engine howled as the pilot struggled against the battering, buffeting winds.

Morgan watched Nias grow pale, his eyes glassy and frightened. The gun wavered in the big man's meaty fist.

When the ship suddenly pitched, listing dangerously, Morgan made his move. His left hand shot out, grabbing for the gun, and he brought his right fist around, landing a haymaker just below Nias's left eye.

The big man squealed as he was driven back against the wall, but his hand remained locked on the gun. He tried to hit Morgan, but the helicopter bucked and they both went tumbling across the seat.

The Devouring

Morgan kept one hand on the gun and his other around Nias's wrist. They struggled and fought, the sounds of their battle lost in the din from the screaming engine.

Trying to gain leverage and force himself down on Nias's chest, Morgan threw his weight forward. His momentum drove Nias's arms back. The gun slammed against an interior support and came free. Morgan grabbed for it just as Roberta screamed and the back of his head exploded. . . .

Morgan was lying on hard, rocky ground when he came around. His face and hands were numb with cold, his eyelashes frosted. Icy froth covered his mouth and the mucus in his nose was stiff. A freight train rumbled threw his head.

"I ought to kill you right now," Nias hissed in his ear.

Morgan opened his eyes and saw a pair of insulated boots inches from his face. Slowly, he pushed himself up.

"Case said to give you these," the big man spat, dropping his gloves and face mask next to him. Morgan groped for them, and slowly, painfully pulled them on.

They were near the peak now. The helicopter was nowhere in sight. Nias held a rifle. His eyes blazed through the slits in his ski mask.

"Get up, asshole!"

Morgan nodded, climbing carefully to his feet. He looked around. They weren't far from the entrance to the tunnel where he had spent the night—so long ago, it now seemed. A large tent had been erected on a level patch of rocky ground. Two of Case's men were clearing a larger area of boulders and large rocks.

Nias motioned toward the tent with the gun. "Case wants to see you."

Morgan stumbled unsteadily toward the tent. Pulling back the flap, he peered into the gloomy interior.

279

"Well, well, well, Blaylock's back among the living once again," Richard Case said sardonically. He and Roberta sat in canvas chairs near a propane-powered heater. "Close the fucking door."

Morgan stepped into the tent and let the flap drop behind him. Pulling off his mask, he looked at Roberta. He saw the worry in her eyes, and then noted the handcuffs that held her wrists together.

"You're lucky, Blaylock," Case said, his expression remaining hard. "I could've blown your head off. If I didn't need to know how to get to those things, I would have."

Ignoring the pain at the back of his head—what the hell was a little more pain?—Morgan forced a smile. "Gosh, Dick, you're a swell guy."

The FBI man made a face. "That's right, Blaylock. Keep playing the role."

Morgan squatted on the ground, rubbing the back of his head.

"Are you okay?" Roberta asked.

"Yeah, I'll live."

"Don't bet money on it," Case muttered.

"I told Richard about the Pruett woman," Roberta said. "I told him what you told me about the cavern."

Morgan nodded. "Good. I'd like to see her out of there."

"Well, then," Case said, sounding quite business-like. "Why don't you tell me how you found those things." As he spoke, he pointed the barrel of his gun at Roberta's temple. She flinched away.

"You don't need to threaten her, Dick," Morgan said evenly. "It's not a state secret."

Case nodded.

"In fact," Morgan continued, relieved to see Case lower the gun, "it was really you who led me to them."

"Really?" Case said, smiling.

"Actually, your rockets."

"Explain."

Morgan did and in detail.

"So," Case said, when Morgan had finished. "Our flying friends have another way in. You found a back door, I take it?"

"Something like that."

Case face grew hard. "Then why don't you tell me where this opening is?"

Morgan chuckled. "You're practically sitting on it."

Case beamed. "I thought returning here would do the trick. You couldn't have gone far the other day. You had to have some kind of shelter." He got up and pulled on his gloves.

"Let's go see this place," he said, motioning Morgan outside with his gun. "Roberta, if you'll promise to be good, I'll let you stay here where it's warm."

She flashed him a nasty look. "Like I'm going to run away."

"Bright girl," he answered, following Morgan out into the raw morning.

The sun was breaking through the clouds. Below, the snowfield was still obscured and the surrounding area looked like a carpet of cotton.

"Where?" Case asked, pulling down his mask and goggles. Morgan pointed to where the rocket had destroyed the small cave.

They made their way to it. Morgan pointed at the skull he had pitched out of the tunnel.

"Very good, Blaylock. You might get to live a while longer at this rate."

"The boulder's been rolled back," Morgan said, indicating the large rock he had moved away from the opening. "They've blocked the entrance."

"Well, let's unblock it, shall we?" Case said, motioning with the gun.

Morgan went to the rock. He saw the scratches in the ground where the creatures' feet had clawed it as they shoved the boulder back in place.

"Do it," Case ordered.

"You're not helping, Dick?"

"Just do it, Blaylock!"

Shaking his head in disgust, Morgan circled his arms around the rock and heaved. The boulder tottered. He sucked in a breath and tried again. His ribs and head were throbbing as his muscles bunched and his boots scraped along the frozen ground. The rock moved and then rolled backward.

"Very good," Case said. He paused. "Jesus, what's that smell?"

Morgan too got a whiff of the foul, fetid air. "Your breath?"

Case started to say something when the roar of the jet helicopter echoed across the valley. Both men glanced into the bright, cold sky.

The helicopter appeared, a large, boxy structure suspended from its midsection.

"What the hell . . . ?" Morgan mumbled.

"Ah," Case cried. "Right on time. Come on, Blaylock, I think you'll appreciate this."

"I'm all goosey, Dick."

The helicopter hovered above the site. Nias held a walkie-talkie, directing the pilot. Other men waited as the cables holding what appeared to be a modular building were uncoiled.

"How the hell did he get it up here in the wind?" Morgan asked, genuinely curious.

"Only from the snowfield, Blaylock," Case said, watching the building descend. "I happen to have a rather nice snow tractor at my disposal. I had the bunker trailered up here early this morning."

"Bunker?"

Case smiled and nodded. "In a manner of speaking. It couldn't withstand a direct assault from those creatures, but then they won't be getting near it."

282

Morgan studied Case. "You're really serious about all this, aren't you?"

Case met Morgan's gaze. "Oh, you have no idea just *how* serious, Blaylock." He motioned with the gun. "Now, you can return to the tent if you like. Just don't try anything cute. If you do, the first bullet goes into Roberta's head."

Morgan obeyed. Inside the relatively warm tent, he removed his mask and gloves.

"How you doing?" he asked the woman.

She smiled at him. "Okay. What's going on?"

He told her.

"He's well financed," Morgan observed. "Helicopters, sophisticated weapons, modular buildings, men. It all costs a lot of money."

"Morgan," Roberta said. "I'm really scared."

He nodded. "I know the feeling."

"No," she said quickly. "I don't mean just about being here. I think . . ."

Morgan sat in the canvas chair next to hers and touched her cheek with his fingers. "What?"

Outside the helicopter roared. They could hear men shouting, and then there was a crunching, grating sound as the modular building was lowered to the frozen ground. In a few moments, the helicopter's thunder grew distant and then faded away completely.

"Richard said something to me after . . . he slugged you," she explained.

"And?"

She looked at him with real fear. "He said he needed me to catch one of . . . those things."

A tight knot formed in the pit of Morgan's stomach. He took Roberta's hand in his own. "I won't let it happen. I promise."

The tent flap was dragged back and Nias walked into the tent, his rifle pointed at them. "Outside."

283

Morgan helped Roberta pull on her mask and gloves and then they followed Nias outside.

Two men were scurrying around the modular building, taking cables bolted into its sides and attaching them to nearby boulders. Morgan noted the powerful spotlights mounted at each of the building's corners.

"Tying it down in case of wind," Richard Case said.

"What's it for?" Roberta asked.

"Shelter. Just basic shelter. Sort of a command post." He gestured out over the cloud-covered snowfield. "There's another building coming up for you."

"Wh . . . what do you mean, Richard?" she asked hesitantly.

"Yeah, Dick," Morgan added. "What's that twisted brain of yours cooked up now?"

The renegade FBI agent glanced first at Morgan and then at Roberta. "I want to catch as many of those things as I can," he said. "And in doing it, I want to make sure none of them are killed or injured if at all possible."

He paused when the helicopter again appeared out of the clouds. It carried yet another, smaller modular building. Case left Morgan and Roberta with Nias and hurried to a spot 50 feet away where two of his men waited for the second structure.

They watched as the helicopter lowered the building and the men began anchoring it to boulders. This one, Morgan saw, didn't sport exterior spotlights.

The helicopter took off and Case returned to the couple.

"There it is," he said to Roberta. "Your new, albeit temporary, home."

She peered at him. "You can't mean what I think you're planning, Richard. It's disgusting!"

Case nodded toward Nias, who in turn stepped closer and pressed the barrel of his rifle against Morgan's back. The FBI agent produced a key and uncuffed Roberta.

The Devouring

"It's really quite simple," he said, reaching in the pocket of his insulated suit and fishing out a small plastic box. "I need to bring those things to us."

"But I showed you how to get into the cavern," Morgan cried, a knot of fear in his stomach. "You can go in there right now. They'll be trapped. They can't come out in the sunlight."

Case nodded. "That's true, Blaylock. I appreciate that you showed me the way in, but don't think for a minute I want to confront those monsters on *their* turf. We'll go in there and have a look around . . . *after* we've got all of them safely imprisoned."

"But the Pruett woman . . . !" Morgan said frantically.

"To hell with her, Blaylock! She's as good as dead now! Maybe, if she's still alive when we decide to check out the cavern, I'll put a bullet between her eyes. Put her out of her misery."

"Bastard!" Roberta screamed.

Case nodded. "I'm sure you'll think even worse of me tonight." He motioned to one of the men near the larger of the two buildings. "Take Ms. Ferris to her new accommodations."

The man grabbed Roberta's arm. She tried to jerk away, but he held firm. Morgan took a step forward, only stopping when Nias jabbed him with the rifle barrel. Case handed the woman's guard the plastic box.

"Be sure to turn it on," he said as the man led Roberta away. He turned back Morgan. "Handy little gadget. Sends out a signal only those critters can hear. I'm not sure if it maddens them with pleasure or pain, but it sure as hell does attract them."

"Don't do this," Morgan hissed.

"I've got to bait the trap," the FBI man answered in mock sincerity.

"You can't use her . . . those things will . . ."

Case nodded. "Precisely." He pointed to the spotlights on the building near them. "Powerful lights. It'll keep

285

them at bay, away from the rest of us. But I'm also afraid they'll stay away from the other building, transmitter or not. So dear Ms. Ferris will be our bait. They want human women, I'll give them one."

"Case . . . !" Morgan screamed.

"Not to worry, Blaylock," Case said nastily. "If my men are worth their salt, they'll drop those things with tranquilizer darts before they have a chance to . . . well, you know."

Morgan glared at Case for another few seconds, then glanced toward Roberta. Her guard was leading her into Case's trap.

"Son of a bitch," he breathed.

Chapter Eighteen

Morgan sat sullenly at the table holding a cup of steaming coffee. With curious detachment, he surveyed his surroundings.

He had to admit the building was an incredible command post, and certainly was more than "basic shelter." It was 20 by 25 feet, and sported fold-down bunks along one wall, a small, propane-powered stove, a self-contained water supply, an array of equipment, including a small radar screen mounted to a counter, and a closet-sized toilet stall. It seemed to be constructed of some tough, lightweight space-age plastic.

They had been inside all afternoon, waiting for sundown. Morgan was restless, caged, but had no choice except to bide his time. Attempting another escape now, trapped on the mountain, would be foolish and suicidal. Besides, how could he hope to overpower Case and his merry little band of goons *and* rescue Roberta *and* still get off the mountain?

Roberta was a pawn in Case's deadly game. Morgan could rail and rave and raise all kinds of hell, but in the end, Case held all the cards.

Morgan knew, only too well, what the creatures would do to her if they managed to get to Roberta.

He shook his head, trying to drive away the dark image of Connie Pruett enfolded in the monster's wings.

The chances were slim that he and Roberta would come out alive. Case's little army had the bearing and cocky confidence of professional soldiers. They sported shaggy hair, tangled beards and an eerie air of men accustomed to violence.

Morgan spent the afternoon trying to gauge them, attempting to ascertain any weaknesses. He listened to their conversation, their jokes, and gradually placed names to faces. Quiet and intense, Tarkington was a powerful man sporting a stark tattoo of a coiled snake on his left cheek. Rosa was small and quick, reminding Morgan of a scurrying alley rat. Little Sam, towering six-four, moved with disarming grace and spoke in a quiet voice. Darkly handsome Dallenbeck, wearing a plastic-encased two of spades on a chain around his neck, displayed a quick temper and *machismo* which Morgan found both cliched and practiced. Sanchez had an ugly white scar running from just above his right eyebrow down the side of his nose, over his lips to the point of his chin. He was anxious and antsy, as if his nerves were frayed. The guy they all called Preacher had eyes that burned with an inner fire bordering on madness. He spent most of his time sprawled on one of the bunks intently reading a well-worn bible.

A real collection of hardcases . . .

Or psychopaths.

Case sat on a chair opposite Morgan, making entries in a small notebook. Nias was on one of the bunks, cleaning his handgun. The other men checked equipment or, save for Preacher, huddled together talking in hushed tones.

"Where'd you find these guys?" Morgan whispered to Case. "Central casting or a psycho ward?"

Case looked up from his notebook and frowned in annoyance. "They're the best, Blaylock. Professionals. Their loyalties are for sale. You pay them enough, and they'll walk through Hell for you."

Morgan smiled crookedly. "That may be exactly what you're asking them to do."

"They can handle it," Case replied dismissively, returning to his notebook.

"You hope."

Case shook his head, but made no reply.

As the sun hovered above the western mountain peaks, an overwhelming sense of apprehension and dread fell over Morgan like a weighty shroud.

"It's time," Case said, closing his notebook. "Nias, you and Tarkington take care of it."

Nias nodded at the tattooed man and, after donning their winter gear, they left the building. As they exited, cold wind rushed in, sucking out the warmth in one huge gulp.

"You might find this amusing, Blaylock," Case said, motioning toward one of the windows.

"I doubt it," Morgan said dryly, getting up and following the FBI agent to the window. He watched as Nias and his companion dragged the body of the dead bat creature a few feet away from the building.

"What're they going to do with that?" Morgan asked as the men pulled off the black plastic and let the wind carry it away.

"Watch," Case answered.

The creature was frozen, its viscera glistening with frost and ice. At some point, its wings had been opened and were now stiff and rigid.

Nias and his companion retrieved a large wooden cross from somewhere and, as Morgan watched in horrid fascination, they placed the bat creature atop it. Using a small sledge hammer and shiny steel spikes, they nailed the thing to the wood. Finished, they lifted it and dropped the lower end of the bizarre crucifix into a pre-dug hole in the frozen ground.

"What's that for, Dick?" Morgan asked. "Playing Pontius Pilate?"

Case almost laughed. "Ah, Blaylock, you do have a twisted mind. Think of it as a scarecrow. With the lights *and* this little display, I think we can keep those things away from us."

Morgan stared at the bat creature hung on the cross. "You're afraid of them, aren't you, Dick? Really afraid."

Case frowned. "I respect them. They're strong and powerful. They've survived for eons." He eyed Morgan. "You *know* what they're capable of. Tell me that last night, when you killed that one, you weren't just lucky."

"I was lucky. That's why coming here was stupid."

Case moved back to the table to retrieve his coffee cup. When he looked at Morgan, there was a disturbing brightness in his eyes and a new intensity in his voice.

"Do you have any idea what those creatures represent? Any idea at all?" he asked.

It was a rhetorical question. Morgan crossed his arms and waited for Case to continue.

"An alternative evolutionary course, Blaylock. Somewhere, in the distant past, those creatures evolved. Humanoid, but not human. For whatever reason, they developed incredible strength, incredible stamina. They've survived for . . . tens of thousands, maybe hundreds of thousands of years! They've never been discovered, never been exposed. Until now! And now, for whatever reason, they've become less discreet, less *invisible*."

Suddenly realizing he was speaking too loudly, Case paused, sipped his coffee and glanced around the room at his men, who in turn lowered their own eyes and returned to whatever they were doing.

The Devouring

"I never got the impression you were such a passionate anthropologist, Dick," Morgan said dryly.

Case glared at him. "What do you know, Blaylock? I've been handling dirty little jobs for Washington for a long time. I've seen too much, done too much. I'm sick of the games, the intrigue, the bullshit! I've put my life—my damned *life*—on the line a dozen times and what's it got me? A lousy pension, if I even live to collect it!"

"How noble," Morgan spat. "You expect me to buy that? You really want me to believe you're some burned-out guardian of freedom who got dumped on by the system? Hell, Dick, you're just another cheap traitor in a suit."

Case glowered. "Really?" He gestured at the dead bat creature hanging frozen on the cross. "Those things represent power, Blaylock. Wealth and power. And a way out! Have you any idea what the *right* people will pay for them? Any idea at all?"

Morgan shook his head. "That's what this is all about? Selling out to the highest bidder?"

Case laughed. "A time-honored American tradition. We all do it. We wheel and deal and negotiate and leverage and frequently worse, to get our piece of the pie. That's what our whole fucking system is about, Blaylock. Power and money. Pimping ourselves to get a crack at the *real* money, the *real* power. You get enough, you have enough and you're fucking invincible, untouchable!"

"So, let me see if I've got this straight," Morgan said, never taking his eyes off Case. "You capture as many of these things as you can, all of them if you're able to, and you sell them to the highest bidder so they can do . . . what? Genetic experiments? Freak shows?"

"Who cares?" Case cried with a dismissive wave of his hand. "Who the hell cares what they do with them? I'm only interested in what they're worth on the open market."

Douglas D. Hawk

Morgan leaned against the wall and shook his head. "So you assembled a small, well-equipped army and went into business."

The FBI agent nodded. "And you know the funny part, Blaylock? Uncle-fucking-Sam is paying for the whole operation! Lock, stock and barrel! You think I don't know what Ferris has been trying to do? Why do you think her boss was suddenly taken ill and then disappeared? Why was she ordered to get off my back?

"Bureaucracy, Blaylock. Pure and simple. If you know how to manipulate the bureaucracy—and believe me, I do—you can accomplish anything. While our few elected officials run around spouting Constitutional this and Bill of Rights that, the bureaucrats *run* the fucking show! No elections, no voter approval. It's all one big Mafia. You learn how it works, recognize the key players, and you can get anything. Anything! But if you get in its way, it'll crush you like an egg. No remorse, no regrets, no apologies. Look at the IRS, the CIA—hell's bells, the FBI. They take guys like you and grind them up every day, just to keep the machinery oiled."

Morgan heaved a sigh. "A very jaded view, Dick. Very twisted."

"You may not like it, you may believe all the pabulum the spin doctors force-feed the country, but it's true and you know it. Either that or you're very stupid and very naive."

They were silent for several long minutes.

"So, Dick," Morgan said finally. "Why have our bat brothers stopped keeping their low profile?"

Case smirked. "Isn't it obvious? No females. No breeding stock. They want to perpetuate the species. So they go after women like Pruett and the one we found with her guts ripped out. They don't want to become extinct."

"You sound as if you think they have more than rudimentary intelligence," Morgan said.

"Don't they?"

Morgan flashed on the grim scene in the cavern. The bat creature holding Connie Pruett had looked at him with an evil, mocking malevolence. It knew it was tormenting the woman and by extension him, and it knew he was powerless to make it stop.

He shrugged. "Maybe they do."

"Of course they do, Blaylock. How could they survive for so long and not have developed intelligence? Not just cunning and survival skills, but real intelligence."

The sun was down now and it was quickly growing dark. One of the men stood and flipped a switch. Lights blazed both inside and outside the building. The creature on the cross was now a dark shadow, a scarecrow backlighted by the powerful spots.

As Nias and Tarkington returned to the building, Morgan glanced outside, saw Roberta's small building still cast in darkness and stepped away from the wall. He turned back to study the FBI agent. He let a smile touch the corner of his mouth. "You know, for all your cynicism, your pity-me martyrdom and your jaded bullshit, you're still just a guy with a small dick, Dick."

Case rose suddenly, spilling his coffee. "Don't push, Blaylock. I can toss you outside and you'll be dead in ten minutes!"

Morgan started to say something, but stopped as a high, undulating cry chilled his blood.

"We got a blip," said Dallenbeck, staring at the small radarscope mounted on one of the counters.

Case shot Morgan a warning look and then stepped to the screen.

"Couple hundred yards away," Dallenbeck told Case without being asked. "It's circling . . . wait! There's a second and third one!"

The FBI agent straightened and offered Morgan a big grin. "Shall we see if our *bait* works?"

Douglas D. Hawk

Morgan swallowed hard and turned to the window. There was still a faint glow on the mountainside from the vanished sun. The darkening sky was now cloudless and clear and as he scanned the peak, he saw a familiar winged shape circling high, like a giant vulture in search of carrion.

A second bat creature appeared, and then a third. Their huge wings and fur-covered bodies were merely black silhouettes against the indigo sky. They swooped and dove and ascended, effortlessly gliding on the frigid currents of air.

"Still only three blips, Case," Dallenbeck said. "And they're still circling. Keeping a safe distance."

"They're studying us," Morgan said flatly.

Case turned to him. "They'll come down." He gestured to Nias. "Get the tranquilizer guns ready. You know where everyone should be positioned."

Nias opened a cupboard and pulled out three large rifles. Morgan had seen forest rangers use tranquilizer guns, but none like these. They were huge. When he saw the cartridges, he understood why. They were twice the size of ordinary ones, and judging by the shell casings, able to deliver a tremendous dose of drugs.

Nias handed one to the Preacher and another to the scar-faced Sanchez.

"Take up your positions," Nias told them as they made final adjustments to their gear and double-checked their weapons. "And watch your asses. You've all seen the videotape. You know what these bastards can do."

They men stepped out into the raw twilight. Wind and ice crystals swirled into the room and again the heat was sucked out. Morgan shivered.

Standing at the window, he watched Nias and the others move steadily away from the building. Sanchez went to the right, Preacher to the left. Moving slowly, they left the circle of light and vanished into the surrounding darkness. Nias moved nearer the crucifix, positioning himself about ten yards to the left of it, his back to the bright light.

In moments, they began radioing in as they assumed their positions.

"Sanchez, position one. Ready."

"Preacher. Position three. I'm set."

"Nias, position two. Ready as I'll ever be."

"You know something, Dick?" Morgan asked. "I think your plan sucks."

"You would, Blaylock."

Morgan turned away from the window. "Seriously. Why are you assuming these bat creatures are going to come down with armed men surrounding the area?"

"They won't know what to expect."

"Wrong!"

Case clamped pressed his lips together. "Why don't you just shut up, Blaylock? Give it a rest."

Morgan was worried. "Listen, Case, you're underestimating those things. You're assuming they don't understand what a rifle is. But they do! Hell, Gruff and I were blazing away at them last night! They know—"

"Shut up!" Case yelled. "Christ, I know what I'm doing!"

Morgan shook his head. Case was going to get his men killed. Their tranquilizer guns might be bigger, but would their darts have much accuracy in this wind? They were good close up, but at a distance . . .

"They're coming in!" growled Rosa at the radar console. "Fast. Damned fast!"

Morgan looked out the window. The quarter moon was just topping the peak, casting the mountainside and the peak in faint, cool light. He saw the three dark shapes dropping out of the sky in a crude V formation. They dove straight down and then veered left.

"Th . . . they're comin' right at me . . . Jesus!" Sanchez screeched over the radio. "They're comin' fast . . . !" The transmission ended with a burst of static and a loud crackle.

Case, already in his insulated snowsuit, bolted for the door. "Damn it! They attacked as a group! I didn't think . . ."

"Case . . . !" Morgan cried as the man dashed outside.

Morgan glanced at the window. What the hell was this madman up to now?

He saw the FBI agent standing at the edge of the bright light, staring at the sky.

"Nias, here!" crackled the speaker. "They've got Sanchez! I . . . I can see one of them carrying him. Shit!"

Morgan craned his neck. He could just make out a dark shape in the moonlit sky. A bat creature, its wings beating hard against the thin air, rose higher and higher. It had Sanchez's shoulders clamped in its taloned feet. The man was thrashing at the creature's body, struggling against the clawed feet.

Case appeared just outside the window. He was gesturing to Nias. The big man nodded, apparently understanding, and aimed his rifle.

Hell of a long shot, Morgan thought.

Nias aimed and fired. The specially prepared tip left a red tracer streak across the sky. At the last possible second, the creature veered away from it. Morgan groaned as it opened its talons and set Sanchez free. The hapless man, clawing at the sky, plunged toward the frozen earth and rocks a hundred feet below.

Morgan turned away, unwilling to watch the man smash against the unforgiving ground.

The bat creature circled, dipped and then dove toward the Preacher. Another of the things, flying inches above the ground, streaked past the building. In one brief instant, Morgan saw its yellow eyes gaze at its crucified brother as its mouth opened in a scream. It turned toward Nias.

"Nias!" Morgan yelled. Rosa and Little Sam, standing next to him at the window, grunted in unison.

"Nias, get down!" Dallenbeck screamed into the radio.

"I'm comin' in!" Nias radioed back.

Morgan watched as the big man turned and started toward the building. Case yelled something at him, motioned for him to stay at his position.

Morgan's head snapped around when he saw a dark, winged shape hurtling out of the sky. It arrowed toward Nias at incredible speed. The clawed feet slashed the air. Nias whirled around, tried to dodge, but too late. The winged creature sank its talons into the man's throat and lifted him into the air as dark jets sprayed across the snow and rock.

Nias struggled, his hulking frame thrashing, his meaty fists lashing out blindly, frantically.

Even as he watched in horror, Morgan realized how amazingly powerful these creatures were. Nias was as big as a pro football lineman and just as solid. That one of these monsters could lift him almost effortlessly underscored their capabilities. Not for the first time, he realized just how lucky he'd been defeating the one at Reed's cabin.

Man and monster vanished into the darkness. Morgan and the others watched, mute and stunned.

Then Nias's body came streaking out of the sky, his snowsuit bright under the harsh lights. His arms and legs still thrashed at the empty air. He smashed on the rocks, bounced like a broken doll and then flopped down the slope.

Morgan turned away from the window.

"Preacher!" Case shouted over the radio, his voice loud and tinny on the speaker. "Get inside. Take cover!"

Case rushed into the building, tearing off his ski mask. "Christ . . . !"

Preacher dashed through the door an instant later, slamming it hard and snapping a heavy lock into place.

"Holy Mary," he panted, his eyes dancing and glistening. "They've come from Hell itself. Satan's angels!"

Morgan and the others turned when they heard Tarkington, now staring out the window, let out a long, low groan.

"Fuckin' monsters!" he snarled.

Morgan stepped to his side and peered into the night. He swallowed hard when saw two of the winged, hunched shapes huddled around Nias's broken body. He watched in horror as one of the things plunged a hooked talon into a staring, sightless eye and fished the orb from its socket. He coughed against the bile suddenly rising to the back of his throat as the creature's tongue flicked the eyeball into its mouth.

"A delicacy, no doubt," Case breathed softly, looking over Morgan's shoulder.

Morgan turned to face the man. "Still think your boys are up to taking these suckers, Dick?"

"Screw you!" Tarkington snarled before Case could answer. "We can handle 'em. Don't think we can't!"

"Doesn't matter what I think," Morgan said bitterly, nodding toward the two creatures. "*They're* your problem, not me."

"They're *your* problem too, Blaylock," Case hissed. "What happens to us, happens to you"—he pointed toward the other modular building—"and to Ferris. Don't forget that."

Morgan started to reply when the building was suddenly, violently rocked by a tremendous blow. Morgan slammed against the wall as Case crashed into him. Tarkington banged into the heavy plexiglass window as Rosa, Dallenbeck and Preacher struggled to keep their balance.

"What the . . . ?"

Another blow smashed the building. A piece of equipment dropped to the floor in a shower of sparks and broken glass.

"Look!" Tarkington yelled. Morgan turned in time to see a dark shape streak out of the sky just before he was tossed to the floor in the aftermath of yet another crashing blow.

"They're comin' after us!" Tarkington cried.

Preacher started strapping on a huge minigun harness. "Satan's beasts are at our door!"

"One of 'em at the other building! Look at that . . . !" Again they were tossed to and fro as the building was slammed.

Terrified for Roberta, Morgan struggled to his knees and looked toward the smaller, lighter structure. One of the creatures was just diving at it. As it neared a wall, it inverted itself, letting its powerful legs ram into the building's tough plastic and fiberglass hull.

Under the blow, the building listed. The cables mooring it to the ground broke free and it began slowly sliding over the loose rock and ice. As it slid, it began rotating ever so slightly.

"Some trap," Morgan snarled, getting to his feet. "They're trying to run us right off the cliff."

Frantically, he grabbed for his snowsuit.

Just then their building was hit again. This time they heard its moorings snap as they were thrown to the front wall. For a long second, the structure tottered on edge and then with a grating screech, it dropped to its side.

Morgan heard someone scream as loose equipment slammed into the surprised men. The lights flickered and went out, plunging them into a frightening darkness.

"We're trapped!" Tarkington yelled. "They've trapped us!"

"The windows," Case cried. "We'll have to go out the windows."

"I'm pinned," Little Sam cried. "The damned console fell on me!"

Others grunted and groaned. Morgan heard heavy objects being shoved aside, heard muttered curses and anguished grunts. In the confusion, he pulled on his insulated suit, mask and gloves.

A light flared. Richard Case, standing amid a tangle of wires, broken glass and smashed equipment, held a battery-powered lantern high above his head.

"Get your shit together!" he shouted. "We've got to take these bastards . . . !"

Case slammed into what had been the ceiling as the building was again assaulted.

Morgan's heart raced as the building began grinding over the rocky escarpment, picking up speed as it shuddered and bounced toward the cliff.

Chapter Nineteen

Roberta tried not to think about what would happen if—or when—the monsters got to her. Only too vividly, she remembered the eviscerated body in the woods while her mind conjured stark images of the horror Morgan had witnessed during his night in the cavern.

It was like trying not to think about a sword suspended above your head or a snake coiled around your feet. The knowledge gave birth to the fear.

Throughout the afternoon she paced the small room or sat in the small building's lone chair waiting for sundown, waiting for *them*. Thankfully, Case had seen fit to remove the handcuffs. It was one thing to be held prisoner, and quite another to be bound like one.

Other than the chair, the interior of the building was spartan to the extreme. There was a counter running along one wall holding a small heater, vented through the ceiling, and a few packages of freeze-dried food. Next to it was a small sink no doubt attached to a limited water reservoir.

A trapdoor in the center of the floor, obviously designed for some other circumstance, intrigued Roberta. She knelt and opened it, only to stare at sharp, fractured rock. Shivering when frigid air seeped through the opening, she immediately closed it.

The one recessed light in the ceiling and the heater built into the wall were apparently run by a compressor mounted somewhere on the outside of the building. It was remarkably quiet, but Roberta could still hear it chugging steadily.

Through the window, she saw the other building and wondered about Morgan. What was he thinking? What was he doing? Would she ever see him again? Would they ever be safe again?

Imprisoned in the room, live bait in a horrible trap, she was as alone and isolated and helpless as she had ever been in her life.

And Roberta was not used to feeling powerless. She had always been the overseer of her own destiny. Her choices were made carefully. She had learned to weigh and calculate every option and alternative. From early in life, she learned that to survive and succeed, she had to maintain control over her own destiny. Although far from being Machiavellian, she was one who calculated the odds.

Yet during the hunt for these strange and horrible creatures, Roberta had become so consumed with the investigation, she had ignored all of her internal alarms, all of the carefully constructed mechanisms specifically developed to protect herself from people like Richard Case.

She should have recognized him for what he was during the first meeting. In retrospect, she had ignored his intensity, his ruthlessness and the near mania with which he had joined the hunt.

For that lapse, she'd first lost control of the project, and now might lose her life.

The Devouring

The thoughts depressed her. She had betrayed herself and the price was high.

Swearing, she got out of the chair and began pacing her cramped prison.

As the sun set, Roberta stopped berating herself long enough to watch Case's men erect the hideous scarecrow.

What insanity were they up to?

The answer became frighteningly evident when the creatures attacked. She was horrified when Sanchez and then Nias were crushed on the rocks, and she heard herself scream when her prison was attacked.

Roberta struggled against her terror when the building began sliding down the slope. If it went over the cliff, there would be no surviving the fall. Yet, with an odd detachment, she knew it would be better to die like that than at the mercy of those *things*.

It was hard to stand as the building bumped and banged down the slope toward the larger structure. On her knees, her hands braced against the windowsill, she watched the dark world outside slowly rotate by.

The overhead light winked out and warm air ceased flowing from the heater. The creatures had likely damaged or destroyed the generator.

Fascinated, Roberta watched as two of the creatures attacked the other building. When they managed to tip it onto its side, she prayed for Morgan.

Suddenly, like an insane race out of a madman's fever dream, the two buildings were sliding together, bumping and banging and bouncing their way toward the ever-nearing cliff.

Roberta's sense of survival kicked in. In spite of her depression, in spite of the sheer hopelessness of the situation, she quite consciously realized she didn't want to die. Not like this, not like a rat in cage. She wanted to live, wanted to see another sunrise, go to another movie, read another book, again make love with Morgan.

"Not like this," she screamed, frantically scanning the dark room for something, anything, to help.

In desperation, she again knelt next to the trapdoor and yanked it open. It was like looking through the rusted floorboards of her college-days car as the rocky ground tumbled and whirled past. Rocks crunched and cracked as the building splintered them and sent tiny pieces of crushed stone bounding through the hole.

Standing, Roberta grabbed the chair and jammed its legs into the opening. She was jerked violently, but managed to hold on. The legs lodged against the back of the small opening. For one brief, heart-stopping minute, wedged against the rock, they slowed and then, with a grating, tortured scream, halted the building's progress.

Roberta's grin faltered when, with an ear-splitting crack, the chair's back legs buckled and the building again began its steady descent toward the cliff.

She raced to the window, knowing it offered no escape. It was heavy plexiglass, mounted into the wall, the brackets hidden under the fiberglass interior.

Roberta couldn't see the other building now. Maybe it had already pitched over the cliff's edge.

In the dim moonlight, she could see the edge of the cliff, marked by a few scattered, small boulders. With each passing second, it loomed closer. It was 30 yards away. Then 20.

Acting on instinct, not sure what she would accomplish, Roberta zipped up her snowsuit, pulled on her gloves and sat down next to the opening in the floor.

Morgan managed to get to his feet, one hand holding the grating over the ceiling light. The others were scrambling around, struggling to maintain their balance, while searching for a way out.

"The window," he yelled. "Somebody blow a hole in the window!"

Preacher, his back pressed against the far wall, ordered

everyone down and then let loose a string of bullets from the minigun. The plexiglass fractured and then shattered.

"Out!" Case yelled. "Everyone get the hell out!"

One by one the men leaped into the darkness. They carried what weapons and supplies they had managed to salvage in the chaos.

Morgan, ignored in the confusion, grabbed an abandoned M-16, a coil of heavy rope, and a knapsack of what he hoped held either ammunition or food or, in the best of all possible worlds, both.

Case was at the window, ready to bail out, when he saw Morgan.

"Drop the gun, Blaylock!"

"You need me!"

"Drop it!"

Morgan had picked his way to the window now. The building was gaining momentum. He didn't have time to play games. With one quick move, he shoved Case out the window. As the startled man tumbled into the night, Morgan heard his name uttered as a curse.

He jumped, landing hard, feeling the sharp stones tear at the snowsuit. The loose rock, disturbed by the passing building, sent him sliding. He dug in his heels, struggled for purchase and finally stopped himself.

Glancing over his shoulder, he saw the building tottering for one brief instant on the edge of the cliff and then slowly, irrevocably tip out of sight. Seconds later, he heard it slam into the rocks and trees below.

Frantically, Morgan scanned the area for the smaller structure, but it too had disappeared. A pang of hopeless despair stabbed his heart.

Roberta was dead, nothing more now than a pulped mess of crushed bone and rent tissue.

He clamped his jaws together. No time for remorse.

In the distance he could hear the other men calling out to one another. They were regrouping.

Morgan flattened himself against the ground.

He heard a rustle above him. A leathery beat against the frigid air. His skin prickled as he anticipated the creature's rending talons embedding themselves in his back. But nothing happened. He glanced up, and saw two dark, winged shapes streaking up the slope.

He heard a tortured scream, and then saw one of the creatures rise into the moonlit, a struggling figure dangling from its powerful legs.

Automatic weapons roared and red tracer bullets, like laser beams, crisscrossed the sky.

The man's screams echoed around the mountain peak. They continued to echo for several seconds after his body smashed against an outcropping of jagged rock.

Morgan knew he couldn't stay in the open much longer. Adjusting the coil of rope, the knapsack and the rifle, he began creeping slowly away from the others. Gunshots punctuated the night. He stayed parallel to the cliff, hoping to circle around until he was on a straight line to the opening where he had spent the long, dark night.

As he crawled across the rocky ground, he heard a movement to his left, near the cliff. Stopping, he pulled the M-16 to his shoulder, flipped off the safety and pointed it down the slope.

In the moonlight, he could just make out a shape sprawled at the edge of the cliff.

"Another move and I'll blow your fucking head off!" he hissed.

He was answered by a sharp, startled intake of breath. "Don't shoot."

Morgan's heart leaped into his throat. "Roberta? Jesus Christ, is that you?"

"Yes."

Quickly, he scrambled to her, clasping her hand and pulling her close.

"I thought you went over the edge."

"Almost," she breathed, clinging to him. "Too damned close."

306

"How the hell did you get out?"

Roberta told him about the trapdoor. "I just waited. When the building started going over and the door was clear, I dropped through."

Morgan shook his head. "How'd you know you weren't just jumping out into space?"

"I didn't," she answered, a little breathlessly. "But if I stayed inside, I *knew* I'd die."

They were quiet for a few moments. "I'm glad you're safe," Morgan told her.

She shook her head. "That's a relative term, isn't it?"

More shots rang out.

"Come on," Morgan said. "We've got to get the hell out of here."

Together, they continued along the edge of the cliff until Morgan stopped.

"Straight up is the passage. Maybe we can get there without being seen."

"Won't Richard and his men try for it too?" Roberta wondered.

"Maybe. But if those shots are any indication, they're still pretty busy with our winged friends. We've got to chance it. We'd never make it off the mountain in the dark and besides . . ."

He paused.

"Morgan?"

He shook his head. "I want to get the Pruett woman out of there, Roberta. If I don't at least try . . . well, I just have to."

She made no response, but fell in behind him as they picked their way slowly and cautiously up the slope.

Tracer bullets continued to streak across the sky and men continued to shout. Occasionally, Morgan glanced to his right. He could see the bat creatures swooping and diving at their antagonists. He had to admit Case and his goon squad were putting up a good fight.

Apparently, neither the men nor the creatures noticed

Douglas D. Hawk

Morgan and Roberta reach the opening. He led her into the depression and showed her the hole leading to the tunnel.

Roberta stared at it for several seconds. "What if . . .if they're waiting in there for us?"

Morgan shook his head. "We'll have to chance it. Besides, it's easier for us to move in the tunnel. Their wings get in the way." He opened the knapsack. "Our luck's still holding." He showed her a large flashlight.

Morgan felt around the opening. "It's been enlarged, I think."

"Meaning?"

"I'm not sure," he answered. "I'll go first." He handed her the knapsack and rope. Fearing either Case or the creatures would see his light, he kept it off. The worst part was thrusting his body through the opening. The darkness and the stench enveloped him and for an instant, Morgan was overcome by memories of his last experience in the narrow tunnel.

Once inside, he switched on the light and flashed it toward the bend in the tunnel. Empty. He let out a long breath.

"Come on," he called to Roberta. Awkwardly, she squeezed through the opening and joined him.

"You know all the fun places," she quipped, looking around.

"Yeah, I'm a regular party guy."

Holding the light and the rifle, Morgan started forward. Roberta followed, grimacing when they rounded the corner and she saw the bones scattered against the walls and across the rough floor.

"Are you sure we can get her out?" Roberta asked as they neared the opening through which the faint, eerie light filtered.

"No. But I've got to try."

They both stopped when they heard a noise behind them. Morgan put a finger to his lips and motioned for

Roberta to stay put. As he started back along the tunnel, she grabbed his arm. When he looked at her she shook her head.

He gestured for her to be still and started creeping back toward the bend. Morgan was halfway there when two huge, luminescent yellow eyes peered from the darkness. The instant the light struck them, they vanished.

"Shit," Morgan hissed. The creatures must have widened the opening as a precaution against just what he and Roberta were doing. He hurried back to her.

"I saw it," she said shakily. "We're trapped."

"Not yet," Morgan answered, still watching the curve in the passage. "But we've got to get the hell out of here. If we get bottled up, it'll only be a matter of time before they take us."

He urged her to the opening. She peered into the dimly lit chamber relishing the rush of warm air across her face.

"Do you see her?" Morgan asked, stilling watching their backs.

"No."

"Okay, maybe she's not in the main cavern. From the look of the place it may be honeycombed with chambers." He handed her the rope. "Here, tie it around your waist. I'll lower you down."

"But . . . what if something's down there waiting?"

Morgan glanced at her. She was pale and drawn. "It'll be okay. I'll be right behind you."

Roberta nodded and forced a weak smile. "Okay, party guy. Let's do it."

Once Roberta had the rope secured around her waist, Morgan wrapped the opposite end around his own. This was the tricky part. He'd have to put down both the gun and the light in order to lower Roberta into the cavern. The creature blocking the other end might suddenly overcome his aversion to the light and attack the intruders.

He placed the flashlight so it shone down the tunnel.

Then, with his gloved hands grasping the rope firmly, he eased Roberta out the opening.

For one instant, swinging free, she feared she was about to fall to the cavern floor, but Morgan held her steady, letting the rope play out slowly.

Feet braced, arm muscles burning, Morgan clamped his jaws together when he heard the creature in the tunnel stir. If the light didn't keep the thing at bay, he'd be easy prey. He chanced a glance just in time to see the terrible face again vanish around the bend.

"You want me," he muttered. "Come get me."

The rope went slack and Morgan relaxed, dragging in great gulps of the warm, rancid air. He thrust his head through the opening.

"Okay?" he hissed.

Roberta was unfastening the rope while glancing around nervously.

"Hey," he called again, still keeping his voice low.

She looked up. "What?"

Morgan touched a finger to his lips to silence her. "I'll be down in a second."

This was the tricky part. He had to find something to which he could anchor the rope and there was nothing immediately available.

Again he heard the creature moving and, retrieving the light, he played the beam toward the end of the tunnel.

"Morgan," Roberta called softly from below. He looked out the opening.

"Hurry," she said. "This isn't much fun."

He nodded.

With nothing else to use to brace the rope, Morgan tied it around the rifle. By positioning it across the opening, he could lower himself and, with any luck, pull it down after him. He hated to risk damaging the weapon, but couldn't stay there much longer. If there was one creature following him, it stood to reason the others would come into the cavern to confront both of them as soon as they could.

Morgan hoped Case and his surviving men were keeping the other creatures busy.

Stuffing the flashlight into the knapsack, knowing the creature would be coming as soon as it realized the light was gone, he positioned himself through the opening and, with some difficulty, wedged the M-16 in place. Just as he gripped the rope and started down, he heard the click of the thing's talons on the stones. It was coming fast.

Clasping the rope tightly, Morgan started sliding down toward the floor. He was just over halfway when he heard Roberta let out a startled gasp. Glancing up, he saw the monster's head thrust out through the hole. Its mouth opened, exposing its razor-sharp teeth and dark, flicking tongue.

"Morgan! Watch out!" Roberta screamed, just as the rope went slack and Morgan felt himself falling toward the floor. He landed hard and rolled, the bottoms of his feet stinging and a loud, sickening *pop* exploding in his leg. A second later, he was wracked by a wave of agonizing pain.

"Oh, God!" Roberta cried, rushing to him.

Teeth gritted, swallowing hard, Morgan rolled on his back.

Roberta pressed a hand against his chest. "Don't move!" She immediately began working up the leg of his snowsuit and probing his ankle. He let out a yelp.

"It's broken, all right," she said.

Just then something landed scant inches from them. They both gave a start.

"Jesus . . ." Morgan breathed, seeing the M-16, its barrel twisted and bent.

Glancing up, they saw the hideous, leering face of the creature. If its mouth could smile, then it was grinning with delight.

"It just bit the rope in two," Roberta said, staring at the thing.

"Yeah," Morgan groaned. "And took care of our only

weapon. We're in a shit sandwich now."

"What're we going to do?"

Morgan grimaced against another jolt of pain. "He can't get to us through the opening. We've got a little time. You got to splint my ankle."

"With what?" she demanded desperately.

"There's got to be something around here. . . ." He stopped as footsteps scraped out of the gloom behind them.

Wide-eyed and frightened, Roberta looked up at the apparition shuffling out of the gloom. Her expression shifted from fear to pained amazement when she saw Connie Pruett staring at them with glazed, uncomprehending eyes.

Morgan turned his head in order to see the woman. Seeing her in the filthy, tattered rags, her flesh streaked with dirt and grime, he felt his stomach tighten.

"Connie," he said softly, trying to ignore the pain in his ankle "Can you hear me?"

Arms dangling at her side, Connie continued to stare at them with dazed, uncomprehending eyes.

"Connie," Morgan said again, keeping his voice low but firm. "We've come to take you out of here."

Something sparked in the woman's eyes.

"It's true," Roberta added. "We're going to take you home."

"Home?" It was whispered. A promise, a dream, something all but forgotten.

"Jesus, Morgan," Roberta breathed. "She's almost catatonic."

From above the creature at the opening cried out, and Connie Pruett froze, backing up a step, her eyes huge and frightened.

"Connie," Morgan said urgently. "We need your help. If you help us, we can take you home."

"Home." The spark in Connie's eyes ignited a tiny fire. The clouds seemed to lift. He mouth began to work as large, fat tears started rolling down her cheeks. "Yes, oh, God, yes. Take me home!"

Roberta stood and put her arm around the other woman's shoulders. "We need you to help us get you out of here. Morgan's hurt. His ankle is broken. Is there something I can use as a splint?"

Connie was thoughtful for a minute, and then she nodded. Tugging on the sleeve of Roberta's snowsuit, she led her across the cavern floor. Near the bubbling pool of water, she pointed toward a pile of stout tree branches.

"Th . . . those should . . . work," Connie said haltingly. Roberta quickly selected two short ones and started back toward Morgan.

Again the creature above them cried out, but this time Connie ignored him.

"Will you help me set his leg, Connie?" she asked, appraising the half-naked woman and absently wondering how much psychotherapy would be required before this trauma could be dealt with and she could resume something approaching a normal life.

Connie nodded.

"How bad is it?" Morgan asked when Roberta again knelt beside him.

"Pretty clean, I think," she answered. "The skin's not broken." She looked up at Connie. "I want you to hold his leg while I set the bone. Can you do that?"

"I . . . I can do it."

Morgan bit on one of the sticks as Connie held his leg and Roberta gripped his foot.

"Ready?" Roberta asked. Morgan nodded.

He thought he was going to pass out when she pulled on his leg. He felt his bones grate together as great electric bolts of pain swept up his leg, exploded in the pit of his stomach and sent his mind reeling. The edges of his vision fuzzed and fractured and blackness enveloped him.

When he came around, his mouth was filled with brackish bile. He spat on the floor and then looked at his leg in amazement. Roberta was just tightening the final binding holding the makeshift splints in place. She had used his knife to shred the canvas knapsack into strips.

"How long was I out?" he asked.

Roberta looked at him and shook her head. "A few minutes. I hope this works."

Morgan glanced around the cavern. "Where's Connie?"

Roberta shook her head. "I don't know. She left while I was hacking up the knapsack."

"Damn, Roberta," Morgan said, exasperated. "We've got to get . . ."

"Here she is," Roberta said, ignoring his outburst.

Connie appeared beside them. She carried a small collection of heavy winter clothing. Some of it was torn with dark stains on the dirty nylon. She had a heavy parka, the back bearing triple gashes, a pair of snow pants, bloodstained on one leg, and a pair of winter boots that looked too large for her small feet.

"They kept these from . . ." Connie didn't finish.

"Good," Morgan nodded. "Get them on and then we'll try to get out of here." He looked at Roberta. "I think I'll need a crutch. The two of you can't carry me out of here."

Roberta was at the pile of wood, speculating on what use the creatures would have for the striped tree branches, and Connie was quickly donning the discarded clothes, when they heard a furious, insane hiss from somewhere close.

Connie froze. She whimpered and the blood drained from her face. She looked at Morgan and he saw the terror and madness there.

Morgan struggled to stand. "Help me, Connie! For God's sake, help me up!"

The woman blinked, shook her head and stood. She took Morgan's offered arm and helped him up.

As the menacing hiss echoed through the room, Roberta

snatched up several of the longer sticks and started back toward Morgan. Her heart was pounding and, racing across the cavern, she felt exposed, vulnerable.

The creature was there in one brief instant. It soared into the cavern, screeching and screaming. Roberta saw it diving at her, and dropped to her knees just as it glided over her head. She went sprawling when a taloned foot slashed the snowsuit just below her left shoulder.

"It's *him!*" Connie cried. "Don't let him get me! Please!"

Morgan kept his arm around the woman's shoulders both for support and to keep her from bolting in panic.

"Roberta!" he yelled. "Watch out!"

The creature made an impossible turn and was again diving at her. She saw it, rolled and was missed by the raking claws by scant inches. As soon as the creature passed, she jumped to her feet and raced toward Morgan and Connie.

"Don't let him . . . get me!" Connie screamed. "Don't!"

The creature circled high, its glistening yellow eyes glaring down at them with what Morgan thought was as malevolent a look as he'd ever seen. It was waiting for them to make the next move.

"What are we going to do?" Roberta asked, her eyes never leaving the flying monster.

Morgan looked at Connie. "Where's the main entrance?"

She shook her head. "I . . . I don't know. I . . . I've only been permitted to move in this cavern and the one next to it."

"Don't they always come here through the other cavern?" he pressed.

The woman nodded.

"Okay, then that's the way we have to go."

"How are we going to get away from him?" Roberta asked.

"Beats the hell out of me," Morgan answered. He took

one of the tree limbs from Connie. "I'll use this one for a crutch. Keep the others, though. They're all we have to defend ourselves."

He looked when the creature again let out a screech.

"What's he waiting for?" Morgan wondered.

"The others," Connie replied. "They know about guns and he's not sure if you have one or not."

Morgan nodded. "Then we'd better get going."

"Wait a minute," Roberta said, digging into the pockets of her snowsuit. She fished out a small waterproof canister for matches.

"Fire," she said. "If we can make a couple of torches . . ."

"With what?" Morgan asked. "We need something that'll burn for quite a while."

"With this," Roberta said triumphantly, holding up a small can of Sterno. "It was in the knapsack. If we put it on some rags . . ."

"Yeah, okay," Morgan said hurriedly. "Use what's left of the knapsack."

With the predatory creature occasionally screeching at them as it continued to circle near the roof of the cavern, Morgan and Roberta quickly made the torches. Once the heavy canvas was tied around the ends of the stout limbs, Roberta smeared them with the thick goo from the Sterno can.

Then, fumbling out a match, she lit it the canvas. Bright yellow flames blossomed.

"Now let's get the hell out of here," Morgan said. "The two of you carry the torches. Give me that other stick. Maybe I can keep the bastard away from us if he attacks again."

They started toward the cavern's exit, but stopped when the creature came flying toward them. Connie screamed. Roberta thrust the torch at it and Morgan took an awkward swing with the stick. The creature veered away from the flames with a reverberating cry of rage.

The Devouring

"Come on," Connie said. "We've got to go." She started toward the opening. Morgan followed her, clumsily struggling with his crutch and immobilized leg. Roberta walked behind him, keeping a close eye on the creature.

It was again circling high, but as they moved toward the opening, it suddenly spiraled and dropped toward them. Its mouth was open, exposing the sharp, daggered teeth.

"Get down," Roberta shouted, dropping to the limestone floor. Connie, covering her head and crying out, followed suit, but Morgan, hampered by his broken leg, clumsy on the crutch, staggered, hopped a few steps and then whirled around just at the creature slammed into his chest.

Warm wetness splashed on his face as a talon traced a groove along his jawline. He was falling—thinking he was dying or already dead. He slammed into a stalactite, and pain erupted up his leg. A scream of rage and anguish—which might have been his own—echoed in the huge cavern. He was squashed to the ground under an unyielding weight . . .

. . . and there was darkness.

Chapter Twenty

Morgan knew he wasn't dead. If he was dead, he wouldn't feel like he was being pureed in a giant blender.

Everything hurt. His leg was an agony. His ribs and chest throbbed and when he tried to speak, a jagged lightning bolt struck the right side of his face.

"Morgan . . . ?"

He nodded. Somewhere near he could hear someone muttering and grunting.

"Thank God," Roberta sighed.

Maybe they weren't still inside that stinking mountain. Maybe they were back in town, in his house, safe, warm.

He forced his eyes open.

"Still here, huh?" he mumbled, trying to ignore the spasms in his face.

Roberta looked down at him. Her face was ashen and he thought she looked a lot older than she had a few hours—days?—ago. Her eyes were cloudy and darkly circled. Tiny lines around her mouth stood out in sharp relief. Tears glistened on her cheeks.

She forced a weak smile. "Yes. I thought you . . . I thought it had . . ." She couldn't say the words.

His memory flooded back and he was swept with panic. "The creature . . ." He tried to push himself up, but his head spun dizzily and he slumped back down, realizing his head had been cradled in Roberta's lap.

There was a wet thumping sound accompanying the muttering and grunting.

"Wh . . . what's that? What happened?"

Roberta raised her eyes and looked beyond them. He turned his head and saw Connie Pruett, one of the long, spear-like tree limbs held in her hands, leaning over the still form of the creature. Again and again she raised the end and drove it into the inert body. Each time she withdrew the gore-splattered end of the stick from the body, she grunted. Her lips moved and unintelligible sounds came out as she rammed the tip home again.

"She's been doing it for several minutes now. She's over the edge."

"How did you manage to kill it?" he asked, awed.

Roberta shook her head. "I'm not sure. It hit you, drove you back, and I just stabbed it with my torch." Her face contorted. "And it screamed. Like nothing I've ever heard. It was terrible."

Morgan probed his face and realized Roberta was hold a rag against the wound. The rag was wet and sticky.

"How bad?"

She shrugged. "Not too deep, but its still bleeding."

Morgan put a hand on her shoulder and started to pull himself up. "We've got to get out of here."

She nodded. "I know. But can you walk? You're not really in any condition . . ."

"Listen," he said urgently. "I'd rather drop dead trying to get out than stay here and wait to get munched by those flying freaks. Help me up."

With some effort, Morgan got up. Roberta gave him his crutch. He took the blood-soaked rag from her and pressed it against the gash.

"Connie," Morgan called to the woman, who was still attacking the lifeless thing. Its stomach and chest were thick with dark blood and viscera. She made no response.

He called to her again, his voice louder and his tone sharper. She paused, leaned against the stick and looked at him. After several long seconds, the crazed gleam in her eyes melted away and she suddenly looked down on the mutilated corpse, gasping, stumbling backward.

"Connie," Roberta said. "Let's go. We've got to go. Now!"

The woman nodded mutely, never taking her eyes off the monster.

How long before the others returned? Morgan wondered. We can't fight them all.

Connie, shoulders slumped, hands quivering, joined them. Silently, she took the one remaining torch and started toward the opening into the next cavern.

It was a smaller than the first, but the air was as warm and smelled just as rancid. Along the wet, glistening walls, piles of bones and rags littered the floor. There was a steady plop of dripping water.

As they moved slowly past a deep cul-de-sac in one wall, Morgan stopped.

"What . . . ?" Roberta said, falling silent when he lifted his hand.

"Hear that?" he asked in whisper.

She listened. Yes, she heard *something*. A tiny cry, a whimper. It was coming from the cul-de-sac.

Morgan started hobbling toward the indentation in the wall. As he drew nearer, he peered into its gloomy interior. In the back there was a pile of rags atop a small mound of twigs and branches.

"Bring the torch," he called. Connie turned and stared at him, but made no effort to move.

"Connie," he called. "I need the light."

Hesitantly, Connie retraced her steps and joined him. When she saw the nest-like affair in the cul-de-sac, she stepped back and shook her head.

"What?" Morgan asked. "What is it?"

"Kill it!" Connie spat. "Kill it!" She bared her teeth and her face twisted into a mask of outrage and disgust.

Gently taking the torch from the woman, Roberta carried it to Morgan. They exchanged worried looks and then moved into the wide, shallow depression.

As soon as she glanced down and saw the source of the mewling cry, she stepped back in horror.

Morgan was transfixed, staring at the thing lying on the heap of shredded clothing and sticks. For a moment, his head felt light and it was with some effort he kept his balance.

"Oh, God, Morgan," Roberta said behind him. "It . . . must be what they . . . cut out of . . . that woman . . ."

The tiny creature was grotesque. Not quite a bat creature, but far from human. Its eyes, neither as large as the other creatures' nor the same saffron color, were almond-shaped, the pupils distinctly human. Its flesh was a light brown and hairless. Its tiny wings were embryonic, folded at its sides. Its clawed "fingers" were distinctly human, as were its plump legs and tiny feet.

It cried out to Morgan. Absently, gazing at the tiny monstrosity in fascinated revulsion, he let the bloody rag fall from his hand. It fluttered into the nest. Something changed in the creature's face. Instantly, its feet swept up, clutched the blood-soaked rag and shoved it into its gapping, lipless mouth. It sucked greedily on the sticky gore.

"Kill it!" Connie Pruett screamed. She was suddenly rushing toward the cul-de-sac, her hands out stretched in claws. Roberta grabbed her, held her back.

Morgan turned from the creature and stared at the women.

"Stop it, Connie! Stop it!" he shouted. The woman ceased her struggles.

She shook her head sadly. "It . . . it's a monster! Just kill it and we can go."

Morgan knew he couldn't kill the thing, nor did he presume he had the right. Regardless of what it was and how it came to be, it was a living thing and he knew, no matter how vile and disgusting he found it, he did not have the kind of callousness necessary to destroy it.

"We'll just leave it," he said quietly.

"NO!" Connie screamed. "Get rid of it. It's evil!"

Morgan looked at Roberta. "Let's get out of here!"

But Connie persisted. "You can't leave it alive! You can't let it become . . . one of those *monsters!* You can't!"

Morgan hobbled to the pair. He touched Connie's arm. "I can't kill it. Do you understand? I can't and I won't let *you*."

Connie pulled away from Roberta. "Why? What good is it? It's just another of those *things!* It's a freak of nature. An abomination before God!"

Roberta reached for the distraught woman, but her hand was brushed aside.

"We have to go, Connie," Roberta said. "We can't waste any more time."

The woman looked first at Roberta and then at Morgan. "Why can't I make you understand? Why won't you listen to me? That thing is evil! Evil!" She clutched her hands to her stomach and slumped to her knees, sobbing bitterly. "It . . . it's what's growing inside of *me!* Evil! EVIL!"

Again, Morgan and Roberta exchanged worried glances.

Connie slammed her right fist into her midsection and then her left.

"Destroy it! Kill it!"

Roberta grabbed the Connie's arms. "Stop, Connie," she said gently. "Don't hurt yourself. Help us get out of here and then we'll take care of . . . what's inside of you. I promise."

Connie looked up, her eyes pleading. "Kill it," she whispered.

Morgan limped to them. "Let's go. We're losing time."

Reluctantly, in defeat, Connie got up, took the torch from Roberta and started leading them around the stalagmites toward the far end of the cavern.

As Morgan hobbled along, he tried not to hear the slurping, sucking sounds coming from the cul-de-sac.

The cavern sloped gradually upward toward yet another opening. This one was smaller, a fracture in the rock, just wide enough for one person to squeeze through.

"I don't know what's beyond here," Connie said in a flat, dead voice. "I . . . I don't remember them bringing me through here."

She thrust the torch through the opening and then sidled through.

"What about that . . . thing back there, Morgan?" Roberta whispered before he started into the narrow opening.

He shook his head. "I don't know. If we get out of here, maybe we can get someone to come back for it. Someone who knows what the hell to do with it."

Roberta looked sad. "In a funny way, I feel . . . sorry for it."

He nodded and began edging his way through the cut in the rock. It was difficult. He had to brace his hands against the rock wall in front of him and hop/shuffle along, keeping his broken leg slightly crooked and taking care not to smack it against any sharp protrusions. Roberta was right behind him, and when they were finally through, she handed him his crutch.

They were now in a darker, cooler chamber. There were only a few phosphorescent streaks in the walls, and Morgan saw none of the bubbling pools of warm water which were plentiful in the other two caverns. There was an acrid, overpowering stink in the room.

Connie's torch flickered in the gentle breeze moving through the chamber. It threw weird, misshapen shadows across the walls and high ceiling.

Wordlessly, the trio began moving deeper into the chamber.

As they trekked up a rise in the rough floor, Connie's right foot slipped out from under her. She let out a small cry as the torch flew from her hand and she fell on her knee.

Morgan and Roberta hurried to her side and helped her to stand. She picked up the torch and held it close to the floor. The flickering flame illuminated a pile of dark feces, flattened on one side.

"Great," Morgan muttered. "We're in their toilet."

"Come on," Roberta prodded. "Let's keep going."

At the top of the rise, the floor leveled for several yards and then began angling downward. As they moved, they constantly sidestepped mounds of foul waste and were forced to pick their way around huge boulders. Morgan thought some of them appeared to have fallen quite recently.

"Just what we need," he mumbled to himself.

"What?" Roberta asked from behind him.

"Nothing." Why give her something else to worry about?

Connie picked her way around the boulders and other obstructions easily. Morgan noticed she was agile and quick and he wondered what kind of person she had been before . . . this? What kind of movies did she like? What kind of books did she read? Did she have a boyfriend? Were her parents still alive?

Depressing. If there was a Hell, it couldn't be much worse than this, could it? And, for all he and Roberta had experienced, for all the nightmares germinating in their subconscious minds, how banal were they compared to the *real* nightmares and terrors Connie Pruett had suffered and might yet suffer?

Reaching the bottom of the incline, they stopped.

"Now where?" Morgan asked, studying the rough, blank wall of rock before them.

Connie Pruett's eyes searched and then she pointed upward. "There."

A narrow ledge, formed when the earth had shifted a few millennia before recorded history, led to a gaping hole in the rock 40 feet above their heads.

Roberta looked at Morgan anxiously. "How will you . . ."

He grinned. "I will."

"But . . ."

"I can do it," he said, forcing a smile.

Connie left the torch leaning against a rock and was moving up the ledge on all fours. It was no more than 18 inches wide, but the rough surface provided plenty of handholds and footholds.

"It's not bad," she called down to them.

Roberta eyed the narrow shelf dubiously. "How are you going to get up that? You can't use your leg."

"I can do it. Trust me."

"Nixon said that."

"Yeah, and we believed him," Morgan said, almost smiling.

Roberta flashed him a brutal look, the torch light flickering in her eyes. "Don't be glib."

He touched her with his free hand. "It'll be okay. I can . . ."

He paused. They both snapped their head upward when they heard Connie gasp. Morgan expected to see her plunging from the ledge. What he saw, instead, chilled him just as much.

Connie stood in the hole, Richard Case clutching her arm, pointing a big handgun at Morgan and Roberta.

"I thought you were both dead," he called down.

"And I'd hoped you were," Morgan shot back.

"You look like shit, Blaylock."

"You must be looking in a mirror, Dick."

The FBI agent's expression shifted. "I'll give you an A for being an asshole, Blaylock."

"How'd you get here, Case?"

The man smiled wolfishly. "We had a guide. A reluctant one, but he got us here." Little Sam appeared behind him, a length of rope held in his massive fist. He tugged on it and one of the creatures, its wings bound to its body and a gag in it mouth, stumbled into view.

"Congratulations, Case," Morgan said nastily. "You caught one."

"That we did. Took us a while. Cost us a few men, but we caught him." He held up one of the transmitters he had used to attract the creatures. "And we can control him with this. Set the pitch just right . . ." He released Connie, who was staring at the captive with horror and contempt, and fiddled with a dial. The creature instantly began thrashing and struggling until it dropped to its knees, shaking its head violently.

"It tames them," Case continued, turning the dial again. The creature slumped.

Morgan felt a wave of pity for the strange, alien thing. It might be savage and dangerous, but it had been struggling for survival. It deserved better than to be tortured. And better than what Case had in mind for its future.

The creature looked up, eyeing Case with such hatred, the FBI man took an involuntary step backward.

"Why come here, Case? You got what you wanted."

"Not by half, Blaylock. Not by half." He looked behind him. "Dallenbeck, keep those two covered."

With a flourish, Dallenbeck appeared beside Case, pointing his M-16 at Roberta and Morgan.

"Kill it!" Connie screamed suddenly, startling the men standing near her. "Kill it! Shoot it!"

Case glared at her. "Shut your mouth!" He looked down at Morgan. "Is this the Pruett woman?"

"Yes."

The Devouring

Case's hand, as quick as a striking rattler, clamped his hand on her jaw and looked into her eyes. "They didn't kill you, so they must have been using you for breeding stock."

Connie stared back, her eyes wide and frightened.

"Don't hurt her, Richard," Roberta cried. "For God's sake, she's been through enough."

Again the wolfish smile touched the FBI man's mouth. He released Connie and glanced down at the pair.

"Hurt her? I wouldn't dream of it. What may be growing inside her is one of the greatest treasures in the world."

Connie covered her mouth with her hand and sagged against the rock. She shook her head. "No! I . . . I won't have . . . I won't carry that *thing!* I . . . I'll kill myself first!"

Morgan sensed what was about to happen. Case must have recognized it too, because his hand shot out just as Connie pushed herself away from the wall and tried to leap from the shelf. He held a wad of the soiled parka. For an instant they tottered on the brink of the high ledge, and were only saved when Dallenbeck grabbed the back of Case's coat and pulled the pair back to the wall.

"Bitch!" Case snarled, spinning the woman around. The open-handed slap echoed in the cavern. "If I didn't need you, I'd give you back to *them!*" He pointed at the bound creature.

Connie Pruett, now firmly in Dallenbeck's grasp, sobbed hysterically. She made no further effort to get away.

"Enough of this shit," Case snapped. "We haven't time to screw around." He looked at Roberta and Morgan. "We're coming down, Blaylock. Then you can take us back to where you found Pruett."

"The only other creature in there is dead," Morgan said. "It's a waste of time."

Case snorted a laugh. "There are others. They'll come back before sunup." He glanced at his wrist watch. "Not that far away. A couple of hours. And when they come back, we'll be ready."

With some difficulty, Case and his men—Little Sam, Dallenbeck and Tarkington—with Connie and the creature in tow, made it down the narrow ledge. The creature thrashed and tugged against the rope, but when Case showed it the transmitter, it became quiet and shuffled defeatedly ahead of Little Sam. Tarkington kept a tight hold on Connie's arm, forcing her ahead of him.

When everyone was down, Case shot Morgan a mocking smile. "Seems you didn't fare all that well. Broken leg, carved-up face. I guess you just aren't the *macho* man you think you are."

Morgan returned the smile. "Naw, I guess not. I'm not interested in impressing other men."

Case's smile faltered. "Lead the way, Blaylock. You fuck around and I'll break your other leg and leave you here to rot."

Like he's going to let us leave here alive, Morgan thought ruefully.

Reluctantly, he and Roberta began retracing their steps. Morgan found the thought of returning to the main chamber, to wait for the return of the other creatures, both depressing and discouraging. They had been so close—so damnably close—to escaping, to leaving this hellhole once and forever . . .

"Why so quiet, Blaylock?" Case asked. Morgan started, not having heard the man come up behind him. "I thought you were never caught without some asinine remark on the tip of your well-oiled tongue," Case continued.

"Blow me, Dick," Morgan barked.

Case laughed. "So glib, so urbane, so *very* much . . . you."

They were silent for some minutes. The only sounds in the cavern were the echoes of their footfalls and an occasional grunt as someone stumbled or fell.

Finally Morgan glanced over his shoulder at the FBI

agent. "Do you really believe someone will *pay* you for these monsters?"

Case smiled. "Absolutely. Think of the possibilities. Genetic research, the military applications, just the sheer volume of information they can generate. Oh, there are so many places where checkbooks, wall safes and numbered bank accounts will fly open. I couldn't possibly count them all."

Morgan chewed on that a minute. "Level with me, Case. Satisfy my curiosity. Where *did* these things come from?" He sensed Case had the answer.

"You really want to know?"

"I wouldn't have asked otherwise."

They were nearing the fissure in the rock leading to the middle cavern—where we left the baby, Morgan reminded himself—and he had to wait until he and Case were through the narrow gap before his question was answered. Case talked while the others edged their way into the cavern.

"Speculation, Blaylock. Conjecture. But based on evidence and logic." He paused to watch Little Sam fairly drag the captured creature through the opening.

"Roberta might have told you about the 'human bat' artifact discovered in Mexico a while back. Very rare, very unique. What she couldn't have told you, because it has never been reported, was the cavern found in New Mexico last year."

Roberta's eyes widened. "And another ceramic bat figure was found there?"

Case nodded. "Now, the one in Mexico was probably Aztec. In fact, the researchers are fairly certain it is. And so was the one found in the new cavern. It had been sealed until something, maybe a earth tremor, opened it."

"But the Aztecs never went that far north," Roberta blurted out. Case silenced her with a wave.

"Of course they didn't. If you'll keep quiet, I'll explain."

Morgan glanced at Roberta. She frowned at the rebuke and lapsed into silence.

"By chance," he continued as Roberta edged closer to Morgan, "the site was practically in the backyard of a retired American army sergeant. Now this sergeant once worked for me."

On something sneaky and covert, Morgan thought, but didn't say. He wanted to hear Case out.

Everyone was through the fissure now. Case glanced around. "Move on. We'll catch up."

Case was warming to the subject, wanting them to know, wanting them to go to the grave knowing how all this came about.

In an odd way, it amused Morgan. Here was this FBI agent, who probably knew more nasty little secrets than the rest of them combined, eager to reveal the details of his darkest secret to a man he hated.

And to a man he was going to kill, Morgan reminded himself. *Dead men tell no tales.*

The others moved into the cavern.

Case glanced toward them. "Well, to make a long story short, Washington put a lid on the find." He looked at Roberta. "Your little operation was called in. All very hush-hush."

"Because of the figurine?" she asked, forgetting about Case's order.

He nodded. "Partially. But mainly because of the creatures. They weren't found in the cave, but there was plenty of evidence they had lived there and for a very long time. With a little testing, the researchers figured they had vacated the place within the previous few months."

Roberta decided to ask another question. "How is it possible that they could have survived underground for so long? If they had ventured out, they would have been discovered by now."

Case looked at her and nodded. "Right. Nobody is sure, but they may have been in a kind of suspended animation.

A long-term hibernation. It's the most reasonable explanation we have. In the cavern we found human bones, artifacts and clothing dating to the late eighteen hundreds, and some going back to the time when Spaniards moved through the area searching for gold."

"They go into suspended animation for a century at a stretch?" Morgan asked, amazed.

Case smiled at him. "Very good, Blaylock. That Neanderthal brain of yours can do some rudimentary deduction."

"Richard, please," Roberta urged. "How did you get involved?"

He snorted a laugh. "Washington was worried people would become hysterical if word leaked out. The FBI was called in to keep a lid on things. It wasn't hard. There were very few researchers involved. They were willing to keep quiet, just to have a chance to investigate the site.

"But when I found out more about these things . . . well . . ." Case shrugged. "Too great an opportunity to be left in the hands of a bunch of long-haired, wild-eyed archaeologists and anthropologists. I decided if someone was going to profit from it, it was going to be me. A little maneuvering here, a little backslapping there and"— he motioned around the cavern—"here we are."

Morgan started to say something, but they heard one of the other men yell to Case.

"Richard, Jesus, you'd better see this," Dallenbeck shouted. "You ain't gonna believe it."

Case frowned. "What is it?" His words bounced off the walls and high ceiling several times before fading.

"You've got to see it for yourself," Dallenbeck answered.

Morgan and Roberta exchanged knowing glances. They'd found the mutant baby.

Chapter Twenty-one

With Dallenbeck's words still reverberating in the cavern, Case took hold of Roberta's arm and glared at Morgan.

"She and I are going ahead. Don't be a hero, Blaylock. Just shuffle on over." With that, he fairly dragged Roberta away.

It wasn't as if Morgan was going to sprint out of the cavern.

His ankle throbbed, while the rest of his injuries were merely dull aches. If he didn't bump his leg against anything, it was tolerable. His thigh muscles, however, were burning and cramping from holding the leg off the floor, and his arm and shoulder were sore from using the make-shift crutch, which in turn did little to ease the perpetual pain in his limbs and chest. The gash on his jaw was now crusted over with blood, but was, by comparison, little more than a minor irritant.

Sighing, Morgan hobbled toward the others. Case and his men were gathered in a knot around the cul-de-sac.

The Devouring

Roberta and Connie sat sullenly on a rock while the bound creature, the rope around its neck still clamped in Little Sam's fist, stood very still, watching the humans peer down at the grotesque form on the rags and twigs.

"This is fantastic," Case said loudly. "Absolutely fantastic." He gestured toward their captive. "These bastards *can* mate with humans. Their DNA is compatible. God, think of the possibilities."

"Think of the perversion," Morgan hissed as he joined Roberta. She gave him a sick, sad look.

"I never knew he was so twisted," she whispered. "I mean, he was arrogant and domineering, but this . . ." She motioned in Case's general direction. "He is definitely psychotic."

"They *have* to kill it," Connie blurted out. "It's evil." She sat near Roberta, her knees drawn up to her chin, her arms circling her legs. Morgan was overwhelmed by an intense need to comfort and protect the woman. She had been so terribly violated and was now so horribly vulnerable.

He had been driven by those motives since he first saw her in the cavern. Saving her, in some measure, would save him from the acute sense of failure. Red Crumley was dead. Charlie Shaw was dead. Jasper McKissik was dead. He hadn't been able to save any of them. They were victims, Connie was a victim.

And Richard Case was victimizing everyone. He was the exploiter, the despoiler, the user. After he had what he wanted, he'd discard all of them with all the concern of a man discarding old shoes.

Morgan felt as powerless as he had at any time in his life.

"We take it with us," Case snapped angrily, pulling Morgan out of his troubled reverie.

"You want me to *carry* that thing?" Tarkington growled. "It's disgusting!"

333

"You'll do it and like it," Case shouted back. "No argument!"

"How the hell are we supposed to get it outta here?" Tarkington shot back. "We don't know what to feed it or how it'll react to the temperature outside."

Morgan saw Case thrust his face close to Tarkington. "Figure it out! I want it with us."

"KILL IT!" Connie Pruett screamed, jumping to her feet. "JUST KILL IT!"

Case glared at her and then looked at Morgan. "Keep her quiet, Blaylock, or so help me, I'll put a bullet through her head." He pointed at the hideous infant. "Now that I have this, I don't really need her."

Roberta reached over and touched Connie. "Please," she whispered. "Don't provoke them further. They'll kill all of us if you do."

Connie turned her head slowly and looked at Roberta with large, accusing eyes. *Why don't you understand?* they asked. Why can't you see that *it* has to be destroyed?

"Please," Roberta repeated. "Let's worry about ourselves for now, okay?"

Connie studied the other woman for a few more seconds, and then again drew up her legs and rested her forehead on her knees.

Morgan watched as Tarkington, his hands encased in heavy gloves, reached into the nest and picked up the squirming, gurgling thing. As he did so, the captured creature made a grunting noise even though his mouth was still gagged.

There was a sudden rush of air above them and simultaneously a frightening eruption of screams.

All eyes turned toward the ceiling just as half-a-dozen bat creatures came shrieking and screaming out of the cavern's gloom. Their cries were of outrage and betrayal.

Three of them, talons raking, jaws snapping, landed among Case and his men. They hissed and spat, and as

The Devouring

Morgan was reaching for Roberta, he saw a geyser of blood spray into the air.

"Get down," he called, tugging awkwardly at Roberta's arm. She and Connie both dropped from the boulder, the latter disappearing around its opposite side.

Something hit Morgan's shoulder with the force of a hammer blow and he stumbled to the cold, damp floor. His leg ignited in a fresh explosion of pain.

Struggling to get up, he heard Roberta scream in terror, and opened his eyes just in time to see her lifted, kicking and thrusting, into the air.

One of the creatures, its taloned feet securely clamped on her shoulders, carried her high above the cavern floor.

Morgan bit his lip and tasted blood as he struggled to his feet. Ignoring the pandemonium around him, he scanned the dark ceiling and walls, but Roberta and her abductor were nowhere in sight.

Several gunshots rang out. Case and his remaining men struggled against attacking monsters, firing their weapons in futile attempts to bring the bat creatures down. Little Sam lay on the stones, his throat ripped wide and his head twisted at an impossible angle. A great puddle of blood was rapidly spreading around his body.

Morgan leaned against a stalagmite, panting for breath. Praying for the pain to subside, he reached for the makeshift crutch.

He had to find Roberta. He had to stop the creature from . . .

Focus! Not on the pain, not on Case and the creatures, but on finding her. Focus on getting to the other cavern.

The creature they had captured was now free of its bonds, the hemp rope bitten in two by one of its comrades. It launched itself at Case, Dallenbeck and Tarkington.

Momentarily ignored, Morgan jammed the crutch under his arm and started toward the distant portal. He saw the freed creature lift off the floor and soar above the embattled men, preparing to exact a measure of revenge.

And then suddenly the attackers screeched and withdrew, rising to circle near the dank cavern's ceiling. Their large, luminescent yellow eyes were locked on Case, who now held the tiny mutant creature by one hand and with the other pressed the barrel of a .45 automatic to its head. No doubt he would kill it, and the creatures knew it. They screamed and howled, but made no further moves toward the men.

Tarkington hastily bound an ugly wound on Dallenbeck's arm. Both men watched Case, whispering softly to one another.

Remarkably, Morgan found himself hopping and hobbling across the cavern without interference. The screaming, raging creatures were too intent on Case, and in turn, the FBI agent's attention was riveted on them.

As he ducked behind stalagmites and piles of fallen debris, Morgan was aware that Connie Pruett was nowhere in sight. She had ducked down behind the boulder and vanished. He hoped she was hiding, safe from further horrors.

But his real concern was for Roberta. He couldn't let those horrors be visited upon her.

"Get out of here, you fuckers!" Case screamed. "Get out or I'll kill this monstrosity!"

The creatures simply screeched back and continued to circle high above their heads.

Morgan's ears rang when Case fired the automatic toward the circling swarm. The bullet sparked against the stone and whined away. The creatures cried out and scattered. One landed on a high ledge. Another dropped to the floor on the opposite side of the cavern. The rest continued to flap and flutter above the humans.

Each jarring step was an agony for Morgan, but he concentrated on the opening into the next, larger cavern. He was close and still he had not been spotted.

He stumbled up a rise, the opening only scant feet away. He started toward it. . . .

The Devouring

"Blaylock!" Case yelled. "Don't move!"

Morgan had come too far to stop now. He lowered his head and, like a crippled bull, charged the opening. A shot exploded. The creatures howled and screamed. Tiny pieces of splintered rock bit into his cheek.

As he ducked into the rock doorway, another sound filled the chamber at his back. A cracking, rolling rumble.

He glanced back, saw tiny pieces of dirt and rock cascading to the floor and stared in amazement as a huge stalactite came rocketing down, fracturing into a thousand pieces when it hit.

Then another fell.

And another.

Behind him, Case was shouting and the creatures were screaming.

And then, with an ear-shattering roar, much of the ceiling gave way, sending unimaginable tons of rock crashing down.

Morgan stumbled backwards, bumped his injured leg and, howling in pain, flopped to the floor.

As the earth collapsed in on itself, great clouds of dirt washed into the other chamber. Morgan coughed and spat and covered his face. His mouth was filled with dust and grit, his eyes watered and he lay there, waiting to feel some massive, unbelievable weight pulp his body.

He might have been there a minute or an hour. He didn't know. But when he opened his eyes and realized he was still alive, he was utterly astounded.

Through the choking cloud of dust, he saw the other chamber littered with piles of fractured rock. Some of the cavern remained as it had been, but near the entrance where he lay, he saw that fully half of the ceiling had given way.

Other than the occasional thud of a rock clattering, the chamber was silent.

With strength he didn't know he had, Morgan struggled to his feet. Standing on one leg, he retrieved his crutch and studied the large chamber. Roberta and the creature were here somewhere.

He started moving into the cavern, constantly scanning the walls, probing into the dark recesses.

"Roberta!" he called and paused, hoping, praying, she would respond.

He heard a muffled squeal.

Morgan couldn't tell where it came from. It bounced softly off the walls and echoed away. He continued to move across the floor.

Then Roberta screamed. It was a wild, frantic cry.

Still unable to pinpoint the location, Morgan hobbled toward the large, bubbling pool of water. As he neared it, he saw movement from the pile of rags where Connie Pruett had slept.

Morgan rounded a stalagmite jutting from the floor and saw them. The creature held Roberta enfolded in its wings, her face forced against its massive chest. She struggled vainly, her arms pinned and her body too restricted to find any leverage.

Morgan stared in mute terror as the monster's gapping mouth opened and its thick black tongue flicked at the side of her neck, as if tasting her.

"Let her go!" Morgan screamed, ignoring the fact that he was unarmed and virtually at the end of his physical strength.

The creature's head snapped up and glared at him, its huge yellow eyes shining and its mouth contorting into a grotesque parody of a grin.

Morgan hobbled closer to the pair, watching as Roberta struggled to turn her head. As quickly as he could, he bent over and picked up a fist-sized stone and without considering the consequences, heaved it at the creature. The thing saw it coming, twisted its head away and let the rock bounce off the uppermost joint on its wing.

It spat and hissed at Morgan, opening its wings, as if in challenge and, for all the world, looking like some infernal demon out of a Hieronymus Bosch painting. It shoved Roberta away, and she stumbled backward against a rock wall. Ignoring her, the creature flapped its powerful wings once—a harsh flutter of leather—and lifted easily into the air. Its eyes never wavered from Morgan.

"Run, Roberta!" Morgan yelled as the creature soared high, banked and came streaking down, its dark talons groping and clutching the air.

With no time to see if she complied, Morgan whipped the crutch from under his arm and, hopped precariously on one foot, holding the crutch like a crude baseball bat. When the creature was near, he swung.

And missed. The thing's reflexes were too finely honed. At the last possible second, it veered away, letting the heavy tree limb swish through the air inches from its body.

The momentum of his swing sent Morgan staggering. He tottered, about to fall, and then felt hands steady him.

"Watch out!" Roberta screamed, her hands around his left arm.

Too late, Morgan saw the creature again diving toward him. In that brief, fleeting instant, he saw the glistening fangs, the flicking tongue, the grasping talons, and then it collided with them and they were both tumbling ass over elbow. Pain exploded everywhere in his body. A tiny, detached part of his mind told him he was now dead, and in one brief millisecond he saw his body lying in a pool of blood, more flesh and blood upon which the creatures would feed. . . .

But he was still alive. The unbelievable surge of pain exploding from his ankle told him that. Dying might be painful, but death was not. He might be dying, but he wasn't dead.

As the red and yellow tracers streaking his vision cleared, he realized the creature had not fallen upon them. It was again flying high, glaring down at them with mocking contempt.

Playing with us, Morgan thought.

You shouldn't play with your food.

"That's insane," he said aloud.

"Come on, Morgan," Roberta cried, trying to get him up.

Standing, leaning against Roberta, Morgan knew his time—their time—was short. His reserves were used up. Even the adrenaline pumping threw his body couldn't sustain him much longer.

"We've got to get out of here, Morgan. It has to be light outside by now. If we can get out of the caves . . ."

"No," he spat. "We'll never make it out. Not with him"—he pointed at the creature—"following us."

"Morgan . . . !"

"We've got to fight it here. We've got to make a stand. The other chamber caved in. Hell, the exit may be blocked." He was panting. Cold sweat chilled him beneath the heavy snowsuit. His throat was raw from dust and grit and his eyes burned. Every wound, every cut and scrape on his body seemed to flare with renewed fire, merging into one throbbing torment.

"We can't run. We fight here and now."

Still the creature circled. Maybe it was waiting for them to make a move, maybe it was waiting for its fellows to join it. Morgan didn't know, nor did he care. He was going to see this through. Win or lose, live or die. He wasn't running anymore.

Roberta, perhaps sensing his resolve, kept hold of his arm and momentarily rested her head on his shoulder.

"Can we beat it?" she asked in a hoarse whisper.

"Hell if I know, but I'm sure going to try."

She patted her pockets. "I still have the matches. Maybe we could make a fire. . . ."

"Good," he said, never taking his eyes off the creature. "What about the Sterno?"

"There's a little left in the can. Not much."

"It'll be enough," Morgan said tonelessly. "There are

rags over there, right?" He nodded to where she had been held by the creature.

Slowly they started edging their way toward the place where Connie Pruett had slept. After they took several steps, the creature screeched and dove. This time they were ready and dropped low as it passed above them. Its talons ripped at Morgan's back, shredding the nylon, but not cutting deep enough to reach his flesh.

"Why doesn't it just take us?" Roberta asked.

"You. It wants you and I think it's afraid if it fights me, either you'll be injured or escape." It was speculation, but made as much sense as anything amid all this insanity.

Even through the thick padding of their winter gear, Morgan felt Roberta shudder.

He glanced up, saw the creature banking above them.

"Okay. Get the Sterno and matches ready. When we get there, I want you to start a fire. Get everything you can find burning."

"Then what?"

He shrugged. "We're playing this by ear, kiddo. We'll just have to make it up as we go along."

They got up, gave the creature another cursory glance and, as quickly as Morgan could move, started toward the niche in the wall. The creature again screamed a warning, but as it wheeled into a dive, they reached the recess. Roberta dropped low and Morgan pressed himself against the wall. Talons scraped the rock near him as the thing's hot breath washed across his face.

"Do it, Roberta!" Morgan hissed.

She was already on her feet, scraping the contents of the Sterno can on the heap of rags. Her fingers trembled as she opened the waterproof match holder and shook several of the matches into her palm.

The creature banked high, turned and screeched.

"Jesus," Morgan breathed, sensing their attacker was through playing games. "Hurry." Still leaning against the wall, he raised the crutch, a meager weapon against his awesome opponent.

Roberta struck a match on the rough rock floor, but the head popped off with a loud hiss. She cursed under her breath and fumbled another one out of her palm.

With all of the amazing speed and maneuverability of its smaller brethren, the bat creature dodged and darted among the stalactites. Its cries echoed from wall to wall, filling the cavern with an unnerving, maddening wail of rage and betrayal.

Roberta dropped the second match and it rolled into a tiny fissure in the rocks. She picked up a third one, held it carefully and struck it on a rock. It flickered and then flared.

The creature whirled around a particularly large hanging stalactite and dove.

Morgan held his crutch in front of him like a spear, ready to impale the monster if given a chance.

The thick goo ignited when Roberta touched the flame to it. The rags danced with fire which spread rapidly over the mound of soiled and rotted clothing, old blankets and tattered canvas.

The creature arrowed toward Morgan, who tensed, his sore muscles protesting, and held the crutch before him.

At the last possible instant, the bat creature veered to Morgan's left, well out of range of the crutch, and dropped to the floor. Hissing and spitting, it darted its yellow eyes from Morgan to the ever-growing fire.

"Be careful," Roberta cried.

"Get behind me," he replied. "It wants you, not me."

As they stared at one another, the flames mounting, heat and smoke filling the rocky niche, a gunshot echoed through the chamber. It was immediately followed by a terrible, inhuman scream of pain.

The creature confronting them opened its wings, ready to take flight, and at that instant Morgan lunged and stumbled forward, driving the makeshift crutch at the monster. The splintered tip, worn sharp from scraping on the rough rock, pierced a jagged hole through the tough, leathery membrane of a wing.

The creature screamed as blood welled from the ragged wound. Then, with a leathery flap, it soared awkwardly into the smoky air. Morgan's crutch tumbled to the ground, one end dripping darkly.

"Somebody's still alive in the other cavern," Roberta said excitedly.

The creature Morgan wounded continued to cry out in pain and rage, finally alighting on a high rocky shelf. It studied its wound and then glared down at them.

At the same instant, another creature fluttered into the cavern. Great globs of blood and viscera leaked from a gaping hole in its middle. Its eyes were stunned and maddened as it screamed and wailed, careening off stalactites and walls. It let out one final, unearthly scream and spun to the floor, hitting with a sickening crunch, bouncing and then flopping against a protruding rock.

Its companion on the ledge bleated mournfully, but remained perched near the cavern's ceiling.

"Now what?" Roberta whispered, staring at the dead creature.

Smoke from their fire was billowing into the rancid air. Already the dim, distant ceiling was becoming thick and cloudy.

"Let's make a couple of torches. Big ones. And try to get the hell out of here."

Moving out of the rock niche, away from the flames, Roberta scanned the area. Near a rock outcropping, partially covered by tiny bits of rock and earth, she found an abandoned ski pole. Picking it up, she wondered absently about its owner, and trembled when she thought about the skulls and bones scattered inside the shaft through which she and Morgan had entered the chamber.

A few feet away, amid a tangled heap of discarded junk—summer shorts, winter coats, gloves, and other reminders of the creatures' other unknown victims—Roberta found the pole's mate.

"These'll work," she said, gathering more rags. As she bound the ends of the poles with strips of cloth, Morgan continued to watch the creature on the ledge.

"He won't be able to stay up there much longer," he muttered, watching the smoke gather and thicken.

"Ready," Roberta said, thrusting the two torches into the flames. They ignited instantly.

Morgan retrieved his crutch and tucked it under his arm. "Let's start running the gauntlet. Whoever's in the other cavern has a gun. If we can reach him . . ."

He stopped and turned as footsteps scraped against the floor.

"Thought I was dead, I'll bet," Richard Case said, his lips twisting in a nasty smile. He leveled an M-16 at the pair. His snowsuit was ripped and torn in a dozen places and covered with a dirt and dust. Blood oozed from a cut at his hairline and trickled down his left cheek. But what Morgan saw first was the wide, wild look in the man's eyes. They were bloodshot and showed white all around the pupils. The madness he had seen in them before was now complete.

"I knew you weren't dead," Morgan lied. "You're too tough to die."

"Fucking right!" Case growled, a demented grin curling his lips. "Too tough and then some."

"Richard," Roberta said quietly. "Why don't we all get out of here. . . ."

"No!" he shouted, swinging the gun toward her. "Not without one of those fuckers alive."

"Aren't they all dead?" Morgan asked.

Case didn't answer for a long moment, and then shrugged. "I killed that one." He nodded toward the body crumpled on the floor. "He was . . . feeding on Tarkington when I regain consciousness after the cave-in. He was *eating* him, for Christ's sake! I gut shot the bastard!"

"What about the others?" Morgan prompted. He needed to know if there was any chance they could get out of here alive.

"Some may have been killed in the cave-in," Case replied. "But there's got to be some of them still alive!"

"Was everybody killed?" Morgan persisted. "The Pruett woman and Dallenbeck?"

The FBI man frowned. "Dallenbeck's dead. I don't know where that crazy broad went. Too bad these blood-suckers didn't eat her." He looked around the cavern. "Any of them in here?"

"One," Roberta said before Morgan could stop her.

"Where?"

Morgan pointed to the high ledge, suddenly realizing it was now empty. "Damn, it was there. Just a minute ago."

They all craned their necks, searching for the wounded creature. If it was still in the smoky chamber, it was well concealed.

"Maybe it went into the other cavern," Roberta offered.

Case nodded. "Fine. That's good. We'll drive it to the entrance. It's light outside now. It can't bear the light. We'll trap it between us and the sunlight. We'll catch the son of a bitch yet!"

Morgan heard the desperation and panic in the man's voice.

"Can't we just go?" Roberta asked wearily. "You can get more men, equipment and come back. . . ."

"No!" Case snarled. "You don't understand shit, Ferris. You never have."

"What do you mean, Case?" Morgan asked, curious.

The FBI man licked his lips and swallowed hard. "This is my last chance! All the money and equipment I've used. I'll never be able to get it again." He continued to search the cavern. "This was a business venture." He shook his head. "And I intend to make it work. Do you understand? If I don't capture one of those flying bastards now, I'll never have another chance."

"Why don't we just get out of here?" Roberta asked again.

"Not without one of them!" Case shot back. "And you, dear Ms. Ferris, are going to be instrumental in its capture."

"No way, Case," Morgan cried, knowing what the man wanted.

The M-16 was leveled at his face. "You're already half dead, Blaylock. If I kill you, it'd be doing you a favor. You either help me or die here and now. Frankly, I don't much give a shit."

Morgan grabbed Roberta's arm, pulled her toward him. "Let it go, Case."

"How touching," the FBI agent said icily. "You've become her champion." He lifted the rifle to his shoulder and took aim at Morgan's head.

"You've got ten seconds to decide, Roberta. You help me or I kill him!"

"Richard . . . !"

"Eight seconds!"

"Oh, God, don't do it," Roberta cried.

"Five seconds!"

"Richard . . . !"

"Two seconds!"

"All right!" she screamed. "All right! All right!"

Case lowered the M-16 and smiled. "That's better. Now, take off your clothes. These monsters seem to like human flesh in a variety of ways."

Chapter Twenty-two

"Case," Morgan said, trying not to reveal his anger and frustration. "It'll never work. They'll know it's a trap. These sons of bitches are shrewd. They won't fall for it."

"Shut up, Blaylock," Case answered. "Of course they will. They need human women to reproduce. One thing the researchers found when they examined the creatures' droppings was a virus of some sort. They think maybe it killed off the females."

Morgan sucked in a deep breath. "But they'll know you're waiting with a gun. They understand guns, Case." He gestured toward the dead creature heaped against the rocks.

The FBI agent waved the rifle, indicating he wanted silence. "It'll work, Blaylock. Don't worry, it'll work!" He glanced at Roberta standing next to Morgan. "Start getting out of your clothes, Ferris."

Roberta stared at him for a second and then at Morgan.

If he expected to see terror in her eyes, he was disappointed. She was furious. Suddenly, she moved away from Morgan.

"I'd rather let you kill me, Richard," she yelled.

Morgan's heart thumped hard when he saw the barrel of the M-16 swing toward Roberta and Case's finger tighten on the trigger. "I have no intention of killing you, Roberta," he cooed.

The M-16 swung away from her and Morgan was again looking down its cruel bore.

"When I can kill Blaylock instead."

For several long, tense moments, the trio stood very still. Case's eyes flickered from Roberta to Morgan and back. And for his part, Morgan was trying to come up with a plan, but his sluggish, exhausted mind had run out of ideas.

"If you kill him," Roberta shouted. "You'll *have* to kill me!"

The rifle remained leveled at Morgan's chest and he sensed his eminent demise. But oddly, he viewed his own death with amazing dispassion. Maybe it was his physical exhaustion or his mental fatigue. Whatever the reason, he just didn't give a damn.

So I die. So what?

"Perhaps," Case replied, his voice deadly calm. "But Blaylock goes first. And slowly." He squinted his eyes against the thickening smoke. "Have you any idea what an M-16 slug does, Roberta? When it hits, it tumbles. I might shoot Blaylock in the leg, blow off a foot. Or maybe I should start by blowing off a few fingers.

"Are you sure you want to watch him die by inches? One piece of his body at a time?"

The blood drained from Roberta's face. "All right, Richard," she said savagely, starting to unbutton her shirt.

Case smiled and lowered the rifle. "Ah, that's so much better. So practical. I thought you'd see it my way, even if Blaylock couldn't." Eyeing Morgan, he shook his head in mock sadness. "She's so much more reasonable than you."

And suddenly Morgan wanted to feel his hands around Richard Case's throat. He wanted to feel his thumbs press into the soft flesh, wanted to hear the man gag and gasp for precious breath, wanted to feel him buck and squirm for air even as his brain died of oxygen starvation.

For the first time in his life, Morgan wanted to kill another human being. And God help him, he wanted this son of a bitch dead!

The fire in the niche was still burning brightly, still issuing a steady flow of thick smoke toward the ceiling. The stalactites now jutted through the smoke like bizarre teeth in the mouth of some monstrous creature.

Roberta was stripped down to her longjohns. Morgan saw her shiver, and knew it probably was not from the temperature. Slowly, she began unbuttoning the white ribbed shirt.

As one, their heads snapped around when they heard the creatures' screeching cries. Above them, just below the drifting smoke, three winged shapes came soaring at them.

Case let out a startled grunt, Roberta gasped and Morgan cursed. The FBI agent swung the rifle around and, without aiming, let loose a quick, three-round burst. The slugs ricocheted off the ceiling, missing all three of the creatures.

With Case's attention diverted, Morgan made his move. He took one quick hop and, dancing on one foot, swung his crutch with all the strength he could muster.

The blow caught Case across the back of his neck. He yelped, slumped to his knees and dropped the M-16. Before he could rise, Morgan brought the thick branch down, breaking it across the man's back.

Roberta was suddenly beside him, clutching at his arm to keep him from falling. She thrust one of the two ski poles, its end still burning, into his hand. As he balanced himself, she raised the second pole high, poised like a matador to deliver a death blow at Case's unprotected back.

Before Roberta could drive the point home, there was a leathery flap, a wash of air, and she was again lifted from the floor, her arms snared in the creature's powerful taloned feet.

Morgan whirled just as a second creature dove at him. In one brief instant, he saw the ragged, bloody hole in the monster's wing. Then, reflexively, he spun away just as the creature tried to grasp him. It missed and soared upward with an angry cry.

Morgan slumped to the floor.

"Fools!" Case snarled, pushing himself to his feet and reaching for the M-16. "You're both . . ."

His sentence went unfinished. Powerful talons locked around his throat and he was heaved off the floor.

Morgan stared in amazement, as the creature carried Case into the smoky air. The man's legs kicked frantically and his hands clawed at the creature's talons gripping his neck.

Morgan watched as the creature banked hard and sent Case smashing against a particularly large stalactite, never releasing the death grip on his throat.

Pulling his eyes away, Morgan crawled toward the M-16. As his fingers wrapped around it, the hair on the back of his neck rose and his back muscles quivered. On instinct, he dropped prone and rolled, vaguely aware of the terrible pain in his leg.

The creature came in low. Its hooked claws hit his midsection and he rolled over twice, almost losing his grip on the rifle. As he flopped on his back, his finger jerked the trigger. The shot was wide, but the creature sprang into the air.

It flapped away. Without aiming, he pointed the M-16 in its general direction and held down the trigger. The rifle bucked in his hands. Red tracers streaked into the smoke. The creature wailed, tottered and then, its wings folded behind its back, plunged toward the rocky floor.

Morgan turned away before the thing smashed headfirst into a mound of rubble.

Panting for breathe, he pushed himself up and leaned against a wall. Frantically scanning the room, he tried to find Roberta and her captor. He could hear her screams, but couldn't see her. What he did see caused him to gag in horror.

Case was sprawled on a rocky ledge, a creature perched on his chest. The FBI agent, weak and dazed, struck futile blows. He let out one terrible, haunting scream when a taloned foot lashed out and plucked his right eye from its socket. The creature popped the orb into its mouth and then extracted the other one.

Morgan lifted the rifle and took aim at the monster now tearing at Case's exposed throat. Gritting his teeth, he squeezed the trigger. The shot pierced the thing's head and, soundlessly, it toppled from the ledge, dragging Case with it. Both bodies hit the floor with a moist thud.

Quickly, Morgan pulled out the rifle's clip. It was empty. Using the M-16 for support he started hopping across the floor. He had to find Roberta before it was too late.

Again, he heard her scream.

Frantically, Morgan moved through the cavern. He let the rifle barrel bang against the rocks; he yelled her name, made as much noise as he could, hoping to draw the creature away from her.

When he was halfway across the room, rounding a large rock formation, he saw Roberta and her tormentor. Her longjohns were tattered and torn. The creature was poised in front of her, its mammoth erection jutting forth likc a demonic weapon. Wings flexing, black tongue flicking over its bared teeth, it danced and pranced around her.

Her back was pressed against a wall, her hands held in front of her trying to ward off the creature.

Morgan was at least 20 yards from them. He knew he had one chance to stop it. If he failed, it would undoubtedly kill him and Roberta would . . .

He pushed the thought away.

Dragging in a deep breath, mustering his remaining strength, Morgan clutched the rifle in both hands like a club and started moving toward the creature. His booted foot scraped and clattered on the floor, but the creature seemed oblivious to everything save the human woman cowering near it.

Morgan was almost there. He tightened his hold on the rifle, readied himself for one final confrontation. Hopping and bouncing, fighting for balance, he raised the rifle over his shoulder. Just as he was about to take his swing, Roberta saw him. Maybe it was something in her eyes, a flicker, shift, but the monster suddenly whirled just as Morgan swung the weapon.

As if in slow motion, Morgan saw the look on the creature's face. Shock. Amazement. Then the rifle's heavy plastic stock smashed into the side of the thing's face. Its head snapped with the blow. It staggered and dropped to its knees.

Morgan lost his balance and fell near the creature. For a second their eyes met, locked. Something passed between them, something ancient and primordial. In that one split second, hunter and prey—Morgan would never really know which was which—exchanged a final, silent acknowledgment.

The creature stood. Blood dripped from a terrible gash on its face. It spread its wings, raised a taloned foot and prepared to deal Morgan a swift death stroke.

He knew it was coming, knew he had done as much, perhaps more than should have been expected. He braced for the final blow. . . .

The creature staggered. Its eyes opened impossibly wide and clouded in shock and surprise. A bubbly, gurgled growl tore from its mouth and then, like a puppet whose strings have been cut, it toppled over, sprawling across Morgan's chest.

Morgan peered over its wings to see Roberta standing stock-still, a huge, blood-splattered rock held in her trembling hands. She looked at him, blinked and let the rock fall.

"Oh, God," she cried, kneeling next to him. Together they rolled the dead thing away and, as if trying to merge into one, they clung together.

How long they sat there, holding each other, muttering meaningless, whispered sounds, neither knew. After a long time, Roberta rose and helped Morgan to his feet.

"We . . . we should try to get out of here," she said quietly, her hysteria gone.

Morgan agreed.

"I'll go get my clothes," she said, starting back to where the now-smoldering fire still sent a column of into the cavern. "I'll get you another crutch," she added as an afterthought.

Morgan could only nod. He was exhausted. Perhaps beyond exhaustion. His eyes were gritty and sore. Every muscle was stiff, every nerve jangled and raw.

He sat there, his mind blank, numb. He couldn't consider what had happened, what would happen. He couldn't think beyond the next breath, the next second. It was enough to be alive.

And then he heard an odd sound and his muscles tensed. Another creature?

Dear God, he prayed. No. No more.

The sound persisted. A metallic scrap. A grunt. And again the sound of metal.

"What is it?" Roberta asked. He glanced up at her, not realizing she had returned.

"I don't know."

"It sounds like it's coming from the other chamber."

They exchanged glances. Maybe someone else had survived the cave-in.

Using another thick, dried tree branch for a crutch, they started toward the entrance to the rubble-strewn cavern.

"What if it . . . one of them?" Roberta whispered.

He shook his head. "I don't know. But if it is, it's hurt. If it could come for us, it would have already found us."

They crept through the opening leading to the other chamber. In the cavern's dim illumination they could see the fresh rubble, the heaps of rock and dirt. The air was still thick with dust and there was the occasional thud of a stone falling from the scarred, fractured ceiling.

"It's coming from the right," Morgan said.

They could still hear the metallic clink, an occasional grunt or incoherent mumble.

As they carefully picked their way through the debris, they saw a huddled shape, crouching on the floor near the wall. Something glinted as the arms rose and then fell.

"Connie?" Roberta called when they were within a few yards of the kneeling woman.

No response. The mumbling continued as did the methodical, almost mechanical motion of her arms. Up and down. Up and down. She held a huge knife clutched in both hands and each time it descended, Morgan and Roberta heard the metal hit rock.

"What the hell is she doing?" Roberta whispered.

"I'm not sure I want to know," Morgan answered.

They came up behind the woman, looking down to where the blunted blade of the knife drove against rock.

Roberta choked and swore. Morgan shook his head.

On the floor in front of the woman, now little more than a mass of butchered, mutilated meat, was the body of the tiny creature. She had hacked it into pieces and was now stabbing the ruined torso.

Morgan reached out and grabbed one of Connie's arms on the upswing. She didn't resist. Carefully, he took the knife out of her fingers. Roberta pulled the woman to her feet and turned her around. Her face was splattered with blood, her eyes as vacant and as devoid of life as those of a corpse. Her lips moved, but no sounds issued from her mouth.

"She's on the la-la-land express," Morgan said dryly, earning a harsh look from Roberta.

He turned from the pair and almost stumbled over Dallenbeck's body. The empty scabbard on the man's belt told him where Connie had found the knife. Trying not to look at the dead man's ripped throat and eyeless sockets, Morgan probed in the backpack. He found a large flashlight and a bag of trail mix.

"Light and food," he muttered, handing both to Roberta.

After they wolfed down the mixture of nuts, dried peas, coconut, and seeds—Connie would eat nothing—they left the cavern.

Later, Morgan couldn't remember much. He recalled going back through the narrow fissure into the third, smaller chamber, then entering another, larger one.

He remembered light and cold and voices. A lot of excited voices. Gruff Ryan was there. He was sure of that. And there were strangers. A lot of strangers. A cast of thousands. Then he was lying inside a snow machine. Someone was talking to him, but what they wanted was a mystery.

He faded in and out of reality for a long time. But even when he was awake, everything had a dream-like quality, an odd flatness, textureless and surreal. Faces blended into faces, words had no meaning.

Morgan floated and drifted and dreamed forever.

Chapter Twenty-three

Morgan limped out the front door of his house, went to the mailbox and fished out a stack of letters and bills. Mostly bills. He returned to the porch, where he flopped down in the metal lawn chair he'd brought out of the garage at the first sign of warm weather. Leaning his cane against the porch railing, he rifled through the envelopes and then tossed them aside.

Methodically, he began massaging his temples and face. He was tired, his back ached—it was time to get a better desk chair—and his eyes felt like two piss holes in the snow. He'd been at the word processor all morning.

The sky was cloudless and amazingly blue and the afternoon breeze was warm and dry. The subtle, sweet scent of lilacs drifted from the bushes blooming along his fence.

Morgan glanced at his mail and then closed his eyes, drawing in a deep breath.

All these months later, and still not a word from Roberta Ferris.

The Devouring

What had happened on the mountain, inside the cavern all seemed so distant now, like the events in another lifetime.

He had awakened in the hospital three days after their rescue. His broken ankle had required extensive surgery and he had worn a series of casts on it until only a few days ago. It felt good to be able to scratch the flesh below his left knee.

He'd asked the nurses and doctors about Roberta, but no one seemed to know anything. She hadn't come to the hospital with him, nor had she left any messages.

When he asked about Connie Pruett, he was told that she had been taken to a hospital back East.

Gruff Ryan, no worse for wear, came to see him every day. At the hospital, recovering from the wound in his back, Ryan had been interviewed by an FBI agent who had a lot of questions to ask about one Richard Case and a lot of misappropriated government equipment.

In turn, Gruff had convinced the agent that, monsters aside, Case was on a killing spree and was holding two of Ryan's friends hostage. Dragging himself out of the hospital, he had led a squad of agents to find Morgan and Roberta. For his efforts, Ryan had spent an extra week in the hospital.

Ryan told Morgan he'd spent hours being debriefed by a group of very intense fellows from Washington.

A few days later, Morgan had a similar experience. He answered all their questions as best he could, but when he asked about Roberta, he got only blank stares in reply.

He was cleared of the murders. Stories were planted in the media that essentially fingered Richard Case for the murders while at the same time distancing the Federal Bureau of Investigation from any involvement. By the time the media frenzy died down, Case was labeled a "rogue agent" and a man who had betrayed both the Bureau and his country.

Douglas D. Hawk

After agreeing to go along with a plausible scenario, Morgan enjoyed a brief time as a media darling. Reporters from Denver and Chicago and other places interviewed him on his harrowing escape from the caverns.

But no one offered to make a TV movie.

After getting out of the hospital, Morgan spent a week moping around, waiting—hoping—Roberta would call. But she hadn't.

The person who did call and then came to the house was a nondescript little government bureaucrat who said his name was Smith. He had a government check for Morgan to cover the cost of his destroyed snow machine and a hefty sum to keep his mouth shut. All Morgan had to do was sign an agreement not to disclose any details of the events in the mountains.

He signed. The money would see him through until he could decide what to do with the rest of his life. He paid off the loan on the tractor and banked the rest.

Finally, with all the gusto he could muster, Morgan planted himself in front of his computer and reentered the violent world of Jackson Black Cloud.

Writing was an effective distraction. When he was trying to figure out how Black Cloud was going to save the girl from the ruthless bank robbers (not to mention get her between his blankets), he momentarily forget about Roberta. And when the writing went well, he could work until he was so tired the nightmare images with their yellow eyes and slashing fangs didn't haunt his sleep.

Other than at the debriefing, Morgan had heard nothing further about the creatures. If any had survived, the feds were keeping quiet about it.

Now, sitting on his porch, enjoying the afternoon, he dozed.

The clunk of a car door jarred him awake some time later. He rubbed his eyes and looked into the bright afternoon.

Maybe he was still dreaming.

The Devouring

Roberta Ferris stood on the sidewalk, next to a small car crammed with boxes and clothes and with a U-Haul trailer hitched to the back. She wore a white summer dress that gave her a look of youth and innocence.

She was studying him, her face worried.

"Hi," she called. "Remember me?"

Using his cane, Morgan lifted himself out of the chair and stepped to the edge of the porch. He swallowed hard, trying to dislodge the lump in his throat.

"Didn't we meet in another lifetime?" he finally asked.

She blushed and lowered her eyes. "I'm sorry, Morgan. I . . . couldn't call or write. There were things . . . I had to do."

He was silent, unable to sort out his conflicting emotions. He couldn't be angry, it would be unfair to her. He didn't own this woman; there was never a commitment. And seeing her there, radiant in the sunlight, reminded him why he had so longed for her, why he had fallen in love with her.

Morgan cleared his throat and nodded toward her car and the trailer. "Leaving the rarefied world of Washington?"

She shook her head. "This is just some of my stuff I left here."

He looked away. "You're heading to a new assignment?"

"In a way, yes."

He couldn't look at her.

"How's the leg?" she asked, taking a tentative step forward.

"Coming along nicely. Doctors think I'll be able to walk without a cane in a month or two."

"That's wonderful."

"Yeah."

"I don't blame you for being angry and hurt, Morgan," Roberta said in a rush. "I wanted to call you. I wanted to write, but I was in Washington. Being debriefed. There were countless questions and reports and interviews. This whole thing was a mess." She drew in a deep breath and looked away, studying the mountains beyond the house.

"Did you read about that presidential aide resigning his position?" she asked.

Morgan thought about it. There had been something in the papers. "I think so."

"He was the one helping Richard. Used White House clout to get everything done. He was a little like Ollie North, only the President was uninvolved. Totally in the dark. If it hadn't been for their fear of public exposure, I think the guy could have ended up before a senate committee or in federal court. As it was, they just destroyed his career and sent him packing."

Roberta sighed, obviously relieved to have it all said.

"Five minutes," Morgan said softly. "That's all it would have taken. Just a five-minute call."

She looked away, brushing at a single tear rolling down her cheek. "I couldn't. I was incommunicado until last week. Why are you making this so hard?"

Morgan couldn't answer that one. Male pride, maybe. Wounded ego.

"What about Connie Pruett?"

Roberta looked at him, her eyes moist and sad. She shook her head. "I don't know. No one would tell me. No one would talk about her. She just vanished."

Morgan glanced down at her, and then held out his hand. She returned his look, smiled and dashed up the steps. They held each other close.

"I quit my job," she whispered after a time. "I told them to stick it up their bureaucratic asses."

"What now?"

She smiled. "I thought maybe we could . . . work that out together."

He nodded. "I think we should go inside and talk about it. We can't just jump into the rest of our lives without a plan."

The Devouring

Roberta nodded. "Good idea. In my spare time, I've been reading those *Half Breed* novels you write. I want to talk about the way that Black Cloud character treats women."

"Oh?"

"Yeah," she said. "I want to know how the writer does his research."

Morgan pulled open the door. "Right this way, ma'am. My research facilities are at your disposal."

Epilogue

The lights were too bright. The white room was stark and sterile and made her uncomfortable. This wasn't the same room she'd been in for so long. Why was she strapped down on the table? Why were her legs elevated?

And why was she in so much pain?

"Everything will be fine," said a woman whose masked face was suddenly thrust into hers. "It'll be over soon, I'm sure."

Where am I?

The contraction hit like a bolt of lightning and she gasped, crying out.

"Breathe. That's right. Now push. Yes, yes, that's good."

"We've got . . . good God . . . we've got the head. Just a little more." The man's voice came from somewhere in front of her. Between her spread legs.

"Push a little more," the woman coaxed. "That's right. Yes, yes."

The Devouring

She pushed and there was pressure, and then it ended and the pain subsided. She swallowed and leaned back, willing her muscles to relax.

Through hazy, blurry eyes, she saw a man dressed in hospital greens rise from in front of her, a bundle in his arms. He glanced at her, his eyes wide with . . . what?

"What . . . what's happening to me?" she asked. Why couldn't she remember? Why was everything so hazy and distant?

"You're fine now," the nurse said. "Everything is fine. We'll finish here and then you can rest."

She closed her eyes. Why can't I remember? Why can't I remember anything?

Connie Pruett.

That's my name.

I'm Connie Pruett.

I worked for NORAMS.

Oh, God. NORAMS. The station . . .

Them . . .

"OH, GOD! OH, DEAR GOD! THE BABY! KILL IT! KILL IT!"

She felt a tiny prick in her arm, and almost immediately her vision fuzzed and the world closed in on her.

And Connie Pruett easily slipped back into the warm, comfortable void where the drugs kept the monsters at bay.

ANIMUS

Ed Kelleher and Harriette Vidal
Bestselling Authors of *The Spell*

He looks like an innocent child, but he is the spawn of hell—a demon seed conceived by the most diabolical powers ever imagined. His loving parents think his coming is a blessing, but they soon fear his birth is a curse that will damn them—and mankind—for all time.

__3473-5 $4.50 US/$5.50 CAN

WILLIAM SCHOELL

WRITES TERRIFYING BOOKS YOU WON'T BE ABLE TO PUT DOWN!

SAURIAN. It emerged mysteriously one night and destroyed the town with unbelievable swiftness. Now the only survivor of the bloodbath found himself being called toward the ruins of his boyhood home, possessed by visions of the centuries-old beast—a gigantic creature that wouldn't rest until the world was crushed by its wrath.

__3248-1 $4.50 US/$5.50 CAN